The Darkness and the Deep

ALINE TEMPLETON

The Darkness and the Deep

HODDER &
STOUGHTON

Copyright © 2006 by Aline Templeton

First published in Great Britain in 2006 by Hodder & Stoughton
A division of Hodder Headline

The right of Aline Templeton to be identified as the Author
of the Work has been asserted by her in accordance with the
Copyright, Designs and Patents Act 1988.

A Hodder and Stoughton Book

1

A CIP catalogue record for this title is available from the British Library

Hardback ISBN 0 340 83856 6
Trade paperback ISBN 0 340 83858 2

Typeset in Plantin Light by Palimpsest Book Production Limited,
Polmont, Stirlingshire.

Printed and bound by
Mackays of Chatham plc, Chatham, Kent

Hodder Headline's policy is to use papers that are natural, renewable
and recyclable products and made from wood grown in sustainable forests.
The logging and manufacturing processes are expected to conform
to the environmental regulations of the country of origin.

Hodder & Stoughton Ltd
A division of Hodder Headline
338 Euston Road
London NW1 3BH

To Alison, Mark and especially Molly,
the first of the next generation, with my love.

A donation is being made to the Royal National
Lifeboat Institution

I

The sea haar came rolling in on an oily swell from the Irish Sea just ahead of the darkness. Now, to the melancholy lowing of the foghorn on the Mull of Galloway, it crept over rocks and bays and low cliffs, stealing light and feature from the landscape. It engulfed the small boat becalmed in the Bay of Luce, then, on its south-west shore, the ancient stone harbour of the port of Knockhaven.

Lights began to appear in the small deep windows of the white-harled houses huddled close along the curve of the shore and in the shops and small terraced houses on either side of the winding ribbon of the steep High Street. They shone from the sprawl of council housing and grey stone villas in the higher, newer part of the town and blazed from the 'executive homes' with sea views, whose picture windows would have found small favour with the original occupants of the little town. Those earliest fishermen derived no romantic satisfaction from gazing out at their workplace and their enemy – even if she was their mistress as well.

The High Street and Shore Street, bypassed by the main coast road which divided Knockhaven roughly into old and new, were quiet this evening after a still, damp day in late September. A couple of cars were parked outside the '8 'til Late' minimart and the chip shop was just starting on its evening trade, but the other shops were preparing to lock up and in the hushed, foggy gloom there was little to tempt last-minute shoppers to linger.

Suddenly, out of the murk a motorbike appeared at the top of the hill, the sound of its racing engine shattering the unnatural silence. It took the bends in the narrow High Street at speed, then, swinging dangerously round the sharp corner into Shore Street, skirted the harbour to stop abruptly where the road ended outside the lifeboat station. A second later its burly rider was running towards the entrance, the key ready in his hand.

Inside the vaulted shed he found the switchboard with the ease of long familiarity and a moment later the building was ablaze with light. He was opening the door to the slipway, blinking in the brilliance of the outside floodlights, when he remembered the new instructions and, swearing under his breath, went back into the secured locker where the maroons were kept. Before he could carry them outside to set them off he heard the squeal of brakes announcing another arrival, then another. Summoned by pager, they would all be on their way now, the mechanic, the second cox, the team on standby, the reserves, the officials.

He set up the first rocket and lit it. It shot into the gloom, its report muffled by the damp air and its light only a sullen, ruddy glow. Timing the interval, he set off the second a minute later.

A small crowd, alerted by the bustle, had gathered already and the sound of the maroons would bring extra onlookers. More cars were snaking down the High Street and along the shore, slowing as the dead-end road became congested.

None of their drivers, intent on the emergency summons, paid any attention to the car that drew up hastily on the main road near the top of the High Street and switched its lights off, waiting until the stream of vehicles turning down to the harbour passed. Then it took off in the opposite direction, heading north out of the town towards the headland which separated the safe harbour of Knockhaven from its treacherous neighbour, the rocky cove known as Fuill's Inlat.

As the street lights came to an end and the car's headlights bounced back off the white wall of the haar, only the light from the dashboard instruments illuminated the grim face of the person at the wheel, driving dangerously blind along the narrow road.

Dr Ashley Randall, her striking, pale blue eyes cold, looked with distaste at the fat woman wedged in the patient's chair to the side of her desk, at her skin which was the colour and texture of oatmeal, at her sly expression and the slack, gossip's mouth.

'By rights,' the woman was saying resentfully, 'I should have stayed in my bed for a home visit instead of trauchling up here with my back giving me gyp every step I took.'

'No, no, Mrs Martin, that's quite the wrong approach to back pain. If you don't exercise it, your back will only get worse. And of course your weight is imposing a considerable strain on it – have I given you one of the leaflets on tackling obesity?' There was no percentage in tact where Aggie Martin was concerned.

Aggie bridled, adjusting her massive bosom. Her expression was mutinous as she said, 'You're aye giving me leaflets but they've never done any good.'

The doctor sighed, tapping slim fingers on the desk. 'I don't suppose they have, if you ignore what they advise. Now, all you need at the moment is regular gentle exercise and a couple of paracetamol if the pain's bad, and I think you will find your back improves in a day or two.'

'What about my prescription?' the woman said belligerently. 'I've a right to a prescription—'

'Not if you don't need one,' Dr Ashley said crisply, getting to her feet as a signal that the consultation was over. 'Now, Mrs Martin—'

An urgent 'beep-beep' interrupted her. With the familiar lurch in her stomach – part excitement, part nerves – she pulled a pager out of her pocket, glanced at it, then spun round to open a cupboard and grab the jacket hanging from a peg inside.

'I'm sorry,' she said with blatant insincerity, 'I'm afraid I have to go – that's a call-out for the lifeboat. I'll have one of the receptionists show you out.'

Then she was out of the door, not giving Aggie the chance to protest that she'd also wanted to discuss the nasty pain she'd had in her stomach after her black-pudding supper last night.

Behind the desk in the foyer, a group of receptionists in their usual gossiping huddle turned to look at her – like cows in a field, Ashley thought contemptuously. She could almost see their jaws rotating. They didn't like her, and she didn't care.

Mobile in hand, she was scrolling to her husband's number as she gave her orders. 'Show Mrs Martin out, would you? It's a lifeboat emergency, so put the rest of my patients on someone else's list. If that's a problem Dr Lewis will come in and help out.'

As the phone was answered, she said, 'Lewis? I'm off on a distress call. They'll phone if they need extra help with my surgery. All right? Bye.'

Then she was through the door, being swallowed up in the fog outside, but not before she heard the eloquent sniff of Muriel Henderson, the oldest receptionist (the one who belonged to the same coven as her mother-in-law) and the 'Poor Dr Lewis!' meant for her ears.

As she flipped on the fog lights and started the engine and her black BMW Z4 responded with its satisfying growling roar, exhilaration fizzed inside her, not only at the prospect of action with an edge of danger but because of the other dangerous hobby she was currently pursuing. Adultery – not a pretty word, but she savoured it as she ran her hand through her hair to fluff out her crop of strawberry-blonde curls. She bit at her lips, too, to bring the colour there; there was no time to stop and put on lipgloss when the target from summons to launch was less than ten minutes, and if she wasn't there in time there were reserves who would jump at the chance to replace her.

Fortunately the Medical Centre, purpose-built in the newer part of the town to the landward side of the main road, was only 500 yards from the High Street in one direction and her own home, in an enclave of modern housing, was not much further in the other, so she hadn't yet missed a launch when she was on standby. Earning her place in the three-man crew had been the only compensation for being stuck in this dismal hole, the only thing that had stopped her from using arsenic, or something more subtle, on Lewis and his mother. Jocasta, Ashley called her privately, and she knew who to blame when Lewis announced he was bringing her back to his childhood home since a vacancy for a GP and a part-timer had become available in the Knockhaven Medical Centre. She'd protested, of course; she'd had a job she'd enjoyed in a hospital in Edinburgh where he'd been in practice before, but Lewis, who gave the impression of being easy-going and amenable when it was anything that didn't matter to him, was blandly implacable when it did.

So he couldn't blame her for choosing to follow her own inclinations. Adultery: she formed the word again with smiling lips.

She was just turning down the High Street when she heard the sound of the maroon and chuckled. That was Ritchie's idea: he'd gone to a meeting of lifeboat Honorary Secretaries and discovered that Fowey, having discontinued the outdated rocket summons years ago like everyone else, had improved the donations total by reinstating it. He'd met with stiff opposition from Willie Duncan, the cox, but he'd got his way. He usually did. Ashley smiled again, reminiscently.

There was a car she didn't recognise in front of her as she reached Shore Street, so she put her hand on the horn and kept it there. With an almost visible start the car pulled aside and she reached the lifeboat shed only moments after the second maroon went off.

It was so gloomy outside that she couldn't any longer see properly what she was doing. Detective Inspector Marjory Fleming stood up from the floor where she had been crouching, painfully straightening out her five-foot-ten frame, and stepped back to survey her work morosely. What a way to spend one of your precious days off! Still holding the paintbrush, she wiped her brow with the back of her forearm which, since it was already spattered with paint, neatly transferred several black smears to her face.

Normally she didn't mind decorating. Normally. She would have said there was always something deeply satisfying about obliterating the battle-scars of daily life and starting all over again with clean, fresh walls, unsullied as yet by accident, carelessness or a stray rugby ball misfielded, something symbolic, even, if you cared to think it through. Something to do with renewal and hope and putting the problems and mistakes of the past behind you.

Today the symbolism was uncomfortably insistent, and it didn't make her happy. Here, in the pretty pink-and-white bedroom under the eaves of the Mains of Craigie farmhouse, the room which had had bright gingham curtains and a patchwork quilt her mother had made, she was obliterating her daughter's childhood with matt black paint.

She blamed herself on two counts: first for promising, six months ago, that Cat could choose her own decor, and second for not getting round to doing it at the time, when Cat's choice would probably have been blue or perhaps, daringly, yellow. Catriona Fleming had never been an adventurous child; her final primary school reports had depicted a model, positively old-fashioned pupil.

God forgive her, Marjory had even said to her husband Bill, over the ritual dram they had at night before his final checking round of the farm, that she couldn't understand how the two of them had managed to produce such a middle-aged child.

Bill, laconic as always, had suggested that perhaps they hadn't been quite as radical in youth as they might like to think now.

'Speak for yourself!' Marjory had retorted, peeved. 'Remember that poster of Alice Cooper I had on my wall?'

'Yes, but did you actually like him, or were you just doing it to wind your parents up?'

After a pregnant pause, Marjory had said venomously, 'Did I ever mention how much I dislike you on these occasions?'

And perhaps that was all Cat was doing too. But black paint!

In the six months between the promise and its fulfilment, at the age of going on thirteen, puberty had hit Cat with the force of a ten-ton truck – breasts, spots, mood-swings, self-absorption and the sort of teenage deafness which means that music is only audible when played at a decibel level which cracks plaster. The abruptness of her metamorphosis had left her parents reeling.

Their first Parents' Evening after Cat's starting at Kirkluce Academy had been another shock. They'd gone in feeling – well, perhaps smug would be the unkind word for it, and emerged shaken and bemused. Her Year Teacher was first, saying delicately that Catriona was, er, undoubtedly an able pupil, at which Bill had smiled and nodded and Marjory, veteran of a thousand interviews where reading between the lines was a required professional skill, stiffened. It got worse from there on: inattention in class, poor time-keeping, sloppy work, unfortunate friendships . . .

And that, Marjory reflected grimly as she put the lid back on the paint tin and immersed the brush in a jam-jar of white spirit, was where the problem lay – with the dreaded Kylie.

Kylie MacEwan had attended one of the dozen or so primary schools that came within the catchment area for Kirkluce Academy, the secondary school in the main market town in Galloway. She lived with her mother, grandmother and two of her uncles in a small estate of council houses on the outskirts of Knockhaven. It was home to many characters of sterling worth, but in Marjory's experience the adult members of the MacEwan clan could not be numbered amongst them. The child's father, whoever he was, seemed to be out of the picture completely.

Kylie had a row of metal hoops round the top of each ear and a glittering nose-stud; there were rumours of other, more intimate piercings too which, in a child of thirteen, was disturbing. Especially when your quiet, innocent daughter was her new best friend.

Marjory could understand how it had happened, and she felt guilty about that as well. The police force was not in general regarded with affection by the young, and after the problems over the foot-and-mouth epidemic last year, Cat had been punished for her mother's role by other farmers' daughters she had known all her life: not with anything as blatant as bullying, just with hurtful exclusion. She had found herself something of a loner in the large secondary school and Kylie, whose precocity made many of the girls uneasy, was in a similar position.

And Kylie, even Cat's mother could see, had a certain glamour. The henna-dyed, short-cropped hair, the plum lipstick and black imitation leather chic she favoured when out of school uniform was heady stuff for an impressionable country girl. And she had charm too; there was a sparkle of mischief in her kohl-outlined brown eyes and the pert little face had a wide mouth which smiled with engaging warmth. Given the family background, Marjory would have had a lot of sympathy with the child if she hadn't so feared her influence on her daughter.

The black bedroom was evidence of this. All black, Cat had said defiantly, as the family sat over supper in the farmhouse kitchen.

'*Black!*' Her mother's astonished response was enough to provoke an explosion.

'Oh, I knew you'd rat on your promise! You didn't mean it, did you, unless I chose something really sad to suit you. I expect you get some sort of tragic kick out of it – ruining my life?' Furious tears pouring down her cheeks, Cat pushed her chair back and jumped up from the table.

Her brother Cameron, still more or less normal at eleven, looked up to say, 'Hey, chill, why don't you?' before returning to his unsophisticated attack on the mountain of spaghetti bolognese on his plate.

'Cat, I didn't say you couldn't have black. You just took me by surprise. But if you're going to behave like a toddler throwing itself into a tantrum, I'm not prepared to discuss it with you. If you want to storm out of the room, do that. You can think it over in your—' The slam of the door interrupted her sentence and Marjory finished it, 'nice pink bedroom', with a rueful grin at Bill.

'Dear God!' he said piously, making a quite unnecessary business of twiddling strands of pasta round his fork.

So black it was, after Cat had cooled down sufficiently to mumble something that could almost, with extreme good-will, be construed as an apology. Rejecting Cat's offer to do it herself, with Kylie's help, Marjory had introduced a white ceiling and white woodwork which hadn't featured in the original colour scheme. Still, if Cat didn't like it, there was always the traditional alternative.

Marjory gave a last look round the half-finished room, shuddered, and shut the door.

The windows of Jackie's, the little hairdresser's salon in one of the warren of narrow streets off the High Street, were opaque with condensation. Inside, there was a cosy fug created by the heat of the hairdryers, and the sickly smell of shampoo and hair-spray almost masked the acrid, ammoniacal fumes from the old-fashioned permanent wave which was being inflicted on old Mrs Barclay, whose thinning white hair was a hedgehog mass of pink curlers and flimsy tissues.

The eponymous Jackie, in a shocking-pink overall like her two assistants, was a woman in her forties, elaborately coiffed herself with improbably black, brittle-looking hair in a French roll. Even through her pancake make-up her cheeks were flushed with the heat as she flicked a steel tail-comb to neaten the wispy strands before soaking them with a sponge and wrapping them in tissue. She was just clamping the last of the curlers in place when the first maroon went off.

'That's the lifeboat!' Her eyes went to her seventeen-year-old daughter, Karyn, who had looked up from her task of sweeping up hair-clippings.

'Oh mercy, that'll be Willie away, will it?' quavered Mrs Barclay. 'It's an awful dangerous business, yon!'

'Och, away you go!' Jackie said robustly. 'They've that many safety features these days it might as well be a pleasure steamer. And a night like this, it'll be a flat calm out there.

It's likely just some poor souls run aground maybe in the fog, and with the radar they've got on the boat it's like working in broad daylight.'

But despite her confident tones, there was some sort of anxiety in her face as she asked Karyn if she'd heard her dad's bike going past.

Karyn shook her head. 'But it's him would have set off the rocket, isn't it?'

'That's right.' The second report sounded as she turned with studied calm to fetch the bottle of lotion to be applied to Mrs Barclay's exposed pink scalp. 'Did you – did you see him at all at lunchtime, Karyn?'

It seemed a casual enough enquiry but her daughter's look was understanding. 'Aye, I did. He was fine, Mum, busy working at the shed and chatting to a couple of the visitors.'

Jackie relaxed visibly. 'That's all right then. Now, don't you fash yourself, Mrs Barclay. Willie's a good cox after all these years being skipper of his own boat, and they know what they're doing.'

'I hope you know what you're doing with that cold stuff you're putting on my head,' the old lady retorted querulously. 'Catch my death, likely.'

Luke Smith stood on the pier, his hands in the pockets of his waterproof trousers, his narrow shoulders hunched, looking disconsolately at the retreating wake of the *Maud and Millicent Dalrymple*. The Knockhaven lifeboat was an Atlantic 75 rigid inflatable, known affectionately as the *Maud'n'Milly* after the two maiden ladies whose generous legacies had provided the money to commission it.

For once, as reserve, he'd actually managed to get there ahead of Rob Anderson – owner of the Anchor Inn in Shore Street, a former naval officer and second cox to Willie Duncan – and had even started to get kitted up by the time Rob arrived. Luke had hoped Willie might have said he'd take him instead; he'd been out on enough training trips, for God's sake, and surely this would have been ideal as his first chance to go 'out on a shout', as the jargon had it – it sounded as if it was just some idiot who'd got himself stranded in the bay. But no, with a jerk of the head Willie, who was never exactly chatty, indicated that there was no point in finishing his preparations. Rob had given him a sympathetic glance as he pulled his own kit out of his locker, but he hadn't offered to stand down, had he? And of course Ashley Randall had been the first crew to arrive after Willie, as she nearly always was. She must cut her patients off in mid-sentence, sometimes.

It was a wonder Willie had accepted her as a permanent member of the crew. A doctor might be useful occasionally but certainly wasn't necessary, and Willie'd been known more than once to repeat the adage that there were three useless things on a lifeboat – a wheelbarrow, a woman and a naval officer. But there he was now, putting out to sea with two out of the three. When Luke had been unwise enough to remark on it to Ashley he'd got the tart reply that Willie was clearly drawing the line at taking the wheelbarrow, which Luke had taken as a gibe about his own competence. And of course where Ashley was concerned it hadn't done her any harm to be a protégée of the Honorary Secretary. If that was all she was, which was a whole other question.

Things really weren't going well for Luke right now. It had all looked so promising on his move to Galloway two years ago; with his interest in outdoor activities, the job teaching geography at Kirkluce Academy had seemed perfect. He was almost at the end of his tether teaching in an inner-city school in Glasgow, a baptism of fire for a first job which had all but broken his nerve. He'd been looking forward to teaching his subject now instead of spending every lesson trying vainly to get the class quiet enough to be able to hear his pearls of wisdom on the subject of the volcanic geology of Iceland.

Somehow, though, it hadn't quite worked out like that. It had been another illusion shattered when he discovered that the gentle country children he'd envisaged were just as unruly and disrespectful of him as their urban counterparts had been. And what was even more galling was that the only thing different was that in Glasgow no one had been able to do much with the kids whereas here he was one of very few members of staff who had serious difficulties with discipline.

He'd assumed, too, that here there wouldn't be the same problems with what was categorised as substance abuse, but the under-age drinking culture was well established and he could see that even in the time he'd been here the drug problem was getting worse. It was seriously depressing.

All in all, if it hadn't been for his involvement with the lifeboat, he'd have been packing it in and looking for another job by now, preferably one which meant he would never again be forced to speak to anyone under the age of twenty. But he'd rented a cottage in one of the higgledy-piggledy lanes which seamed the old part of the fishing town, hoping he might be able to afford to buy a dinghy and do a bit of sailing, and then heard the lifeboat legends in the pub, tales of rescues and failed rescues, of waves like walls of water and winds that tore the breath from your throat – high romance, in this pedestrian age! And these men were respected, heroes, almost. Luke hungered for respect.

It was the proudest moment of his life when he got the letter accepting him for training. It made you one of them, entitled to sit around the crew room at the station, to take training courses at RNLI Cowes, to go out on exercises as one of the crew, waving to people who stopped to watch the launch admiringly, and it all gave you back some of the self-respect that seeped out of you day after day in the classroom.

Yet here, too, he was beginning to doubt himself. 'Always the bridesmaid, eh?' a grinning mechanic had said to him as they assisted at the launch, checking the chains as the *Maud'n'Milly* was eased down the slipway into the deep water at its foot. It wasn't fair, after all his hard work to pass every training course he'd been to.

The *Maud'n'Milly* was out of sight now. Luke turned gloomily to walk back into the shed, then hearing a burst of mocking laughter looked round. A small group of spectators – about fifty, perhaps – was still gathered at the head of the pier and among them, he could see several youths. It was too foggy to identify them clearly, but he didn't need to – it would be some of his Year 12 pupils, including, most likely, his bête noire, Nathan Rettie, who was Rob Anderson's sixteen-year-old stepson. Luke had had a major run-in with him resulting in Nat's suspension, which had looked like a victory at the time. But Luke had paid for it afterwards – oh yes, he had paid.

With what he hoped was dignity he straightened his shoulders and turned to go in. He heard something whistle past his head and as a pebble struck the wall of the shed in front of him, spun round. The boys, still laughing, were moving off and there was nothing he could do, nothing that wouldn't make him look even more foolish and impotent than he already did.

'There's that car coming back up again, Ron.' The woman dropped the curtain and came away from the window of the cottage at the top of the road down to Fuill's Inlat.

Her husband, engrossed in a football match on television, grunted.

'Wonder what it would be doing there, a night like this? Driving too fast, anyway, when you can hardly see your hand in front of your face. It's barely been five minutes down there – what do you think it's doing?'

He sighed, then said repressively, 'One of the workmen, probably, from those new houses they're building. Forgotten his hammer or something and gone back to fetch it.'

'I suppose that's the sort of thing we'll have to put up with all the time once they sell them.' Her tone was fretful. 'That'll be the end of our peace and quiet. It'll be like Piccadilly Circus before they're finished.'

The exaggeration earned her an exasperated glance, then Ron went back to his football, sunk in gloom. Ayr United were losing again.

2

A wind had got up, pulling and tearing the fog to rags of wispy cloud, dull grey against the night sky, with the first stars starting to show through. The *Maud'n'Milly* was roaring back across the harbour, a small speedboat bouncing jauntily on a tow-line behind her.

Waiting on the pier under the arc lights, Ritchie Elder, Honorary Secretary of the Knockhaven lifeboat, made an imposing figure in his navy and red lifeboat sweatshirt: a big man, broad-shouldered but spare, with a fine head of well-cut iron-grey hair and a complexion still tanned from his most recent Caribbean cruise. His eyes were very blue and his uncompromising jawline suggested a man who knew what he wanted and how to get it, a suggestion confirmed by his success in having Elder's Executive Homes built the way he decreed, at the price he set and in the time he specified. His business methods, he was wont to remark, might not make him popular but they had made him rich, and you could always buy friends.

It was a relief every time to see 'his' boat's safe return. Acceding to the coastguard's request to launch the lifeboat hadn't been a difficult decision tonight but sending a crew out into savage seas on a mission of mercy could sometimes be a heavy responsibility. In the ultimate analysis the cox had the final say on safety, of course, but he'd never yet heard of a cox who'd refused to take the boat out in answer to a distress call.

The *Maud'n'Milly* came alongside and tied up. A middle-aged man and woman, wrapped in silver survival blankets, were sitting in the stern; the woman got shakily to her feet as Willie Duncan cut the engines then came forward to help her climb the iron rungs of the ladder up to the pier. Overweight and clumsy, she had almost to be hoisted up, and Elder went forward to crouch at the top, holding out his hand for her to grasp as she negotiated the awkward gap between the ladder and the pier.

'There you are, safe now,' he said, putting a comforting arm round her shoulders to steady her as she tried to find her land legs again.

Baleful eyes glared up at him. 'No thanks to *him* if I am,' she said, directing a smouldering glance over her shoulder at the sheepish-looking man who had followed her up the ladder, rather unfortunately still sporting a yachting cap with 'Skipper' on the front in large letters.

Stifling a grin, Elder escorted her to the shed where she could get a cup of tea and the chance to pursue her quarrel in comfort, then went back to the boat. 'How did it go?' he called down.

Ashley Randall had taken off her helmet and her hair was curling wildly in the damp. With her cheeks pink from the fresh wind, she looked up smiling from her task of coiling ropes. In the harsh illumination he could see her eyes sparkling, with excitement, probably. Retrospective or in anticipation?

'Piece of cake,' she said. 'Believe it or not, he ran out of petrol, then they drifted and the fog came down and he'd no charts or anything, so she decided they were going to drift on to rocks and be wrecked. She'd been announcing this at the top of her voice for about an hour before we arrived, as far as I could gather.'

'Can't say she looked the sort of girl I'd choose to run out of petrol with myself, but there's no accounting for tastes. OK, Willie? Shall I get them into position to winch her up?'

Duncan had started the engines again. 'Fine,' he said over his shoulder, and Ashley climbed neatly up the ladder to stand beside Elder on the pier, her yellow oilskin open under the orange Crewsaver life-jacket. Rob Anderson, who had jumped aboard the little speedboat to tie it up, appeared from a ladder further along and came towards them, unfastening his.

'I'll just get off now if you don't mind, sir. Katy's single-handed in the bar tonight and I'll get Brownie points if I'm back before the evening rush starts. You'll get the full report from Willie.'

'Now *there's* a thought,' Elder said dryly and the other man laughed.

'Well, from Ashley, then. Not that there's much to tell, really – just the standard incompetent stuff. Shouldn't be let out without a keeper, some folk.'

He disappeared into the shed to take off the rest of his kit. People were gathering by the slipway now to watch Willie perform the skilled operation of lining up the keel so that the winching cable could be attached, leaving Elder and Ashley alone together. Instinctively they moved out from the pool of light where they had been standing but took up positions an ostentatious two feet apart. That was close enough, though, for her to hear him murmur, 'Tonight?'

Her eyes danced up at him. 'I'll need to phone my husband to tell him I'm back.' She spoke loudly enough to be heard by anyone interested enough to be listening. 'He always worries, bless him.'

This time, instead of his mobile, she dialled their home number and after a moment switched off. 'Oh dear,' she said carefully, 'he must have gone round to his mother's for supper. I'd better not disturb them, in case they're eating.'

Her eyes met his in perfect understanding, then they both went over to watch as the cable tightened and the *Maud'n'Milly* was winched gradually out of the water.

'How was Willie?' There was a shade of anxiety in his voice. She had shared her concerns with him some time ago.

'No problem tonight,' she assured him. 'And look at the way he brought her in there – Rob's all right for a second cox, but he'd make a meal of doing that. Willie knows the coast like the back of his hand too – you can't have the same knowledge after living here for only three years. And in any case Rob'll never be half the seaman Willie is, whatever state he's in.'

'Difference between spending your life at sea on a destroyer and being skipper of a trawler, I suppose. Still, don't take any risks with your personal safety – or anyone else's.'

'Oh, I promise. But there isn't anyone to touch him when it comes to tricky manoeuvres.'

'Oh, I don't know.' He wasn't looking at her, but he was smiling. 'I rather fancy myself in that field as well.'

'And that's *another* one, away down!' The woman reached the window a little too late to see the car which had passed on the road down to Fuill's Inlat. 'There must have been a gey lot of hammers forgotten, according to you, Ron!'

'It'll be rare exercise for you, Jeanie, jumping up and down all evening after they've sold those houses.' He was in a thoroughly bad mood after his team's defeat. 'You'd better get used to it, that's all I can say.'

'And look – that's someone else turning in off the main road!' Jeanie's voice was shrill. 'One of these great big daft things like wee lorries on great big wheels.'

He was almost interested. 'That'll be the Heid Bummer – that man Elder. He's got one of those big Mitsubishis. They've that showhouse down there that's opening soon – he's maybe giving someone a wee keek at it.'

'So we're going to have to thole them being up and down the road all night as well as all day? The works traffic's been bad enough but if it's starting at night now too – well, I'll just have to phone the Council again, though they're nothing but a set of useless articles.'

Suddenly, Ron jumped to his feet and went out of the room. She stared after him; he reappeared a moment later with a wodge of cotton wool in his hand.

'Shove that in your lugs so you can't hear them,' he said brutally. 'Either that or the next time I go to that bathroom cabinet I'm bringing back the sticking-plaster to put across your mouth.'

He looked, Dorothy Randall thought, tired and somehow strained tonight, and the eternal flame of her hatred for her daughter-in-law burned that little bit brighter as she sat over supper with her son in her Victorian villa, The Hollies, up at the back of Knockhaven. She had lit the candles in the plate candelabra on the reproduction Georgian dining-table; the room, with its Regency-striped wallpaper, always looked particularly warm and welcoming, she thought, with the candles lit and the thick red velvet curtains drawn across the bay window.

It had been a real scramble following his phone call, with all she had to do, but somehow she'd got his meal prepared and still had time to change into a smart blue twin-set, with her pearls of course, and its matching wool skirt, but she'd managed. She always prided herself on looking calm and well turned-out for her son – without, of course, in any way compromising her standards. Ashley's idea of taking trouble over food seemed to consist of scooping a ready-meal on to a dish instead of serving it straight from its foil container, and Lewis, poor love, did enjoy proper home cooking, nicely presented.

Tonight, with only a couple of hours' notice, she'd just had to take an apple pie out of the freezer and put two steaks into the microwave to defrost. She didn't like doing that, but at least it was quick, and she'd served it daintily with a sprig of parsley and a cheese sauce for the cauliflower – he'd always enjoyed that. And she enjoyed watching him eat, watching his clever, doctor's hands slice so neatly across the grain of the meat. She devoured her son with her eyes, her own steak barely touched, as if the sight of him were sustenance enough. He was so beautiful, with his dark waving hair and blue eyes with those long, thick lashes like a girl's – and such a good boy too, coming back to be near his mother in the teeth of opposition from the harpy who had somehow managed to snare him. Oh, he didn't say much – Lewis had always been one to keep his own counsel – but his mother could guess what That Woman would have put him through. He was too good, that was the problem, allowing her to walk all over him with her constant demands. Oh, she heard all about the way she behaved in the surgery from Muriel Henderson – and how she behaved outside it too, by all accounts.

Did he know what they were all saying, know how she was making a fool of him? And of her mother-in-law too; no one would say anything to Lewis directly, but there were people bold enough to make broad hints, veiled in mock-sympathy ('It can't be easy for poor Dr Lewis, his wife being so taken up with her lifeboat friends'), which had necessitated some cold and steely snubbing.

She hadn't dared tell him herself. She and Lewis were close, but she had never been invited to discuss his marriage. Though she could see sometimes that things were difficult, he kept his problems to himself, just as he always had even as a little boy, and she had spent years concealing her opinion of Ashley so that the woman could have no excuse for creating a breach. If she'd got it wrong, if Lewis blamed the messenger for the message, it would have undone the careful work of years without any certainty of success in ending this disastrous marriage which was obviously never going to provide Lewis with the son he deserved, the grandchild she so hungered for. Ashley, as she had laughingly told Dorothy, wasn't the maternal type.

'It was your day off today, wasn't it? Did they have to call you in to cover for Ashley?' Muriel had told her how often *that* happened.

He shook his head. 'She did warn me to expect a phone call, but it would have been a bit tricky if they had wanted me. I'd been walking from St Ninian's Cave over to the Isle of Whithorn – looking down towards Burrow Head it was quite spectacular to watch the landscape disappearing as the fog started rolling in – but by the time I got back from there surgery would probably have been over.'

'What time will the poor girl get home tonight?' Dorothy spoke with determined brightness. 'It's such a *demanding* hobby, isn't it?'

Lewis sighed. 'I don't think she sees it quite in those terms. A hobby's something you can give up if it stops being amusing. She describes it as being almost a vocation – the call of the sea, that sort of thing.' He gave a wry smile. 'Frankly, from the symptoms it looks to me more like an addiction.'

'I suppose it must be like belonging to a very special club, isn't it? Now, that is very addictive – do you remember how when you were little it was always terribly important to belong to whichever secret club was the thing of the moment, with all the passwords and secret rituals?'

'Good gracious, Mother, how long ago was that? But yes, I do remember – what fun it was!' He smiled reminiscently.

She cut a piece off her own steak with apparent concentration, saying casually, 'And, of course, you do form very close friendships when you're involved in something like that, don't you? I'm sure, with that atmosphere of excitement and tension, dealing with life-and-death situations, it creates special bonds with the people you're working with, very *intimate* relationships—'

She had gone too far. Lewis looked up sharply, his blue eyes cold. 'Oh, I think Ashley's pretty savvy about handling that sort of thing.

'That was a very good steak, Mother. Was it from the butcher's in Shore Street? Ashley and I always use lack of time as an excuse for buying ready-meals but actually steak's the ultimate convenience food.'

'And it tastes *so* much nicer, doesn't it?' Dorothy rose to collect the plates. 'And it's my own apple pie to follow. With proper custard, of course.'

So he had heard something. If there were . . . developments, how would she play it? As she went through to the kitchen, her mind was buzzing.

Ashley Randall sat on the end of the super king-size bed in the sumptuous master bedroom of the Elder's Executive Homes showhouse, fastening her lacy white bra. In the en suite bathroom, Ritchie Elder was carefully combing his hair in front of the mirror with its star's dressing room-style lighting.

'I do apologise that the water isn't connected for a shower,' he called over his shoulder. 'It just might give rise to questions if I insisted. There was a bit of chat as it was because I had the house furnished so early.'

'Lewis will probably be still at his mother's anyway. If he's back I can just say I didn't stop for a shower at the shed because I was so keen to get back to him.'

'He'll believe you?'

'He always believes what I tell him. It's the thing I like best about him.'

Elder came out of the bathroom. 'Are you sure? He's not a fool.'

'No, he's not a fool. He's just supremely complacent – thinks the world was arranged for his benefit and can't imagine that anything could possibly happen which would interfere with his image of the way things should be.'

She stood up to put on her cream silk blouse. He came across to her and put his arms round her from behind, undoing the buttons she had been fastening and nuzzling her neck. She smiled, but disengaged herself. '*No*, Ritchie!' she scolded with mock severity. 'We're pushing our luck already.' She refastened her shirt, stepped neatly into the trousers of her suit and did them up too.

Elder sighed. 'If you insist. When can I hope to see you again?'

'Well – can't rely on another call-out soon, can we?' She looked about her at the luxurious room, the soft lights, the deep-pile carpet, the faux fur throw on the acreage of the bed. 'And what are we going to do when the sales start for the estate? It must be very soon now. Going anywhere public's too risky, with us both being so well-known round here, and I'm definitely past the age of making out in the back of a car. Even if it is a top-of-the-range Mitsubishi!'

'Mmm. I'll have to work something out. Actually . . .'

They went to opposite sides of the bed to straighten the covers and the throw and plump up the pillows and cushions. After a second he went on, 'Look, I wonder if we need to find some time to talk things through? I've been thinking, lately – we might not want to go on for ever like this.'

Ashley's heart gave a thump of excitement. Yes! But she was too clever to sound anything but cool. 'I don't know,

Ritchie. We're brilliant together, but there's an awful lot to consider – Lewis, Joanna . . .'

'More top-level discussions, then? As soon as possible?'

He came round to take her in his arms again and this time she melted into his embrace.

Rob Anderson slid in behind the bar in the Anchor and with a wink at the man waiting to be served on the other side of the counter, came silently up behind his wife Katy, who was filling a glass from the optic of whisky in the corner, and pinched her charmingly rounded rear.

She jumped and gave a squeal of protest. 'Rob Anderson, look what you've made me do! This was supposed to be a single and now it's a double, thanks to you, you daft eejit!' She looked with affectionate exasperation at her grinning husband and took her revenge by reaching up from her diminutive height to pull the full black beard he had sported since his days in the Navy.

'No loss what a friend gets, eh, Doddie? The extra's on the house.' He took the glass from her and slid it across to the appreciative customer.

'You weren't out long,' she said, pulling the pint of Special to go with it.

'No – just a wee fella who'd bought himself a boat and didn't know his anchor from his engine. His wife was giving him laldie when I left and if you ask me he'll be lucky to get a shottie playing with boats in his bath from now on.

'Were you busy earlier?' He looked round; the bar was quiet enough at the moment, with half a dozen people at the tables and three of the regulars watching the television in the corner, expressing their disgust at Ayr United's defeat.

'No, very quiet. The weather's probably kept them at home.'

'It's clearing now.' Rob picked up a dish-towel and began to dry the tumblers upside down on the draining board beside the sink. 'We'll maybe get a rush later now the match is over.'

'Yes.' Katy sounded distracted and he looked at her sharply. 'All right, love?'

'Yes, fine. Well, at least – Rob, have you seen Nat this evening?'

'Nat?' Oh God, not problems again! He adored his wife of four years, and the proof of that was taking on Nat, who took after his unpleasant father and was the stepson from hell. But Katy suffered enough without him adding to it by complaining about the little creep. 'Why, did you want him for something?'

'No, not really. Oh, he should be in doing his homework, of course, but I've stopped crying for the moon. No, he went out around the time the maroons went off and I haven't seen him since. He's – he's taken my car again and he didn't come in for his tea.'

Rob had already told her what he thought she should do about Nat's joyriding habits. Trying to hide the keys simply wasn't enough; Nat always managed to find out where she put them. He needed a short, sharp lesson, but her fear that he'd kill himself – and somebody else as well – wasn't great enough to persuade her to report him to the police and have him end up with a criminal record. This time, he ducked the issue.

'Probably got chips instead. And now I think about it, there was a group of lads hanging around the shed when we came back – he could have been with them. He'll turn up when he's hungry.'

And he mustn't even allow himself to wish that Nat had done a runner, because it would break Katy's heart. Not that Nat wasn't all set to break it anyway.

As Ritchie Elder parked the Mitsubishi outside Bayview House, he glanced up at the impressive, pseudo-Palladian frontage with its pillared porch. It was, of course, one of his own Executive Homes, only built on a uniquely lavish scale on a site about a mile south of Knockhaven by the main coast road which, as a prospectus would say, boasted spectacular sea views. It was a statement about his status as local lad made good.

One wing was dedicated to a swimming pool, sauna and gym area, a double-height temple to the Gods of Fitness and the Body Beautiful, of which cult Joanna seemed to be becoming a High Priestess. The lights were on there now; no doubt she was exercising. He wondered, sometimes, if she ever did anything else nowadays.

He'd married a girl with the face of a Dresden shepherdess and a delicate physique, ready to be the perfect wife for a man who was Going Places, with no inconvenient ambition except to be hostess for him and mother to his children. Unfortunately, the delicate physique had recently proved not up to the second of these tasks.

He was disappointed, admittedly – what man wouldn't like a son to carry on the name and the business? – but there were many compensations for being childfree. Joanna, on the other hand, was distraught. It seemed that despite wanting for nothing in terms of luxury and comfort, her life was pointless if the outcome wasn't small, squally, smelly things to mother. He'd suggested puppies; she'd looked at him as if he was a monster.

The lights were on in the gym area. She'd be pounding away on the treadmill, no doubt, although she had thinned down to little more than bones and whipcord muscle already. Ashley somehow managed to stay seriously fit while retaining those silken rounded curves that could drive a man mad. Hastily, he tried to think of something else. It was getting harder and harder to think about anything except Ashley.

He wasn't often unsure of himself, but then he'd never

had a woman like Ashley, so cool, so self-possessed. She could just be using him, as he had used half a dozen other women, to add a little spice to married life. This was the first time he'd ever seriously considered the hideous and expensive business of divorce; Ashley might turn him down flat, of course, but even so it probably wasn't too soon to sound out a competent lawyer.

He took the stairs to his bedroom two at a time. A swim last thing at night was a useful habit he'd developed over his unfaithful years, and he changed into swimming trunks, put on a towelling robe and padded downstairs and along to the pool area.

Joanna was, indeed, on the treadmill when he came in. These last few weeks, she'd seemed to live on it. She was wearing turquoise shorts and a white T-shirt, her Nikes thudding away on the moving belt. She was sweating profusely, her neat-featured face contorted in what looked like extreme agony. She raised her hand in greeting as he came in, then flicked a switch to allow her to slow down. 'Eleven miles,' she gasped as she stopped, labouring for breath.

Ritchie picked up a towel from a chair and threw it at her. 'You're sweating like a pig,' he said brutally, then walked past her to execute a competent shallow dive into the pool and began ploughing up and down in an elegant, economical crawl.

Watching her husband, Joanna Elder rubbed her face, her neck, her shoulders and under her arms. She had punished her body – her pathetic, treacherous body – for its failures to the point where conceiving would have been beyond it anyway.

Ritchie thought her problem was not having children to mother; he was wrong. She *needed* children, for security. Without children, she was only Ritchie Elder's wife – his present wife. Hardly an assured position. Oh, she had always known about his infidelities, but equally she knew that until now none of them had been serious. She could still look in the mirror in the morning and see Mrs Ritchie Elder looking back at her.

Her parents had a newsagent's shop in Dumfries where she'd helped, not very enthusiastically, and she'd done a bit of local modelling though she wasn't tall enough for the real stuff. She'd never had a proper job, the sort that gave you status of your own, and she'd never been very good at friendship either, somehow. It all seemed like awfully hard work, listening to the boring problems girlfriends always had. So marrying Ritchie had been the perfect answer: it provided money, position, a social life, everything she'd ever wanted – as long as she was his wife. If Ritchie divorced her, it wasn't just the money, though of course she'd be doing her best to take care of that; it would be like falling into a vacuum that would suck the breath from her body.

There were rumours which even she had been hearing, for ages now. And she was scared. She was terribly, terribly scared.

It was five o'clock in the morning when the crying started. It began softly, whimpers at first, but soon it was anguished, heart-wrenching.

She'd tried to ignore it when it woke her at first, shut her eyes, tried to sink back into sleep again. She pulled the pillow over her head to try to blot out the sound, reminded herself of what she'd been advised – no, instructed to do.

It was hopeless. Completely impossible. Laura Harvey switched on the light, blinking blearily at the clock. She got up, shoving her feet into the slippers by the side of her bed, and grabbed a dressing gown; there were the first hints of cold weather ahead in the chill of the night air.

The sound of her movement seemed to provoke even more distress. The cries rose in pitch and intensity as she opened the door of the kitchen in her rented cottage and switched on the light.

One corner of the kitchen, the one nearest the radiator, had been barricaded off with a deep wooden plank. Over the top of it, a little black nose and two furry ears appeared, then disappeared, then appeared again as their owner bounced up and down. Laura went over to it. 'You're very, very naughty,' she said reproachfully.

The collie pup on the other side of the barricade began a frantic wagging of its stumpy, pointed tail, while still emitting 'Yow-yow-yows!' of distress. The comfortable basket by the radiator was empty, the old duvet which had lined it was lying on the floor oozing feathers, and the hot-water bottle, concealed below it to substitute for the warmth of a mother and four siblings, had deflated in a large pool of water. There was another, more sinister, wet patch too on the newspaper covering the floor.

'Daisy, this is ridiculous. Marjory told me I just had to ignore you, but how could I when you're making that sort of noise?' She bent forward to scoop up the portly little creature, cradling it against her.

The effect was magical. The noise stopped instantly, the warm, furry head butted against her, and a tiny pink tongue tried frantically to lick whatever flesh was available.

Laura was entranced. 'Oh, poor baby! Are you missing your mum?' she crooned idiotically as the puppy snuggled into her arms and indicated that in these circumstances she was prepared to go back to sleep. At least Laura retained enough common sense to say, 'Oh no you don't! Outside first, if I'm going to take your basket through to my bedroom. And you'd better take on board that you're going to have to settle there, with no more nonsense.'

Daisy, daughter of Meg of Mains of Craigie, seemed unimpressed by the outdoors at this hour of the morning. Eventually, after a long chilly wait for nature to take its course, Laura deemed that it was prudent to bring her back inside. Puppy in one hand, basket and what was left of the duvet in the other, she went back upstairs to the bedroom, settled the puppy in one corner, and climbed thankfully back into bed.

She was almost dropping off when the crying started again. Too tired to think of discipline, Laura groped her way across the room, grabbed the squirming Daisy and dumped her on the end of the bed.

'Now, since it's the first night you can sleep there. Just don't tell Marjory, that's all.'

Daisy waited a few minutes, then wriggled up the bed until she was cosily settled in contact with her new best friend, her head tucked comfortably under Laura's chin. Entirely satisfied by this adjustment to the pecking order, she sighed pleasurably and fell asleep.

3

The spicy, delectable smell of home-baking wafted through the kitchen of Enid Davis's modest terraced house in Knockhaven High Street. With one of the changes of mood so typical of this south-west corner of Scotland, yesterday's grey dankness had given way to a clear autumn morning with the sunshine making golden pools of light on the blue vinyl floor.

Enid had wakened early – she rarely slept well – and put a batch of rock cakes in to bake while she had her usual cup of weak tea and toast with her home-made marmalade. They should be ready now; she opened the oven door and took out the tray, viewing them with satisfaction – all golden-brown and glistening with the demerara sugar she had sprinkled on top. There was a clean dish-towel waiting to receive them and she lifted the buns into it, folded it neatly, then put the bundle into a basket standing ready on the worktop.

It was an old-fashioned kitchen, bare of the usual knick-knacks, and immaculately kept. She hadn't been able to afford to replace the chipped blue and cream formica units but she was good at DIY and she'd fitted the new vinyl to the floor and painted the walls cream so that at least it was clean and functional, which was all that mattered. She enjoyed cooking still, even if doing it for one was a depressing business.

Now, she went over to the mirror she'd fixed to the back

of the kitchen door and, though it was neat enough already, brushed the straight, light-brown hair which she wore in a longish bob, powdered her nose and put on some pale coral lipstick. She sighed. There was nothing wrong with her looks: she had regular features, a good skin and really quite pretty grey eyes. She looked neat, efficient – and wholly un-memorable, the sort of person you could be introduced to and not recognise the next time you met her. Not that she wanted to make a spectacle of herself; it was just that this was yet another instance of the terrible unfairness of life, the way other people, like Ashley Randall for instance, should have it all – looks, status, a good husband and not a care in the world – and not even appreciate it.

Enid glanced at her watch, then rapidly gathered up her handbag, her basket and the coat she had laid out ready on the back of a chair. It would only take her a few minutes to walk to the Knockhaven Medical Centre, leaving a good half-hour before the doctors would start arriving and the doors had to be opened to patients at half-past eight. When she was on the early shift she liked to have plenty of time to deal with messages on the answerphone and check the appointments before that.

And sometimes, if she was lucky, Dr Lewis would be in early too. He was such a kind, sympathetic man: she always felt better when the day started with a chat to him, and on the days when she brought in baking for the receptionists' elevenses she could rely on him stopping with his nose twitching as he passed the reception desk. He'd said before that rock cakes were his favourites, and there was one thing certain – that *she* wouldn't bother herself to make them for him at home.

Her mouth twisted into a bitter line. It would do Ashley Randall good to live with Enid's ex-husband for a bit. They could have a competition to see which of them could be more cruel and selfish and insensitive to anyone else's feelings. And unfaithful, too – oh yes, the receptionists all knew how she was going on. And poor Mrs Randall knew now too; Muriel Henderson had felt she ought to be told. Though of course she'd seen through her daughter-in-law long before that, Muriel said, and she'd gone through agonies watching her son suffer, being ordered around like a slave, with no proper home life, and now being cheated on. Enid hadn't much time for Muriel, but she approved of Mrs Randall – she was a devoted mother and a nice woman who always had a word for you when she came into the Medical Centre, not like Dr Ashley, who treated everyone behind the desk like dirt. Some days, when things got on top of Enid, she just felt like telling the stuck-up bitch what she could do and walking out.

But that was stupid. She'd left her home up on the West Coast north of Glasgow to get away from her broken marriage and her painful memories; almost broken herself, it had taken finding the job here a few years ago to give her a new sense of purpose, and she wasn't about to squander that in a fit of temper. She should be used to controlling her feelings by now. With a final pat to her hair and a neatening tug at her navy skirt, she picked up the basket and went out.

She arrived at the surgery first, as she always liked to do. She was listening to the answerphone messages when Muriel Henderson arrived, sniffing the air.

Muriel was the most senior of the four receptionists employed at the Knockhaven Medical Centre. In her fifties, she was divorced with two children who had imitated her husband in making an early escape. She had lived in Knockhaven all her life and with her local connections had an intelligence-gathering service which would have had the KGB queuing up for lessons. 'The trouble with Muriel,' one of the doctors had been heard to say, 'is that she sees the practice as her own little police state.'

Disliking her was the aversion that dare not speak its name and Enid smiled, as everyone always did, in response to Muriel's jovial greeting.

'Goodness me, Enid, you've been at it again, haven't you, you terrible woman, with me trying to keep on my diet! Did you spend all your time off baking? And you know the doctors'll be down on you like a ton of bricks – it's the obesity clinic this morning, and that smell's like waving a bottle of whisky around at an AA meeting!'

'I'm thinking of sending you on a diversity course, Tam.'

Detective Sergeant Tam MacNee's swarthy face, pitted from teenage acne, took on an expression of horror. Dressed in his customary plain-clothes uniform of black leather jacket, white T-shirt and jeans, he had just come into DI Fleming's office; he kept hold of the door handle as if ready to bolt back out again at any moment.

'Tell me you're kidding me, boss,' he pleaded. 'This is just a wind-up, eh?'

Fleming kept her face serious. 'It's something we're all supposed to do. It's to stamp out racism, sexism, politically incorrect language—'

'Look!' Letting go of the door, MacNee came to sit opposite her, leaning earnestly across the desk. 'See Wilson and Macdonald from the crime desk? Went on that course a couple of weeks ago, right? And here's me going into a meeting with them about shoplifting yesterday. They're both from Edinburgh, so what does Wilson say? "Here, he's from Glasgow – who let him in?" And Macdonald goes, "Sorry, he could speak English so I didn't realise." That's how much good it does.'

'I didn't say it did any good. I just said it's one of the boxes we need to tick. There's a slot available and I think I should send you on it. Unless . . .'

'Unless?' MacNee's eyes narrowed. 'What's the deal?'

'Oh, there isn't one, really. It's just you could maybe—'

MacNee relaxed visibly, sitting back in the chair. 'Oh, we're talking *blackmail*, are we? Oh, I'm jake with that. I've a thing or two up my sleeve I could use myself if I have to.'

He wasn't wrong there. There were one or two revelations he could make, from the early days when they were partners in a squad car, that would be worth good money down in the CID room.

She grinned, putting up her thumbs and saying, 'Keys?' in the traditional Scottish playground signal of truce. 'The thing is, you know Charlotte Nisbet's getting married and going to live in Stirling? We've got a replacement coming.'

'So I should bloody well hope. We're spread as thin as fish paste on a Morningside sandwich as it is.'

'It's a man.'

'Fair enough. And?'

'He's moving here from Edinburgh.'

'So? I've a forgiving nature. I even bought Wilson a pint last night.'

'He's English.'

There was an appreciable pause. MacNee sighed. 'Even so, he *might* be all right.'

Fleming pounced, like a cat which after waiting a long time in the grass has at last seen the fieldmouse twitch. 'That's exactly my point, Tam. Diversity course.'

'It was a joke, for any favour.'

'I know. You're supposed to get trained not to make jokes like that.'

He stared at her, flatly disbelieving. 'Are you serious, Marjory?'

'We-ell, of course not entirely. I'm not saying you can't have a bit of a laugh. If we stopped everyone making jokes at someone else's expense a deathly silence would fall on the whole place. But you know as well as I do about anti-English feeling.'

'And you don't think the English lad would come to you complaining about discrimination if I was rude to everyone except him?' MacNee's tone was dry.

'The problem is that jokes are a helluva lot funnier when you're an insider. It can just be a short step from there to downright bullying. You've seen the cases in the Press where English folk claim they've been victimised at work.'

'If he thinks he needs special consideration from his fellow officers, what's he going to do if there's a brawl when he's making a couple of arrests? Tell them to cut it out, chaps, in a pan-loaf voice?'

'I've no reason to suppose he thinks any such thing.' Fleming's voice took on a steely edge. 'He's coming to us with the highest recommendation from the St Leonard's Street HQ in Edinburgh. He's got a lot of experience of the drugs scene and you know how we're struggling with that at the moment.'

MacNee grunted. 'We're doing our best—'

'But it's getting worse, that's the point. Oh sure, so we're picking up the kids smoking a joint – now they get a Fiscal fine which they don't pay anyway. They just grin and walk away without so much as a note on the file, let alone a criminal record. They know we can't touch them – why would they cooperate with us to close down the supply lines? We're not containing it, Tam, are we?'

'We know what a lot of the problem is – there's too many lads around here unemployed. With the foot-and-mouth last year, and them that should know better deciding to hand all our fishing rights to Spain and send the boats to the breaker's yard – well, Satan finds mischief for idle hands, as my nan used to say any time she saw me sitting down. They've risk in their blood, these fisher folk, and supposing they're short of money, with easy access to a wee boat . . . Well, some of them are just suppliers waiting for someone to tell them how to do it.'

'I know that, Tam. But theories aren't enough. We need a high-profile arrest or two to put the frighteners on them.'

'I'm working on it.' His tone was defensive.

'I know that too. I'm not criticising, this is just a situation where we need all the help we can get. We need everyone to work together as a team and what we don't need is the whole initiative coming unstuck, either because this guy feels uncomfortable and applies for a transfer back, or because you come to his contribution with a hostile attitude. The Super isn't at all happy.'

'Who is?' MacNee shrugged, his face set in a hard, in-different line. 'Was there anything else, or was it just to get me to promise to be a good wee boy?'

'Tam . . .' she said uncomfortably. She hadn't handled this well; it had been meant to be a light-hearted warning to lay off the English jokes and somehow it had got out of hand. 'He's just another copper to be treated decently.'

He went to the door. 'Seems more as if he's "*a gentleman who held the patent for his honours immediately from Almighty God*",' he quoted acidly. 'I'd maybe have thought you could trust me to behave professionally but never mind.' The door was shut pointedly behind him.

Fleming hadn't even had the heart to point to the box that stood on her desk to collect the fines she'd imposed on him for quoting Burns. She always thought that wretched man – Tam's idol – had a lot to answer for when it came to the less admirable Scots characteristics, like the aggressive 'wha's-like-us-damn'-few-and-they're-a'-deid' attitude. If they just banned the Burns personality cult, Braveheart and the Old Firm matches, it would do wonders for the Scots' reputation for chippiness and prejudice.

It vexed her, though. Tam was not only her most useful officer, he had seen her through in the days when she was a raw recruit and had watched her progress past him up the promotion ladder without resentment or envy. She relied on him, too, for the street-wisdom he'd acquired in his unregenerate youth in Glasgow, before he fell in love with Bunty, who came from this corner of the world and who, generous in nature as in girth, had sorted him out, married him and brought him back home in much the same spirit as she rescued homeless dogs and one-eyed kittens.

It had been Donald Bailey who'd insisted on a pre-emptive strike. The Superintendent, while being, as he assured Fleming with his usual pomposity, 'fully apprised of MacNee's value to the Force', was nonetheless anxious that the rough places should be made plain for the advent of DC Jonathan Kingsley. Kingsley, he explained, had got into conversation with Assistant Chief Constable Paula Donald at a conference on drugs and impressed her mightily. It was she who had suggested the transfer.

In Fleming's jaundiced opinion it wouldn't be hard to impress the ACC if you were a reasonably personable young man. On the other hand, as Tam might say, even so he *could* have something substantial to contribute to their struggle against the flood of drugs – everything from cannabis and ecstasy to heroin and crack cocaine – which had hit this quiet rural area particularly hard over the last few years.

Tam's analysis was shrewd enough. There was anecdotal evidence to suggest that at least one of the trafficking routes was through the ports in the south of Galloway, with the

stuff coming in via Ireland. He was right, too, that it was
hard for lads with a seafaring tradition who would have
grown up in the expectation of getting not only a job, but
one that would satisfy the young man's need to live life on
the edge without having to join the Army or buy an over-
powered motorbike. And somehow, the evil, invisible men
had found them and now there was a direct channel of
destruction straight to the heart of the rural community
Fleming had grown up in, and loved so well.

Surely it had all been easier when her father had been
a sergeant in the same police station where she was now
an inspector? But perhaps not; perhaps each generation
of law-enforcement officers saw apocalypse in the vices of
the day.

Oh God! Was she really getting that old? She needed a
talk with Laura Harvey; it was good to have acquired a
younger friend who could give her a sense of perspective
on this, who could remind her how Socrates had despaired
of the manners and morals of the younger generation in
his day too. Marjory had used that argument against her
own old-fashioned father in the days when she had a starry-
eyed belief in progress; she was terribly afraid she might
be against it now, and there wasn't a more middle-aged
attitude than that.

She might drop in on Laura on her way home tonight.
She'd been delighted that a contract for psychology-based
articles with a Sunday broadsheet – and, Marjory guessed,
a fairly substantial income from her dead parents' estate –
had allowed Laura to decide to settle in Kirkluce. It was
handy having her there when you wanted to pick her brains
and anyway, Marjory was keen to see how Daisy was sett-
ling into her new home. Daisy had been Bill's present to
Laura, who had used her psychotherapist's skills during the
foot-and-mouth epidemic to persuade him to grieve over his

slaughtered herds as he needed to do, but also to put it all behind him and move on.

Daisy was a considerable gift. Meg, her mother, had a reputation in sheepdog trials which meant that her pups would sell at a substantial premium, and money was tight in the Fleming household at the moment. But it was important for Bill's pride that his gratitude should be commensurate with the favour received.

'We'll have to keep an eye on Laura, though,' he warned Marjory. 'I've picked that pup carefully. She's the sociable one in the litter – you don't want a one-man dog unless you're going to work it – but she's a bright wee smout. Laura will have to see she's not bored, or there'll be trouble. And she'll have Laura wrapped round her little finger if she doesn't watch out, and it's a cruel thing to let any dog get away with that. They need to know you're boss – you tell Laura that.'

It would be fun to see how Laura and her Daisy were getting on. It would take Marjory's mind off her professional problems – and perhaps Laura would even have a few psychological tips to give her about how to deal with wee Weegie hard men who were feeling threatened.

And that was even before she had broken it to Tam that Jonathan Kingsley was a graduate entry to the profession. If she were to be honest, she felt a bit threatened by that herself.

'But where were you last night, Nat?' Katy Anderson persisted, prodding the onions in the frying pan. She was cooking him a beefburger for his tea; he liked them, and if she was going to have an unpleasant confrontation with her son it made sense to avoid an argument about what he was meant to be eating at the same time.

Nathan Rettie, at the kitchen table and apparently deeply

absorbed in the sports pages of a red-top, muttered, 'Oh, nowhere, just out.' He was big for sixteen, dark and heavily built like his father, and his face with its fiery plague of adolescent spots was eloquent testimony to the hormones raging within. He had a row of silver rings in one ear and another ring through his eyebrow which his mother couldn't look at without wincing.

'Out where?'

He looked up then, his brown eyes blazing. 'Quit nagging, Ma, OK? I'm not some kid who gets told what to do.'

At the aggression in his tone, bad memories stirred. It took a lot of courage for her to say, 'You are when it's my car you've taken and you're too young to drive.'

'Oh, turn me in to the police, why don't you? That's what *he* wants, isn't it? Well, you know what you can do, both of you!' He proceeded to tell her, his voice rising as the torrent of obscenities went on.

Feeling almost physically battered by the onslaught, terrified that the outcome would be what it had so often been in the past with his violent father, Katy shrank back instinctively against the wall of the kitchen. When the door suddenly burst open and Rob appeared she gave a sob of pure relief, despite having told him as usual to leave her alone to deal with her son.

Nat was a well-grown lad but Rob was a big man, thickset and powerful. He was wearing a polo shirt which didn't conceal the muscles of his chest and upper arms, painstakingly maintained with weight-training, and with his black beard and thunderous expression he was an intimidating figure.

'What the hell is going on?' he demanded. 'Don't you dare speak to your mother like that! If you think you can bully her because you're bigger and stronger than she is, just remember who's standing at her back.'

Nat, cut off in mid-flow, shrank back in his seat, licking lips that were suddenly dry as he recollected other confrontations with a dominant male. 'If you lay a finger on me, I'll shop you,' he whined, eyes narrowed in hatred for his mother's husband.

Anderson looked down at him contemptuously. 'I wouldn't soil my hands. I've kept out of this until now because I agreed that your behaviour was to be your mother's business. But she's my wife now, and by treating her like that you've made it mine.

'You're living under my roof and I'm going to spell out what that means. You're civil to your mother, for a start. You behave decently at school. And if you so much as touch her car keys again, I call the police, whatever she says.

'Those are the rules. And if you don't like them, you can go back to your father. As I recall, you didn't much like living with him before.'

That touched a raw spot. When his mother, fearing for her life, had left, Nat had chosen to stay. But the family home rapidly grew squalid; there was never any food in the house, or money to buy it with unless Nat managed to nick some from his father before he spent it down the pub. Then, without his mother to act as a punchbag, it was Nat himself who came in for the drunken beatings . . . And it could be a good life with just his mother, if it wasn't for the bastard standing over him, waiting for him to speak, to submit.

Well, he wasn't going to give him that satisfaction. He pushed back his chair and got up, then with a final defiant stare went out of the kitchen and slammed the door.

Katy burst into tears. Rob went over and took her in his arms, patting her soothingly as if she were a frightened child. 'I don't know if I've made things better or worse,' he said ruefully. 'But I meant it, Katy. We've tried it your way – waiting for him to come round to me while I look a total prat – and he resents me like fury anyway. He might as well have something to resent me for.'

She was still shaking. 'It was like one of his father's rages. I really expected him to come and hit me. I know it's not working, trying to be non-confrontational and understanding – it just makes him despise me. But Rob, you wouldn't really send him back to Dave, would you?'

Rob sighed. 'No, of course not. But maybe I could see if they still have a press gang in the Naval Recruitment section. A spell below decks would do him a power of good.'

Tam MacNee took up his position on the mat, his eyes half-shut in concentration, drew back his hand, then with elegant precision launched the dart to finish the game with a double top.

There was a roar of applause from his fellow-members of the Cutty Sark's darts team and its travelling support from Kirkluce, as Tam sealed their victory over their counter-parts in the Anchor Inn. It was a long-standing fixture, played alternately in these two salubrious venues, and the Anchormen, as they called themselves, had been four up over the series; Tam's efforts for the Cutty Sark's Warlocks, demonstrating delicate judgement and a fine restraint unknown to his namesake Tam o' Shanter on a much ear-lier festive occasion, had at least done something to reduce the shameful deficit.

The group gathered around the darts board to watch the solemn presentation of the original pound note wagered on the first game, now framed so that it could hang in a place of honour behind the victors' bar. Gradually they drifted off into smaller groups, talking and guffawing as the air grew thick with smoke and the jugs of beer had to be filled up with a regularity which Katy Anderson, in charge of pulling it, swore would leave her with a sore shoulder tomorrow.

Tam turned aside to pick up the pullover he had stripped off for that final throw. It had been knitted for him by Bunty and he took it to every darts match as a sort of mascot, even if the darts board on the front – a real labour of love and a serious challenge even to a knitter of Bunty's redoubtable skill – made it sit oddly with his usual sartorial style, which was understated to the point of being laconic.

He was enjoying the evening. It had taken his mind off the problem at work, the first time he'd really fallen out with his boss. He and Marjory went back a long way; he counted himself a friend of the family and had shared many a pleasant wee bevvy down the pub with '*the hardy son of rustic toil*', as he liked to call Bill. He'd watched uncomfortably last year as the stress of Marjory's position as a police officer in a hostile farming community took its toll on her marriage and admired Marjory's toughness, even when, he suspected, she was hurting badly – still was, to some extent, if you asked him. She always got a wee bit tight-lipped when you asked her how things were at the farm.

He'd been friend enough, on a good few occasions since she made rank, to tell her bluntly to her face when there was a problem brewing that was of her own making, and however little she might have liked it she'd been big enough to be grateful. This was the first time he'd ever felt she'd joined the management side, playing bloody stupid games instead of coming at him straight. He didn't like it, and he'd resented her suggesting he'd have been heavy-handed in his dealings with an English colleague. Even if it was true. OK, especially if it was true, but he didn't want to think about that now.

A pint was thrust into his hand as he rejoined his team-mates, responded to the usual witticisms about 'banging up' the opposition, 'nicking' the prize and even (from a solicitor who was no slouch with the arrows himself) 'causing alarm and fear to the lieges', then slid quietly away. He was looking for someone: spotting his quarry, he moved in.

'Willie!' he said, positioning himself with a neat and un-obtrusive flick of the shoulders next to Willie Duncan, member of the defeated Anchormen and cox of the Knockhaven lifeboat. 'Haven't seen you since the last time we lined up on the mat. How're you doing, pal?'

Duncan, perched on a high stool in the farthest corner of the bar, shifted uneasily. With the wall to one side and MacNee on the other, there was no escape. 'Fine, Tam, fine,' he said weakly.

'Here – you're not the man you were with the arrows, are you? I mind you had us by the short and curlies last time.'

The group Willie had been part of was still talking, but its focal point seemed somehow to have shifted. MacNee put his elbow on the bar now with an apparently casual move-ment which effectively pinned Duncan into his corner. This was piling on the pressure, and he could see his victim start to shift uneasily on the bar stool.

Willie looked down into his beer. 'We all have our off days.'

The bloodshot eyes hadn't escaped MacNee. 'Don't expect you care as much as you used to, Willie? Don't expect you care about anything all that much these days? Money, maybe, but not a lot else.'

It was with a visible effort that Willie made himself sound angry. 'Here, what are you saying, MacNee?'

MacNee gave his trademark, mirthless smile. 'You're feeling pretty mellow right now, eh, Willie? Well, get this – when you're thon way, your judgement's shot to hell. Suppose that pager in your pocket there goes and you're on a call for the lifeboat. Suppose it's a wee thing tricky out there. Suppose you've other folks' lives hanging on your reactions. Still feeling mellow, Willie?'

The shutters came down. 'You're daft, MacNee. Daft or drunk. Don't know what you're havering about.'

'Aye, do you!' MacNee's reply was as swift and sharp as his winning dart. 'Dead men on your conscience, Willie. Think about it.

'Get this.' His tone changed. 'We can turn a blind eye to the occasional joint. But you're not a fool – you know as well as I do the other stuff that comes with it. You know who brings it in and where it comes from. And there's lads out there having their lives ruined, lads you'd have had on your boat if there was any fishing left. Don't think I don't see why you want to put up two fingers to the system – I'm with you on that, but this isn't how to do it. Who is it, Willie? Between ourselves – no one has to know. Just a name, that's all. I only need the end of the thread.'

Tam could smell fear and he knew he was on a loser. 'I don't know what the hell you think you mean,' Willie blustered. Then he got off the bar stool, pushed MacNee rudely aside and rejoined the group, leaving Tam to grimace ruefully. Then he shrugged, finished what was in his glass and went in search of the man with the beer jug.

'How's Daisy?' Bill Fleming demanded, handing his wife a heavy cut-crystal tumbler with half-an-inch of Bladnoch whisky in the bottom. She was sitting in her usual place at this time of night, in the low-ceilinged sitting room which ran from front to back of the Mains of Craigie farmhouse, her long legs curled under her in one of the deep, comfortable armchairs that they were always talking about replacing with something less shabby but somehow never did. Apple-wood logs – almost the last from the old tree in the orchard they'd had to cut down last year – were crackling in the fireplace, scenting the room with their spicy smoke, and Meg the collie, liberated from the cares of motherhood, lay stretched out in front of it, not quite asleep but with her eyes half-closed in blissful relaxation.

Marjory laughed. 'Oh dear! I don't think Laura quite understands. She had Daisy in her bed last night – not just *on* her bed, but cuddled up with her under the blankets.'

Bill wasn't amused. 'She can't let her get away with that! If she doesn't start the way she means to go on she'll have a delinquent dog on her hands.'

'Don't think I didn't tell her. Daisy was having a wonderful time when I saw her, on and off the chairs, racing round the furniture when Laura tried to catch her. And of course Laura thought it was terribly funny that she was so cheeky.'

'And her a psychologist!'

'Only human. I don't think her training extended to dogs. I had a little word with Daisy myself and she was a bit chastened after that. I've told Laura she's to leave her in the kitchen no matter how she screams and I've told her I'll be able to tell from Daisy's behaviour whether she's done it or not. And I've also told her she'll have you to answer to if she ruins the dog.'

'Good. I suppose if the worst comes to the worst we can bring Daisy back here for a bit and Meg'll knock some manners into her.' Meg, at the sound of her name, raised her head.

'Look at that, now you've upset her. She's been revelling in her regained freedom.' Marjory took a sip of her Scotch. 'Laura's good about people, though. You know I told you about this new man, Jonathan Kingsley?'

Bill nodded. 'And you were worrying about how to handle Tam.'

'Right. Well, I tried to do it in a jokey way, and all I

managed to do was put his back up. I was telling Laura, and she thought joking about it might have put the whole thing in the wrong context. If I'd said to him that this guy was going to be an important member of the team and I was worried about how other people might react, I'd have been more likely to get him on side.'

'We-ell.' Bill was uneasy. 'He's the one who was going to be the biggest problem – we all know that. Isn't what Laura's suggesting a bit underhand?'

'Manipulative, anyway,' Marjory agreed. 'It's a damning word, but isn't that what management has to be about? The humorous approach was manipulative too, it just wasn't successful.'

'So did she have a suggestion for what would work?'

Marjory sighed. '20/20 hindsight's easy, but it's never as simple as that, is it? It was a help to talk it over with Laura but where you go from where I am now—'

'If all else fails, you could try saying you weren't straight with him and you're sorry.' Bill finished his whisky and got up abruptly. 'I'm just going to do the rounds. You've shut in the hens, haven't you?'

With Meg, galvanised into activity, at his heels, he went out, leaving Marjory to stare into the fire where the logs were burning away to ash. That was all she needed – for the man she loved and the woman who had become her good friend to be at odds. But then, of course, it was notoriously hard to forgive someone for doing you a huge favour.

Bill still wasn't the cheerful, easy-going fellow he had been before the foot-and-mouth epidemic had taken its toll. He was better, much better, so that a lot of the time she could convince herself that everything was back to normal, very nearly. But perhaps 'normal' meant something different now, and tonight Bill had almost sounded jealous. And perhaps, since he had always been her confidant and adviser, she had been insensitive in admitting that she had another counsellor.

Marjory sighed. Somehow she'd managed to upset the most important man in her personal life and the most important in her professional life at the same time. Not a good day. She finished her drink, barely tasting it, and got up. The room felt cold now and it wasn't entirely due to the dying fire.

Anyway, she'd have to see to it that Laura got a grip on training Daisy. Bill would never forgive her if she spoiled a good dog.

4

A breath of fresh autumn air gusted into the reception area of the Galloway Police Headquarters as Marjory Fleming swung open the door on her way into work. It was well into October now and a clear, cold morning with a strong wind blowing and the brown and russet leaves, lying in deep drifts on the pavement outside, were being snatched up to dance in crazy spirals.

She nodded curtly to the desk sergeant and the young constable on duty behind the counter, then headed for the stairs to her office, the heels of her plain, low-heeled court shoes clicking briskly on the tiled floor.

PC Langlands, looking after the tall retreating figure of the DI, now taking the stairs athletically two at a time, pulled a face at Sergeant Naismith. 'Who's stolen her scone? Big Marge is usually cheery enough unless she's on the warpath. And I'll tell you who else is going round looking like a wet weekend in Rothesay – Tam MacNee.'

Naismith, with fifteen years of police experience, not to mention a fair few Scotch pies, under his expansive belt, was always a reliable source of station gossip. 'Ah well, you see, there's this English lad just come as a DC, one of those fast-track, high-flyer types out to make a bit of a splash, no doubt, and show us teuchters where we're getting it wrong, so Marge has her knickers in a twist about that, seemingly. And Tam's fallen out with her – he's not saying why but he's called her "ma'am" twice in Macdonald's hearing.'

'Bad as that, eh? Heavy stuff. Best keep our heads down till it blows over then.'

The sergeant gave the benign nod of a teacher with an apt pupil. 'Oh, you're learning, laddie!' Just as he spoke, the outside door burst open again on a savage gust of wind and a flurry of dead leaves was swept in. He tutted.

'See that woman – she's never shut the door properly behind her. Away and close it, Sandy, and try and hoosh those leaves back out. The wind's fair getting up out there.'

Detective Constable Tansy Kerr, standing uneasily in front of the DI's desk, bit her lip and studied the twizzled laces of her deck shoes. Under her urchin-cut hair, tinted dark red with a blonde streak at the front, her naturally pale skin was a shade or two paler than usual. 'Yes, ma'am, sorry, ma'am,' she mumbled.

'As somebody said to me once, Kerr, "Damn your sorrow, just don't do it again." You weren't on top of the facts of the case when you went into the witness box and the defence agent had you for breakfast. There's the Fiscal snorting flames and we've got Hughie Fowler back on the streets. Not only has the cost of a court case been wasted, it's going to cost police time to bang him up again when he commits his next offence, which should be any minute now. Anything you want to say?'

Tansy Kerr swallowed. 'No excuse. I was just careless. Sorry.'

Fleming's stern expression relaxed a fraction. 'All right, Tansy. We all understand that sort of mistake can happen. Once. Now get back to the coalface.'

'Thanks, boss,' she said fervently, and went out. With the door shut behind her, she collapsed against the wall just as PC Macdonald appeared, coming along the corridor escorting a good-looking, fair young man in a city suit.

'Phew!' Kerr said. 'I got out alive. Do the teeth marks show?'

Andy Macdonald grinned. 'Only round the jugular. This is Jonathan Kingsley, the new DC. Jonathan, Tansy Kerr.'

She regarded him with some curiosity. There had been quite a bit of talk about him in the CID room, with Tam MacNee noticeably tight-lipped. He looked a bit of a stuffed shirt but that was maybe just the suit. They shook hands.

'Well, good luck,' she said as Macdonald knocked on DI Fleming's door. 'Maybe now Big Marge has had her fix of blood she'll be sweetness and light.'

Looking at the young man waiting to be invited to take a seat with an air of calm self-possession, Fleming could understand why the ACC, a susceptible lady, had been impressed.

Jonathan Kingsley. His CV was on the desk in front of her: age twenty-six, school in Derbyshire, good degree in chemistry from Edinburgh University, three years' police service. He'd had an early success, playing an important part in busting a drugs ring by going undercover and passing himself off as a student.

It wouldn't have been difficult. He looked much younger than his years, being slight and fair, with a sharp-featured, intelligent face; his grey eyes were, at the moment at least, cool and watchful. There was something about the set of the mouth she couldn't quite read – arrogance, cussedness perhaps? The smart suit he was wearing looked expensive and she could only hope this was in honour of his interview with her. He'd stick out like a sore thumb if he went around here looking as if he was trying to find a Starbuck's.

Fleming came round the desk to shake his hand. He was fractionally shorter than she was.

'DC Kingsley. Good to have you join us. I hope you're

not going to find it too quiet here in the sticks, after the big city.'

Damn, why had she said that? It sounded touchy, defensive.

He had a pleasant smile which gave absolutely nothing away. 'Not at all. I like the area – I've sailed a bit down here.'

At least he spoke the flat, Estuary English standard with the young and not with a 'plum-in-the-mouth' accent, but even so Fleming groaned inwardly. A yachtie as well as a graduate and an Englishman who looked as if he'd be as much use as a schoolkid if things turned nasty – how was that going to play with the lads downstairs?

She made the usual perfunctory enquiries about accommodation and other practicalities, then moved on to his experience of the Edinburgh drugs scene and found herself, like the ACC, impressed. He knew his stuff. She'd read endless papers and reports on the subject, of course, with increasing concentration lately as drug-taking, once seen as an urban blight, had taken deep and deadly root in her own patch. She'd even attended a course on the problem, but that was no substitute for hands-on experience. Kingsley's scientific background, too, was clearly an advantage; he was outlining some of the lab procedures now.

'You mean,' she asked, 'that given two samples of a drug it would be possible to state categorically that they came from the same source?'

'Pretty much. Under analysis there would be features – a comparable level of adulteration, for instance – which would indicate they were at least from the same batch.'

'Right. So say we had three drugs finds in different places in the district, we could expect the labs to tell us whether they all came from the same supplier or from three different ones? Establish a sort of tracking pattern?'

'It could do. You just need to get your hands on the stuff.'

'Which was presumably where your undercover work in Edinburgh came in? Unfortunately, you'd find that a bit tricky here.'

He looked a surprised enquiry.

'In a rural community, where everyone knows everyone, you tend to be a marked man. The criminal fraternity will make it their business to clock you as soon as possible, though you've probably got a few weeks' grace. But then of course the other thing – I hate to be personal, but it's your accent. It's not like Edinburgh where they've almost as many English students as Scots ones – you'd stick out like a sore thumb if you started hanging about in the bars here.'

Kingsley smiled. 'Oh, I don't have to talk like this. I've been assured that my Scots accent is pretty convincing.'

Fleming tried not to wince noticeably. She'd heard too many Englishmen smugly doing a 'see-you-Jimmie' and never would be too soon to hear another one. 'I'm sure it is,' she said hastily, 'but I think we'll pass on that one.'

He gave a shrug. 'Suit yoursel'. It's no' a problem.'

She stared at him. He'd got it absolutely right: not implausibly broad, the merest hint of a sing-song intonation and those lazily dropped final letters. 'You're good,' she admitted.

'Self-protection. It saved a lot of hassle in the Edinburgh pubs on an International Saturday when England had won, kept me out of quite a few fights, I reckon, and then of course it came in handy professionally as well. I was always a good mimic – got into a lot of trouble that way when I was at school.'

'Did you, indeed?' Fleming said dryly. 'I can imagine a "Big Marge" impression going down very well here. Did you know they call me Big Marge?'

For the first time he showed signs of being rattled. 'Er – er,' he stammered.

She enjoyed that. 'I like to tell myself it's affectionate. That's affectionate as in, "She's OK unless you screw up when there was an alternative." All right?'

He nodded slowly. 'Message understood.'

'Thanks, Jonathan. Now, can you find your way back to the CID room? Good. I've had them sort out some files for you to read to bring you up to speed. Oh, and by the way – I wouldn't go displaying your linguistic skills until they know you a bit better. They might think you were taking the mickey.'

And was she entirely sure that he wouldn't be? When he left, Fleming got up from her desk and walked over to the window of her office. It was on the fourth floor; she had a view out over the roofs of the market town of Kirkluce and down into the main street. The sun was still shining, but now it was a troubled sky with gold-tinged, purplish clouds massing over to the west, and a blustering wind was stripping the dying leaves from the branches of the trees lining the pavement below. In farming, you lived close to the weather; Fleming could see now all the signs of a gathering storm. She tried to resist the temptation to see it as symbolic.

It wasn't easy to know what to make of the new officer. He was highly intelligent, that was for sure, and he'd come from a specialist drugs unit, something they didn't have the manpower to run here. He might bring a more cutting edge to the drugs operation which was presently at the head of her agenda, and he was undoubtedly a very cool customer, not the sort to allow himself to be riled by the more abrasive members of the team. Like Tam.

Tam was still standing on his dignity. She'd tried to frame a suitable apology but it was difficult; it wasn't the words she had used which had caused the trouble, it was Tam's inferring from them that she was accusing him of being unprofessional. She'd told him she hadn't meant that and received only an uncompromising 'No, likely not,' in response, but she couldn't say she'd been wrong to think his treatment of an English colleague might be insensitive. She knew damn well it would have been, and so did he; he would see an apology of that nature as despicably insincere. And he'd be right. Stalemate.

The ringing of the phone on her desk made her jump and look at her watch. Was that really ten o'clock already? She hadn't time to waste worrying about Tam's wounded feelings. She'd just go on treating him as she always did and sooner or later he'd unbend. Surely.

Jon Kingsley settled down in a corner of the CID room, an untidy pile of files beside him. He'd taken off his jacket and draped it over the back of his chair with his tie in the pocket, then unbuttoned the collar of his shirt. The natives seemed relatively friendly: Tansy Kerr had brought him a cup of coffee, looking a bit more cheerful now than she had immediately after her mauling from Big Marge.

Big Marge. It was the first time he'd had a woman boss and he wasn't sure what that was going to be like. She had a formidable presence: that was partly her height – he had felt dwarfed beside her, though he was around average height for a man – but there was something about those shrewd hazel eyes too which made you feel as if she could look further into you than you would choose to have anyone do. Tough-minded and down-to-earth as well, he reckoned, unlike his previous DI, who prided himself on being a hard man who never missed a trick, but fell like timber for a well-chosen line. From what he had already gathered, playing games with DI Fleming would be a high-risk occupation, but there would be ways to handle her too, of course, once he'd sussed out what they were.

If he wanted to get off to a good start, he'd better get on with reading through this lot. He took a swig of coffee, then had a preliminary sift through the contents of the folders, most of which seemed to relate tò the on-going drugs investigation, code-named Operation Songbird. His lips twitched appreciatively at the name; in this line of work the breakthrough seldom came if you couldn't find a canary who was prepared to sing.

He picked up the most recent file of reports first. They seemed to be going on a theory that the stuff was coming in through fishing ports in the south of the area – presumably he'd find the evidence this was based on as he worked back through. The name Knockhaven featured, and one of the most recent additions was from DS Tam MacNee who'd been pursuing one Willie Duncan these last couple of days.

Tam MacNee – he'd met him. Short, stocky chap, thick Glasgow accent, pitted skin and a gap between his front teeth when he smiled, which he hadn't, much, and certainly not at his new colleague. The perfectly balanced Scotsman, no doubt, with a chip on both shoulders where the English were concerned. The other detectives had been severally pleasant, inquisitive, offhand or preoccupied, with only MacNee giving off vibes of controlled hostility. He clearly carried a lot of clout round here too, more than the other DS he'd met, Greig Allan who seemed a rather colourless individual.

Well, usual new boy's rules: keep your head below the parapet, speak when you're spoken to and get on with your work. He addressed himself to the job, speed-reading the history of the investigation, until Tansy Kerr took pity on him and offered to take him down to the canteen for lunch.

★　　★　　★

Ashley Randall unwrapped the sandwiches it had been her turn to collect from the '8 'til Late', to be consumed at home during their usually brief lunch-hour. Lewis was back ahead of her and had already laid out the plates on the glass table in their sleek, minimalist kitchen with its state-of-the-art cooking appliances, though the only one which showed much evidence of use was the microwave.

He was pouring Badoit into two glasses. 'I'm going to have to eat and run today. I've promised Martin a consultation before afternoon surgery.'

'What is it this time – heart disease or cancer?' Ashley had very little sympathy with Martin Matthews, their hypochondriac partner. 'You should refer him to me. I'd prescribe a low-fat, no-alcohol, strict-exercise regime and he'd make a miraculous overnight recovery.'

Lewis glanced at her with an expression she couldn't quite read. 'Oh, you're probably right. On the other hand, you have to remember that he's very popular with the patients and he's a good colleague. You know how often he's been happy to cover for you when you have lifeboat duty.'

Ashley was setting out the sandwiches; her hand hovered for a fraction of a second before she completed the action. Then, 'That reminds me,' she said, her voice casual, 'I've got an extra meeting tonight. Willie phoned – some new regulations have come through and he wants to discuss them. To tell you the truth, I think what he means is he can't understand them. He's fine when he's at the helm but his lips tend to move when he's reading.'

Under her thick gold lashes she watched him narrowly. With his usual deliberateness he was addressing himself to a prawn sandwich with reduced-fat mayonnaise; he said only, 'Really? We'd better have an early supper then.'

'Fine. I'll pick something up,' she offered quickly. 'I was planning to go for a run before my two-thirty clinic, but not in this weather.' She glanced through the French windows which gave on to wooden decking, sheltered by the leg of their L-shaped ranch-style house, but even so being blasted by the gale. It was pouring now, great billowing squalls of rain which rattled on the windowpanes like hailstones.

'You'd better hope it's just a meeting tonight and not a call-out,' Lewis observed. 'I certainly wouldn't fancy going out in that.'

His wife shuddered. 'I've told you before – don't say it! You only need to let the thought enter your mind and it prompts some dangerous lunatic somewhere to head for the rocks.'

'Such superstition – and you a rational scientist!' he mocked her, then added seriously, 'But tell me about Willie – is he all right? I'd Jackie in today, complaining about headaches, and then it was the usual "By the way, doctor," just as she was leaving. She's very worried about him.'

Ashley's smooth brow furrowed. 'Yes, I'm worried too. It's nothing stronger than cannabis, as far as I can tell, but I've a nasty feeling his usage has increased. I sense he's under a lot of strain, for some reason, and I tried tackling him head on – he simply lied about it, of course. But I'm keeping a very watchful eye and so far he's been OK when he's been on call. Trust me – I wouldn't go out with a hopped-up cox.'

'I should hope not.' Lewis, still with the last bit of his sand-wich in his hand, stood up. 'I'd better go. Supper at – what, half-past six?'

As the door shut behind him, Ashley sank back in her chair and closed her eyes, breathing a sigh of relief. It was a nervous business, this lying. Lewis always seemed oblivious – but could she be sure? He was, as Ritchie had reminded her, no fool, and he had always been so self-contained that she had long ago given up the struggle to work out what he was thinking. She suspected that most of the time it wasn't very interesting, at least to her. But what she didn't want was the embarrassment of accidental discovery, and there was always the chance that Lewis might be talking to Willie, or Jackie even, and happen to mention a meeting which, of course, wasn't taking place. They'd been careful up to now; she was pretty sure no one else knew, since if there was gossip in the village Jocasta would be the first to find out through Gossip Queen Muriel at the reception desk or her other little favourite, the mouse-like Enid, who had a crush on Lewis that was positively comical.

Still, there shouldn't be too many more of these uncomfortable occasions. The showhouse had opened to the public now and there wasn't even a corner of the site where she and Ritchie could meet safely, with buyers trampling round the finished houses – which had, gratifyingly, made Ritchie keener than ever.

Originally it had been the old 'my-wife-doesn't-understand-me' line, but now it had reached the 'if-I-have-to-watch-her-doing-that-once-more-I-shan't-be-responsible-for-my-actions' stage. A marriage was over in all but name by the time the husband could spend ten minutes describing the irritating way his wife brushed her teeth.

She'd begun the affair as – what? A hobby? A secret revenge on Lewis for bringing her to Knockhaven where, without the distraction of friends and city life, she had found herself living with a reserved, bloodless stranger in a claustrophobic society? Certainly, there had been nothing to stop her refusing to come with him, or even fleeing back to Edinburgh – nothing except the humiliation of admitting that her marriage had failed and suffering the sympathy of 'friends' who had envied her the charming, clever, good-looking doctor husband.

It was all so ragingly, hog-whimperingly *dull!* She wasn't in love with Ritchie – but then, had she ever been in love with Lewis? She had never been convinced that love was anything more than a fig leaf to cover up some pretty basic human instincts – and certainly Ritchie satisfied most of those, where she was concerned.

Tonight they were actually risking meeting for a drink in a pub about three miles away; he was, she could tell, going to ask her point-blank if she would leave Lewis. She'd be interested, in an abstract sort of way, to see if he would be offering marriage. Probably, since he had a penchant for respectability and one's place in the community.

So what was she going to say? Even if this was where he'd grown up, he'd have to agree to find another community to be respectable in, since Ashley could hardly go on working afterwards in the Knockhaven practice where Lewis had more or less created his own personal fiefdom. Ritchie had said to her there wasn't the demand for more than another one or at most two developments in this area anyway; he'd started checking out the coast of Ireland, only an hour from Stranraer, where he had contacts and there were good prospects. So he could run his business just as easily from Glasgow where Ashley could get a hospital job again and where there were theatres and galleries and shops and easy access to airports for the sort of exotic holidays Lewis had never found time for them to take. She'd always appreciated the good things of life and having serious wealth would be a delicious new experience.

She would miss the lifeboat, of course: there was something in her that responded viscerally to the raw, elemental struggle between feeble man and the unbounded force of the sea, where it was only the skill to keep a cockleshell above the waves instead of below, the mastery of amazing technology and the courage to defy the terrifying gods of wind and water that could work, in combination, to snatch from them the victims of their anger. Oh God, yes, she would miss that.

Still, there would be many compensations. Apart from anything else, Ritchie's mother was dead. She'd checked.

There really wasn't any doubt. Her answer had to be yes.

Luke Smith, his head pounding, his heart racing, dived into the staffroom and shut the door. It was mercifully empty, non-pupil-contact-modules (free periods, as they used to be called) having all but disappeared from teachers' timetables.

He collapsed into a chair and buried his face in his hands. He felt as if he had been flayed, very slowly, strip by strip, until he was standing in front of the class containing Nat Rettie and his friends not merely naked but without any skin to cover his shrinking, bleeding flesh.

What on earth had possessed him to confront them? He should know his place by now, know that the titular authority being a teacher gave him carried no clout in the bear-pit of the Year 12 classroom. You could only govern by consent unless you could dominate by the force of your personality, which he couldn't – oh God, he couldn't even begin! And what they had all consented to today was Nat's flouting of Luke's every instruction, baying him on, bolstering his defiance with their raucous laughter. Until the end.

That was when Nat, taking advantage of a break in the laughter, flung at Luke the word 'paedophile'.

There was immediate, stunned silence. Among all the obscenities, all the crude, offensive language which was their daily currency, this was the one word left with the power to shock. The air became electric with tension.

Luke's mouth went dry so that he had to lick his lips before he could speak. 'What – what did you say?' he stammered foolishly, as if he hadn't heard the word which was now branded into his mind for ever.

'Paedophile. Don't act stupid – my girlfriend's speaking to the Child Protection Officer this afternoon.'

Luke could barely frame the words. 'Your girlfriend – who is she?'

'You mean there's others you've touched up as well?'

The response to that was totally unnerving, a sort of growling, hissing swell of anger from the class. Nat glanced round them, a smirking sneer on his face. 'She's Kylie MacEwan. But it sounds as if she's not the only one. She's thirteen, you dirty old man!'

Luke knew he should have stood his ground, defended himself, laughed at such a ridiculous charge. He knew the girl by sight, largely because there had been anxious discussions at staff meetings about the problems she was presenting – including her relationship with Nat – but he didn't teach her, had never spoken to her, far less been alone with her. He should have declared that immediately. He didn't. What every teacher most dreads had happened and he was frozen with the horror of it all.

He had fled the classroom, knowing from the rising decibel level that Nat had caused a sensation. The story would be circulated without even his denial to counter it.

The next thing he ought to do was see his union representative and Fiona Walker, the pleasant, sensible, middle-aged mother of three who combined teaching French with her role as Child Protection Officer. Fiona, surely, would understand the evil game Nat was playing. No one could possibly take such a ludicrous allegation seriously.

But she would have to. They all knew that. They all knew what an allegation of this sort meant: immediate suspension, with the attendant publicity, which would only be lifted if the child could be persuaded to admit that it was a malicious fabrication, or a court cleared you, months later. One or the other happened in 95 per cent of cases, but your life was ruined anyway. He had seen the ordeal inflicted on a blameless colleague in Glasgow, who'd had a breakdown and never worked again.

He couldn't face it. Not yet, not until he had to. A bell pealed, announcing the end of a lesson. Usually it was music to Luke's ears; now it was a warning that in another moment or two he would no longer be alone. It wouldn't take his colleagues long to hear the scandalous story.

A minute later he was in his car, heading for his home in Knockhaven with the instinct of a wounded animal.

5

Willie Duncan glanced at his watch. Five o'clock: time to lock up the lifeboat shed and head up the hill home to his tea. His last chore, as always, was to glance over the *Maud'n'Milly*, lying in readiness at the top of the slipway, to check that all equipment was in place, and he climbed in over the nylon tubes which, on top of a glass-reinforced plastic hull, formed the sides of the boat – such as they were. It looked such a flimsy, vulnerable construction, with no superstructure at all to protect its crew from the effects of severe weather, and yet it was one of the fastest boats in the RNLI fleet, flexible and highly effective for inshore operations.

The old shed was full of shadows; Willie never wasted money by putting on all the lights when he was there by himself. There was talk of a new building, with all mod cons, but that would never have the atmosphere of this great vaulted space. It was creaking and groaning now like a ship in the gale but he barely heard it, any more than he noticed the smell of the creosote which coated its timbers or the dry dustiness of the coils of rope. As he mechanically performed his check, his mind was on the problem which had gnawed at him for days now.

When the side door opened, letting in a blast of cold, fresh air and the sound of the storm, he didn't need to turn his head to see who was standing there. He felt the man's presence as an animal senses a stalking predator, and his hand, resting on the rail by the helmsman's seat, gripped it until the knuckles showed white.

Tam MacNee stepped inside, shaking himself like a wet dog. His dark hair was plastered to his head and water streamed down the black leather bomber jacket. He had to shout to make himself heard above the roaring sea and the wind.

'Fine weather, eh, Willie? You'll be hoping they've all had the gumption to tie up safe in harbour tonight.'

Duncan turned to look at him sourly. 'Shut the bloody door. With you outby.'

MacNee complied with only the first part of the request, then walked round the boat to the farther side, where a crew room, a galley, changing rooms and a workshop had been constructed within the soaring central space, along with shelves and a counter for the inevitable souvenir stall. 'Now, now, that's not very nice, is it? Come on and we can have a wee chat.'

Duncan ignored him, making a meaningless check on the first-aid pack. If he said nothing, even MacNee would have to give up, surely.

There was no sign of it, though. Whistling through his teeth, MacNee took the opportunity to inspect the lifeboat souvenirs, stacked in a case ready to lay out the following day to tempt any passing tourist. 'I doubt you'll be missing your sales target, with this rain. I wonder if maybe Bunty would fancy a tea-towel?'

'We're closed.' Abandoning his tactics before they had a chance of success, Duncan climbed out of the boat. Keeping his voice level, he said, 'I'm away to lock up now. Are you wanting shut out or shut in?'

'I'll come with you. Buy you a drink, even – don't say I'm not good to you.'

'Will you, hell!' His hands were shaking and he could see that MacNee, watching him clinically, had noticed that.

'Feart to be seen with the polis, Willie? Now, what way would a fine, upstanding man like yourself need to be feart?'

'I'm not feart. Just like to choose my company.' It sounded hollow, even to his own ears.

'See you, Willie!' MacNee stepped in close. The cox was a big, burly man who might in other circumstances have described MacNee as a shilpit wee fella, but that slight frame exuded a menacing physicality that made him take a step back.

MacNee smiled his unsettling, gap-toothed grin. 'I'm here today, son, and I was here yesterday and I'll be here tomorrow and the day after that. I always quite like to take a wee run down the coast. Sooner or later you're going to tell me "*the honest, open, naked truth*", as the Great Man says, so why not make it sooner and save the aggro?'

'I've nothing to tell you about, MacNee. And this is harassment – I could complain . . .' He knew it was bluster and MacNee made no response, only raising a sceptical eyebrow.

It helped, being angry. 'Anyway, you've no right being in here without a warrant. I'm telling you to get out.'

MacNee shrugged. 'Have it your own way. But I've tried nice, and I'm warning you, it's nasty from here on in. You see, in dirty stuff like this what you need to do is work out where to put the pressure, and I've done that. You are the weakest link, Willie. Goodbye.'

Willie saw MacNee silhouetted in the doorway as he went out into the dark fury of the storm like, he thought with uncharacteristic fancifulness, a demon returning to hell. He hurried to lock the door behind him, then retreated, shaking, to the crew room.

Had anyone seen MacNee coming here? Had he been spotted in his company any time over these last few nerve-racking days? He had denied being afraid, but it wasn't true, except in so much as he was less 'feart' than terrified.

He should have said right at the start that MacNee was sniffing round, but no one was trusted and any contact with the police could be taken as suspicious. He knew what had happened to the lad from Ayr who'd thought he could play both ends to the middle – he'd had a nasty accident falling into the harbour one night.

The terrible thing was, Willie was beginning to feel there might be comfort in talking to MacNee. He was getting in deeper and deeper; if he told him now before it got any worse, took his punishment and got it over with . . . But it wouldn't be over. They had people inside too, and even if he survived the jail, they'd be waiting for him when he got out.

He felt sick. He could almost hear his nerves twanging as he went over and over it in his head, like a fox in a trap gnawing frantically at its foot in an effort to escape. There was only one thing now that gave him any respite from the agony of his fears. He glanced out of the window at the livid sky, heard the rushing of wind and water; it was tempting fate on a night like this, but, he told himself, if he didn't take something that would calm his nerves, he'd be useless anyway. He fumbled in his pocket for the tin and the cigarette papers.

Jackie saved his tea for him in the oven but the bridie, beans and chips were pretty well welded to the plate by the time he got home. Not that he cared much.

The pub wasn't the sort of place Ashley Randall normally frequented, with its shabby paintwork and the lights of gambling machines flickering through the windows. Indeed, she couldn't remember having been in a place like this since her student days when you went wherever the beer was cheapest. She parked as close to the door as she could, then pulled a soft scarf over her head and ran for shelter from the teeming rain. Inside, she pulled it off and shook it, looking round for Ritchie.

He had chosen a table in the corner farthest from the bar; it wasn't exactly cosy, with an uncurtained window beside it rattling in the force of the wind, but he was certainly right that here they were unlikely to be recognised. It was Friday night and there was a raucous group clustered round the bar, celebrating something or other; Ritchie was served by a young barmaid who barely glanced at him, delivering the vodka and tonics as if irritated by this intrusion on her social life.

When he came back he set them down on the smeary zinc top of the table with a grimace. 'The tonic came out of a pump, I'm afraid. It's probably disgusting.'

Ashley gave him a glinting smile. 'I'm not really here for the beer.'

'No,' he agreed. 'No, nor am I.' He looked down at his hands, rolling the glass between his fingers. 'Ashley, I haven't long, and I don't suppose you have either. They're expecting me at the site and I've told Joanna that's where I'll be.

'We're trapped by circumstances at the moment. I know that I don't want it to go on like this,' he indicated their seedy surroundings with distate, 'and I know it could all get hideously messy if this comes out accidentally. What I don't know is what you want – is this meant to be just a casual affair, or do you feel the way I do?'

He looked around him again, and grimaced. 'This isn't exactly how I'd choose to do this. I'd have preferred the whole soft lights, sweet music, vintage champagne bit before I went down on one knee with the solitaire in my hand.' He was still nervously playing with his glass.

She looked at him from under her lashes, then leaning across the table covered his restless hands with her slim, manicured one. 'Later will do,' she murmured.

He stared at her, those very blue eyes suddenly wide. 'Ashley – oh God, Ashley! You'll marry me? That's fantastic—'

His phone rang. They both jumped. It had an irritating, chirpy *da-da-dee-da, da-da-dee-da* ring and he swore savagely as he took it out of his pocket.

'A thousand to one that's Joanna. She has a talent that amounts to genius for being a pain in the arse. Oh! No, it's – hello?'

His face, dark with irritation, had changed. 'What? For God's sake, on a night like this?'

Immediately Ashley was bolt upright, staring at him as if that might enable her to hear the conversation at the other end. Ritchie's eyes met hers soberly as he listened in silence for what seemed a long time. Then he said, 'I see. What's the forecast? Right.'

He put his hand to his furrowed brow and closed his eyes briefly. His voice was heavy as he said reluctantly, 'I can't do anything other than agree. Carry on.'

Ashley was on her feet before he had disconnected. He explained rapidly. 'It's a Spanish trawler. Fishing in the Irish Sea, ran before the gale into Luce Bay looking for shelter. But they've lost power and now with the direction of the wind they're at risk of being driven on to a lee shore. There's no hope of putting up a chopper to take them off at the moment, apparently. The coastguards have called out Portpatrick and Stranraer, but it'll take a while for them to get there round the Mull of Galloway. They want us to go and stand by in case the crew needs taken off before either of the bigger boats arrives.

'I could have refused, I suppose – it's pretty challenging out there for an inshore boat—'

'Don't be bloody silly,' Ashley snapped. 'We've been out in worse than that. What is it – Force 7, gusting 8?'

'I know, I know. It's just difficult, seeing you go . . .' He sighed, getting up. 'Still, that's the job. The only good thing is that the wind's forecast to ease down in the next hour or two, if they've got it right. But a south-wester – you know how much worse that makes it.'

Ashley's pager went off. 'That's the call. I'm on my way. We need to talk – I'll call you tomorrow.'

'Right. Look, I'd better go into the site office on the way past – the coastguard phoned the home number first and Joanna told them that's where I was. I'll check in with the girls and pretend to have been moving round between the houses. I hope I can get to the shed before the launch, but if not . . . Ashley, for God's sake, take care!' He kissed her, and was aware that she was somewhere else already.

'Naturally,' she said, and went to the door.

He called after her, 'You did say yes, didn't you?'

She glanced back over her shoulder, her light blue eyes very bright. 'Oh, I said yes all right!'

Ritchie followed her to the door. Her head down, she ran to the car, started the engine and roared off into the darkness. He stood in the rain watching the red tail-lights until they disappeared.

The Anchor Inn was busy this evening. Katy Anderson loved it when it was like that; it was hard work, of course, but the crack was always good and you got a real laugh. Now she knew so many of the regulars and the local people, it felt a bit like giving a party and being paid for it. It was a great life and sometimes she still couldn't believe her luck in finding Rob, the sort of good man and loving husband she had once bitterly decided didn't exist. Glancing along the bar to smile in his direction, she saw that he was coming towards her, looking serious.

'Your car's parked in front of the garage, isn't it? Where are the keys?'

Her smile faded. 'At the back of the cutlery drawer. Oh, Rob, not a call-out – on a night like this!'

He took her face in his hands and kissed her. 'You're not to worry,' he said firmly. 'We know what we're doing.' Then he was gone.

She looked after him, her happy evening ruined. She wouldn't know a second's peace of mind until he walked back through that door.

It opened and he came back in. He was wearing a yellow oilskin jacket and he was scowling. 'They're not there. I'll murder that bloody kid when I get my hands on him. I'll take mine.'

Then he was gone again, before she could even frame an apology, make an excuse . . .

But she didn't want to make an excuse. She'd made too many excuses for her son in the past and it was time he faced up to the consequences of his actions. She was angry, very angry.

'Can you hang on a wee minute while I make a phone call?' she asked the elderly fisherman who had been waiting patiently at the bar.

He smiled sympathetically. 'Aye, lass, no problem. And don't you go fashing yourself about Rob – he's a canny man.'

She bit her lip and tried to smile. 'I know that. But it's a wicked night.'

'Och, I've seen worse.'

She tried to comfort herself with that as she looked at the card by the phone in the corner of the bar and dialled the number of the police station.

When his pager went, Luke Smith looked up dully, confused by the sound. He was sitting in the dark, with only the moaning of the wind around the thick walls of his cottage for company, so sunk in despair that he had no idea how much time had passed.

He had waited for the inevitable call from the school but

the phone had remained silent. The Head and the Child Protection Officer were probably discussing it; they'd send for him tomorrow, no doubt, and tell him he was suspended and to stay away until further notice. Not that he would ever set foot in a classroom again, whatever happened.

Then the police enquiry would begin. It would operate on the premise that, whatever he said in his own defence, it was the child who must be believed, because of course the official line was that children never told lies. Didn't these people *remember* being a child?

And even if, by some miracle, justice did prevail, he would be forever tainted. His parents – what would they feel? Oh, they'd say they believed him, of course, and would stand up for their son, but would there always be a lingering doubt that perhaps they had produced a monster?

He just couldn't bear it. What was the point in struggling on like this? He could see no way out, no future which promised anything but more pain. His next decision was easy; the hard part was working out how best to achieve release from a life which had become intolerable.

There wasn't enough paracetamol in the bathroom to provide an overdose – they sold them in small packets these days for that very reason – and though there was a sharp knife in the kitchen drawer he shrank from the idea of slitting his wrists. He'd always been squeamish about blood and he didn't like the thought of the pain either. He just wanted everything to stop, all the elaborate systems that kept his heart beating and his lungs full of air and his mind active with these torturing thoughts, so that he could slip quietly away and not feel anything any more.

When the pager sounded its urgent summons, he didn't move for a moment. It seemed to have nothing to do with him. How could he possibly go out and face anyone, let alone the crew whose respect he had struggled so hard to gain?

But then, if he went . . . Suddenly it was all clear in his head. It was quite possible – likely, even – that they wouldn't yet have heard the terrible accusation, and if he answered the summons there was a chance, just a chance, that this time someone might be held up and he could go out with the boat. It would solve everything.

Of course he wouldn't endanger anyone's life, but once they were safely on their way back he could just quickly take off his life-jacket and step over the side. In a high sea, that would be that.

And if, as usual, he was rejected, he'd walk out along the arm of steep rocks that sheltered the harbour and step off into the waves which would be boiling below.

He hadn't a moment to waste. Leaping into action, he jumped up and without even pausing to grab a jacket, hurried out.

'Good gracious, Luke, you're soaked to the skin!' Ashley Randall, stepping out of her car and shrugging herself into a hooded waterproof jacket, stared in astonishment as Luke Smith came past her in his shirt sleeves, without even a jersey.

He looked down as if surprised to find the thin fabric saturated and clinging to his skin. 'Oh,' he said vaguely, 'I was in a hurry. I forgot to pick up a coat.'

'You'd better run, then,' she urged him and, as he broke obediently into a trot, jogged along beside him. Just then, the loud bang of a maroon went off and she frowned. 'That's very late, surely? Willie must have forgotten – he's meant to send them up immediately the call comes through. The Hon Sec won't be pleased!'

She enjoyed mentioning his name impersonally like this, enjoyed the exercise of deception while she hugged her secret. Might she miss that, she wondered, once it all came out?

The second maroon soared into the sky above the harbour

just as she reached the shed. All the lights were on, inside and out, and a team was already rolling back the doors in preparation for the launch. She could see the chief mechanic collecting up the maroon cases; he must have realised Willie had slipped up. Through the open door of the crew room she could see Rob Anderson was already kitted up, and she hurried across, looking about for Willie as she did so. He would usually be in the boat by now but he wasn't there.

A dozen people were milling around in the centre of the shed and it took her a moment to spot the cox. He was holding a coastguard printout and he was still, strangely enough, wearing his ordinary clothes.

Puzzled, Ashley hesitated. Had there been some further message she didn't know about, that one of the offshore lifeboats had got to the area more quickly than expected, perhaps? And of course, she remembered belatedly, she wasn't supposed to know anything about it at all.

'Willie?' She came up behind him. 'Are we going for a launch?'

He turned slowly. 'Aye, that's right,' he said. 'A launch. Spanish – Spanish boat in trouble. Have to get there before they hit rocks.' His bloodshot eyes had a glassy stare, the pupils pinpoints.

Ashley gazed at him in horror. She could smell the sickly-sweet smell of cannabis on his clothes. 'For God's sake! Willie, you're stoned!'

He shook his head, again slowly. 'Nothing the matter with me. That's just daft.' He giggled foolishly.

The man hadn't just had a few puffs. He'd smoked enough to reach the lethargic stage and it would be hours – if not days – before he was clean. 'Rob!' Ashley called sharply. 'Rob, get over here!'

Rob, uneasy already at the cox's strange lack of urgency, crossed the floor at a run, taking off the helmet he had been fastening.

'He's completely out of it. Totally unfit to cox,' she told him.

'You're joking?' It wasn't a question, though; he looked with disgust at the other man who was now blinking at them in mild enquiry. 'What the hell do we do about this?'

'You take over, Rob, I suppose.' Ashley tried to sound positive. They were a team, after all, and for a team to be effective you had to have complete faith in one another. But her eyes went involuntarily to the open doors beyond which, theatrically illuminated, she could see the choppiness of the sea even here in the harbour and the spray being flung up into the air beyond the harbour wall.

He followed her eyes. 'Can you trust me, out in that?' She saw him swallow hard. 'I haven't Willie's experience – and we'll need to take Luke. There's no reason not to.' He glanced back towards the young man, standing uncertainly in the crew room doorway, still in his wet clothes. Somehow his appearance didn't inspire confidence.

Her voice was harsh. 'Then let's get on with it.'

'Unless, as acting cox, I refuse to launch.'

She didn't lack courage. 'Of course you can't!' she said fiercely. 'We'd never live it down.'

'No, we wouldn't.' Rob took a deep breath and squared his shoulders as if bracing himself to take a sudden heavy weight. 'Right! Let's move it!'

He assumed command with the ease of long training. As he contacted the coastguard, Ashley ran over to the changing room, sweeping Luke along with her as she went to kit up. It did cross her mind that he was less excited at being told his chance had come at last than she would have expected him to be, but she put it down to nervousness. Anyway, she had other things on her mind.

Ten minutes later, they were on their way. As they reached the harbour bar and the cross-sea smacked into the boat,

Rob opened the throttle and headed out across the bay. As always, the powerful thrust of the two outboard motors thrilled Ashley; she could feel the surge of adrenaline as the spray hit her face.

It was still an evil night, with the wind driving the rain almost horizontally into their faces and a sullen, lumpy sea with only the tops of the waves foam-capped, but she turned to Luke as they sat clinging to the rail behind the helmsman's seat and grinned. 'This is what it's all about!' she said happily into the radio microphone in her helmet and heard Rob laugh. It came to her that it was in these moments of exhilaration edged with danger that she came closest to real joy.

Luke didn't reply. She saw that he was staring into the waves – nervous about his first real operation, perhaps.

Five minutes later, Ritchie Elder's Mitsubishi drew up on the pier. They had been looking out for him; Jason Channell, the chief mechanic, came out to meet him as he jumped down from the driver's seat.

'Have they gone yet?' Elder shouted above the noise of the sea.

'Aye, they're away.' The man came up to him. 'But they're away without Willie.'

'*What?*'

As they stood bareheaded in the heavy rain Channell told him, with some trepidation, what had happened. He had expected the Honorary Secretary to be upset, angry, even. He hadn't expected raw, naked fury. He cringed under the onslaught.

It was a full minute before Elder managed to get himself back under control. He stood, shaking, oblivious to the rain streaking his face like tears.

Then he said, so quietly that the other man had to strain to hear him, 'Get Duncan out of there before I go in. If I see him at this moment, he's a dead man.'

And somehow, that was more scary than the shouting. The mechanic hurried to do as he was told.

On the steep headland curving out to the south of Fuill's Inlat, a green light was flashing in the darkness. On the other side of the narrow bay the ruin of a stone shed, built on a lower, flatter stretch of shoreline, had a red light fixed to one gable, shining steadily. Between the two, waves boiled over savagely pointed rocks, sending up intermittent fountains of spray in a beautiful, deadly display of power.

And in the stormy darkness a car was being driven back up the narrow road from the bay, keeping to an unobtrusively cautious speed.

6

It wasn't, in the end, as tough as Rob Anderson had been afraid it would be. As forecast, the wind had eased and veered a little too so that the Spanish trawler, while still in serious difficulties, was in no immediate danger. They had been able to circle her, keeping a watching brief to reassure the crew until the *Mary Eileen Millar*, the Tyne Class offshore lifeboat from Portpatrick, arrived to relieve the Knockhaven crew of their responsibility.

'OK,' Rob radioed cheerfully to the coastguard. 'Tell them we'll be heading off to tuck the *Maud'n'Milly* up for the night.'

'All right for some,' came back a gloomy message from his opposite number. 'The *Mary Eileen*'s no spring chicken and it's past her bedtime but she's in for a heavy session by the looks of things.'

Grinning, Rob swung the boat round and headed for home across Luce Bay. There was still a heavy sea and in the frequent rainstorms visibility was diabolical, but they were running with the wind more or less behind them now. The worst was over, he hadn't screwed up, and when Ashley's voice said in his ear, 'Nice work, Rob,' his confidence soared. He glanced at the weatherproof watch Katy had given him; with any luck, they'd be back before closing time, which would be a good thing. Katy always worried herself silly when he was out on a shout.

Behind him, Ashley sat quietly, automatically adjusting her

body to the jarring of the boat as they smacked through the cresting waves. Her excitement was ebbing now and she wondered, elegiacally, if this might be her last ever trip as lifeboat crew. Was Ritchie worth what she was giving up? Was anyone worth it?

Although, she thought suddenly, it needn't be Glasgow she suggested to him as their new home. What if it was somewhere like Ayr, say? There was always a demand for doctors and experienced lifeboat crew; if she could persuade him to move there, she could have the best of both worlds. A delicious vision of her future brought a small, secret smile to her lips.

He'd be waiting at the shed, of course. There might even be a chance of a few private words then in the general confusion of getting the boat out of the water, and she'd have the excuse of needing to discuss the situation regarding Willie. She glanced about her, screwing up her eyes to try to get some idea of where they were. She could just see lights along the shore behind them; that would be Port William, she judged. Not far to go then, though another nasty squall had hit them and they'd have to stay close inshore to pick up the leading lights for the harbour.

Ashley became aware that Luke was shifting restlessly in his seat. He had barely said a word, making only monosyllabic replies to anything directly addressed to him; Ashley had put it down to seasickness, and having suffered from it herself once – though only once – knew that not throwing up took every atom of concentration.

She leaned across to him. 'Won't be long now. Hang in there!'

He didn't turn his head, or even seem to notice that she had spoken to him, and Ashley eyed him warily. He would be smart enough to lean out over the side if the worst came to the worst, wouldn't he?

Luke was fiddling with the fastening of his Crewsaver life-jacket with the integral harness that kept crew attached to the boat if they went overboard, for operational reasons or otherwise. It must be constricting his suffering stomach, Ashley surmised, but he couldn't be allowed to release it. In a boat bucking like this one it was much too dangerous.

'Luke!' she said sharply. 'Be sick if you have to be, but don't—'

He snapped the release, shrugged off the jacket and stood up unsteadily.

Feeling the shift of movement, Rob turned his head in alarm. 'You stupid bugger! Sit down!' he yelled. 'That's an order – you'll have us over!'

Ashley flung herself across, grabbing at Luke with both hands and dragging him back. Unbalanced, he fell back into the seat and she threw her weight across his knees, trying to pin him down.

Luke was crying now. 'Just let me go,' he begged. 'I'm going over the side. Leave me – don't come back looking.'

Rob swore. 'Christ, he's suicidal! Ashley, can you cope?'

'Just,' she managed, through gritted teeth. 'How much further?'

'I'm looking for the lights now.' Rapidly over the radio he described the situation to the shore control room, peering towards the land through the fog of rain and flying spume.

Luke was struggling fiercely. Ashley was a fit young woman but he was taller and stronger; it was only by using her bodyweight across his legs and clinging, almost upside down, to one of the iron grab handles on the boat's side that she was able to stop him standing up. She couldn't do that for ever.

'For God's sake, Rob, are we nearly there?' she screamed.

Like an answer to prayer, Rob saw a row of lights high

above sea-level. They were well past Port William, and Knockhaven, with its villas up on the cliff-top, was the next coastal village. 'Five minutes, max,' he said, easing back the throttle; no point in being in such a hurry you missed the harbour.

And yes, there were the harbour lights now, just visible through the drifting veils of rain: the green one flashing on the higher rocks to the south which encircled the harbour protectively, the red fixed light to the north on the side of the lifeboat shed.

'I've got a fix on the harbour lights now,' he announced, 'We're heading in. Two minutes.'

He heard Ashley gasp, 'Thank God!' followed by a cry of heart-rending misery and despair from Luke. *Poor lad*, Rob thought as he opened the throttle again and swept round the curve of the rocks into the harbour.

But where were the familiar, welcoming lights of the village? Where—

The waves, boiling to and fro in the seething cauldron of Fuill's Inlat, seized the *Maud'n'Milly*, lifting her into the air with contemptuous ease to smash her down on the teeth of the jagged rocks beneath. Ashley's scream of terror, the sound of the ripping of the nylon tubes and the rush of escaping air were the last things Rob heard before the shock of the icy water hit him and he too was snatched up, only to be tossed aside like a toy flung down in a toddler's tantrum.

When Hamish Raeburn reached the punchline of his story about the farmer and the agricultural adviser from the Ministry – 'I don't mind you taking away one of my sheep if you want, but that's the collie you've got' – Marjory Fleming laughed heartily, a little more heartily than the old joke warranted, perhaps, but it was the laughter of happiness.

They were sitting having kitchen supper with their closest neighbours, whose farm, like Mains of Craigie, was just a few miles from Kirkluce. Nothing elaborate: beef raised locally followed by Kirstie's Aga meringues. Just an ordinary, pleasant evening, like so many they had spent in the past in this cosy room, with the huge pine dresser which had belonged to Hamish's grandmother and now displayed the Wemyss ware Kirstie's mother had collected over a lifetime of finely judged auction bids at the local roups. Bunches of the dried flowers Kirstie grew to sell to the smartest flower-shop in Kirkluce hung from a pulley overhead and a couple of dogs were snoring contentedly in a big basket next to the dark blue Aga.

Yes, just an unremarkable evening with old friends – except that this was the first invitation Marjory had received to another farm since last year's foot-and-mouth epidemic, when she had so wretchedly found herself enforcing a government policy which was seen as pointless, insensitive and wantonly destructive of rural life.

It was only now, with wounds starting to heal a little, that Marjory was finding acceptance again. Most of the farmers' wives would actually speak to her when they met her in the street or the local supermarket, but friendships had been bruised if not broken, so Marjory had been deeply grateful for Kirstie's somewhat tentative invitation. She'd accepted it, though, as if this were no more than the casual reciprocal hospitality which had been the basis of their long connection.

She had come tonight resolved to steer clear of all controversial subjects, but somehow the warmth of the familiar room, where they had talked through so many problems over the years, seemed to thaw any cold feelings. She found herself pouring out the pent-up misery of the last year, and found, too, that Hamish and Kirstie were still – or perhaps, once more – the understanding friends they had been. It was balm to Marjory's wounded soul, and it was good to see that Bill was listening to her with the sympathetic affection she would once have taken completely for granted. She had begun to wonder if she would ever see that look on his face again.

The men embarked on some discussion of National Farmers' Union politics. Helping Kirstie to clear, Marjory seized the opportunity to air her worries about Cat; the Raeburns' three girls were some years older, and Kirstie, with considerable experience of teenage problems, had always been a source of comfort and sound advice. She chuckled at the story of the black bedroom.

'This I have to see! But honestly, Marjory, girls at that age—'

She was interrupted by the ringing of her guest's work phone. For a second Marjory made no move to answer it, wanting to wail like a child, 'No! It isn't *fair!*' She had given instructions that tonight, for once, she wasn't on call except in the direst emergency.

And already the mood was broken; everyone had stopped talking and in the silence she could feel the distance between their life and hers open up again. She fished the phone out of her bag, looking at the inoffensive object with loathing, said, 'Excuse me,' and took it to the far end of the room.

'This had better be good,' she said tersely.

'Depends what you mean by good.' It was Tam MacNee's voice. 'The Knockhaven lifeboat's been wrecked.'

'Wrecked?' she said blankly.

'Went into Fuill's Inlat instead of the harbour. They don't know why.'

She knew Fuill's Inlat, the wicked little cove near Knockhaven whose approach from the sea mimicked the contours of the port's harbour. Surely every local sailor knew too?

'But the cox—'

'Acting cox, apparently. Willie Duncan was stoned out of his mind, but maybe they'd have been better with him even so.'

'Any fatalities?'

'Two, definite. One still alive so far, but they're not hopeful.'

'That's awful. I'm on my way. No, I don't need a car – it was my turn to drive anyway.' She clicked off the phone and turned slowly, her mind already on the job ahead.

At the table they had politely pretended not to be listening, but now the three faces turned to her expectantly. 'Problems?' Bill asked.

'Grim. The Knockhaven lifeboat's gone down, with loss of life. I'll have to go.'

Kirstie looked stricken. 'Oh no! How – how terrible! And there was me just doing some baking today to put in the freezer for your mother's stall at the lifeboat coffee morning next week! Do they know who was on it?'

Marjory, already picking up her handbag, shook her head. 'No information as yet. Oh, I am sorry, Kirstie. It's been such a lovely evening – I hate to break it up.' She looked wistfully round the pleasant domestic scene, at the coffee cups waiting on the table beside the crystal tumblers and the bottle of Bladnoch, at Bill getting reluctantly to his feet.

'Bill, why don't you stay?' she urged. 'It's a bit fierce to walk back on a night like this, but we can rise to a taxi, surely?'

'No, no. Now, if this had happened before we got to the meringues, it might be different, but . . .' They all laughed, but their farewells were subdued.

Marjory started the car and drove off miserably. She had been so happy to have had the chance to be just another farmer's wife again, instead of someone with a difficult, demanding and high-powered job. And she was dragging Bill away from the sort of convivial evening he loved, which, thanks to that job, had been denied him for so long. Was this going to set them back again, just when she had thought—

Bill reached across to cover her hand on the steering wheel with his. 'I'm maybe wrong, but I just wonder if you're worrying that I'm upset about having to cut the evening short? I'm not. This is a disaster for Knockhaven – for the whole area. There isn't a community in Galloway that doesn't feel the lifeboat's special – look at the way even Kirstie, living the best part of twenty miles away, was baking to help raise funds. It's going to be tough, and it's you and your lot are going to have to pick up the pieces.

'Listening to what you said tonight about what you went through last year, I was ashamed that you've never said that to me – I suppose, because I've been clinging on to some sort of stupid grievance as if it was a comfort blanket. You've a hard job and I'm afraid I've made it harder. I'm sorry.' He picked up her hand and kissed it.

She felt a lump in her throat. 'Oh, Bill,' she said, and bit her lip. Then, because they'd never been the kind to wallow in sentiment, she went on lightly, 'Didn't someone once say love meant never having to say you're sorry?'

'Someone daft, then,' Bill said darkly, and they both laughed, comforted and comfortable and at ease with each other once more.

'Don't wait up,' she said as she dropped him, and in the rain and darkness set off for the winding coast road to the stricken town.

*   *   *

Luke Smith looked surprisingly tranquil. His eyes were closed and his face below the white helmet was unscarred; only the blue-grey colour of his skin and a trace of froth around his still soft, almost childish mouth suggested unnatural death. The odd angle of his head, though, and the smashed limbs visible through great rents in his weatherproof clothing were evidence of the brute violence inflicted on his body by waves dashing it on to the jagged rocks.

He was not, Tam MacNee noted, wearing a life-jacket, so the chances were that he had drowned before the worst of the injuries happened. The rescuers had laid him up here on the stony shore beyond the tide-line, but hadn't taken time even to cover the corpse; they were battling now to reach another yellow-jacketed figure on the exposed rocks to the southern side, having to resist the sucking undertow of the waves sweeping over them as they groped desperately for handholds to cling to. It was agonisingly slow work.

MacNee was standing on the raised edge of the bay, looking down into Fuill's Inlat. There had been a serious delay on the way down – an accident had been blocking the road a couple of miles north since early evening – but the ambulances were mercifully in place now, parked on the road at the top on the apron which had been newly surfaced to service Elder's Executive Homes. A rough track led from it to an old tumbledown stone shed down at the shore and they had managed to get half a dozen cars down here, parking them so that their headlights were trained on the operation below.

It was close to high tide now. Waves were raging to and fro within the confined space of the cove, gaining force as they bounced off its sides. Shredded remains of the lifeboat's orange buoyancy tubes had been pitched up on rocks and shore, incongruously cheerful against the dark boulders and the black menace of the swirling sea, and other debris – rails, broken plastic, ropes – was bobbing in the edge of the waves. The rigid hull of the boat was wedged upside down in the centre of a group of rocks towards the northern side, their knife-edged points showing above foaming water. There was a figure in yellow there too, limp as a rag doll, its helmeted head being submerged as the waves rose, reappearing as they fell back.

They had reached their objective now, were manhandling the sagging form rapidly back along the rescue chain they had established. MacNee saw a couple of the men bend over to check, then a shout went up. An unused stretcher was waiting just above the waterline; a moment later, the victim was strapped to it and four of them were rushing up the hill to one of the two waiting ambulances at the top. It took off at speed a few minutes later, lights flashing.

As they went past, MacNee caught only a glimpse of a man's face, deathly pale above his dark beard, his eyes half-open, with scars and gashes still trickling blood. Rob Anderson; the last time he'd seen him, Rob had been playing the jovial host at the Anchor. 'He was the lucky one, thrown clear,' one of the bearers muttered to MacNee. It wasn't, from the look of him, the word MacNee would have chosen.

They were firing a line across the narrow bay now, securing it midway up the rocks at the southern side and positioning it so that it ran close to where the wreck and that other body lay, dead for a certainty. At the other side, more willing hands fixed it to the landward side of the ruined shed. The tide was on the turn now and more rocks were beginning to show above the still-angry water, giving precarious access; clipped to the line, a man set off. He slipped once, managed to right himself, and then reached the wreck, establishing with some difficulty a secure foothold in one of the crannies between rocks. When he snatched the body from the water's deadly embrace it looked as small as a child's, and with it slung over his shoulder in a fireman's lift he retraced his steps. The weight made balance more difficult and twice he slipped into the water, but secured by the line could scramble to safety and at last deposited his sad burden on the shore.

There was no haste this time. The rest of the rescue team came over, but with a brief glance averted their eyes. MacNee saw one of them double up to vomit into the sea.

They carried her up sombrely to lay her beside Luke. MacNee knew who Ashley Randall was but had never met her; even if he had, he would have been unable to recognise her, except perhaps from the curling wisps of saturated fair hair clinging round the face which was so demolished by the blows it had taken as to be nothing more than a bloody pulp. Despite having served his time in traffic, he had never got used to graphic demonstrations of the fragility of human flesh; MacNee turned away, his own gut churning.

Raised voices caught his attention and he followed the sound to the road at the top of the bluff where a big 4x4 was parked under a street light. The driver's door was standing open and a tall, powerful-looking man was wrestling with two others who seemed to be trying to control him. MacNee set off at a run but almost immediately the struggle was over; the big man, his head bowed, was being helped round to the passenger seat while the other man got in and prepared to drive it away.

MacNee stopped. He had long ago learned that 'If it ain't broke, don't fix it' is a wise motto for any policeman; he walked on again, slowly enough not to reach the top before the car was driven away.

'Aye, aye, Tam! Bad business, this!'

Turning his head, MacNee saw Jason Channell, one of the Anchormen he had recently played at darts and chief mechanic to the lifeboat, coming up the track behind him in one of the cars which had been supplying light. He had stopped and rolled down his window.

'Bad, right enough.' MacNee jerked his head towards the disappearing car. 'What was all that about?'

'That's the Honorary Secretary. Elder – you know, him that's built these.' Channell indicated the five new houses, still blazing light. 'He went clean gyte this evening when he heard it was Rob taking charge instead of Willie. He was like a hen on a hot griddle all evening and when the news came through he was out the shed and along here with the rescue party, yelling and swearing and getting in the way. Then he kinda collapsed and we got him back in his car but it looks like he maybe took another turn just now.'

MacNee frowned. 'I've never come across the man, but surely he's a reputation for being a bit of a hard man?'

'Aye, well, there's a story going round that him and the wee doctor were having a carry-on. He maybe wasn't keen about his fancy piece going out on a night as fierce as this with just the acting cox.'

'Rob? Good man, wasn't he?'

'I'd have said he was probably safe enough. But maybe Elder knew something we didn't – I can't see Willie being such a gomeril as to go into Fuill's Inlat.'

'But Rob obviously was.'

Channell scratched his head. 'Beats me. There's something funny about all this. They'll be able to tell you better along at the shed. I wasn't by the radio when it all went wrong – just there was a gey lot of shouting and we were on our way along here.'

'Fine. I'll have to phone my inspector anyway. She's on a night out – she'll not be pleased.'

The other man nodded, and drove on. The cortege bearing the bodies on stretchers, covered now, was plodding wearily up the hill to the second ambulance; other dispirited, silent men were getting back into the minibus that had brought them along. The cars which had been at the bottom of the track were lurching slowly up it now.

MacNee made his phone call, looking back down into the cove as he spoke to Fleming. Two of the team were packing up equipment; another had gone to reclaim the line from the higher side of the narrow bay. Watching him idly as he detached it, MacNee's eye was caught by something.

Out at the point of the rocky ridge, behind and above where the man had been working, there was a flash of green light, then a moment later, another, and after the same interval, another. Whatever was emitting it was concealed by the bulk of the rocks – was it some sort of warning beacon visible from the sea, perhaps, to mark the danger of this entrance? He had finished his call and was still watching it when one of the men carrying equipment reached him, and he was curious enough to ask him about it.

'That green light flashing there –' he indicated it, 'is that a warning light that the cox should have seen?'

The man followed the direction of his pointing finger, then said blankly, 'There shouldn't be a light there at all. Drew! Tommy!' he shouted to the men below. 'What's that light out on the end of the rocks there? Come up here and you'll see it.'

The two men climbed up to join them. 'My God!' one exclaimed. 'Green, flashing light! That's what you look for, coming into Knockhaven harbour!'

They took off at a run, heading in opposite directions, two along the flattish top of the ridge towards where the light was coming from and the other to the farther side beyond the shed, to see if he could get a view across. He reached his objective first; MacNee heard him shout and wave to recall them, but couldn't hear what he said. He hurried down to the edge of the retreating sea himself and reached it just as the three men came back together.

'What did you see, Tommy?' one demanded.

Tommy's face was grim. 'Some bastard's done this deliberately, Drew.'

'Done what?' MacNee demanded.

'There's a fixed red light on the end gable of that shed. There's a green flashing light higher up on the other side. That's the pattern of leading lights that tells you you're on course for the entrance to the harbour at Knockhaven.'

Drew said slowly, 'I thought it was queer – Rob's a wise-like man. Though you'd expect to see the lights from the houses on the cliff before Knockhaven on your way in – you'd have thought he'd have maybe wondered about that.'

'Look up there.' MacNee gestured to the little development fringing the bay. 'They've only just opened this up. It's probably the first time they've had the lights on like that. You could easy mistake them – forget there were houses here at all.'

There was a heavy silence. 'Right enough,' one of the men said.

'Don't touch anything,' MacNee warned them. 'I'll get someone down to secure the site.'

'I'll radio the coastguard to put out a warning to shipping,' Drew said. 'We're not wanting anyone else landing in here.'

They fetched the line and coiled it up, then, with the last of the equipment, plodded tiredly up the hill. MacNee, summoning some unlucky constable for a cold, unpleasant night of duty, looked down at the sad remains of the *Maud'n'Milly*. '"*On Life's rough ocean luckless starr'd,*"' he murmured, then, 'Control? I've a rare job here for somebody.'

★   ★   ★

By the time Marjory Fleming arrived after the twenty-minute drive down the coast, it was raining only fitfully and the wind was dropping. By half-past midnight on any normal night, most of the douce folk of Knockhaven would be either preparing for bed or in bed already, but tonight lights blazed from the windows and the streets were thronged with people, talking in sober groups or, as Marjory found when she reached the brilliantly illuminated lifeboat shed, just watching in silence. As she wound down her window to speak to the constable controlling access to the pier, she could hear a woman sobbing.

There were two patrol cars parked there already, blue lights revolving, and she spotted MacNee in earnest conversation with a couple of uniforms. He detached himself and came towards her.

'I got a slightly fuller briefing on the way down,' she told him. 'Any relatives here?'

'No. Luke Smith's parents have been informed, but they live in Edinburgh. Ashley Randall's husband was at the scene with his mother, apparently, but they didn't hang about after the body was recovered. Rob Anderson's wife's gone to the hospital, but he's in a bad way.'

'If he made a mistake as crass as that I doubt if he'll have the will to live,' Fleming said crisply. 'So who do I need to see? The Honorary Secretary, I suppose, since he's technically in charge.'

'That's Ritchie Elder – local boy made good, so-called self-made man. God likely wouldn't want to take responsibility.'

'Must be in quite a state, with an accident like this happening on his watch.'

'You could say that,' MacNee said dryly, then, as Fleming made to go into the shed, went on, 'but hold your horses! It's a wee bittie complicated. They've packed him off home. Seems there may have been a touch of the hochmagandy going on with Ashley Randall and he's not himself just at the moment.'

'Ah. Difficult situation.'

'That's not the half of it. I noticed this green light flashing when I was over at Fuill's Inlat and when they investigated they found someone had rigged up lights at the entrance to the cove.'

'You're not telling me this *wasn't* a tragic mistake?'

'They're the same as the lights that lead you into Knockhaven harbour.'

Fleming stared at him, aghast. 'You mean we're looking for someone who deliberately tried to wreck the *lifeboat*?'

'Hard to see what else it could mean. And with the way these things happen, the cox radioed that the teacher laddie was in a state, wanting to throw himself overboard, so they were distracted trying to restrain him just as they headed in.'

Fleming groaned. It was almost a truism that if things were bad, something else would happen that made them worse. Experience should have hardened her by now, both to the cruelty of fate and human wickedness, but the *lifeboat*! People die tragically every day, but in any locality with towns and villages where men go down to the sea in ships, the lifeboat service has a special place in the community's heart and the loss of two, or perhaps three, lives in this context would have a particular resonance. The thought that this could have been the result of a deliberate act was hugely shocking.

'Vandals, I suppose,' she said bitterly. 'We've become the sort of sick society where kids get their kicks out of trying to derail trains and dropping rocks off bridges on to passing cars.'

'Could be. I was having a wee word with some of the locals,' MacNee nodded to the group by the police cars, 'and it seems they're looking for Rob Anderson's stepson. His mother reported he'd taken her car without permission and he's under age. He's a young tearaway and there's no love lost between him and Rob. You might just wonder . . .'

'Aye. You might. Tell them to take him in for questioning when they catch up with him. I'll go and have a word with them inside but I doubt there's much we can do before morning. Is the accident scene secured? Thanks, you've done a good job here.

'Now away and get your beauty sleep, Tam.' She smiled at him hopefully, but he just touched a finger to an imaginary forelock.

'Right. I'll be off then. Goodnight, boss.'

At least he hadn't called her ma'am. With a sigh, Fleming went over to the open door of the shed.

It was a long, cold, boring night when you were sitting in a patrol car by yourself in the darkness in a deserted bay, looking out over a bare shore with only the eerie flashes of a green light for company, and around three in the morning even that stopped. There hadn't been a sign of movement since PC Keith Ingles came on duty and he only realised he'd fallen asleep when the sound of a car's engine wakened him.

He had parked the car at the further end of the area in front of the little row of houses, in darkness now. Still fuddled with sleep, he turned and saw a car's headlights sweep round the corner and had to shut his eyes again as the beam caught him full in the face. The car braked sharply, and when he could see again it had disappeared back round the corner. A moment later he heard it take off fast towards the main road.

His first instinct was to go after it, but his orders were to stay here. He reached for his radio and reported the incident, though without any description of the car's make, far less its number, this was more an exercise in clearing his lines than anything else.

He settled back into his seat, hunching his shoulders uncomfortably. He'd been saving his last Mars bar, but perhaps now was the time to eat it. It was meant to give you energy and it wouldn't do to be caught snoring when the next shift arrived.

7

Marjory Fleming pulled on her overalls on top of her work clothes – an appropriately sober grey trouser suit over a black polo-neck – and glanced anxiously out of the window. The wind had dropped and it looked like being a fine autumn day but there was storm debris all over the lawn: leaves and twigs and even small branches broken from the garden trees.

Normally when there was a strong wind she checked the henhouse last thing to make sure it was secure, but it had been so late when she got back last night that she hadn't a thought of anything except getting her head down. She'd crept in as quietly as she could so as not to wake Bill, but as she slipped shivering into bed he had turned over, gathering her cold body to his warm one in a close embrace. 'Welcome home,' he had murmured, and he hadn't only meant from Knockhaven.

Marjory normally snatched an extra ten minutes after Bill had got up but today she was too anxious about her chookies to wait until after breakfast as usual to feed them. If the roof had lifted off or something . . . She beat a tattoo on the children's doors, reaching in to switch on their lights and waiting for some sign of life before she hurried downstairs.

As she walked down towards the old walled orchard on the slope behind the Mains of Craigie farmhouse which was the hens' domain, she could see that a huge branch from one of the twisted, lichened apple trees had been torn away. They were old trees now, not good for much except producing scabby windfalls for the hens to peck at. They had pretty pink-and-white blossom in spring, though, and when one of them fell victim to a winter storm provided the sweet-scented logs for the fire that Marjory loved. Perhaps they should be planting replacements, but making apple jelly and chutney and quantities of apple pies for the freezer wasn't really her scene and the last thing she needed was something else to ratchet up her guilt about domestic inadequacy.

The henhouse at least was unscathed, though as she watched its occupants shove and squawk their way out she thought that it had probably taken quite a battering in the night. They seemed unsettled: Tony, the rooster, instead of shaking his wattle and crowing, immediately began preening ruffled feathers, while Cherie, the aggressive alpha hen, seemed to be giving him dirty looks as if holding him personally responsible for her disturbed night.

Marjory stood watching them affectionately for a moment, as she always liked to do. The social bickering, squawking protests, crooning exclamations of surprise and delight when their morning scratchings turned up some succulent titbit: her daily glimpse of their feathered world was somehow infinitely soothing.

At last, reluctantly, she fetched the pail of mash and tipped it out for them, leaving them to their pecking-order squabbles as she collected eggs, then went back up towards the farmhouse. The sun wasn't fully up but the sky was a pearly colour and after the rain everything looked freshly minted, as if promising a cleansed and better world. But Marjory had no illusions about the day ahead: same old world, same old problems, with some new ones added.

The dormer windows of the old stone farmhouse, up there under eaves like pointed eyebrows, were the children's bedrooms; in Cammie's the light was off, which probably meant he was downstairs having breakfast since it was unlikely he would actually have got up to switch it off then gone back to bed. Cat's was still on, so – unless she'd defied parental wrath by leaving it burning – she was most probably standing in front of the mirror in her black bedroom, trying to work out how much make-up she could risk applying without having one of her brutal parents sending her back to wash her face before school.

Marjory saw Bill cross the yard just ahead of her and by the time she reached the kitchen he was standing looking at breakfast television. They were just finishing an item about the Knockhaven lifeboat disaster; Cameron had even suspended his attack on a heaped bowl of honey-nut cornflakes to watch.

'Hey, Mum!' he greeted her. 'They're talking about Knockhaven! They've just been talking to Forbes MacRobert's mum. I know her!' He was still young enough for the novelty of involvement with momentous events to outweigh any consideration of their nature.

'Yes, I know.' Marjory went to switch on the kettle for tea. 'You'll probably hear about it at school. One of the crew who was drowned was a teacher at Kirkluce Academy – Luke Smith. I expect Cat knows him.'

An expression of distaste crossed Cammie's face. 'Him? Oh, he's just a rotten old paedophile.'

His parents exchanged startled glances. '*What?*' said Marjory, and Bill added warningly, 'Cammie, I hope you know what you're saying. If this is just some silly rumour going round among the kids—'

'It's not!' the boy protested. 'Greg Baxter's sister's in Nat Rettie's class and she came for Greg after school yesterday and she said Nat said his girlfriend – you know, Kylie MacEwan – was going to see someone to complain.'

In stunned silence Marjory tried to assimilate what she had heard. The Kylie MacEwan angle was unwelcome in itself; from what she had so recently heard about Nat Rettie he was the last person she would want to have any sort of contact with Cat's close friend. Then other things began to slot into place: if Luke was going to be under investigation for paedophilia it would explain why he had been suicidal, and it did suggest, too, that the trap set for the lifeboat might not simply be mindless vandalism. If the boat contained not only the man who you believed had abused your girlfriend but also the stepfather you hated, you had quite a solid motive. And you might even have hoped it would simply be written down as an accident – which it might well have been, if it weren't for Tam's sharp-eyed observation. Well, they had circulated details on the car Nat was driving; even if he hadn't turned up at home last night it shouldn't take them long to find him.

The kitchen door opened and Cat slid herself round it as unobtrusively as possible. She'd got on some new, ash-pale foundation and some state-of-the-art lash-lengthening mascara and she was horrified to find that all eyes were upon her.

But for once her mother didn't seem to notice. 'Cat, do you know anything about Kylie having problems with one of the teachers at the school?'

Bill shot her a warning glance and Marjory, realising she had spoken like a police officer instead of a mother, softened her tone. 'Sorry, darling, I didn't mean that to sound aggressive. It's just that Cammie said one of your teachers had been accused of abusing Kylie – Luke Smith.'

Cat gave her brother a contemptuous look. 'What does *he* know? He's still in baby school, anyway.'

'Did you see Kylie yesterday after school? Did she say anything to you about that?'

'Yes. And no.'

Cat looked so indifferent that Marjory yearned to shake her. With some difficulty, she said calmly, 'According to

Cammie, it was something to do with Nat Rettie. Do you know him?'

This time Cat did react. An uncomfortable flush coloured the pale cheeks. 'Spoken to him. So?' Her tone was defensive and she made a business out of picking up a cereal bowl and a packet of Special K then, shaking out a tiny pile of the flakes, sat down at the table with an air of unconcern.

Marjory sat down opposite. 'Cat, this is something very serious. Last night the Knockhaven lifeboat was wrecked and Mr Smith was one of two people who lost their lives. I need to know if he had problems at school, problems with Kylie.'

It was good to see that under that hard exterior – what had the child got on her face and why did there seem to be furry caterpillars attached to her eyelids? – her tender-hearted daughter still existed.

Cat's eyes filled with tears. 'Oh no! Not the *Maud'n'Milly*!' she cried. 'I went out on her last summer when Gran was helping at the lifeboat fête and the crew were really, really nice! That's awful!'

'Yes, it's all very sad. So – did Kylie ever say anything about Mr Smith?'

'Don't think she even knew him. He didn't teach us.'

'And she didn't mention having gone to complain about him yesterday?'

'She couldn't have. We were, like, together all afternoon?' The teenspeak had returned and she went on, 'That's just little kiddie Cammie telling porkies.'

Cammie, outraged, shouted, 'I'm not, Mum – just ask Drew's sister!'

Bill, as so often a silent observer, intervened with his usual decisiveness. 'That's enough, you two. Cat, there's no excuse for deliberate rudeness. No, don't get up and flounce out. And take a proper helping of cereal – you're not going to school without breakfast.'

If she had said that, Marjory reflected ruefully, there would have been a scene, but mercifully Cat would still take it from her father. She had filled up her bowl and seemed to be eating obediently now, thank goodness; the last thing her mother needed on top of everything else was a daughter with an ambition to be anorexic.

She brewed the tea, her mind already racing ahead to the instructions she would be giving at the morning briefing. The uniforms would be assigned to interviewing anyone and everyone, but there were areas she wanted covered by her own team. Someone must go to the hospital: that had better be Tansy Kerr, since Katy Anderson would probably still be with her husband and a female officer would be more appropriate. Jon Kingsley could go to the school – she'd need to brief him on Cammie's story – and then go down to Knockhaven to talk to Lewis Randall, and find out how much he knew about his wife's goings-on. She'd have to tell her Superintendent, Donald Bailey, the bad news, and she wasn't looking forward to *that*. He was inclined to take anything that disrupted the smooth running of his Force and the balance-sheet projections as a personal affront, and blame the messenger.

Then, of course, if they picked up Nat Rettie—

'Marjory!' Bill's voice broke in. 'Were you actually planning to pour out the tea or just to swirl it around in the pot?'

With a conscience-stricken start she apologised. 'I was just—'

'Oh, I can imagine what you were just doing,' Bill said with mock severity, but his smile was sympathetic.

She smiled back. 'I think I'll take Tam in the car with me when I go down to Knockhaven. That way he can't walk away when I start trying to build bridges. I'm going to take your advice – tell him straight out that he's nairra-nebbit and all I was doing was telling him to keep a civil tongue in his head.'

'*Nairra-nebbit*? Where on earth did you dig that one up from?'

Marjory grinned. 'Good, isn't it? One of my mother's words – it means bigoted. And if I hadn't been daft enough to try to use tact on a Glaswegian, none of this would have happened.'

'And who's being nairra-nebbit now?'

It was only after breakfast, when Marjory was doing a lightning clear of the dishes before taking the children with her to school, that she noticed the telltale traces of cereal round the sink drain. She had vaguely noticed Cat get up from the table but, absorbed in conversation with Bill, she hadn't looked at her bowl. With a sudden twinge of anxiety she wondered how much Cat had actually eaten, after all. They'd have to watch her much more carefully in future.

The room for patients' relatives at the hospital had been arranged with comfortable chairs, pictures and a light, pretty colour scheme, but its impersonal cheerfulness, the backdrop to so many of its occupants' darkest hours, did not register with Katy Anderson. Her eyes were so swollen she could hardly see and she had no idea how long she had been sitting in the prison of her misery. Kindly nurses had popped in from time to time, making her fresh cups of tea which she obediently sipped then left to get cold, and she thought she might have dozed from time to time, though she couldn't be sure.

Rob, when she had been allowed in to see him last night, was drifting in and out of consciousness and connected up with wires and tubes to frightening-looking machines. He had some deep gashes on his face but she couldn't see any other injuries; he had opened his eyes and recognised her, even muttered a few words, but she could see he was somewhere far, far away from her, somewhere that her tear-choked pleas couldn't reach.

They wouldn't let her stay long. They were working on him, they told her, hoping to get him stabilised so they could operate to deal with his internal injuries. But she could tell they weren't hopeful; the young doctor who had talked to her had explained gently that there was no guarantee that he would survive surgery.

'What's – what's the alternative?' Katy had asked, white-lipped.

'We-ell . . .' His reply was awkward and she knew what *that* meant.

All through the dreadful, interminable night she had looked up every time the door opened but it was never the visitor she was waiting for and at the same time dreading. Now it was a young woman with dark red hair streaked blonde at the front, wearing jeans and a hooded top. Katy looked at her blankly.

'Mrs Anderson? I'm DC Kerr.' She flashed a photo card in a plastic holder, then came over to sit down beside Katy. 'Is there any news of your husband this morning?'

Katy licked dry lips. 'I think they must still be operating. Surely they'll be finished soon?'

'They'll be doing everything they can for him, I know that.' From her accent, the policewoman sounded like a local girl; she had a low, pleasant voice. 'It's tough, but try not to worry too much. They're pretty good at their job, these guys.' Her calmness was reassuring.

'Do you know yet what happened?' The question had been haunting Katy all night. 'How did they go in there? Rob knew about Fuill's Inlat – everyone knew!'

'We've people checking it out now. Our inspector's away down to Knockhaven this morning and I'm sure we'll get some answers soon.'

'And—' Katy licked her lips again. 'The others? What happened to the rest of the crew? I know Rob was coxing because Willie didn't go, but what about Ashley? And was the other one Luke? They couldn't tell me here at the hospital.'

Couldn't – or wouldn't, more like, Tansy Kerr reflected bitterly. Who wanted to be the person to tell a woman that two people had died when her husband had been at the helm? She'd had a drink in the Anchor herself a couple of times; Katy was a nice woman, and he by all accounts had been a nice man. 'Yes, Luke, that's right. I'm afraid they were both dead when they got to them.'

Katy bowed her head and Kerr could see the cracked lips quivering. 'Did he know what he'd done?'

'I – I don't know.' Changing the subject swiftly, Kerr said, as neutrally as she could, 'Mrs Anderson – Katy – can I just ask if you've seen your son at all?'

'Nat?' She looked startled at the name, as if the thought of her son hadn't crossed her mind since she heard about Rob. Now, she was remembering what she had done and she put her hand to her head. 'Oh dear! I was so angry last night, before— And I'd been so worried, too, about him joyriding. But maybe I shouldn't have told the police he'd taken my car, informed on him—'

'Don't blame yourself,' Kerr said firmly. 'How would you have felt if he'd come to harm because you hadn't stopped him?'

Katy drew a shuddering sigh. 'Or harmed someone else. That's what Rob said – he was very strict about it. Oh, what shall I do if – if—' Mentioning her husband brought tears, welling up and splashing silently down her cheeks.

'But you haven't seen Nat?' Kerr persisted gently.

'No. He's probably back at home by now.' Picking up a tissue from the box to mop her sore-looking cheeks, she obviously wasn't interested in his whereabouts.

The detective scribbled a note discreetly. Then she said, 'Katy, can I just ask you, was Rob able to speak to you last night – tell you anything at all about what happened?'

'Not – not really.' She was finding it hard to keep control. 'He was so weak – just muttered something about the lights—'

'Can you remember his words, exactly?'

'He kept saying, "My fault, my fault."' She couldn't speak for a moment and it was only with an obvious effort that she managed to go on. 'And it was – sort of like he didn't understand, was puzzled. "The lights were there," I think that was what he said. He said that once or twice – maybe, like, "There *were* lights." Then he said something about three of them – "Three of them – too many, too many." And then about it being his fault again.'

Kerr scribbled the words in her book. 'You're being so brave, Katy – this is really helpful. Was there anything else?'

The woman frowned, as if seeing a picture that Tansy couldn't see, of a man only just holding on to life, murmuring words that might be his last. Then she shook her head. 'Just that. He sort of repeated that kind of thing, once or twice, and there were one or two words I couldn't make out. Then when they made me go he opened his eyes and said, "Katy, love—"'

She began to sob and with a lump in her own throat Tansy looked round, saw a little sink in one corner and fetched a glass of water, more as a distraction than anything else. She clasped the woman's hands round it, persuading her to take a sip. Her own voice wasn't quite steady as she said, 'I know. It's awful. But hang on, there's always hope—'

And then the door opened and Tansy did not need the jerk of the nurse's head indicating that she should make herself scarce to tell her that the doctor standing behind her in the doorway was bringing the news that would kill that hope stone-dead, as dead as Katy Anderson's husband.

'*Nairra-nebbit?*'

She had surprised Tam into laughter, as she had hoped she would; that was a good start.

'For God's sake, Marjory,' he went on, 'why could you not just have said at the outset that if I pit the heid on him for being English you'd have my guts for garters, same's you usually do?'

'It's what I meant, right enough. I just thought I'd try for a wee bit more delicacy.'

'Did I never tell you the story about the fella from Maryhill who was asked why he punched his pal in the stomach instead of the jaw? He said, "I was tryin' to be subtle, ken?" That's what we call delicacy in Glasgow.'

'That's fine. Next time I promise I'll begin by saying, "See you, you Weegie bastard . . ." OK?' It was good to be back on insult terms again. 'Now listen to this.' She told him what Cammie had said and he pursed his lips in a silent whistle.

'That would figure, eh? They've not found him yet, have they, so I'll maybe take a wee shufti round the Anchor in case he's there but keeping his head down.'

'Good idea. I've got Ritchie Elder to see at the lifeboat shed and I'll have a word with anyone else who's there. Then I want to go to Fuill's Inlat – see how they're getting on. You've been dealing with Willie Duncan so you'd better go and see him. He could be rattled enough by what's happened to be vulnerable to your unique brand of persuasion.'

'That's supposing the effects have worn off by now. He'll maybe still be so relaxed he doesn't care.'

But Willie was anything but relaxed. When he opened the door of his house, his eyes red and watery, he reacted to MacNee as if he had seen Old Nick himself.

'Get away from me, MacNee! I'm having nothing to do with you! Now leave me alone or I'm making a complaint.' He was yelling like a madman.

A second later, an astonished MacNee was staring at a slammed door. It had been so unexpected he hadn't even reacted fast enough to put his foot in to stop it closing; indeed, he could count himself lucky not to have lost the end of his nose. He took a step back and stood surveying the situation, pondering his next move.

He could hear that Willie was still on the other side of the door; was that even sobbing he could hear? Well, it wasn't dignified, but . . .

MacNee dropped to his knees on the doorstep and pushed open the letter-box. On the other side the brushes of a draught-excluder blocked his view but he called in the voice of sweet reason, 'Willie, you know fine we're going to have to talk to you about what happened yesterday. Why not do it the easy way instead of the hard way? If you give me a voluntary statement now we won't have to send someone to bring you in for questioning.'

'Do what you like. Just get off my doorstep.' There was the sound of retreating footsteps, then an inner door slammed. Standing up self-consciously, MacNee bent to brush the knees of his jeans and heard a mocking titter behind him. He swung round, his face reddening as he recognised the man who had recognised him. He was one of the local stringers for the *Scottish Sun*, a thin youth with acne and a weasel face. Pond-scum.

He was smirking. 'I knew things were bad but I didn't realise the Busies were having to resort to prayer,' he sneered.

'You'd be better putting up a wee word or two yourself.' MacNee was fully signed up to the principle of getting your retaliation in first. 'I've been hearing rumours about your leisure activities and if I decide to look into them a little more closely it'll be you needing divine assistance to stay out of trouble.'

He walked away, the journalist looking uneasily at his jaunty, retreating back. Perhaps it wasn't such a good story after all.

Fleming was early for her appointment with Ritchie Elder but Jason Channell, the lifeboat's chief mechanic, seemed almost desperate to talk to her; indeed, from the way he was pouring out his version of the previous night's events, it probably counted as therapy. He was unshaven and hollow-eyed, clearly grieving for his comrades and exhausted from his efforts of the night before. She suspected he hadn't even gone to bed.

Much of what he said had been covered by Tam's report to her, but clearly since then there had been a lot of talk and speculation about the mystery surrounding the fate of the *Maud'n'Milly*, and the curiously uncontrolled behaviour of the Hon Sec as well. This last was, presumably, irrelevant to the main issue, but she was interested nevertheless. She knew Elder's reputation, and in any new enquiry jarring elements were worth investigating, even if only to get them out of the way. She'd definitely want to put that to Elder when he arrived, and almost on that thought the door of the shed opened.

Ritchie Elder this morning was a different man from the ranting wreck of the previous night. He was wearing a pale grey cashmere polo-neck over dark grey trousers, having obviously made a similar sartorial judgement to Marjory's own. His striking blue eyes did, indeed, look somewhat puffy, but he was perfectly calm and immaculately clean-shaven, with not a hair of his thick, iron-grey crop out of place.

'Inspector. How do you do?' He didn't look pleased to find her there already, deep in conversation with Channell. She thought she even caught a flicker of anger, but he favoured her with a nicely judged smile: pleasant enough, though of course constrained by the atmosphere of tragedy. 'You'll forgive us if everything is a little disordered this morning. Last night's disaster has left us all reeling, I'm afraid, and the phone's going mad – reporters, head office, the chair of the Friends of the Lifeboat, the coastguard . . .

'Still, come into my office – it's just a cubby hole, but I can unplug the phone so we won't be disturbed and you can tell me how best we can help you get to the bottom of all this.'

Feeling as if she had been deluged in treacle, Fleming followed him. The room in question had been partitioned off from the main shed and was indeed, as Elder had indicated, very small, with room only for a desk with a swivel seat behind it, a filing cabinet and a couple of upright chairs. A shelved wall held file boxes, manuals and untidy piles of reports and brochures. He waved her suavely to a seat, then, taking up his place in the swivel chair, leaned back and said, 'Now, shoot!'

It was a good performance of the 'great-man-being-gracious-to-humble-copper' role, and it riled the hell out of her. She'd been wondering where to begin; now, at his invitation to shoot, she took aim squarely below the belt.

'Mr Elder, perhaps I can start by asking about your affair with Dr Ashley Randall, who, I understand, is one of the victims?'

She failed to rattle him. The only visible reaction was one of sardonic amusement. 'Dear me, Inspector, don't tell me you've been listening to local gossip?'

'That's how we get some of our most useful information.'

'And a great deal of misinformation, as I'm sure you would be the first to acknowledge.' He smiled ruefully, then, putting his hands on the desk, palms upward in the classic gesture of openness, went on, 'Actually, as I said to my wife this morning, I was expecting this. You were bound to hear it somewhere and I'm glad it's cropped up right at the start so that I can knock it on the head.

'If you've ever lived in a village, Inspector, you'll know what it's like. Ashley Randall is – was,' he corrected himself, with what could almost have been a trace of human emotion, 'a very attractive young woman. She and I, through our lifeboat work, were naturally enough thrown together and of course the tongues started wagging. It only takes one person saying, "I wonder if . . ." and the next person says, "Mrs So-and-So says . . ." and on it goes.

'I'm not going to deny I got on well with Ashley. We'd a lot of interests in common and if you were accusing me of having the occasional flirtatious conversation I'd have to put my hands up. Flirting with a pretty woman is surely one of life's innocent pleasures.

'But!' The steel in his voice reminded Fleming of his business reputation. 'If I hear that allegations are being made about our relationship, allegations which would of course deeply distress my wife and Dr Randall's husband, I shall sue – the Press, you, whoever. So if you are planning publicly to pursue that line, you'd better have convincing proof of something beyond normal social activity. Is that clear?'

'Perfectly.' It had been a side-issue anyway and it was never wise to charge in without an army of facts at your back. Still, there was nothing to stop her using such evidence as she did have. 'I understand that you were distraught last night and had to be restrained?'

Fleming thought she saw the muscles in his jaw tighten but he said lightly, 'Guilty as charged on that one, I'm afraid. Perhaps you can imagine what it feels like to be responsible for giving an order which sends out friends and fellow-workers to their death?'

'Of course. But it seems you were uncontrolled earlier, when you heard that Willie Duncan was unable to go out with the boat?'

This time there was no mistake about the tightened jaw.

'I was very angry, yes. Intemperate, even. Willie and I go back a long way and it was a serious betrayal of trust. As I believe I said at the time, if I could have got my hands on him, I would probably have killed him.'

He was covering all the bases and there was nothing more to be gained by pursuing that line either; she changed tack. 'You were unhappy about Rob Anderson's capabilities as acting cox?'

As he paused, weighing his words, Fleming had the sense of someone regrouping after a hard-fought skirmish. Which was interesting.

'Rob Anderson,' he said slowly at last, 'was a thoroughly good man and he's done all the appropriate training. But as a naval officer you don't have to fly by the seat of your pants, whereas Willie has the sea in his blood. He used to fish out of Stranraer, until the quotas came in, but he still goes out with a creel two or three times a week. He knows these waters like the back of his hand.

'This was the first time Rob had had to take the helm. It shouldn't have had to be on a night like last night, at a moment's notice.'

'Were you aware of the situation as it developed last night?'

'Naturally.' She saw him run a finger round the neck of his sweater as if to loosen it. He was finding it hard to talk about this, which again was interesting; it hadn't bothered Jason Channell.

'I was by the communications desk, listening in as usual. It had been, in the event, a perfectly straightforward operation and we were all just chatting among ourselves as we waited for them to get back. Then all hell broke loose – you know about Luke Smith?'

Fleming nodded and Elder went on, 'He was another of my worries last night, but only because the boy was inexperienced. He was totally dedicated – never missed a call-out, worked to pass every course he needed, been on a dozen training exercises – there was no reason why he shouldn't go.

'To be honest with you, I have to say he never struck me as particularly impressive, and someone said he wasn't making much of a fist at teaching. But frankly, the way kids are today I couldn't blame him. How they can get anyone to go into teaching beats me, with the yobs they're dealing with, all snarling, "You can't touch me!" I'd touch them, all right!'

She wasn't up for digressions about the state of modern education. 'So this came as a shock to you? He had no history of depression?'

'A shock not just to me. It was clear that this was a bolt from the blue for Rob and Ashley as well. She was hanging on to him, screaming, and Rob was trying to get in as quickly as possible. Presumably that's how it all went wrong, though I still don't understand—'

'How did you discover what had happened?'

'Rob said he'd picked up the harbour lights and was on his way in. Some of us hurried out, ready to help restrain Smith, if that was needed, and I remember thinking it was odd we couldn't see them yet. Then they started yelling from inside the shed – they'd heard Ashley scream . . .' He was sweating as he described it, Fleming noticed clinically.

'The coastguard got a fix on them and of course we realised then . . . I jumped into the car and got out there immediately – it was terrible, terrible!'

He bent his head, shuddering, and for the first time Fleming felt real pity for the man. This, for whatever reason, was going to haunt him for the rest of his life. 'I'm sorry to have to take you through all that,' she said, getting up. 'I won't trouble you further at the moment, sir, but thank you for your cooperation.'

Elder visibly pulled himself together. 'There were one or

two questions I was hoping to have answers to before you go, Inspector. I would like some indication of the direction and present progress of police enquiries. I shall need to know exactly what went wrong—'

'Of course,' Fleming said smoothly. 'The investigation at the site is going on at the moment – in fact, I'm on my way there now to check what's happening. But as you will understand, we're not yet in a position to give any answers. Thank you for your time.'

Elder didn't get up to show her out. He looked drained and exhausted, almost like an actor after a demanding performance, and as she shut the door she saw him bend down to open the bottom drawer of the filing cabinet. She would bet that what was filed there came in a glass bottle.

So what was that all about? It was natural enough that in his position the loss of the lifeboat which was technically in his charge would be a devastating blow, and natural too that if he was having a clandestine affair he would be worried about scandal. But was there something more to it than that?

Of course, it was probably a line that would never need to be pursued, once they had got hold of Nat Rettie, but she was thoughtful as she left the shed.

8

There was an almost visible pall of mourning over the town as Tam MacNee walked down the narrow wynd between high walls which led from the end of Willie Duncan's street to the irregular square of buildings behind the Anchor Inn, the raucous screams of the gulls overhead a shocking intrusion on the strange, heavy silence. MacNee usually enjoyed it when his business took him to one of the coastal areas which was part of Galloway Constabulary's wide rural district, but this wasn't the day for admiring a seascape.

When he reached the sea-front, the only traffic seemed to be to and from the lifeboat shed; the streets were almost deserted and several of the shops were shut. Where a knot of people gathered it was for a brief, muted conversation before they went soberly on; here in this close-knit community there was no public sign of any salacious enjoyment of sensation.

The Anchor was shut up, as it would be anyway at this time of day. It had a double frontage and a door on to Shore Street, but access to the Andersons' flat was from behind, and after glancing in the window at the empty bar MacNee went back round to the square again. The Anchor had a garage and a small yard with empty barrels and stacked crates down one side, as well as a pocket-handkerchief lawn which had a straggling cherry-tree in the middle with a bird-feeder hung on a low bough; a blue-tit and a sparrow flew off at MacNee's approach.

The back of the inn looked as blank as the front, showing no sign of life. He looked sharply at the drawn curtains at a window on the first floor, but that of course didn't prove that anyone had spent the night there. He inspected the garage, trying the handle of the side door. It was locked, but there was a tiny window, grimy and cobwebbed. He bent down to peer in.

There was a car inside. He hadn't seen the report about it and anyway couldn't read the number plate, but this was a small green Peugeot, the sort of thing you might well run as a second car. So had Nat Rettie quietly come home and gone to bed without being spotted? MacNee went over and rang the doorbell, a long, authoritative ring, then stepped back to observe the curtains. There was no sign of movement; he rang again, three or four times, then had another look. Still nothing.

That, of course, didn't prove anything either. At this time of day the boy should actually be in school, though Tam would be very surprised if he was. From Control, he got confirmation of the car's make, passed on his own suspicion that the boy could be inside, then walked on thoughtfully towards the lifeboat shed.

He'd known the Andersons ever since they took over the pub and he liked them both. He had a particularly soft spot for cheerful, bonny Katy, so happy in her work and just daft about her husband, poor wee soul. Tam wasn't much given to empathy, or 'going saft' as he was more likely to put it, but he couldn't help wondering what it would do to her if she lost her husband and then found out that it was her son who had engineered not only his death but the deaths of two other innocent people. It didn't bear thinking about.

Fleming was coming out of the building as he approached it, provoking a flurry of movement in a group standing idly on the pier, with notebooks and cameras. He saw her smile

– well, bare her teeth, anyway – then speak to them briefly before heading for her car. They followed her like a cloud of flies, shouting questions which she ignored.

MacNee was ready to jump in when she paused to pick him up, driving off again before he had even slammed the door.

Headmasters hadn't been as young as this when he was at school – at least his certainly hadn't. Feeling the weight of his twenty-six years, DC Jonathan Kingsley followed the head-master of Kirkluce Academy through to his office. The man looked not much older than he was himself and he was wearing quite a sharp suit with a Paul Smith shirt open at the neck.

'Peter Morton,' he replied to Kingsley's introduction, waving him to a seat. 'This is a very sad business, isn't it? We're all in shock here. Luke was a good lad – gave a lot to the school, and to the community, of course, with his lifeboat service. Tragic that it all had to end this way. Coffee?'

'Tragic,' Kingsley echoed, and expressed a preference for black, no sugar. This was, he reflected as Morton passed this on to his secretary, a curious way to describe someone recently outed as a predatory paedophile, but he'd heard before of the reluctance of headmasters to involve their school in that sort of scandal. Did Morton see Luke's death as a heaven-sent way out of a nasty, messy situation?

If he did, then the man was wasted as a headmaster. The London stage was crying out for people with that sort of acting talent. When Kingsley said, 'I gather there were some problems with him?' Morton's only reaction was a rueful smile.

'Oh dear. Yes, I'm afraid he was having difficulty with dis-cipline. Such a shame – he was so enthusiastic about his sub-ject, so ready to help with extra-curricular activities, but I'm afraid kids today don't have much respect for these virtues. We were doing all we could to help him, of course, but—'

'Did you have any complaints about him?'

The man's untroubled eyes met his squarely. 'Not that many. A couple of conscientious parents were worried about how much their children were being allowed to learn in his class, but that was all. No, quite honestly the main problem was what the kids were doing to him. He was getting a pretty hard time from some of them. To tell you the truth, we were beginning to wonder if he was in the wrong profession.'

You had to go for it. 'Were there any allegations of child abuse?' Kingsley asked baldly.

The transformation was remarkable. Morton jumped as if someone had jabbed him with a needle. 'Child abuse! No, never! Have you had a complaint?' He certainly wasn't untroubled now.

'We have information that yesterday a child made a complaint that she had been abused by Mr Smith.'

'Good God! Well, if so it never reached me.' He was pressing numbers on his phone as he spoke. 'Sarah? Would you find Mrs Walker for me – ask her to come to my office as a matter of urgency? Thanks.'

He replaced the receiver. 'She's the Child Protection Officer, but I can't imagine that if there had been a complaint like that she wouldn't have come straight to me. There's a strict protocol – Luke would have had to be suspended immediately.'

The pause, as they waited for Mrs Walker to appear, was going to be awkward. The other question on Kingsley's list – the whereabouts of Nat Rettie – seemed a good way of filling it.

Morton turned to his computer, scanning through files. 'The absent list should be here, unless Sarah hasn't had a chance to compile it yet. Oh yes, here we are. Nat Rettie

isn't in today – natural enough, I suppose, in the circumstances.' He closed the file, then looked up sharply, his face
suddenly alive with suspicion.

'Oh, hang about! These allegations wouldn't have anything
to do with Nat Rettie, would they?'

Kingsley didn't confirm it, but he didn't deny it, either.

'Rettie,' the headmaster went on, 'was conducting a
vendetta against Smith. I suspended him once on the basis
of a report from Luke and ever since he's been out for revenge.
Ah, here's Fiona.'

The woman who came in was middle-aged and slightly
overweight, with a kind, motherly face. She had obviously
been crying; she looked enquiringly at Kingsley as Morton
performed the introductions and explained.

'The officer has heard that a girl made a complaint of
abuse yesterday against Luke Smith. Did it reach you?'

A look of unfeigned horror crossed Fiona Walker's face.
'*Luke*? No, no, of course not! I'd have come to you straight
away, and so would any other member of staff. But who—'

'The detective won't confirm it, but I suspect that Nat
Rettie's behind this. So the girl, no doubt, will be—'

'Kylie MacEwan,' Fiona supplied grimly. 'Of course we have
to deal with this totally professionally, but if it's anything other
than another stage in Rettie's war of attrition, I'll be astounded.
Probably the only person abusing Kylie is Nat himself.' Then,
with tears in her eyes, she went on, 'And you know what
they're saying, Peter? They're saying that it happened partly
because Luke was trying to throw himself overboard and they
were distracted, trying to stop him.'

It crossed the detective's mind uneasily that perhaps this
new kind of Head wasn't as different from the old kind as
you might imagine when Morton turned a gimlet eye on
him. 'Is this true?'

It would be on the news today anyway. 'Yes, that he was

trying to commit suicide. There would have been other factors, of course.'

'And about Kylie and Nat?' Fiona pressed him.

'I can't discuss that, but what I can say is that I shall be wanting to talk to Kylie.'

'You and me both,' Morton said with feeling. 'Oh, don't worry, Constable. We'll play it by the book.'

'I'm sure you will, sir,' Kingsley got up. 'I've got another preliminary interview to do, but I'll come back later with a woman officer and talk to the girl formally then. And if Nat Rettie turns up, you will let us know?'

That had all shed an interesting light on the information received. The teachers were an impressive pair, and if Kingsley had to put money on it, he'd back their analysis of the situation. Still, you couldn't be too careful with Child Protection issues; he took the precaution of contacting the Social Work Department, though by the time he found the number and tracked down the appropriate person, he discovered she had been informed already. Yes, Morton and Walker were definitely a class act.

It was a heartbreakingly beautiful day now as Fleming drove the short distance along the coast road between Knockhaven and Fuill's Inlat, high above the shore. A periwinkle sky had clouds like lace doilies and the gannets, wings folded, were performing their arrow dives into a sea that was Prussian blue, artistically edged with a few white-crested waves. Yesterday's storm had subsided to a comfortable swell, like some monster sated by its swallowed prey.

The scene at Fuill's Inlat was in stark contrast to this benign innocence. The tide was out and the deadly rocks were now no more than picturesque boulders, lapped by waves which sparkled in the sunshine, but all around them and strewn on the shore was the detritus of last night's disaster: ropes, engine parts, white plastic buoys, shreds of orange nylon. There were black slicks of oil in the pools left by the retreating tide and as Fleming stepped down to the water's edge on the pebble beach a bedraggled RNLI pennant was washed up at her feet. Her mouth twisted; she felt nauseated by the wickedness, the waste, the awful injustice that a mission to save the lives of others should end like this. The sick mind of the perpetrator seemed to have tainted with evil even the salty freshness of the air.

There were half a dozen SOCOs in their white overalls here, painstakingly gathering up and bagging whatever might be considered evidence, and lifeboat officials were present too, sombrely watching the operation. Normally this would have waited until the investigating officer had viewed the scene, but in these circumstances Fleming had instructed that they should go ahead.

As Fleming and MacNee went towards them, the crime scene manager who had been directing the activities of a photographer came over, with an enquiring look. When Fleming had identified herself, he said, 'Ah! We've got something here that might interest you.' He turned to pick up two large plastic evidence bags which had been tagged and parked on the ridge of springy grass behind the beach.

'We found these on either side of the bay, one on the higher rocks to the south there, the other in a niche at the side of that tumbledown shed. Facing out to sea, green one set to flash, red one a steady beam. Not working now – battery run down, I'd guess.'

They looked at the exhibits. They were beacon-shaped lanterns on a sturdy plastic base, one with green glass, the other red.

'Where would you get lights like that?' Fleming wondered. 'Ship's chandler's, perhaps? We might get a lead out of that.'

The SOCO shook his head. 'The colour's just glass paint.

Sort of thing my wife gets at the craft shop – she's into Tiffany lamps. Otherwise they're just the standard sort of light you might use for camping – look, there's a searchlight in the base too. Very practical.'

'Not any sort of specialist store then?' MacNee asked gloomily.

'Could be Halfords, Milletts, Argos catalogue, even—'

MacNee pounced. 'If it was a catalogue purchase they'd have records, wouldn't they? We might get at it that way.'

Fleming, with a housewife's more specialist knowledge, looked doubtful. 'I hate to be a wet blanket, but there's definitely an Argos store in Dumfries. One in Ayr as well, probably, and a Halfords. It would be easy enough to get them from there without leaving a purchase record. Have you picked up anything from the sites where the lights were set up?'

'Not a lot. Nothing from the rocks, right down to the shoreline, but they're checking the side of the shed now. It's not hopeful, though – no smooth surfaces.'

'What about the lights themselves?'

'We've dusted them, but nothing's come up. The lab boys'll maybe be able to turn up something more for you.'

'We can always hope,' Fleming said, then as the man went back to his work she and MacNee slowly climbed the track together.

'That's it, then, isn't it?' she said heavily. 'It's definitely murder. Someone planned all that, carefully and cleverly. They put these in place when they knew the lifeboat had gone out in poor visibility—'

'So someone with links to the crew, like Rettie?'

Fleming frowned. 'I think I remember they went back to firing maroons, like in the old days – publicity stunt, basically. So anyone within earshot would know there was a call-out.

'These things would only have a limited battery life, so you'd have to be there to set them going. You'd know the battery would run down a few hours later and if everything went according to plan and you managed to wreck the boat, the chances are no one would even notice before you managed to remove them. And if it hadn't been for you spotting them the chances are we'd just have put it down to human error.'

'They couldn't have known Willie was stoned and Luke was suicidal, mind. Or even that the boat would be coming back from the north not the south,' MacNee pointed out.

'That's true. But on a night like last night, close enough to home for them not to be running on instruments, it had at least a chance of success. And supposing the attempt failed, what were the risks? If the boat didn't come round that way, you could try again. If it did, but survived to report fake lights, what's the most that would happen? There'd be a lot of shocked comment about vandals, we'd try to trace the lights and probably fail, then because no one had come to harm we'd drop it. Not worth the manpower.'

'Right enough. And if you were watching, and saw the boat come back, you could even recover the evidence long before anyone else could get there. But is it not all kinda subtle for the likes of Rettie, though?'

'I'm probably over-refining. He may not have thought anything, except that he'd a chance to get two people he hated in one go.'

'Mmm.' She noticed Tam was frowning but before she could ask him why, PC Langlands appeared, heading towards them. He had been detailed to question staff at the on-site office of Elder's Executive Homes to find out if they'd noticed anything the night before, and establish a list of visitors to the houses.

'Any luck, Sandy?'

He pulled a face. 'No, boss, except I've a list of people who came to see the houses last night to follow up – eleven couples, plus the staff here. But the two girls in the office didn't see anything at all. With it being such a horrible night they'd the curtains drawn and the lights on to make the show-house look cosy, and the lights were on in all the empty houses too. And if you were getting out of a car with that gale blowing, you wouldn't stop to admire the view, would you?' He was looking crestfallen; he was still young enough, Fleming reflected, to cherish high hopes of a breakthrough even when conducting the most routine questioning.

'That's fine, Sandy,' she said encouragingly. 'You may find when you work through your list that one of the visitors spotted something useful. Whoever put those lights there had to get from here down to the shore during the time the houses were being shown and you might well have been peering out at the view from one of the empty houses if you were plan-ning to buy it.' She took the list from him and scanned it. 'Oh – Ritchie Elder was here, was he?'

'The girls didn't see him until he was just going. He came into the office to say he'd to go to the lifeboat shed, but appar-ently he'd been going round the houses earlier chatting up the punters.'

'Right. OK, Sandy – good luck.' As they walked back to the car, Fleming said, 'So Elder was here, at the scene? I've got an odd feeling about that man. Something doesn't quite fit.'

'I'll tell you the other thing that doesn't fit. If Rettie did this to get his old man and his teacher, how could he know Smith would be going out? This was all set up well in advance.'

Fleming stopped. 'Of course he couldn't. If he knew at all, it could only have been at the very last minute. I should have focused on that myself – I've just had about twenty-three different things on my mind.' Then, walking on, she added,

'But again, we could be making too much of this. The object may have been to get Anderson, and Smith was just a bonus, as he would see it. Still, the sooner we get our hands on him the better.'

Kylie MacEwan's pert little face was a study in sullenness as she came into the headmaster's office. Her regulation school skirt had been abbreviated to well above the knee; her shirt, worn outside it, was only just long enough to cover her midriff and open at the neck with a loosely knotted tie draped round it. She looked distrustfully at the two people she did know, and more distrustfully at the one she didn't, a tired-looking woman in her forties with long, straggling grey hair escaping from a clasp at the back and thick glasses which magnified anxious-looking brown eyes. They were sitting round a small coffee table in one corner of the room, at the social worker's request – 'So much less confrontational than sitting behind a desk!'

'Sit down, Kylie.' Peter Morton gestured to the one vacant chair. 'This is Mrs Barnett. She's from the Social Work Department and—'

'We just want to have a little chat with you, Kylie dear,' she interrupted. 'Nothing to make you at all uncomfortable – just a chat.'

Kylie dear favoured her with a contemptuous look which spoke volumes about her opinion of social workers in general and this one in particular. She sat down with arms folded and legs crossed, her body language a study in resistance.

'Has something – happened to you recently? Something which upset you?'

The guarded eyes, fringed by lashes thick with blue mascara, flicked across the adults' faces. 'Nuh.'

'I know that you may not want to talk about it, that you may feel guilty it happened, that people will blame you instead of him. But it's not like that!' The woman was leaning forward earnestly, as if she would have liked to take one of the hands so firmly tucked into Kylie's armpits.

Morton and Fiona Walker both thought they could read alarm in the girl's eyes but she only muttered, 'Don't know what you're on about.' Her jaws began to move rhythmically.

The headmaster stepped in. 'Kylie, gum out, please.' He took a tissue from a box on the table and handed it to her; she grudgingly removed the offending substance. 'Right,' he continued, 'I can see you're wondering what we're talking about, so I think we should be a bit more direct. Did you ever have any problems with Mr Smith?'

There was no mistaking the child's surprise. 'Him? Nuh.'

'Kylie, are you sure, dear?' Mrs Barnett broke in. 'Was his behaviour to you ever – inappropriate?'

She sniggered. 'Like to see him try! He's a right tosser.'

'Was, Kylie.' Morton spoke quietly. 'I expect you have heard he died in the lifeboat disaster?'

He succeeded in shaming her. There was a flush under the pale make-up as she said defensively, 'Yeah, well – whatever.'

Fiona Walker, silent thus far, leaned forward. Her kindly face was stern as she said, 'Kylie, I've been speaking to some of the older girls. Nat Rettie said in class yesterday that you were coming to me to accuse Mr Smith of child abuse—'

'We don't use that word, *accuse*,' the social worker protested, but was ignored.

'Is that true?' Fiona persisted.

At the mention of his name, Kylie became visibly agitated. 'I dunno,' she mumbled, her head bent.

'Is – it – true?'

Mrs Barnett fluttered, 'Well, *really*—' but before she could say more, Kylie looked up.

'Nuh! 'Course it wasn't. Nat would just be, like, mucking about.'

'Mucking about!' Fiona's eyes flashed anger, but before

she could say anything more, Morton's cool, authoritative voice overruled her.

'Thank you, Kylie. I think that's all we need to know at the moment.' He looked enquiringly at Mrs Barnett, who shook her head. Kylie needed no second bidding; she was through the door faster than a weasel into a hole in a dyke.

Morton turned to the social worker. 'Are you satisfied that no abuse has occurred?'

'I suppose so.' It was a grudging admission; reluctant to accept total defeat, she went on, 'But she looks to me like a child who has problems. What's the background like?'

Morton and Walker exchanged glances. 'How interesting you should ask,' he said smoothly. 'We've been rather worried about her relationship with Nat Rettie – he's over sixteen, and you probably noticed her reaction when you asked her if anything had happened to her recently. Shall I ask my secretary to find us some coffee?'

When the door eventually shut behind Mrs Barnett, Morton said with reprehensible satisfaction, 'The MacEwans aren't going to be pleased. They've got enough problems to have that woman wished on them for a month. I don't know – it would be good to think she might manage to achieve something useful, but what I certainly do know is that this won't have made Kylie a happy bunny.'

'Yes,' Fiona agreed, then her eyes filled. 'But Luke's still dead, isn't he?'

The woman who answered the door of 8 Mayfield Grove in response to DC Kingsley's knock was in her mid-sixties, he judged, a fit-looking woman and what one might unkindly describe as well-preserved. Her well-cut hair was tinted a tasteful pale gold, her face was discreetly made-up and she was smartly dressed in a pink sweater with a pink-checked tweed skirt, the matching scarf round her neck held in place with a heavy gold cameo. She looked at him as if he were a double-glazing salesman even after he had shown his card and given her the boyish smile which usually got a favourable response from mature ladies.

'My son, Dr Randall, is at his surgery. He is a very dedicated doctor who would not allow any personal circumstance, however tragic, to keep him from his duty to his patients and his colleagues.'

There was certainly no sign of these tragic circumstances in her own face or demeanour. Intrigued, Kingsley said, 'How very brave of him. I wonder if you could spare me a few minutes, just to fill in the background?' Reading a glacial refusal in her face, he added cleverly, 'It might spare him some distress if I didn't need to go through it all with him.'

She hesitated. 'Oh, very well,' she agreed at last, stepping aside to let him enter the hall.

It was a modern house, situated in the small network of roads forming a modern housing development off the main road which roughly divided Knockhaven into old and new. It was sparsely furnished; the sitting room Mrs Randall led him into had a black leather suite, an expensive-looking perspex coffee table, a bleached wood and glass unit down one wall and very little else apart from a large plasma-screen television. On the mantelpiece above the living gas fire in its chrome surround there was a large glass sculpture of a swan and three abstract oils in pale colours hung on the cream walls. The only photograph was a large, very glamorous shot of someone who looked rather like Nicole Kidman: Ashley Randall, Kingsley assumed.

You couldn't readily imagine having a cosy evening in with a takeaway in front of *Big Brother*. Ashley Randall didn't look to have been much of a home-maker and her mother-in-law looked around disparagingly as she ushered him in.

'I suppose we can sit here. It's not exactly—' She broke

off her sentence with a sigh, then perched on the edge of one of the leather seats as if dissociating herself from any connection with it.

'It's very kind of you to spare me the time on what must be a very difficult day for you as well as your son,' Kingsley grovelled shamelessly, and was rewarded with a wintry smile.

'Of course. My son's wife was a very able woman. She will be a great loss.'

A fulsome tribute! 'Had they been married long?'

'Six years.' Six years too many, her tone implied.

'And am I right that they had no children?'

She compressed thin lips, carefully outlined in dark pink lipstick. 'My daughter-in-law was very much a career girl.'

'That must have been something of a disappointment for you,' Kingsley prompted sympathetically.

'It certainly was. My son would make a wonderful father, wonderful, but to tell you the truth I doubt if he would ever have managed to persuade Ashley. She was a very sel—' She cut off the word and substituted, '*determined* person and she had her work and the lifeboat, of course. That seemed to take up a great deal of her time and energy.'

'It must sometimes have been quite tricky to combine with her duties as a doctor. The practice must have been very understanding.'

At this evidence of right-thinking, Mrs Randall thawed visibly. 'Oh, I can't tell you how often poor Lewis gave up his time off to cover for her! I used to think he was quite exhausted sometimes, but of course *she* never even seemed to notice.'

The claws were definitely starting to show now. 'Were they unhappy together?'

'Oh no, no! Certainly not!' This was taking it a step too far, obviously – a less than perfect marriage might reflect badly on her perfect son. 'They were a devoted couple, absolutely devoted.'

He retreated. 'So last night's events must have been a devastating shock. Were you together when it happened?'

He tried to make the question sound entirely casual, but she was no fool. He saw her stiffen. 'Why should you want to know? Surely it could be of no possible relevance to an accident enquiry where either my son or I was when it happened?'

'Oh, I'm just trying to get a picture of the sequence of events,' he soothed her, but she was on her feet.

'I think I have told you everything that could be helpful. As you can imagine, there are a lot of personal matters to deal with. You must excuse me.'

Kingsley took his dismissal gracefully, favoured her with another of his most charming smiles and left.

Back in his car, he settled down to make notes of the conversation. He had listened intently at the morning briefing, and to what DI Fleming had said to him afterwards about the rumour her son had picked up. Her faulty reasoning – that Smith could have been one of Rettie's targets – had struck him immediately but he calculated that picking her up on it wouldn't make him flavour of the month. She wouldn't enjoy having her most junior officer pointing out a blind spot; he'd save it for later so she could be impressed without feeling so directly challenged by his superior analytic skills.

What Morton had told him about Rettie made Kingsley inclined to believe the boy was more the tormentor of a hapless victim than the avenger of wrongs, though of course he'd need to interview the girl to check out the headmaster's theory. Not that it actually put Rettie in the clear; killing off a hated stepfather was a good enough motive, but you had to keep a very open mind at this stage.

The gossip about Ashley Randall's relationship with Ritchie Elder could mean that her husband had a pretty solid motive too – and the woman he had just talked to opened up another scenario. She adored her son, hated his wife – Oedipal-type stuff, or what? And she'd reacted with instant hostility to his faux-innocent request for alibi information.

Yes, this was his chance to show that a case like this needed a more sophisticated approach than it was likely to get out here in the boondocks where their idea of police work was pursuing the obvious. There were three people in that boat and he would point out at the next briefing that there was still a long way to go before you could assume you knew who was the intended victim. That ought to be good for a few gold stars.

And then it struck him. There was, of course, a fourth victim: the man who wasn't there.

9

'Now, my dearie, are you certain sure you're not wanting me to come in with you – make you a wee cup of tea, maybe?' The woman's elderly, weather-beaten face was creased in concern as she parked the car in the square at the back of the Anchor Inn.

Katy Anderson, unnaturally calm and tearless now, moistened her dry, chapped lips. 'I'll be fine, Jean. Thank you for coming to the hospital.'

Her neighbour patted the hands Katy had clasped tight in her lap. 'How would I not? Do you not mind how often you took me to see Dougie when he'd his operation last winter, and the weather so bad I was scared to drive myself? Now, Dougie and me'll away back in the afternoon to fetch Rob's car, so you've no need to worry about that. And I've made an appointment with Dr Matthews for you – four o'clock. He's real nice, so see and not forget.'

'I'm not ill,' Katy said, but in the face of such inexorable kindness she was too weary to resist.

'Of course you're not, pet. But he'll be able to give you a wee something just to get you over the shock. Would you like me to take you?'

'Oh no. No, thank you. Honestly.' Katy opened the car door, almost frantic to escape from the suffocating solicitude. If she could just have peace, just sit in the silence of her own home, maybe she wouldn't fall apart and start screaming. She still hadn't taken it in; it was all just words,

words which she recognised were slashing away at her heart, but she was numb. They said when you were stabbed you didn't feel pain or even see blood at first. She needed to get inside before the bleeding started.

She was shaking so much it was hard to fit the key in the lock; it took both hands and a lot of determination before the door was open and she was inside. The silent house seemed expectant, as if now she had come back her busy, happy life would begin again. They had painted the hall and stair-case together, she and Rob, sunshine-yellow to replace dark beige wallpaper, which changed it completely. He had trans-formed her life with sunny warmth in just the same way.

Katy had only just left Nat's father when they met; she was still raw from the misery of it all, still ashamed and con-vinced that it was in some way her fault, that she was the sort of person who wasn't entitled to happiness. It had taken Rob some time to convince her that everyone had times of great unhappiness, things they blamed themselves for, but it didn't mean that this was for ever. 'Every day is the first day of the rest of your life,' had been one of his mottoes, and though of course she knew it was a cliché, it had helped, then. It didn't help now. It *really* didn't help to think about what the rest of her life would be.

Her limbs leaden, Katy dragged herself up the stairs to the flat. In the kitchen, everything looked absolutely normal. It seemed all wrong; if the table had been overturned, the chairs broken and the pretty china she had set on the shelves with such pleasure smashed on the floor, it would have been more fitting. How could something as unimportant as a tea-set still be whole and unharmed while Rob, Rob . . . ?

The newspaper was open at the sports page, lying on the table where he had been reading it before they opened up last night. Their coffee mugs stood on the draining board, waiting to be washed. All the signs of home-life briefly interrupted, soon to be resumed. Or not, as it had turned out.

What was she to do now? Make a cup of tea – that was the accepted thing. But she'd lost count of the number of cups of tea she'd been offered last night – as if they had any effect beyond making the other person feel less helpless in the face of your suffering. She didn't want tea.

She didn't want brandy either – that other treatment for shock. She knew all too well what could happen if you chose that route.

Go to bed? Perhaps that would be best. She hadn't slept all night, couldn't imagine sleeping now – could hardly imagine ever sleeping again in the big bed where she and Rob had made love and talked and cuddled and laughed. Rob: she felt, suddenly, a knife-twist of pain in her heart, gasping with the suddenness of it. Yes, perhaps she should get herself to bed before the numb disbelief wore off altogether and she was felled by grief. Wearily she climbed the narrow stairs to the upper floor.

She was just outside her bedroom when she heard a door open downstairs and for a second her heart beat crazily. Rob – it was all a mistake . . . Then, dully, she remembered her son, whose bedroom was at the back on the first floor.

Nat came up the stairs wearing boxer shorts and a faded black T-shirt with the legend 'SuperStud' – an improbable boast, taken in conjunction with his acned skin, straggling stubble and scowling expression.

'Where've you been? There's something going on – police cars and stuff.'

'The lifeboat went down. Rob's dead.' Her lips felt stiff as she framed the words.

Nat went very still and his eyes narrowed. 'What happened?'

She didn't answer, just turned to go into her room. He took two strides across the landing to bar her way with his arm. 'Hold on. Some guy came here this morning. Plain clothes but you could tell he was the Filth. Was he looking for me?'

It was hard to focus her mind. 'Police – I don't know. Shouldn't you be at school?'

'Slept in. Weren't here to get me up, were you?' He lowered his face towards hers menacingly. 'You didn't go and sick them on to me just because I took a lend of your car, did you? Because—'

He was threatening her, just the way his father used to, and suddenly she was angry, furiously angry, and it felt good.

'Yes!' she yelled in his face, startling him. 'Yes, I did. And if you end up in prison, that's fine by me. I've tried to do my best for you, God knows I've tried, but all you want to do is bully me. You did everything to spoil the time I had with Rob and it was so short, so short! He was a good man, a decent man, who wanted to help you to stop making a mess of your life and you threw it back in his face. You couldn't even say you were sorry when I told you he was dead.

'Get out of my way. I can't stand the sight of you.' She struck out at him, slamming down with her full force on the arm that was blocking her way. Nat lurched back, rubbing his injury; the door shut, a key turned, and he heard the sound of frantic weeping on the other side.

He chewed his lip uncertainly, staring at the door with a cold feeling in the pit of his stomach. He'd never seen his mother like this. It would have been sodding Rob's idea to shop him for taking the car last night; he'd changed her ideas in a way that didn't suit Nat at all but now, with him permanently off the scene, it should have been easy enough to put her back in her place.

Her fury had scared him. What if the man being dead wasn't enough – what if she stopped his allowance, threw him out anyway? What would he do then? He wasn't going back to his father, to be his skivvy and a punchbag when he was drunk, and at his age you couldn't live on social security. With the references he'd get from school he wouldn't get a job either. He'd be on the streets, or living in a hostel with stinking old winos.

It was a mistake not to have said he was sorry. That was what had wound her up. He could take her a cup of tea now, find something good to say about the man even if it stuck in his throat, say he'd just been too gob-smacked to say anything before – maybe she'd buy that. And he could say he was going in to school – she always went mental when he took a day off, so she might chill a bit after that. Then he could maybe make her call off the Pigs, say she'd made a mistake, that she'd just forgotten where she'd parked the car.

He went back into his room and dressed in his school uniform grey trousers and white shirt. He was tying the tie the stupid buggers insisted you wore as loosely as he dared – he didn't want to fall foul of Morton today – and he was on his way downstairs when he heard the ring at the doorbell, accompanied by a tattoo on the knocker.

It didn't take a genius to work out who that was and his stomach lurched. There was no point in ignoring it this time. He'd just have to deny everything flatly. There wasn't a thing they could prove.

The sun was pouring into the poolside area of the Elders' house and Joanna, on one of the lime-green padded loungers, was luxuriating in its warmth. She stretched like a cat in her pink one-piece, her eyes half-closed.

On the low table beside her was a deep wicker tray with the remains of a hearty breakfast; she had eaten two croissants smothered with Normandy butter and strawberry preserve and drunk three cappuccinos. At the farther side of the pool, where the gym equipment was, the treadmill stood idle.

This late in the day, she would usually have completed a workout and run several miles, but she didn't need to exercise today. The gnawing fear which possessed her, which only seemed to disappear when physical effort was so gruelling that she could think of nothing else, had gone.

She'd been hungry this morning too, which she hadn't been for weeks and weeks. She was well aware that Ritchie found her emaciated body repellent – she didn't like to look at the knobbly joints, the stick-like arms and legs herself – but she hadn't been able to do anything about it. She had to exercise to control the fear; she couldn't eat because it formed a cold, hard lump in her stomach. She could eat now and get rounded and feminine again, the way Ritchie liked his woman to be. She'd gone a little crazy when she realised that the security of children could never be hers, and she'd lost sight of her primary duty – to keep Ritchie happy. That had brought her perilously close to losing everything and Joanna wasn't going to allow it to happen again.

He'd slipped quietly out of bed this morning, avoiding her, of course. She'd gone down last night when she heard his car just after midnight; he'd been pale and dishevelled, and she had listened to his disjointed account of the disaster, plying him with brandy and womanly sympathy until he said he was ready to go to bed. She'd made him take a sleeping pill and tactfully pretended to be asleep when she heard him blundering about in the morning.

The important thing was not to crowd him. He mustn't have a chance, in his present state, to say something that could never be taken back. If he blurted out his feelings for that bitch who was now, thankfully, dead, Joanna would never get their marriage stuck back together again. He had to believe that she had suspected nothing; he had to be brought to depend on her sympathy and support.

Ritchie would need excuses for his emotion; *her* funeral, for instance, would be a danger-point, but with any luck it would be a combined ceremony for all three crew and Joanna could reassure him that manly grief on the part of the Honorary Secretary, bearing his terrible burden of responsibility, was entirely appropriate.

And once all this was behind them, when she'd regained her figure and her confidence, she'd take him away for a holiday – Goa, perhaps, or the Maldives. A glamorous resort with sun and sand where surely the sex part of the package couldn't help but come right.

Ritchie wouldn't change. He'd go on having affairs, but an understanding wife who knew when to turn a blind eye would be a positive asset. And if anything like the Ashley Randall thing came along again she'd make damn sure it didn't have a chance to take root. She'd had her own stupidity and self-absorption to blame.

Even so, her eyes went to the gleaming machines at the farther end of the pool. Like an alcoholic seeing a whisky bottle, she felt a sudden, desperate yearning, but she fought it down. It was nearly eleven o'clock; her cleaners would be having their elevenses. She picked up the white towelling robe lying on the table beside her and got up. She could go to the kitchen and nick one of the chocolate biscuits she kept for them and catch up on what they were saying in the village at the same time. It should be red-hot stuff this morning.

There seemed to be a public meeting going on when DC Kingsley arrived at the Knockhaven Medical Centre, a little after half-past two. The entrance was open-plan, with a waiting area lined with blue padded benches and a table untidily strewn with dog-eared magazines, while a corridor at the farther end led to the consulting rooms. A basket of children's toys occupied one corner and the whole of the back was office space, separated from the public by a reception desk round which half a dozen women were clustered, their backs to the door, apparently being addressed by the bulky woman on the business side. She was in late middle age with tightly permed hair, protuberant eyes and a thin-lipped mouth a little enlarged by plum-coloured lipstick. The contours of her bosom suggested corsetry of the most architectural sort and, taken in conjunction with the gun-metal grey of her acrylic jersey, reminded Kingsley irresistibly of the prow of a battleship. The name-badge she wore said 'Muriel Henderson'.

'And now he's been taken away to the police station in Kirkluce. Is that not awful for the poor soul – her own son under suspicion?'

There was a communal intake of breath and a few shocked murmurs, though no one had the temerity to interrupt while Muriel held the floor. She was going on, 'Mind you, I was speaking to someone who'd been speaking to Jackie Duncan and she said Jackie said Willie said—'

As Kingsley approached the desk, she broke off. Six heads swivelled as one, looking accusingly at the intruder who had interrupted this gossip fest just as a particularly savoury morsel was about to be served up.

'Yes? Can I help you?' From Muriel's tone, he might have come bursting into her private sitting room.

He flashed his warrant-card and an insinuating smile. It was, he hoped, only the card which had the effect of dispersing the group; like bath bubbles brought into contact with a bar of soap, they melted away as if uncomfortable at having their gluttony exposed to official scrutiny. It was a fine sight: six not insubstantial ladies trying to become invisible.

The smile, however, did seem to be having its intended effect. Muriel Henderson's manner became almost gracious.

'You'll be here because of – the tragedy, no doubt.' She delivered this in suitably mournful tones, with downcast eyes, the effect being only slightly spoiled by the anticipatory way in which she licked her lips.

'I was hoping to have a word with Dr Randall, when he's free. I understand he came into work today.'

'Indeed yes. Poor Dr Lewis! But you can be sure he'll always put his patients first, above everything else. We're just doing our best to make things as easy as possible for him.' She raised her voice. 'Aren't we, Enid?'

Kingsley hadn't noticed the other woman who was quietly working at a computer screen in the corner of the office area beside another younger woman who was putting letters into envelopes. She looked up at her name. 'Oh – oh yes. We're all so sorry for him. I'm just going to take him in some tea when he's finished with this patient.'

'That's right, dear. You do that. And you've made some of your rock cakes for him, haven't you?' Then, turning back to Kingsley, she lowered her voice and said, 'Went back specially to do it in her lunch hour, after she heard what had happened. Just between you and me, got a bit of a crush on Dr Lewis, poor Enid. Not that he'd ever have thought of looking at anyone but that wife of his.'

Alert to her tone of voice, Kingsley prompted, 'And was Dr Ashley perhaps not quite as dedicated as he was?'

'Dedicated!' Licensed to spit poison, Muriel reared up like a cobra. 'It was just self, self, self with that woman! I know she's dead, but I speak as I find.'

He'd heard enough about Ashley from her mother-in-law and he hadn't time to encourage Muriel along those lines when he needed to get back to Kirkluce to meet up with Tansy Kerr to interview Kylie MacEwan before the end of the school day. He moved her on deftly.

'I couldn't help overhearing as I came in – you were saying something about Willie Duncan?'

For the first time she looked flustered. 'Oh dearie me, that was just some story that's going round the town.'

'It's always useful to us to know what people are saying, even if it's not true.'

'Oh, it's true, right enough!' She bridled at the suggestion of flawed intelligence. 'It was Willie's wife Jackie said it – she says he's been scared stiff ever since last night, says it should have been him, and they'll get him somehow. There!'

Playing the daft laddie, Kingsley said, 'They—?'

He got a very old-fashioned look. 'Oh, maybe the police don't know, but everyone else does. Those drugs people he's got himself mixed up with, whoever they are – scum, anyway. You mark my words, it's nothing to do with that wee toe-rag you've arrested. Nat Rettie hasn't the brains for something like this. You'll see who's responsible right enough when Willie's found in the harbour with a stone tied round his feet.'

Kingsley's face remained impassive, but his mind was racing. It was incredible how much this woman – and presumably therefore the whole town – knew about what was going on. Could she be right? Could this be tied up with the drugs scene that was his particular brief? It could be his chance for a second major coup.

He was opening his mouth to ask another question when a door opened and an elderly man came out saying, 'Thanks, Dr Lewis.' Enid looked up from her computer and jumped to her feet, a hint of colour in her pale skin.

'I'll just make his tea and take it in. If you'd like to go in now, Constable –'

He might as well. There probably wasn't anything more of use Muriel could tell him. 'Thanks so much, Mrs Henderson. You've been most helpful,' he said, and she beamed on him as he went to tap on the door.

The man sitting at the desk was very good-looking, but in a curiously bland way. The blue eyes, the smooth dark hair, the classic profile ticked all the boxes but somehow suggested that if character was not actually lacking it was somehow withheld from the observer.

He rose courteously to shake hands with Kingsley, waving him to a chair. He was looking tired and strained, though there were no other visible signs of grief, and the questions Kingsley asked, taking him through the events of the previous night, were answered readily and calmly enough. He had expected his wife to be going out to a meeting, had eaten an early supper with her then gone to work in his study on a report he needed to write up. He'd had an uninterrupted evening, no visitors, no phone calls, until the one telling him of the disaster. He hadn't been aware of the lifeboat call-out, he said.

'I gather they still fire maroons here – you didn't hear them go off?' Kingsley pressed him. 'Is your house within earshot?'

'Normally, yes. But with the storm last night . . .' He shrugged. 'My room is at the back, and I had music playing. I was concentrating, too – I might simply not have registered the sound.' Then, as the door opened, 'Ah, Enid! Is that tea – and are those your rock buns? You spoil me, you know.'

The glowing smile the woman gave him left Kingsley in no doubt that Muriel had been right about her colleague's feelings, and about her boss's too. Enid was a pleasant-looking woman, and when animated as she was just now, even pretty in her quiet way, but it was obvious that Randall had more interest in the buns than in their maker, and even so was doing no more than toying with the one on his plate.

Kingsley put down his notebook and bit into his own. They were good, certainly, and judging by the glimpse he had got this morning, Randall would have a much more comfortable home-life with this one. Maybe she'd run him down in the end, but he wouldn't bet on it.

He still hadn't tackled the most contentious question. It wasn't the easiest thing to put to a man who had just lost his wife, but it had to be done.

'I'm sorry, I do have to ask you this, sir. There are rumours that your wife was having a relationship with the Secretary of the lifeboat, Mr Elder. Was this true?'

'Oh dear.' He looked wearier than ever. 'You've been talking to Muriel, have you? She told my mother that, I'm sure. It was all very difficult.

'Ashley and I had a happy and fulfilling marriage. She had a good working relationship with Ritchie, who was in some sense her boss, and we saw him and his wife socially – I knew him from way back – and that was enough to set people talking. It doesn't take much in a place like this.

'I'm afraid Muriel never really got on with Ashley and per-haps you've gathered what she's like – she has a wicked tongue, together with a prurient mind. I wish I could sack her, but the collateral damage would be too extensive.'

Was it what the man genuinely believed to be the case? Or what he had decided to believe? Or what he knew to be false? It was impossible to tell.

'Did you ever tackle your wife about it?'

For the first time the man smiled. 'You didn't know my wife, Constable Kingsley. To ask Ashley to deny one of Muriel Henderson's rumours would be like taking the pin out of a grenade, and I like a quiet life.'

There was nothing more to ask. Kingsley thanked him and left, little wiser about Ashley Randall's husband than he had been when he went in.

The women were back around the desk again, their heads together as Muriel talked to them with her voice discreetly lowered this time. Behind them, a man holding a form stood ignored, but as Kingsley passed Muriel looked up to give him a 'favoured friend' smile and told him not to hesitate to come back if there was anything else she could help any of the officers with.

He smiled back. This was a source he wasn't about to share with anyone.

'How are you on video nasties?' Tam MacNee came into DI Fleming's fourth-floor office and put a cassette on the desk. 'I've brought you a copy of the official tape.'

Fleming looked up from the paperwork she was trying to clear from her already over-burdened desk before the avalanche of information from the new case descended on it.

'Listen, when you've watched Donald Bailey react to being told that no, the wreck of the lifeboat couldn't have been an accident, yes, three people have died, yes, the Press will be seriously interested, yes, it's complicated and no, we can't just charge Nat Rettie without further proof and have done with it, *The Texas Chain-saw Massacre* would seem like *Mary Poppins*. Is this the Rettie interview?'

'Tansy and I had a go at him earlier this afternoon.' MacNee put the cassette into the small combination TV/VCR which stood on a shelf in the corner of the room and clicked the remote control.

'And?'

'See for yourself.'

MacNee had spooled past the formal identification pro-cedure at the beginning of the tape; it began with Tansy Kerr's question, 'So what were you doing last night, Nat?'

It was always a curious experience, watching a video taken by a fixed camera in black-and-white. It confounded an expectation built on sophisticated colour and lighting and zoom and close-up, so that the film took on the unreal aspect of a theatrical performance. Here, under flat fluorescent light, the props were a table, chairs, a bottle of water and glasses; the actors were an unprepossessing youth in what might loosely be described as school uniform on one side of the table facing a young woman wearing jeans and a hooded sweater, and a man in a black leather jacket and white T-shirt leaning back in his chair with a darkly sardonic expression.

The boy's eyes went anxiously towards him before he answered the woman's question with a sullen, 'Nothing.'

Kerr laughed with apparently genuine amusement, then jerked her head towards her colleague. 'I bet him that's what you'd say. He said you'd say, "None of your business."' She turned to MacNee, holding out her hand; he silently reached into a pocket and took out 10p which he gave to her expressionlessly. 'Had to be one or the other. So let's cut the crap and start again.

'What were you doing last night, Nat?'

This had visibly thrown him, but he was still truculent. 'I was just out. What's wrong with that? Got a right to go out if I want to.'

'Not when you're driving your mother's car without licence or insurance.'

'I wasn't. Never touched it.'

'Oh, I think you did, Nat. We all think you did, don't we, Tam?'

MacNee didn't speak. Again, Rettie's eyes flickered towards him and Fleming, watching, realised that her own eyes were being constantly drawn to the silent, withdrawn figure which somehow managed to emit menace.

The youth shifted in his chair. In the harsh light Fleming could see his brow had begun to glisten with sweat. 'Look, it was my mum.' His tone was ingratiating now. 'Gets sort of confused. She'd gone and parked it somewhere then forgot and next thing, she's, like, blaming me. See?'

'And why would she think of blaming you, Nat?' Kerr asked innocently. 'You're not old enough to drive, are you?'

His eyes narrowed in concentration, signalling calculation as clearly as if he had written it on a board and held it above his head. After a prolonged pause he said, 'OK, I'm not saying I didn't maybe once take a shot at driving her car, just for a bet. Just, like, round the block. She gave me grief so I packed it in.'

'Not what we heard, is it, Tam? We heard she shopped you because she got sick fed up of you doing it.'

He scowled. 'Silly cow!'

'So you were out in the car last night, Nat. Right?' Kerr's voice was persuasive.

'No! I sodding told you I wasn't. She parked it some-where—'

'So how'd it get back in the garage this morning, then?' MacNee, still lounging in his chair, cut in, his voice harsh.

Rettie put up a hand to wipe his forehead. 'Dunno. She remembered and fetched it—'

'Don't – play – silly – buggers – with – me!' Separating his words for emphasis, MacNee leaned across the table sud-denly, then thumped down his fist, making Rettie, and the glasses, jump. 'We know you took that car. Think about it – if that isn't beyond you. Yours'll be the top fingerprints on the key, the steering wheel, the door handle.

'Anyway, do you think the CID gives a monkey's about some moronic juvenile joyriding? You're here under suspi-cion of engineering the wreck of the lifeboat with the loss of three lives – especially your stepfather's. No love lost there, eh? We're talking about triple murder, laddie.' He smiled, terribly, then leaned back in his seat again.

Nat had been alarmed before; now he was visibly afraid.

Fleming could see his Adam's apple bobbing up and down as he gulped. 'Here – you're trying to stitch me up! I never – I've got my rights! I want a lawyer—'

Again MacNee smiled. 'Dear me, you've been watching too many episodes of *The Bill.* You're in Scotland now. The rules say we've hours yet for a nice cosy chat before we have to bring outsiders into it. And if you want a pal's advice, you'll tell us everything instead of having it dragged out of you. I always thought I should maybe have been a dentist – I'd have been rare at pulling teeth.'

Rettie was ashen now. 'I never,' he insisted. 'I wouldn't do a thing like that!'

'All right.' Kerr took over again. 'You never. You wouldn't. OK, Nat. Do yourself a favour and tell us what you did do.'

This time he didn't look towards MacNee before he answered, as if he was frightened of what he would see in his face. 'I – I – OK, I took the sodding car. Just got fed up, ken, stuck in that house all the time by myself. Didn't do any harm, just went a wee drive round—'

'Who with, Nat?' Kerr positively cooed the alibi request, but that set him off again.

'No one. Just by myself, OK?' He grabbed for a glass and the water and his hands were shaking as he poured it out.

Kerr and MacNee exchanged glances. 'By yourself, Nat?' she said.

'Yeah. Yeah, that's right.'

'Look, you don't have to cover up. Anyone who was with you isn't in trouble.'

MacNee cut across her. 'You're lying, Rettie. My constable here, she's a nice person and she thinks you're protecting someone. I don't. You're looking after number one, aren't you? What were you after – spot of breaking and entering, maybe? Better tell us that than taking the rap for murder.'

'I never! Look, I – I had my girlfriend with me—'

'Girlfriend? Doing the dirty on someone, is she? Scared of her bloke?' MacNee was pushing him. Then he stopped. 'Hang about,' he said slowly. 'I wonder what put it into your head to call Luke Smith a paedophile, eh? What age is your girlfriend, Rettie?'

The picture Fleming was looking at seemed to go into freeze-frame: Rettie, gaping; MacNee, staring at Rettie's face as if he could bore a hole into his mind; Kerr, startled. Then it started to move again.

'Thirteen,' Rettie blurted out. 'But we weren't, like, doing anything. She was just there. She'll tell you—'

MacNee snapped off the machine. 'And that was it. Under-age sex, and he's over sixteen. An adult.'

'Kylie MacEwan,' Fleming said heavily.

'How did you know that?'

'Friend of Cat's, I'm sorry to say.' She sighed. 'That's my problem. But you were good.'

'Can't get used to this kind of stuff.' Disgust was plain in MacNee's face. 'In my day, it was your pals' mums you fancied, not their kid sisters. But I wanted you to see Tansy doing her stuff. She's good, isn't she? A wee cracker!'

'You're a classic team – nice cop, nasty cop. Maybe you could do it the other way round sometime?' Fleming suggested innocently, then grinned at his reaction. 'Did you really have a bet about what he'd say?'

'Would I be that daft? That was a wee bit of improvisation. I got the 10p back, mind. In fact, now I think of it –' He drew it out with a flourish and dropped it in the box on her desk marked 'Burns fines'. 'For when I need another quote.'

She groaned. 'Oh God, it'll be like waiting for the other shoe to drop!' Then she said soberly, 'Well, it doesn't look as if it was him, does it?'

'Nuh. So where does that leave us?'

'With a wide open field, that's where. I keep thinking about the tales you hear on every harsh coastline about wreckers in the old days – you know, local people who would use lights to lure a ship on to the rocks in a storm so they could loot the cargo. But of course the only cargo a lifeboat carries is human.

'Give it a bit of thought, Tam. I want a case conference tomorrow, so sort out your ideas. Jon Kingsley should have quite a bit of useful input – he's been seeing a few of the main players today.'

'I hope he'll let us all have the benefit.' The constraint was back. With a nod, MacNee went out, leaving Fleming to frown at the closed door before she went back to the report on her desk. She was going to be late tonight; she'd have to phone Bill and warn him, but she thought she might take half an hour off to go and see Laura. She wanted her ideas on the profile of the person who could do this, and ten minutes playing with Daisy would be light relief in a heavy day.

10

Muriel Henderson had taken her tea-break and Enid Davis was on the reception desk when Katy Anderson arrived, a little early for her four o'clock appointment. She drifted in like a ghost, oblivious to the sympathetic glances of other patients in the waiting room who recognised her, as if she had her being in a different dimension. The pallor of her face was in startling contrast to her fiercely red-rimmed eyes, which seemed to be having difficulty in focusing on Enid as she came up to the desk.

Enid recognised the stigmata of wretchedness. It was like seeing again a familiar domestic landscape which even today was clearly visible to her, though at a distance; now she was only an occasional visitor.

'Dr Matthews is running a bit late, I'm afraid,' she said gently. 'Would you like to sit in the waiting room there?'

'Yes. Yes of course.' Katy turned, obedient as a zombie, as if, had she been asked to lie on the floor, she'd have done that too without question. A woman with a small child pulled it on to her knee to make room for Katy on one of the padded benches, then leaned across to pat her knee.

Enid saw Katy's automatic, meaningless smile. These people offering their sympathy were looking for a connecting response of gratitude for their kind concern, when in fact most of them, you could tell, had either an unhealthy desire to be associated with sensation or a wish to bask in the sunshine of their own benevolence. All the time their greedy eyes were performing a sort of visual rape.

'Is she here yet?' Muriel's voice, speaking in her ear, gave Enid a start. She wasn't due back on duty for another quarter of an hour, and it wasn't like Muriel to cut short her tea-break – on the contrary. The reason was clear enough, though: she was eagerly scanning the waiting room until she spotted Katy, her eyes blank and her hands folded in her lap.

'Oh, there she is! Goodness me, Enid, how could you think of letting the poor soul sit out there in the waiting room with everyone staring!' She was opening the door from the office area as she spoke, surging out and across to where Katy was sitting. The woman looked up in bewilderment as Muriel took both her hands.

'Katy, my dear, you shouldn't be out here, you in a state like this! Come away through the back – there's tea made, and you can just wait there quiet for a bit till Dr Matthews can see you. He's had a bit of a backlog to deal with – poor Dr Ashley's surgery, you know.'

There were one or two meaningful looks exchanged by waiting patients as Muriel led her victim away, a lamb to the slaughter. Two minutes later, Cara Christie, another recep-tionist who had also been on her break, appeared at Enid's side. 'I'll take over. You go and have your break now – I just can't stand it. It's like watching a cat bring in a mouse to play with and not being able to stop it.'

'Oh dear,' Enid said faintly, 'I don't suppose I can, either.' But she yielded her place to Cara and went through a door at the back into the staff sitting room.

It was a small room with a coffee table and half a dozen chairs with wooden arms and multi-coloured cushioned seats. Coat pegs and lockers had been fitted behind the door and there was a sink, mini-fridge, microwave and kettle in one corner with cupboards above, but not much else except a tray of mugs and plates. Muriel had inserted a mug of tea into Katy's hands, which she was holding as if it were nothing to do with her. Muriel was talking, with the air of one who as yet has been able to elicit little response.

'You won't be able to take it in yet, dear – it's the shock, you see. But you know,' she leaned forward confidentially, 'you've got to think positive – isn't that right, Enid? It all might be for the best, after what happened to Dr Ashley and that poor young teacher.'

Enid, pouring out her own tea, went rigid. Katy, her voice roughened by tears, croaked, 'I don't think he knew.'

'Oh, take it from me, he did, dear! Bob MacNally – you know, he was in the rescue party – he said to me Rob asked as they were putting him in the ambulance, and they had to tell him. That would really take away your will to live, wouldn't it? And of course he would know there would have to be an enquiry too . . .'

Katy closed her eyes. 'Oh God,' she breathed.

'He wouldn't have been strong enough to tell you how it happened, though, would he? No?' As Katy made no reply, or indeed showed any sign that she had heard the question, Enid, sitting quietly down opposite with her own mug of tea, saw Muriel's lips purse in irritation. But she wasn't easily daunted.

Continuing her relentless pursuit, she said in a voice sugared with concern, 'And what about your Nat? Have the police gone and charged him?'

'Nat?' Katy frowned, almost as if the name was unfamiliar to her. Then she said, 'Oh, you mean with taking the car? I – I should never have told them, probably. I was angry – I suppose I'll have to speak to them about it—'

Muriel oozed synthetic sympathy. 'No, no, dear! You know – with rigging up the lights that wrecked the boat!'

If her object had been to provoke a response, she achieved

it. Katy's eyes shot wide open, as if she were a sleepwalker rudely awakened.

'What are you saying?' she cried wildly. 'Are you saying that my son – that Nat murdered Rob? And – and the others . . . ? Is that what you're telling me?'

Alarmed by her own success, Muriel said hastily, 'That's not what I was saying! I was just saying the police think that, but you know them – get everything wrong. If you ask me, Nat had nothing to do with it—'

Katy wasn't listening. She had jumped to her feet. 'What shall I do? What shall I do?' she kept saying distractedly, showing all the signs of incipient hysteria.

Muriel, with her eye on the clock, exclaimed, 'Oh, for goodness sake! Dr Matthews'll be ready to see her any minute! We'll need to calm her down or she'll go saying terrible things to him about us.'

'Us?' Enid was tempted to reply, but said instead, 'You go back to the desk, Muriel. She'll maybe be better just on her own with me.'

Muriel, her face flushed a mottled red, needed no second invitation; she escaped with only an anxious glance over her shoulder at Katy, who was pacing to and fro, wringing her hands and taking the short, shallow breaths that lead to hyperventilation.

Placing herself in her path, Enid took her shoulders in firm hands, almost forcing her back into her chair. 'Put your hands to your face and breathe into them,' she instructed with quiet authority. 'Now, slower. Slower.' She talked evenly and calmly until the gasping stopped, then sat down beside the trembling woman.

'Listen to me. Don't pay any attention to Muriel. She's an evil woman. She knows perfectly well it wasn't your son who did it. It's all to do with the drugs business – Willie Duncan was a dealer and he'd only himself to blame if they were out to get him. Don't let her upset you. You know your own son. Every mother does.'

'That's – that's the problem. He's turning out to be his father, all over again. And his father was a bad man.' Her lips were quivering.

Taken aback, Enid said, 'Sometimes, you know, youngsters go through bad patches, but he's your own flesh and blood, after all. You can't think straight at the moment – you're in shock. So put what Muriel said out of your mind. She enjoys making people unhappy. I heard her myself telling the police that she knew it wasn't Nat.'

'You're – you're very kind. It's – it's bad enough already, but believing that—' She shuddered.

There was a tap on the door and a worried-looking Muriel put her head round the door. 'That's Dr Matthews ready to see you now.'

Katy nodded, then got up. 'Thank you,' she said as she went out. 'You've been very understanding.'

'Well done, Enid!' Muriel eyed her colleague with some respect. 'Poor soul – I thought she was well away, there!'

Enid opened her mouth, then, with her usual caution, shut it again. She'd seen, all too often, what happened to people who got across Muriel Henderson.

The cottage which Laura Harvey had rented unfurnished was in a quiet street parallel to Kirkluce High Street, one of a terrace all painted in pastel colours, green and blue and pink and mauve – 'Like a row of fondant fancies,' as she had laughingly said to Marjory Fleming. The front door opened directly into a sitting room with a deep-set window to the front and a pine staircase rising at one side to two bedrooms and a bathroom; behind lay the kitchen with a door to an enclosed garden, ideal for a collie puppy with an enquiring mind and an adventurous spirit.

Laura had furnished it with a sure touch which Marjory hugely admired. She and Bill had never exactly furnished the farmhouse, it had just sort of happened, with bits and pieces handed down through the family or acquired, as necessary, over the years. But when she had said that ruefully to her friend, Laura had only laughed.

'When I go to your house, I feel enfolded by it. You've got a home, Marjory – I've got furniture in a rented property.'

Even so, Marjory thought when she had greeted her friend and the exuberant Daisy – firmly in that order, to stress their respective hierarchical positions – it was a delightfully welcoming room. The walls were a pale buttery cream and the sofa, pushed against the back wall, was upholstered in teddy-bear brown plush with a blue cashmere throw which echoed the blue in curtains and cushions and another couple of chairs. One corner was arranged with a pine desk and a computer as an office area where Laura could work on her articles and the book arising out of them which she had been commissioned to write. On the stripped pine floor, an oriental rug in blue, brown, cream and terracotta lay in front of a fireplace which, while it might not be authentic Victorian, was doing its best. This evening a cheerful log fire was burning.

Daisy, in an ecstasy of recognition, was bouncing up and down at her one-time owner. 'And how's my grand-dog behaving?' Marjory enquired.

'Wonderful!' Laura glowed with pride. 'Practically house-trained, sits, lies down – briefly—'

Looking down at the eager little dog, Marjory said firmly, 'Sit, Daisy!' then, as the plump rear-end made contact with the floor, crouched down to fuss her with extravagant praise.

'She's a clever wee thing. Have you worked out who's boss yet?'

'I am – I think. But we're definitely still in negotiation. Drink?'

Marjory shook her head. 'I wish I could but I've got to go back in. I really came to pick your brains.'

Laura's face sobered. 'This tragic lifeboat business, I suppose? Was it really wrecked? You never know how much to believe of what you hear.'

'Oh, it's true enough, sadly. Someone deliberately rigged up lights in imitation of the leading lights at Knockhaven harbour in Fuill's Inlat – that's Fool's Inlet to you, so-called because the entrance to it from the sea mimics the harbour's contours. There were dreadful conditions, of course, and added to that the regular cox was too stoned to perform and the reserve tried to throw himself overboard on the way home.'

'That's what Mrs Moncrieff told me over the fence this afternoon. She's got a sister in Knockhaven. But you've made an arrest, haven't you?'

Marjory stared at her. 'See villages! MI5 shouldn't be doing its recruiting at Cambridge, you know. Get a few of the local wifies on the job and there wouldn't be a terrorist whose mother's maiden name they couldn't tell you.'

'I'm not convinced they'd be totally reliable when it came to compliance with the Official Secrets Act,' Laura pointed out. 'So what about this boy you've arrested?'

'Nothing to do with it, as far as we can make out at this stage. He'd been joyriding in the car with an under-age girlfriend – friend of Cat's, unfortunately – and we're investigating. Not that I think we'll have anything to go on – slap on the wrist for the car and that will be it.'

'So?'

'So. What sort of person would do such a foul thing? The *lifeboat* – well, I'm sure you know how people feel about the service round here.'

'Mmm.' Laura, curled up on the sofa, wound her finger in a strand of fair hair escaping from its clasp at the back and frowned as she considered the question. The fire crackled and there was a tiny snore from Daisy asleep on the rug, worn out by her duties as greeter. Marjory waited, watching her friend.

Laura was the antithesis of Marjory in appearance, small, blonde and neatly made, with grey-blue eyes. She was also clever with clothes; that pink and grey scarf she was wearing casually looked exactly right with her sweater. Marjory sighed quietly; when she put on a scarf, it always ended up looking like a neck poultice.

At last Laura said, 'A vandal's the obvious one – the usual wanton pleasure in destruction. Do I get the impression you've rejected that idea?'

'It's unlikely. Vandalism tends to be spur-of-the-moment, seemed-like-a-good-idea-at-the-time when everyone's drunk. It's not often planned. But this was, quite elaborately. The lamps had been specially prepared with glass paint and they'd only a battery life of a few hours so there had to be a question of timing too. The other thing is, it was only by chance that the lights were discovered. The perpetrator would have hoped to have it written off as an accident – vandals want people to know it's their handiwork.'

Laura absorbed that. 'So you're talking about planning to cause three deaths. You'd have to wonder about a grudge against the lifeboat service – was there someone they failed to save, perhaps? Or maybe someone who wanted to join the crew and got turned down?'

'Easy enough to check. But Laura, you have to be talking local. This guy had to know about Fuill's Inlat, had to be on hand to wait for a call-out on a night when the weather was bad enough to give it a chance of success – he couldn't know their problem would be compounded by Willie Duncan and Luke Smith. And off the top of my head, I can't think of any failed rescue in recent years and I'd be almost bound to know.

'Suppose it isn't a nutter with a grudge. Suppose we're looking for someone with a personal motive. What's he like? Or she, I suppose you have to say – why can't the language have a neutral pronoun?'

'Case-profiling is bad enough – don't get me started on grammar! But you're asking me what kind of person would kill three people, related only through the job they do, if it turns out to be not about the job? They could be directly connected in some other way – you'll be looking into that?'

Fleming nodded.

'And if not . . .' Laura lapsed into thought again. Then she said, slowly, 'There are the psychopaths, who kill for enjoyment. It doesn't tend to be at arm's length, though, like this – they want to see their victim suffer. Or at least show off their deadly skill and power, like the snipers in America. And again, it would be pointless if people didn't know so weren't afraid. Creating what looks like an accident is logical only if the idea is to get away with it.

'But if this is a person who had a motive for killing one of the crew, and had no scruples about the innocents involved, then you're looking for someone who, if they're not actually psychopathic, has an abnormal degree of detachment. Most normal people who kill – if anyone who kills can be described as fully normal – either do it in a fit of rage, without calculation, or appoint themselves judge and jury and decide the victim deserves to die. To take two other lives as well, incidentally, for the sake of your hatred, vengeance, gain, whatever, means that you have, to say the least of it, an unnaturally solipsistic view of the world.'

'Solipsistic? I know I should know—'

'Selfish, to a pathological degree. A sort of tunnel vision which excludes everything except your wants, needs, desires.'

'Male, female?'

Laura smiled wryly. 'I know women who would tell you

that solipsism comes with the genes where men are concerned. But no, I couldn't say one was more likely than the other.'

Marjory sighed. 'It was worth a try. If we could eliminate fifty per cent of our suspects it would be a good start. But thanks, Laura – you're very good at setting things out so I can get them clear in my own mind. I'll put someone on to sifting through the records of the local lifeboats and see if anything turns up – nice job for the uniforms!'

She glanced at her watch. 'I really need to be getting back. Goodbye, Daisy!'

At the mention of her name, the little dog looked up drowsily, then dropped her head again as if the effort was simply too much. The two women laughed and Marjory got to her feet.

'That's cleared my mind for the briefing tomorrow. We really ought to have you on the strength.'

She was in her car with the engine running when her conscience smote her. It was two or three days since she had been to see her parents, and with the way things were going she wasn't likely to have more spare time in the immediate future. Reaching the main road she turned right, out of town towards the Lairds' pleasant retirement bungalow five miles away.

Janet Laird was, as usual, busy in the kitchen when Marjory Fleming arrived. She could hear the sound of the TV from behind the sitting-room door; when she looked in, her father Angus, long retired after many years as an institution in the Galloway Constabulary, was blankly watching a quiz show. He grunted without turning his head when she said, 'Hello, Dad,' and she retreated with a grimace of concern. It wasn't good for him, this mindless viewing, and she'd told him that. She could almost hear the brain cells dying, but her father wasn't the man to listen to the daughter who should have been a son and who could never, however hard she tried, gain recognition for her achievements in the career she had chosen, almost consciously, in the hope of pleasing him.

Her mother, when Marjory opened the kitchen door, was sitting at the table with a pen in her hand, frowning over a list she was making, but she looked up with a smile when she saw her daughter. She was a sweet-faced woman with plump cheeks and warm brown eyes under a halo of white curls; she greeted her with, 'Hello, dearie! Well, what have you been doing today?' just as she had when Marjory was coming in from school with her hair in pigtails. 'It's a terrible business, that, about the lifeboat.'

Marjory sat down opposite her mother and stole a biscuit from the batch that was cooling on a rack on the table. 'What are you up to?'

Janet sighed. 'It was to have been the Knockhaven lifeboat coffee morning next week and I was doing the baking stall. I'm trying to write down all the folk I need to contact to tell them we're to do the catering at the funeral instead, when the word comes through that it can go ahead. You'd not really want the kind of frivolous things, like chocolate crispies and toffee apples, for a funeral.'

The macabre combination of ideas was darkly humorous but Marjory managed not to smile. 'No,' she agreed. 'No. But Mum, do you know what they've decided about the funeral? Is it to be a joint service?'

Janet looked at her with surprise. 'My goodness, are you asking me? I'd have thought the police would be the first to know.'

The jungle drums had been at it again. 'Nobody ever tells me anything,' Marjory said bitterly, then heard what she had said. Why was it that whenever she came home she reverted to being fifteen, and touchy with it?

Her mother said, in precisely the soothing tone she had used then, 'I expect there'll be a note coming through to your desk. No, they'd a meeting this morning at the lifeboat shed in Knockhaven and they contacted the families. They've all agreed on a service, with private interments later, and all the high heid yins are coming. So us on the Ladies' Committee'll need to make sure everything's just right.'

Then her face crumpled. 'But it's awful sad we're having to do it. Those poor, poor folks! But you'll see that whoever did this is caught and punished, won't you, Marjory?'

She looked at her daughter with the perfect confidence which only a loving and uncritical nature and an unshakeable belief in the inevitability of justice could bring to such a demand.

Marjory, with this added burden of maternal expectation, said hollowly, 'That's what I'm there to do! Actually, I just dropped in on my way back to HQ. There'll be some reports I want to read before tomorrow.'

Janet registered distress. 'Did you get a proper tea? No? Well, you'll not leave this house till I've made you a nice sandwich. And you'd better take the Tin – I'll just fill it while you're eating that. The bairns always like these biscuits, and I've a bit of Bill's favourite fruit cake . . .'

As Janet bustled about, cutting slices of bread and home-cooked ham, putting baking into the Tin, a battered receptacle which made its journeys out to Mains of Craigie full and came back empty, Marjory sat at the kitchen table, a child again, indulging herself in the foolish feeling that with her mother still there to see to it, nothing could go too badly wrong in her world.

As Lewis Randall wearily opened the front door of 8 Mayfield Grove, he was assailed by the unusual smell of cooking. He stopped dead, then closed the door behind him with a sigh.

It hadn't been an easy day. Not that his patients had been difficult – far from it – but being on the receiving end of so much sympathy and kid-glove treatment was an exhausting business, and all that had kept him going was the promise of a silent house and a very stiff gin. He'd been expecting a call from his mother offering food and solace at The Hollies, which he had decided to refuse; he hadn't expected to find her making herself at home in his kitchen, though perhaps he should have.

Like most sons, Lewis had an ambivalent relationship with his mother. They were close, undeniably; he had been the man of the house since his father's death when Lewis was ten and she had lovingly supported him every step of the long way to a medical degree. Her total belief in him and her fierce devotion had always been there as a bulwark against a hostile world.

He'd come back to Knockhaven partly for her sake, mainly for his own. Here, on his own patch, he was uncritically accepted, and there was no doubt that, thanks perhaps to his upbringing, he was much more comfortable where he wasn't constantly challenged to be more dynamic, more pro-active. He liked things the way they were; he was what he was.

There had never been a problem with his mother. Whatever he had wanted, even Ashley, was all right with her.

Ashley. Despite their years of marriage and their close working relationship, she had been a mystery to him since the day she had astonished him by accepting his proposal. But then, he hadn't been looking for a wife who, in the clichéd phrase 'understood' him either. His mother's understanding was quite enough – too much, sometimes. His mother—

'Darling! There you are. Has it been an awful day? Why don't you go into your study and have a drink? Let me know when you're ready for supper.' Dorothy Randall kissed him, then without another word went back into the kitchen.

He looked after her, a twisted smile on his lips. She had always had this talent for being undemanding, for knowing without his having to tell her what his feelings were. He could sit quietly in solitude with his drink for as long as he needed to, confident that there would be no reproaches that the food had been spoiled; almost against his will he felt a sense of comfort. Food and a mother's care were so closely linked, it was almost as if the savoury fragrance coming from the kitchen was love made manifest.

Dorothy was very much on edge, though, he realised as they sat at the bleached oak table in the dining room, so seldom used in his married life. She fiddled restlessly with the cutlery and talked too much, about everything except the thing that was uppermost in both their minds, barely waiting for his responses. At last, when he had refused cheese and they were sitting over coffee, he said gently, 'Mother, I don't mind talking about it. We have to, in fact. There are all sorts of details—'

As if this permission had turned on a tap, it all came pouring out. 'Oh, Lewis, I'm so frightened! Have they told you – they've discovered it wasn't an accident! And this very morning I had a policeman here, oh, all very nice, very polite, but then I realised he was trying to find out what your movements were! He suspects you, Lewis! You're the husband, you're always the first person they suspect when someone's – someone's murdered! And when they find out about Ashley and that dreadful man—'

'Mother!' The steeliness in his tone brought her up short. 'I wish you would stop being so friendly with Muriel Henderson. She runs to you with every piece of malicious gossip going. That is beneath contempt and I refuse to discuss it.'

It was a sign of her agitation that even his annoyance did not deter her. 'But Lewis, you must! We must decide what to do when they come next time, asking these terrible questions. I've been thinking about it all day. We must say that we were together last night, that you came up to see me and were here from the time of the rockets going off to just before they phoned you at home. No one will know.'

He stared at her. 'You're not being serious, are you? Lying to the police – that's madness! If you wanted to create suspicion in their minds, that's the best way to do it.'

'They wouldn't know!' Dorothy protested, high colour staining her cheeks. 'I could say it with total confidence. You must agree, Lewis, you must! You read all about these miscarriages of justice – I know you didn't do it and if that's what it takes to divert their attention away from you I have no scruples.'

Lewis shook his head. 'I can't believe that you're saying that. Anyway, there's no point. A policeman interviewed me this afternoon and I told him I was here by myself.'

She looked stricken, her colour draining away. 'Oh Lewis, you didn't! But then they'll – they'll . . .' She trailed into silence without finishing her sentence.

'They'll what, Mother?'

'Oh – nothing.' She got up and began clearing the plates off the table. 'It's done now, isn't it?'

I I

The temperature had fallen sharply overnight. In Kirkluce High Street, the pavements were rimed with frost and a wind with an icy edge to it was whipping round the corners, savaging the last limp rags of golden leaves and tearing them away to reveal the stark winter anatomy of the plane trees.

Above, at her fourth-floor office window, Marjory Fleming was looking down on the final act of the Rape of the Leaves without seeing it, her fingers unconsciously beating an anxious tattoo on the window-ledge. It was Saturday, but all weekend leave had been cancelled. At the morning briefing she had set up a meeting with Tam MacNee, Tansy Kerr and Jonathan Kingsley; they should be arriving in five minutes.

It was clear already that this wasn't going to prove an easy investigation. The high profile of the case meant that she had a nervous Superintendent getting more twitchy by the hour, and she couldn't see there being the straightforward, common motive for the deaths that he would have liked. On her shoulders, too, lay the burden of community expectation which her mother had expressed last night; it was, quite simply, unthinkable that the victims of such an outrage should be denied the justice of a conviction.

Even at the briefing, which had included additional manpower from the Dumfriesshire Force, you could almost smell the anger in the air. When she had asked for suggestions for a convenience name to attach to the perpetrator, a PC had growled, 'What's wrong with "Bastard"?' to a groundswell of approval. They'd settled on the more neutral 'Wrecker', but Fleming was uneasy. She could understand their feelings, shared them, even, but anger is a bad master in police work; she'd have to keep a tight rein on this one to avoid some fired-up copper fitting up a suspect without a lot more than 'Someone must have done it; this is someone; therefore he must have done it' to go on.

She had outlined the situation succinctly and set out her priorities: she gave a nod to the general grudge theory and arranged for checks to be made at all local lifeboat stations, but she didn't try to pretend that it wasn't simply, in her opinion, an elimination exercise; the main thrust of the investigation would be within Knockhaven and its immediate surroundings to the south, the main road north of Fuill's Inlat having been blocked by an accident at the relevant time.

On a whiteboard she had sketched up a sequence chart, starting from the earlier purchase and preparation of the lamps, then the coastguard's call at 7.05 p.m. and maroons going off at 7.15, the journey to set up the lights between that time and the wreck of the boat just after 10, the rescue attempts which finished around midnight and the rapid appearance and disappearance of the car at 3.15 a.m.

Very deliberately, Fleming had kept it all short and very much to the point. Heated opinions and wild speculation from the floor were not invited and now they were all being given her list of detailed assignments: checks on the lamps and on craft shops selling glass paint; interviews with visitors to Elder's houses; follow-ups to the phone calls already inundating the extra lines with information which, with feeling running so high, would probably be even more well-meaning and time-wasting than usual; experiments with maroons to define the limits of the area where they were audible; questions to coastguards and support teams to establish exactly who, outside those limits, might have immediate access to call-out information.

With MacNee, Kingsley and Kerr, Fleming planned to go into the delicate area of suspects and motives. In a situation like this you couldn't be too careful; the sledgehammer approach might have worked with Nat Rettie but when it came to families who had recently suffered bereavement it was a scalpel job. These were her sharpest operators and she wanted them working together as a team, even if it was a high-risk strategy, with Tam still going stiff-legged as a hostile tyke any time he was around Kingsley. So she'd just have to slap them about, wouldn't she, until they saw sense. Fun, fun, fun!

The tap on the door came at precisely ten o'clock and Fleming watched with interest as they filed in. It was Kingsley who opened the door and stood back to let Kerr enter ahead of him, then walked through it himself, leaving MacNee to bring up the rear. There were two padded chairs on the opposite side of her desk and several upright ones round a table in the corner; Kerr, glancing back at MacNee, took one of the padded chairs a little hesitantly, and Kingsley took the other with no hesitation at all. MacNee, instead of pulling up a hard chair, perched on the edge of the table, which gave him the height advantage. Kingsley glanced back at him, then rapidly away again, as if registering that he had missed a trick. Such jockeying for position was all very amusing, unless it was your thankless task to make them work together.

Fleming began without preamble. 'I asked you to come this morning because I want to use you as a task force, working on possible motives and just getting suspects talking – someone else can take formal statements. I want you sharing theories, insights, ideas. The first thing we have to remember, of course, is that Willie Duncan has to be considered as well as the others – in my view, ahead of Luke Smith.'

Was it her imagination, or was that a look of surprise or even irritation on Kingsley's face? Surely he couldn't have imagined that he was the only one who would think of such an obvious point? If so, he would have to be disabused of that sort of arrogant assumption, sharpish. For the moment, however, Fleming went on smoothly, 'In fact, I hope it's going to be possible to discount Luke completely. No one, including himself, could have known he'd be on that boat. And when I saw the tape of the interview with Rettie yesterday – nice work, Tansy – I had the impression he wasn't in any position to push a paedophilia allegation.'

'The girl denies it flatly,' Kingsley said. 'And believe you me, he'd have been taking his life in his hands coming on to that one. Tough cookie.'

'The staff should get danger money,' Kerr agreed. 'And a bonus at the end of the week if they haven't actually slapped her cocky little face.'

Thinking of Cat, Fleming had to swallow hard. 'Right. I'll make a note to have someone check out his previous background in Glasgow, but are you satisfied there are no problems at the Academy here, Jon?'

'Squeaky clean, as far as I can tell.'

'Then we run all the checks on his personal life and unless that throws up something unexpected we eliminate him quietly from consideration.'

As she paused to draw breath, Kingsley stepped in. 'So that leaves us with Duncan, Ashley Randall and Rob Anderson.' MacNee's lip curled at the younger man's blatant effort to make his mark as he went on, 'I've spoken to Dr and Mrs Randall Senior, but I'll admit I didn't get far. Maybe someone else could take a pop at it – he might be more forthcoming if he wasn't in his own surgery, perhaps.

'Quite honestly, I'd like to go after Duncan. Drugs are

clearly involved somewhere and I'm up to speed – sorry, no pun intended – on that sort of stuff.'

Fleming's eyes went to MacNee's face. She saw the muscles in his jaw clench, then he said flatly, 'That's my patch.'

Kingsley half-turned in his chair. 'I know that. But face it, Tam – you haven't really got anywhere, have you? We're not in competition –' *Oh no?* Fleming thought, '– and perhaps Operation Songbird needs a fresh eye, a new approach.'

MacNee ignored him, speaking directly across his head to Fleming. 'It's up to you, boss. You decide our details.'

Kerr shifted uneasily in her seat – not surprisingly, with verbal bullets whizzing about her head – and Fleming felt hollow inside. She hadn't expected quite such a sudden shoot-out, though with hindsight she should have.

The worst part of it was that Kingsley was right. Tam had told her yesterday about Willie locking the door against him and it made sense to see if someone else could persuade him to talk. As a friend, she didn't want to humiliate Tam in front of this pushy young man but as a police officer she had a different duty. She made a split-second decision.

'Tam, Willie's not talking to you for some reason. He's someone who has survived what could possibly have been an attempt on his life and we have to make the most of that. Jon, I want you to have a shot at persuading him to tell you what's going on, but that's the limit of your brief. Tam's still running Operation Songbird. All right?'

She could see MacNee wasn't happy, but neither was Kingsley, which probably meant she'd got it about right. A left and a right had always worked with her children ('Don't hit your sister, Cammie. But you just stop provoking him, Cat').

After a moment MacNee said, with impressive fair-mindedness, 'Right enough, I wasn't getting anywhere with Willie, and "*facts are chiels that winna ding*".' Then he added hastily, 'And I've paid for that one already.'

Fleming laughed, with some relief, as did Kerr, but she didn't make any attempt to explain the joke to Kingsley, who was looking puzzled. A sense of being at a disadvantage might teach him something he needed to learn.

'OK, that's settled. Now, Tansy, you spoke to Mrs Anderson at the hospital, didn't you?'

'I'm just filing my report, boss. She's in pieces, poor woman – I'm not sure I'll get much from her, but I could do a bit of digging round the neighbours.'

'Anything come out of the interview?'

Tansy frowned. 'Don't think so. Apparently he went on a bit about the lights and feeling guilty and that he loved her, that sort of thing. He wasn't really making sense – muttering about three lights when there were only two, weren't there?'

Fleming nodded. 'Yes, two. But hardly surprising that he was confused. And Tam – the Randalls. Have you done a report, Jon?'

'Not yet. I've filed the Kylie MacEwan/Nat Rettie school stuff but I haven't had time to write up my notes on the Randall interviews.'

'Fine. Hand your notes over to Tam, and he can take them forward.'

Kingsley would have to learn not to show his emotions quite so clearly; she read resistance in the young face even as he said smoothly, 'Sure, I'll get something on paper for him.'

He needed a lesson. Now. 'Watch my lips, Jon. Hand over your notes to Tam. As they stand. Neither of you has time to waste faffing about and as you said yourself, you're not in competition.'

He looked as startled as if the chair he was sitting on had suddenly bitten his bottom. 'But,' he said, then as he encountered the look from her which had turned better men than he to stone, turned bright red and muttered, 'Sorry, ma'am. I'll do that.'

Fleming allowed the pause to lengthen long enough to make sure he was acutely uncomfortable, then said sweetly, 'Oh yes, I think you will.

'Now, what I really want you to look for is anything that doesn't feel right. Behaviour that's inappropriate, whether overreactive or underreactive. Don't be afraid to follow your noses. And my nose tells me there's something about Ritchie Elder. You're going to be talking to the Randalls, Tam – try and see what you can suss out about Ashley and Elder. Get Lewis Randall out of the surgery, as Jon suggests. Then you just might try for a little chat with Elder's wife – after all, she can't have been too happy about it either.

'The other thing to keep at the back of your mind is that there could be some link beyond the lifeboat. Does anything suggest Ashley was involved in the drugs business with Willie, say? Was she having an affair with Rob as well? My gut feeling is that it's unlikely, but be alert for any pointers.

'Thanks, everyone. Report back to me directly if there's anything you think offers a lead.'

Kingsley left with some alacrity, not waiting this time for Tansy Kerr to precede him. She too left looking as if she couldn't get out fast enough. MacNee, on the other hand, lowered himself from the table with dignity and no undue haste.

'Stop smirking, Tam.'

MacNee turned a bland face to her. 'I'm not smirking! How am I smirking?'

'You're smirking inside,' she accused him, and he grinned, then followed the others out.

The notes MacNee found himself holding – set down on his desk with a bad grace and 'I'll want them back tonight' – were in two sets, torn from a constable's page-numbered notebook. That was probably a disciplinary offence in itself.

Pages 23–26 had a few lines relating to the visit to Kirkluce Academy, then went on to jottings about an interview with Dorothy Randall which concluded, with suspicious abruptness, on the bottom of page 26. There were then three pages missing: page 33 started mid-phrase, 'wife to go to meeting', then continued noting what Dr Lewis Randall had said. It finished half-way down page 36, which went on to dealing with Kylie MacEwan.

So what was Kingsley keeping to himself? A strong lead, presumably, but what was it? It could be something that Dorothy Randall had said. From the tone of the notes, the interview had been coming to an end, but often enough the best stuff came when you were on your way to the door and they'd relaxed.

Against that was the fact that Kingsley had pretty much handed the Randalls to MacNee on a plate and he wouldn't have done that if he hadn't thought he'd gnawed all the meat off the bones already. So had something Dorothy said pointed him in another direction altogether?

Or had it been nothing to do with her? Was it some other source Kingsley was so jealously protecting, some info which had suggested that this was all about drugs, which would explain why he was so keen to follow up that line? Tam could, of course, use his superior rank to order Kingsley to hand over the missing pages; if he refused, as most likely he would, MacNee would be within his rights to refer it up. But the distaste for telling tales to teacher was deeply ingrained. In the school he'd gone to – Glasgow, inner-city, run-down and demoralised – more people carried knives than carried pencils and only folk with a death-wish clyped. You just made it your business to screw the bastard next time round. He'd learned that from his English teacher, the only recognisably human member of staff, who had also somehow managed to instil in his scruffy, undersized pupil his own passion for

Scotland's Bard. On both counts, Tam felt he owed him a debt of gratitude.

So for the moment he could only settle for what he'd been given and he applied himself to reading the sketchy notes carefully, with particular attention to what lay between the lines. They were competent, certainly. In fact, if he was to be fair, they were more than competent. Despite their brevity they conveyed not only information but assessment; he had, for instance, emphasised Dorothy Randall's sensitivity to alibi-style questions and MacNee made a mental note to press that button when he saw her and see if it gave a skirl.

What came across from the notes on Lewis Randall was a certain frustration. You had to take a long, hard look at the husband of any murdered woman but Kingsley clearly hadn't decided by the end of the interview whether he was more or less suspicious. He was, to use the hoary old newspaper term, baffled. MacNee liked that. Gave him something to aim at.

It was a rare day for the twenty-five-minute run down the coast anyway. Was there anywhere bonnier than Galloway on a fine, cold, clear autumn morning, and the sea with its rafts of orange seaweed glinting so bright it made your eyes water? The caravan sites weren't so bonny, maybe: ugly metal townships down near the shore, deserted now the summer families had gone.

As he drove along the low-lying road which skirted the bay towards Port William, he saw, pulling out from the sheltering stone arms of harbour walls, a small boat laden with pots for lobsters and crabs. He watched its progress with a jaundiced eye; he'd long had his suspicions that what came up when the pots were lifted again wasn't always waving its claws, but despite a few Customs raids they'd never struck lucky. Too many mobile phones, too many helpful watchers on shore.

His mind went to Willie Duncan. The boss had been right, little as he had liked her decision. His approach, which he still reckoned would over time have worn the man down into unburdening himself to his Uncle Tam, had been undermined by what had happened, and maybe Kingsley would have better luck. It would be worth the dunt to his pride if something useful emerged – always supposing Kingsley could be persuaded to share it with what the boss had so optimistically described as the team.

Tansy Kerr didn't know Knockhaven very well. She'd been in the Anchor a couple of times for a drink with friends but she'd never come in daylight and she hadn't paid much attention to her surroundings at the time. She looked about her now. Behind her, on the upper side of the main road which bisected the town, there were the pompous Victorian villas which held themselves aloof from the smaller, older houses huddled irregularly below it, but whose neighbours now were a modern development and a small council estate. It was a typical small Scottish town of perhaps two and a half thousand, three thousand souls, a nice wee place, with quaint little streets and wynds going up from the exposed Shore Street, which had shops on one side and a low sea wall on the other. The sluice holes at regular intervals showed how often the demarcation line between land and sea was breached: there were actually pebbles, sand and drying strands of seaweed lying in the road, and beside one or two doors damp sandbags were still out.

Growing up in an inland town where a storm meant no more than a nasty day and possibly, at worst, a slate off your roof, Tansy had never considered what an intimate relationship you'd have with the sea, living in a place like this. It'd be your friend and your enemy, giving with one hand, taking away with the other. Beautiful and deadly. Irresistible, compelling.

She could feel the tug of its compulsion herself. Though she should be seeking out scraps to make the patchwork story of Rob Anderson's life, she swung her legs over the wall and let herself down on to the sloping concrete apron shoring it up, and from there on to the shale shore with its patches of rough, dark sand. The sea was calm enough today; teasing waves made darts at her feet and ahead the blank horizon faded into a haze of dusty gold. To her right, the long blue headland of the Mull of Galloway, curved at the end like a beckoning finger, marked the farther limit of Luce Bay.

Tansy picked up a flat stone and tried to send it skimming across the water. It made two brave skips then sank feebly in a swirl of bubbles. A bit like any ideas she'd had so far about the investigation she was engaged on at the moment. She wasn't happy.

It wasn't exactly Jon Kingsley's fault. Tam was being a right pain and you couldn't expect Jon to go round working out what might put Tam's back up before he opened his mouth. But somehow she just had a feeling Jon was trying to set him up, make him look bad in the boss's eyes, though personally she reckoned he'd have more chance of convincing David Beckham he'd look better with a short back-and-sides, cords and a cardigan. And though she had more years of service than Jon did, she felt with slight resentment that he was behaving as if he had seniority.

Jon had done his best to muscle in on the drugs scene, which made it kind of obvious he was backing that as the motive. He could even be right, in which case her enquiries, and Tam's, were only filling in time till he made his spectacular arrest to the applause of the dazzled plods of the Galloway Constabulary. Not.

Anyway, she ought to be getting on with it. She'd given up smoking a couple of weeks back and her vital supply of chewing-gum was running out; she could home in on the most promising-looking shop and get into conversation on the back of her purchase. Local shops always knew what was going on.

Just as she turned to go, she saw something glinting at her feet: an iridescent shell, flat and round, with a neat, tiny hole near its centre. Was that what they called a silver dollar? She picked it up and slipped it into the pocket of her jeans, just for luck.

The Hollies, the Victorian villa belonging to Dorothy Randall, stood in a substantial garden in one of the quieter streets up at the back of Knockhaven. MacNee paused for a moment at its entrance, two old grey stone pillars guarding a short gravel drive which led to the main door at the side of the building and to the garage beyond.

To the left, on the other side of a low brick wall of much more recent date, was a bungalow which looked as if it might have been built on ground sold off from the larger property. It had side windows overlooking The Hollies' front drive and MacNee eyed it thoughtfully. Chances were the owners would be out at work, but it was worth a try. The indirect approach often paid dividends.

He was in luck. A minute after he rang the bell, he heard halting footsteps and then the door was opened by an elderly woman. She was leaning on a stick but her eyes were bright and, once he had shown ID, full of curiosity. She waved him in eagerly and he followed, suppressing a smile. The challenge with this one wasn't going to be persuading her to talk, it would be framing his questions so that the rumour wasn't sent racing round that the doctor and his mother were prime suspects.

When he emerged ten minutes later, he was still trying to suppress a smile, this time of satisfaction. He had, he reckoned, managed to convince her that he was asking about any strange vehicles that might have been hanging about on Thursday, and more importantly he had some useful information to carry forward to his interview with Dorothy Randall.

It was very gratifying for DC Kingsley to find himself being greeted at the lifeboat station by a relaxed and cooperative Willie Duncan and invited to take a seat in the crew room. Never a talkative man, Duncan was still perfectly happy to express the revulsion of the whole community and the wickedness of the person who had done such a thing, or, as he put it, 'Scunnered, we all were. He's a limb of Satan, that one.'

It was less gratifying to find that he was flatly denying that he could be considered a target.

'Och no! Who's been telling you havers like that?' His tone was genial.

'I understood that you were heard to say you were very worried.'

The man's weather-beaten face reddened slightly, but he said only, 'With all yon going on, I maybe said something daft.'

'And why would you do that?'

Willie shrugged. 'I was upset. Rob and Ashley – we'd been out there all weathers. And that young teacher laddie—'

'Oh yes. Luke Smith. Died because of you, really, didn't he?' Kingsley spoke with calculated brutality. 'If you hadn't been out of it, he wouldn't have been there at all, would he?'

The colour in Willie's face deepened but he said only, 'Black lies. I'd a sore head – one of those migraine things—'

'Not what I heard.'

All trace of geniality had vanished. 'Well, you can stuff it, then.'

'The fact is, this whole thing's about drugs, isn't it, Duncan? They were after you, for some reason. What were you trying to do – set up in business for yourself, or something?'

The man got up from his chair and walked to the door. 'I'm not needing this,' he said flatly. 'I've said my piece. That's all.'

Kingsley followed him. 'Had a word with them, Duncan, have you? They've told you that you got it wrong, that they'd no hand in this.'

Willie stopped dead, then without turning round walked out into the main hall. Two ladies, standing beside the souvenir stall, looked up with interest as the two men appeared.

Kingsley walked past Willie, then turned to stand in his way. 'That's what they've told you. But speaking as a friend, I tell you what you've got to ask yourself, Willie – do you believe them?'

He turned on his heel and left, but not before he had noted, with satisfaction, that the other man's hands were trembling.

Dorothy Randall looked at the warrant-card held out for her inspection, then at the man in the leather jacket and jeans who was holding it, in horrified disbelief. 'Detective Sergeant MacNee?' she repeated. She didn't add, '*You!* A policeman?' but the thought-bubble was all but visible.

'Yes, madam. Sorry to trouble you – just one or two wee queries you could maybe help us with.' He knew the type: middle-class, brought up to believe the police are our friends, on their high horse the minute a copper starts doing his job anywhere near them.

'I cooperated fully with the officer yesterday. I have nothing further to add to what I said to him.'

'Oh, he was just one of our *junior* constables.' MacNee enjoyed saying that. 'My inspector felt you should be allocated a more *senior* officer.' These '*high, exalted, virtuous dames*' always fell for the idea of preferential treatment.

She didn't. Dorothy's blue eyes were shrewd and cold, and the way the thin lips, under the pastel-pink lipstick, tightened showed that she was under no illusion as to the significance of a second visit.

'I suppose you had better come in.' Her back poker-rigid, she led the way to the lounge, a large, bay-windowed room at the front of the house.

It looked just as he would have predicted from its owner's tweedy-smart appearance – a gold dralon three-piece suite with deep, silky fringes, matching velvet drapes and twee figurines of dainty ladies with billowing skirts on the mantelpiece reflected in the mirror behind – but on one side of the door there was also a large, well-filled bookcase. MacNee wasn't much of a reader himself but these were clearly a cut above the Mills and Boon romances Bunty favoured. He'd have to see and not underestimate this one.

Without waiting to be asked, he took a seat on the sofa and got out his notebook. 'Yes, do sit down,' she said acidly as she positioned herself in an elaborate wooden carver with a tapestry seat. The fireplace held only an ornamental brass firescreen in the shape of a fan but the room was still uncomfortably hot.

MacNee began mildly enough. 'No doubt you'll have heard by now that we are treating the wreck of the lifeboat as suspicious.'

Dorothy inclined her head. 'That seems to be what they're saying in the village. Not that those of us most intimately affected have been officially informed.'

Hoity-toity, eh? But MacNee had a habit of watching hands – often less well controlled than faces – and Dorothy Randall's hands, the nails well-manicured and coated with clear varnish, were gripping the edge of the chair arms.

Time to cut the cackle. 'You didn't get on with your daughter-in-law, did you?'

He'd expected a defensive reaction. Instead she said, 'No, I didn't.'

MacNee blinked. It was a bit like heading the ball towards the goal and finding the other side didn't plan to defend it. He lined up another shot. 'What did you quarrel about?'

'We didn't.'

'Never?'

Her response to his incredulity was flat. 'Never.'

From Kingsley's notes, she'd not been so backward in coming forward about this yesterday. If she was reacting so differently today, she'd been thinking about it, preparing herself for another visit, maybe.

'Did it not make you angry, her cheating on your son with Ritchie Elder?'

Her hands were curling like claws on the chair arm now but she said scornfully, 'I don't pay any attention to gossip.'

'You'd heard it, though?'

'It was widespread.'

'So your son would have heard it, believed it, maybe. That's not a bad motive for killing your wife, especially if you'd planned it to look like an accident—'

'No!' The word was forced out of her. 'He would never – he didn't believe it, anyway. This is ridiculous!'

She was getting her dander up. Good. 'And then there's you, Mrs Randall. Did you believe it? Did you think she was making a fool of you all? You told DC Kingsley you fancied being a granny, and while she was around there weren't going to be any kids, were there? And was she maybe getting between you and your son, too? You must have been very close, the two of you, him coming back to work here and all . . .'

The provocation strategy didn't work. Dorothy compressed her lips so tightly that they all but disappeared, as if she were afraid of what might emerge from them. Then, though her voice was taut with anger, she said only, 'This is entirely absurd – a complete farrago of nonsense. If this is some sort of stupid police technique—'

'No, no. Just giving you a keek at the way we're thinking.' At least he'd managed to shake her; he was beginning to make the weather now. He went on, 'And what did you do, when you went out that evening? Take a wee trip up to Fuill's Inlat, to set up the lanterns once you knew there was a call-out?'

'Lanterns? I don't know what you're talking about. I didn't go out until my son and I went to the scene of the tragedy.'

'So you were here in the house all evening.'

'Yes.'

'Alone?'

'Yes, alone.'

'Your son wasn't here, then?'

After a barely perceptible pause she said, 'No.'

'And you'd no visitors? No phone calls?'

'Not as far as I remember.'

Dorothy had made her replies firmly. He could see from her face that she thought she was being believed. 'Right,' he said. 'So you couldn't possibly have been at Fuill's Inlat, being in all evening like you were?'

'No.' The response came straight back.

'No?'

'I told you, no!' She was more uncertain now, watching him from under those hooded lids.

MacNee said, conversationally, 'You're lying, Mrs Randall.'

'L-lying?' He had her on the run now. She had turned pale; her hands were twisting the ends of the chair arms as if they were door handles. 'How dare you—'

'Och, it's not hard to be brave when you've got someone by the short hairs,' he drawled. 'Tell me about you going out.'

'I – I,' she licked her dry lips, 'I don't know why you should think I was out.'

'Eyewitness.' He was fairly enjoying this; he'd better watch and not get carried away with himself.

'If someone told you that, they were mistaken, that's all.'

MacNee made a pantomime of consulting his notebook. 'Just after the maroons went off, you drove out in your car.'

'That old witch next door – she spends her life spying on me!' Dorothy's face clouded over with fury, but she hadn't lost the place. 'Of course, she gets very confused, you know—'

'Funny, she didn't sound confused about this. She'd make a good witness. Very clear.'

Dorothy paused, breathing fast, calculation showing in her face. Then she said, carefully, 'I did go out, very briefly. I'd forgotten all about it at first – that was why I didn't mention it. Then, when you started making all these wild accusations, I thought I would be foolish to admit to it. I knew it was totally innocent, but you were clearly planning to make something of it. Just as you are now. And I would point out I wasn't making this statement under oath.'

She was good. Oh, she was good. With a certain reluctant admiration MacNee went on, 'So where did you go, on this brief expedition that wasn't to Fuill's Inlat – unless, of course, we find another eyewitness and you mind that you went there after all?'

'All I did,' she said with dignity, 'was pop down to Lewis's house. I do that so often, you see, I barely think of it as going out. When I heard the maroons, I thought I'd go round to see if he wanted to come up for a meal or something.'

'Could you not have phoned?' He'd read Kingsley's notes: Lewis Randall had denied having any visitors or phone calls. She was, he hoped, walking into a trap she had made for herself.

'I didn't want to interrupt if he was working. He might have felt obliged to accept – he's always been such a caring son.' Dorothy was definitely warming to her story now. 'This way I wouldn't disturb him. I drove down to the house then walked round the back to his study, where the lights were on. He was very busy at his desk so I just got back into the car and drove home.'

Damn, damn, damn! MacNee's own lips compressed with irritation; he hated being outflanked and he wasn't giving up. 'So you would have been away for – what? Five minutes?'

'I should think so, more or less.'

'So if someone said it was longer than that, they'd be lying?' In fact, the helpful neighbour had unhelpfully become engrossed in her favourite soap and had been unable to say when the car returned.

'Confused, anyway, as I said before.'

MacNee got up, putting his notebook away, and she too rose. Her tone was gracious as she said, 'I'm sorry, Sergeant, it was foolish of me not to be entirely open with you once I remembered my little expedition.' It was clear she thought the worst was over.

'Oh, worse than foolish, Mrs Randall.' Tam smiled, and her face changed. 'You see,' he went on, 'us lot have nasty suspicious minds. When someone tells us black lies we wonder why and start sniffing around because, you see, innocent folk tell the truth even when no one asks them to swear on the Bible. I think we're going to be getting to know each other quite a lot better.'

'Is that a threat, Sergeant?' The thin lips were quivering now.

'Och, not at all! Think of it as a promise.' He went to the door, still smiling, and as he did so his eye was caught by a book in the big bookcase.

'Tide tables, Mrs Randall? You a sailor?'

'I – I used to crew for my husband and son, a few years ago.'

'But you've never thrown them away, though they're no use to you now?'

She wasn't slow to recognise the significance of his query. 'There are dozens of books there that I haven't looked at for years! I don't throw books away!' she protested wildly.

'Very wise. You never know when they may come in handy.' MacNee walked away from her agitated protests and let himself out, shutting the front door behind him with self-satisfied delicacy.

Pondering on his interview with Willie Duncan, Jon Kingsley

walked back from the lifeboat shed along Shore Street. His suggestion that someone had told Willie he wasn't the intended victim had hit the nail on the head – the man's reaction proved it. But it didn't prove that reassurance was true.

Jon didn't want it to be true. He badly wanted to believe that this was all part of the drugs scene he knew and understood. If it weren't, he was in unknown – he had almost said enemy – territory where MacNee and Kerr had the advantage because of their familiarity with the slow, boring process of getting people to talk, then talking to more people, then sifting what they said, swirling it all around like a panhandler hoping for a gold nugget among the dross. He was a young man in a hurry; he liked the dangerous buzz of undercover work and the fireworks of the police raid once you had suckered them in. He'd been lucky in that last operation but there were too many other bright young men doing much the same thing in the big cities and he was going to have to stand in line for promotion, so he'd taken the gamble that in a small local force he could make rank quickly then ask for a transfer back. But if this wasn't about drugs . . .

Deep in his thoughts and scowling moodily, Jon didn't notice the woman coming along the pavement towards him until she said, 'Cheer up! It may never happen!'

'Tansy! Any joy?' He switched on a smile instantly.

Kerr wrinkled her nose. 'I'm on my third cup of weak supermarket instant coffee, and all anyone's said is that Rob Anderson was a diamond geezer who adored his wife, and the only person who got across him was his ratbag stepson. His wife – still in shock, poor thing – speaks to a blameless life.

'Oh, there was this wifie told me some bloke he chucked out of the pub a couple of weeks ago said he'd get him, then just when I thought I'd a lead she goes, "Aye, but he was a

wee thing fou' at the time. He's really a douce enough laddie."
I'll have to check him out, but I'm not exactly hopeful. If
everyone bounced for being lairy committed multiple murder
we'd be knee-deep in bodies every Sunday morning.'

Kingsley grinned. 'So I needn't expect a call to help you
make a dramatic arrest, then?'

'You could say. Just more foot-slogging. What about you?'

'Oh, Duncan was happy enough to talk to me. Just not
about anything remotely useful.'

'Story of my life. I'd better away and get on with it. Where
are you headed?'

'Not sure. Probably back to HQ, to record my non-existent
progress. I've yesterday's report on the Randalls to write up
as well, when Tam deigns to give me back my notes.'

Kerr either didn't hear or chose to ignore the bitterness
in his tone, unwrapping a stick of chewing-gum as she went
on her way.

Kingsley glanced at his watch. It was nearly half-past
twelve; the doctors' surgery probably closed around then on
a Saturday. Was there any chance he might catch Muriel
Henderson leaving for home? She might not be on duty but
it was worth a try. He hurried back to his car.

Tam MacNee, eating the pie and crisps he had bought from
the '8 'til Late', was heading towards the Elders' desirable
residence on the coast road south of Knockhaven. He wasn't
sure who he might find there – Elder alone, Mrs alone, the
two of them together, or frustratingly, no one at all.

As he turned in at the entrance to Bayview House, he
pursed his lips in a silent whistle. Elder must be doing all
right: the porch with its massive pillars alone must have cost
about the same as the MacNees' three-bedroom villa. A
powder-blue Mercedes coupé was parked outside and
through the huge windows of the wing to the left he could

see tables and loungers round a swimming pool that looked bigger than the public one in Kirkluce, not that he was intimately acquainted with it. In MacNee's view water's place was in a bath with a wee rubber duck on top.

The woman who answered the door was a surprise. He'd expected someone glamorous enough to match these surroundings but she was short and a bit overweight, wearing black trousers and a green top with the 'Cotton Traders' logo.

'Mrs Elder?' He held up his ID card and the woman snorted with laughter.

'You think! No, she's through the house. I just get to clean it. You'd better come in.'

'Big job you've got.' MacNee followed her across a spacious hall, its main feature a curving staircase with an elaborate wrought-iron balustrade at one side.

'There's the three of us, mornings. It's not bad – there's a bit of company and the money's good. She expects things done right but she's not for ever on your back. And she'll sit and have a cup of coffee and a blether like anyone else.'

'Is Mr Elder in?'

She paused, not averse to a bit of the gab. Carefully lowering her voice, she said, 'We've barely seen him since all this happened. It's maybe just lifeboat stuff – you know he's kind of in charge? – but he's been in a rare state. We all think—' She stopped. 'But maybe I shouldn't—'

'Ashley Randall?' he prompted.

'Aye. And her a doctor, too! We've all been fair scandalised.' There was pleasurable horror in her tone.

'Did you ever see any evidence? Her coming to the house, maybe, when Mrs Elder wasn't there?'

All he got was a scornful 'Naw! Far too canny, that pair, to let anyone catch them at it.'

'So how did you know what was going on?'

This time, there was a pitying look. 'Everyone knew. I'd

better take you in.' She knocked on a door at the back of the hall. 'Mrs Elder? That's the polis to see you.'

So yet again, all that Tam had was evidence that there had been gossip, which in a place like this was like saying there was a bit of traffic in London. Was it at all possible that the 'affair' had been based on rumour and nothing else?

The reception he got on this visit was in marked contrast to his earlier assignment. As he came into the light, airy, modern room with its pale wood floors, huge cream leather sofas and big windows on to a patio with tubs full of winter pansies, a woman got up and came towards him, her hand outstretched. She was too skinny for MacNee's taste – he liked a bit of an armful – but you'd have to say she was pretty enough, with that kind of glossy look you can buy if you're rich enough. She was a bit like the china ladies on Dorothy Randall's mantelpiece with her neat features and a wee rosebud mouth; she had highlighted blonde hair and she was making good use of the sweeping lashes round her big grey eyes as she looked up at MacNee.

'You'll have come about this awful lifeboat thing. I'm afraid Ritchie's not here but if I can be of any help—'

'It was really you I came to see, Mrs Elder.'

It didn't faze her. 'I'm flattered. Come and sit down and I'll get Rhona to bring us some coffee. And those muffins Davina made this morning – unless you greedy lot finished them, Rhona?'

Rhona denied the accusation demurely enough but MacNee noticed a repressed smile. He wasn't sure how a muffin would sit on top of pie and crisps, but in the interests of a cosy atmosphere he'd maybe have to force himself.

Joanna Elder was chattering on. 'It's been terrible for my husband. I didn't know Rob or Luke but I know Ritchie really valued them both. And Lewis and Ashley Randall were such good friends of ours, dedicated doctors, too – it's a serious blow to the community. Then there's been the Press – we've had to switch off the phone – and of course the police enquiry on top of that. I still can't get my head round the idea that it wasn't an accident. I suppose you're absolutely sure?'

After Dorothy Randall's reticence, this avalanche of information left MacNee feeling almost battered. 'I'm afraid so,' he murmured.

'I can't imagine how anyone could do this. Vandals, possibly – but I hear that you think it's something to do with drugs? My ladies here always keep me up to date with what's going on. Oh, Rhona, thank you so much.'

Rhona set down a tray with a cafetière and a plate piled with chocolate muffins. MacNee accepted one, then was surprised when Joanna took one herself. From the look of her, he wouldn't have guessed she was into chocolate muffins. But she ate it greedily and then to his astonishment helped herself to another one before he'd even peeled off the paper case on his. At least it stopped her talking long enough to let him put in a question.

'It must have been kind of a difficult night. When did you hear what was happening? Did you know there'd been a call-out?'

'The coastguard phoned here first so I told them to contact Ritchie's mobile. He'd had to go to the new houses because they were having a special open night for prospective buyers and he'd left earlier. Then later one of the reserve crew phoned explaining Ritchie would be late.'

MacNee jotted that down. 'You didn't speak directly to Mr Elder?'

Joanna shook her head. 'I knew he'd be very involved in the rescue – he didn't need me interrupting.'

'And you didn't go along to Fuill's Inlat yourself? Offer your support?' MacNee persisted.

'Do you think I'd have been welcome? They're serious pros, these guys, and the last thing they need is useless bystanders wringing their hands and getting in the way. No, I had a quiet night in, in front of the telly, until my husband came home and then, of course, we were up till the wee small hours – he was much too upset to go to bed, as you can imagine.' Her eyes were wide and innocent.

He decided to go straight to the point. 'Mrs Elder—'

'Oh, Joanna, please.'

He ignored her. 'Were you aware of the rumour that Ashley Randall and your husband were having an affair?'

'No! Is that what they're saying?' She sounded amused. 'Not that it surprises me. Ashley was a bit of a flirt, and in this place that's all it would take. No, I assure you Ritchie and I have a very happy marriage. In fact,' she indicated a pile of coloured brochures on the table at her side, 'we've been discussing a holiday when this is all over. Ritchie's going to need a break – he's been so stressed that I'm positively worried about him.' Her voice was level, but she was folding one of the discarded paper cases on her plate smaller and smaller.

MacNee's instinct as a street-fighter was to go head-to-head, but Marjory had told him often enough that you caught more flies with honey than with vinegar. She'd have been proud of him so far and he didn't want to put Joanna on the defensive before he had more to go on. He got up.

'Thanks, Mrs Elder. You've been very helpful. And the muffins were great.'

'I'll pass that on to Davina. I can't resist them, myself.' She led the way to the door.

'So just to recap. Your husband left at – what? Half-past six or so?' She nodded. 'And he arrived back—?'

'Oh, well after midnight, poor man.'

'And you were here all evening?'

'Absolutely.' The grey eyes were guileless, as they had been throughout the conversation. You'd swear she couldn't utter an untruth, what with all those lumps of butter unmelted in her mouth. And it might be the truth, at that. But there was still something about her flawless presentation that had MacNee's antennae not so much twitching as doing a Highland fling.

Out in the hall, Rhona was busy with some dusting and looked up as they came out. 'Do you want me to show the sergeant out, Mrs Elder?'

Joanna shrugged. 'Fine. Thanks, Rhona. And goodbye, Sergeant. I hope I told you everything you wanted?'

'And more,' MacNee assured her gravely. She went back into her sitting room as Rhona escorted him to the front door. Her presence in the hall hadn't looked like coincidence to him and he waited with interest to see what was on her mind.

Sure enough, she looked over her shoulder to make sure her boss was safely out of the way, then said, 'We were just having a chat in the kitchen – you know you asked me about Mr Elder? None of us ever saw anything, but I tell you what's weird. She's barely been eating a morsel for weeks now and spending half the day working out, but since all this happened she's been stuffing her face and never looked near the gym. We were wondering if she's maybe pregnant – eating for two, ken? – but it's a funny thing even so.'

'With Davina's muffins I can't blame her,' MacNee said lightly. 'But tell me, Rhona, did any of you ever say anything to Mrs Elder about Dr Randall?'

'Not exactly . . .'

MacNee raised his eyebrows.

Rhona looked uncomfortable. 'Well, if you ask me he's a right bastard. Davina just gave her a wee hint a few weeks ago. It's not right if the wife's the last one to know.'

Even if you haven't a shred of proof that there's any truth in it. The ethics of the gossip circuit! But MacNee said only, 'What did she say?'

'Nothing much. Just sort of went a bit pink and let on she didn't understand. But she knew fine what Davina was saying.'

And had Joanna's starving herself, MacNee wondered as he got back into his car, dated from the time of Davina's 'wee hint'? If your husband was serious about another woman, meaning that you were going to lose a grand lifestyle like this, it would fairly put you off your food, right enough.

So his instincts hadn't been wrong; she'd certainly lied about her ignorance of the rumours. Had she lied to him about anything else?

Muriel Henderson locked the side door, then followed Enid Davis down the path. It was only just half-past twelve, but the doctors had pushed the patients through in good time this morning, so anything else could just wait till Monday. She'd been keen to get away promptly. It was the first time she'd ever been over the threshold of Enid's house so she was pleased about the invitation to lunch. Well, she'd sort of invited herself, really, but then Enid was a quiet wee soul who probably wouldn't have liked to ask.

They were crossing the road when a car appeared, slowing down as it reached the surgery. She clicked her tongue in irritation. 'If that's someone needing a repeat prescription and they think we're going back to open up for them, they've another think coming,' she said belligerently. Her expression was one of uncompromising hostility until the car stopped and she saw who was driving.

'Oh, it's you, Constable! I thought you were one of the patients – they're awful inconsiderate nowadays! I nearly gave you a right telling-off!'

'I'm glad I escaped that!' DC Kingsley laughed as he got

out of the car – he really was a nice-looking lad! 'I was in Knockhaven anyway and I just thought I'd drop in and see how you were getting on. But I see you're on your way home. I don't want to detain you . . .'

Considerate, too. She beamed at him. 'Och, not at all. We're just away round to Enid's house down the High Street there for a bit of lunch, aren't we, Enid?' As Enid murmured agreement, she went on, 'Actually, there was something that might interest you – you know what they're saying now?'

Muriel could almost see his ears prick up. 'It's all over the village. Willie says it was all just havers about him being scared, he was just upset about it all. Says it was definitely nothing to do with him. What do you think of that?'

He wasn't impressed. 'Oh yes, I've heard that too.'

Piqued, she went on, 'But do you see what that means? If it wasn't those drugs people, it has to have been someone else!'

'Yes, I suppose it must.' The signs of impatience were obvious.

Perhaps he wasn't such a nice young man after all. 'The point is, it could be someone local, someone we all know. It's not a nice thought, that. Enough to make your flesh creep.'

'Yes, I suppose it is.'

He didn't seem as shocked as he ought to be. Disappointed, Muriel sniffed. 'Time we were getting along, *if* you'll excuse us . . .'

With only a brief 'Thanks,' he jumped back into the car and drove off, a bit too fast. 'Well!' Muriel said pettishly. 'That's the last time I put myself out for *him*!'

It wasn't the last of Muriel's disappointments. Enid hadn't made much of an effort for lunch, just tinned soup and ham rolls, when Muriel had been looking forward to some of her cooking. She hadn't even been offered a wee sherry, just some home-made lemon squash. *Lemon squash!*

The table had been set in the kitchen too and despite Muriel's hints Enid didn't show her round the house. She'd said, 'What's your sitting room like?' but when Enid just said, 'Small,' even Muriel didn't quite have the nerve to demand to inspect it.

And there weren't any family photographs or anything to look at. There was one photo on the wall, a view of a loch and hills behind, but since Muriel knew already that Enid came from somewhere up the West Coast it was hardly worth the effort she was having to make just to keep the conversation going. You'd have thought Enid grudged the very food Muriel was putting in her mouth. *Not* a very gracious hostess.

So, when Enid brought her a mug of instant coffee – and not so much as a biscuit to go with it – it was with a certain malice that she said, 'You'll have your big chance now, Enid, won't you?'

Enid looked at her blankly. 'What do you mean?'

Muriel giggled. 'With Dr Lewis, of course! Now he's rid of that wife of his he'll be wanting someone who can look after him properly.'

Colour rose in Enid's cheeks. She said stiffly, 'Please don't go making stupid remarks like that, Muriel. I like Dr Lewis, yes, and I don't think Dr Ashley was a good wife to him. She was a right bitch, if you ask me.'

She paid no attention to Muriel's shocked gasp. 'But it doesn't mean I've any plan to take her place and quite honestly I don't think he'd so much as look at me. I'm not deluding myself that I'm his sort. You don't think so either, so I'd be grateful if you'd stop all this, right now.'

'Well, really!' Muriel's cheeks had gone bright red. 'I've never been so insulted in my life!' She set down her mug on the table with a bang and stood up. Picking up her coat and bag from the table, she went on, 'I've tried to be a friend to you, Enid, because you don't seem to have many friends.

And after today I'm not surprised. Thank you for the *snack.*'
She laid emphasis on the last word – she wasn't going to call
it lunch – and went out, slamming the door behind her.

She felt positively stunned. Meek little Enid, turning on
her like that! Mind you, she'd always said still waters ran
deep and she'd believe she was capable of anything after this.
If they'd seen the way Enid had looked at her they wouldn't
be searching around to find someone capable of multiple
murder.

After all, it wasn't natural Enid should be so touchy, was
it, when Muriel had just been teasing her in a jokey kind of
way. Maybe there was more to it; maybe she and Dr Lewis
had something going on after all. Perhaps she should just
mention it to that young policeman, even if she had decided
to be pretty frosty if he came round again. After all, helping
the police was her civic duty.

Pleased with her own public-spiritedness, she walked back
across the main road to her own, much more satisfactory
bungalow in Mayfield Gardens where you had a better class of
neighbour – like Dr Lewis, just round the corner – instead
of the riff-raff you found in the lower town.

13

'Eternal Father, strong to save,
Whose arm hath bound the restless wave,
Who bidd'st the mighty ocean deep
Its own appointed limits keep . . .'

The voices, led by the muted strains of a silver band, wavered on the damp air. Beneath a leaden sky the crowd surrounded the lifeboat shed and filled its pier, then spilled out along Shore Street, falling silent at the end of the hymn so that the only sound was the moaning of the green-black sea. On a dais in front of the shed the minister, black-robed, raised his hand in the final blessing and the crowd mutely fell aside to allow the three coffins, draped in lifeboat flags and shouldered by men in lifeboat blazers, passage to the waiting hearses.

Behind came the chief mourners: Luke Smith's parents, his mother leaning heavily on her husband's arm as if she could barely stand unsupported; Katy Anderson, alone, white-faced, tearless and blank-eyed; Lewis Randall, his face sombre and unrevealing, with his mother in a well-cut coat and black felt hat with a dipping brim. Luke's parents were taking him directly back home for burial and Ashley was to be cremated at a private ceremony in Stranraer later. Only Rob Anderson would lie in the local cemetery, but there would be a big attendance at the graveside.

Slowly the rest of the crowd began to drift away, most

people heading up the hill to the town hall, where the ladies of the Lifeboat Committee had provided tea. Links in this rural area were strong and they came from all over the area, from Kirkluce to the north, Whithorn to the south, Wigtown in the west and a dozen other small communities in between.

Marjory Fleming stood to one side, observing. MacNee, Kerr and Kingsley would all be doing the same somewhere, although she couldn't see any of them. She could see Nat Rettie, though, who'd been released without charge for the moment at least, standing near the front in his school uniform, with his hands in his pockets and his head lowered. She saw too with dismay the distinctive hennaed head of Kylie MacEwan beside him.

No one was speaking to them; indeed, a little space had been left round about as if no one was willing to risk even coincidental association. Kylie had confirmed that they had been together that evening, though her assertion that they hadn't been doing anything except 'just talking a bit' didn't exactly instil confidence in the reliability of her evidence. And, thought Marjory anxiously, what effect could all this be having on her own Cat?

But her domestic worries would have to wait. She was here to work. Professionally, she wasn't happy, and that was an understatement on a par with saying the new Scottish Parliament seemed to be going a wee bit over budget. The forty-eight hours after the murders, in which most cases are solved if they're to be solved at all, were long gone. There had been unprecedented levels of public support and information, yet here she was over a week later, having sifted through a volume of evidence which had sent her computer into one of its periodic fits of nervous exhaustion and threatened to do the same to its operator, no further forward.

The golden rule of crime investigation, 'Every contact leaves a trace', was about as relevant here as a copy of the words of the Red Flag at a New Labour Party conference. Despite the reams of information from the scene of crime team and the pathologist giving impressively precise details about the wreck and the deaths, it was really no more than a fatal accident report. The murderer's contact was limited to those two lamps placed at the scene, and Fleming would be willing to bet her egg money that all the lab report would produce was a sophisticated chemical analysis of the paints used, naming in the last line a popular commercial brand, available in your nearest B&Q.

There was always the other time-honoured principle, 'Who benefits?', but as the Super had said to her with more than an edge of impatience in his voice, 'You don't seem even to have worked out who the victim is in this case, Marjory, let alone the murderer.' This was, she had to admit, kind of an important weakness in their investigation.

Eyewitnesses seemed the only hope. There was certainly no lack of willingness from the public: judging by what had crossed her desk every man, woman and child in the relevant area – and a good number who weren't – had chipped in with their tuppence-worth. Fleming's personal favourite was the woman who had phoned to say that her dog, ten miles away in Whithorn, had suddenly sat up and howled, 'just when those poor souls would be perishing'! Perhaps it wasn't that funny. They were just grasping at anything that fractionally alleviated the gloom.

Given the planning, the Wrecker must have checked out the site at least once, probably more often than that. But under cover of darkness, say, who would notice a torch beam on that isolated shore? Or even in daylight, days or weeks ago, who would remember an innocent rambler scaling the rocks? It was only by chance that Tam had spotted the lamps.

And if the plan had failed? If the more experienced Duncan had been at the helm, if Anderson hadn't been distracted, if the lifeboat had come safe home, would the Wrecker even now be working on a new one?

Yes, Fleming thought with sudden conviction, yes. It would be another low-risk scheme you could walk away from. And that, she suddenly thought, was the key to it – the Wrecker's determination not to pay for the crime. Laura's term, pathologically solipsistic, had highlighted that: common as the instinct for self-interest may be, this was the cold-blooded sacrifice of two lives – innocent by any standard – for no reason other than improving your chances of getting away with eliminating a third. So perhaps she'd moved a step closer to knowing what the Wrecker was like, which didn't, unfortunately, answer the 'Who?' or 'Why?' questions.

You didn't, normally, have to know why, except for professional satisfaction. Why anyone did anything was always highly speculative and all you needed in court was hard evidence against them, but this case, with its lack of any form of hard evidence, was different. In this case, motive was all they had to guide them to the victim, never mind the perpetrator.

The village was awash with rumour and counter-rumour. It was all to do with drugs. It was nothing to do with drugs. Lewis Randall had done it because his wife was having an affair with Ritchie Elder. The doctor would *never* do a thing like that and anyway, people just said there was an affair. Joanna Elder had been behaving strangely – or maybe it was natural enough, if the rumour about her husband was true . . .

And now Kingsley had come back with a new one, that Randall had been having a relationship with Enid Davis, one of the surgery receptionists. They'd have to follow up on that one too, because the trouble was that you couldn't ever dismiss a story out of hand. Small-town gossips had the dirty habit of occasional accuracy.

What hadn't emerged was a shred of hard evidence. There

was Jon's belief (she'd almost said determination) that it was all drugs-related and Tam's assertion that both women he had interviewed had been lying about something. Tansy hadn't come up with much that was useful yet, and both men agreed that interviewing Lewis Randall was, as MacNee put it, like talking to Teflon – 'It all just slides off.'

And that was the problem at the moment: everything sliding off. Nothing seemed to stick, nothing held together to offer even a coherent theory, while she was under pressure from every side – not least from the occupants of the car which was passing her now as she walked up the hill.

Chief Constable Menzies and Superintendent Donald Bailey were sitting in the back, resplendent in their best uniforms. She turned, her hand half-raised in greeting, but Donald, on her side of the car, didn't see her. Or ignored her, quite likely. She wasn't flavour of the month at the moment.

Don was desperate for a quick result and he wasn't going to get it on this one; however hard he pushed, she wasn't going to be bounced into ill-considered action. He was very keen, too keen, perhaps, on the drugs theory, Kingsley somehow having managed to bend his ear about it. It was neat, plausible, and he liked the idea that cracking the murder case might smash the drugs ring at the same time, killing two birds for the price of one budgetary stone.

But whatever Jon might say, Fleming wasn't ready to go along with it – not yet, anyway. It just didn't smell right; you'd only to think of that case in Ayr, a young man who'd been dumb enough to tangle with the big boys and ended up with two broken legs after being pushed into the harbour. It wasn't subtle, it wasn't elaborately planned and, while he had declared afterwards that it had been an accident, no one was in any doubt that this was a message, loud and clear, 'Don't mess with us.'

Today, if things had gone as the Wrecker intended, this would only have been a service mourning another tragic accident at sea. Marjory could almost feel a mind, a someone out there – someone in this crowd, even – who was cunning, ruthless, totally self-absorbed, and now – afraid? Someone who knew the lifeboat had been called out: well, sound tests had shown that was most of Knockhaven. Someone familiar with the tides: you'd only to take a walk along the shore. Someone who knew the pattern of the leading lights coming into Knockhaven harbour: Tansy had been able to check them out in *Reid's Almanac* in the local library. Someone who hated enough, or loved enough, or was frightened or greedy enough to kill three people to get one . . . She sighed. A hamster probably got pretty sick of going round and round in a wheel getting nowhere as well.

The town hall was a handsome Edwardian building with a gallery across one end and a stage at the other. Trestle tables had been set out to line the walls, laden with plates of the sandwiches, scones and shortbread apparently deemed suitably sombre; tea and coffee were being dispensed from a line of urns just below the stage.

Marjory spotted her mother almost immediately, directing operations to replenish empty plates, and was starting to make her way towards her through the milling throng when Bill's voice at her shoulder hailed her: 'Hello, stranger!'

She turned with a smile to kiss him, wincing inwardly. She hadn't got home for supper once since all this happened and this morning Cat, coming into the kitchen, had given a small shriek and cried, 'Who is this strange woman? Oh yes, I remember – she used to be my mother.' Bill had said Cat seemed to be eating all right, but if his daughter was being devious he would be no match for her.

'Quite a turnout, isn't it?' Bill said. 'Janet's in her element, mind you, queen-beeing around. She's got half of Galloway roped in to help with serving the tea and on baking duties – even Laura's made scones though I'd have to say if she'd told me they were pancakes I wouldn't have argued. She's over there.'

Marjory waved to her friend, then went to speak to her mother. Enid Davis would probably be here somewhere, and perhaps even Joanna Elder as well; Janet always seemed to know everyone, and having been so involved in the organisation for today she might be able to point them out.

Janet delivered the information unhesitatingly. They were part of her army of workers and like any good commander she knew who they were and where they were. 'That's Enid, there, doing the teas. They closed the surgery, of course, as a mark of respect, and the receptionists came to ask what they could do so we put them on the urns. That's Cara Christie, and there's Muriel Henderson, look – spending most of her time blethering as far as I can see.'

Enid Davis wasn't blethering. A pleasant-looking woman, neatly dressed in a navy suit, she was filling polystyrene cups with quiet efficiency and handing them out to a seemingly unending queue. The rumour about her and Lewis Randall seemed improbable on the face of it, but perhaps after a beautiful, selfish and (allegedly) unfaithful wife you might fancy a change.

'And that's Joanna Elder over there – bonny woman, isn't she?' Janet broke off. 'Annie, you'll need to bring through more shortbread. They've been at those plates like gannets.'

Joanna Elder was, indeed, bonny. Wearing a silk blouse of palest pink under a Chanel-style black bouclé wool suit with chunky gold jewellery, she was nibbling a scone as she stood behind one of the tables. She was enviably slim and certainly didn't look as if the death of the woman she had described to Tam as a close friend had caused her too many sleepless nights. It was hard to imagine such a dainty creature scrambling over rocks in darkness – but of course she was probably seriously fit, given the gym and the swimming pool.

Another surge of arrivals obviously marked the end of the burial service for Rob Anderson. Fleming saw that Lewis Randall and his mother were among them, stiff and awkward-looking. Rob must have been his patient so they would have felt reluctantly obliged to put in a token appearance here before the journey to the crematorium. She studied the man with interest; even at this distance you got the impression of an impenetrable reserve.

Following them was a little knot of people clustered round Katy Anderson and the crowd parted respectfully as they went down the hall. A short, burly man had his arm round the widow's shoulders and Ritchie Elder, looking tired and drawn, was just behind as they reached the urn where Enid Davis was serving tea.

The women seemed to know each other. Fleming saw what was almost a smile come to Katy's face and she began a low-voiced conversation with Enid as one of the men took a cup of tea from her and put it into Katy's hand. A few minutes later Joanna Elder went across and seemed to be offering formal condolences.

Her work of identification finished, Fleming glanced round the hall. There was quite a number of people she knew but, though they might nod and smile politely, they avoided conversation. She was marked out as being here in her official capacity and the police failure to reassure a shaken and anxious community with an immediate arrest was being laid at her door. And perhaps they were right, at that. It was a bad feeling.

There was nothing more useful she could do and there would be the usual mountain of paperwork on her desk; if she planned to be home for supper tonight it would make sense to go back and tackle it now. Tam and Tansy were still here; she'd spotted Tam talking to a group of older men and Tansy, having drifted around with a cup in her hand discreetly eavesdropping, was now speaking to Katy Anderson, Enid Davis and Joanna Elder. It would be interesting to hear her report; a good girl, Tansy, and learning all the time.

Fleming couldn't see Jon, though. He seemed to play his cards very close to his chest and it was fair enough for Tam to hint that he wasn't a team player. But the reports he'd turned in were good stuff and if you wanted to use intelligent people you had to give them the chance to prove themselves.

She was just on the point of looking for Bill again to say goodbye when there was a loud banging on a table. The man she had seen with Katy Anderson was on the platform, waiting for silence. 'That's never Willie Duncan going to make a speech!' she heard someone say incredulously.

He began by denying it. 'I'm not making a speech. I'm just saying Katy here'll be needing a wee hand in the pub for the next bit. I'm doing tomorrow night and down there's a list you can put your name to.' He stepped down, his reputation for taciturnity untarnished, and from all across the hall men started forward to volunteer.

Fleming smiled. There were drawbacks to village life, but the generosity of the support you got at times like this more than made up for them. And she didn't envy Willie's job tomorrow night; the pub would be packed to the doors. It wasn't often you had solidarity as an excuse for a few wee bevvies.

No doubt Tam would be putting in for a surveillance detail on that one, but if he thought he was going to get overtime he'd another think coming. A couple of halves of shandy on the taxpayer was her best offer.

Ritchie Elder's eyes were fixed steadfastly on the road as he drove home with his wife after the funeral tea, but his mind was far away. They would be committing her body to the flames now, Ashley's soft, exquisite body, the source of so much delight. His throat constricted; with a physical effort he set his jaw and suppressed the emotion which had left him weeping night after night. They had told him what she'd looked like when they found her and he wished they hadn't. It all seemed to have got worse, not better, after the first shock wore off, and he could almost feel his self-control disintegrating.

He'd moved into one of the spare rooms, making the excuse that with so much on his mind he wasn't sleeping well and didn't want to disturb Joanna. He hadn't said that waking from a restless dream of Ashley, alive and warm and responsive, to touch alien female flesh was intolerable. The dreams where Ashley was cold and dead, with a featureless horror which had been her face, were worse.

Joanna hadn't demurred. Joanna had been smiling and sympathetic, understanding about his all too evident distress. The responsibility, she had murmured, the Press . . .

He'd accepted that response with unreflective gratitude. In his life to date, reflection had been something to do with mirrors and you only went in for analysis if you were a chemist. The game was every man for himself; you dealt with problems with buccaneering zest and when you went to bed you fell asleep immediately after you made love to whoever was lying next to you.

He'd let Ashley, somehow, slip under his guard and he was paying for it now. Wakefulness, in the black hours between midnight and dawn, was a new experience. Suddenly, stealthily, he was being encircled by the emotions he had never even recognised before: love and grief and now fear – fear, fear, fear.

Even in the darkness he felt he was being watched, as if he were under a spotlight while They lurked in the darkness beyond. A woman's face with a cold, penetrating gaze kept coming into his mind, the face of the policewoman who had interviewed him the day after the wreck. He had never had a problem dealing with women. If they stood up to him when he tried to browbeat them, he rather liked it. They wouldn't win the argument, but they could have a bit of fun struggling.

She hadn't bothered to take him on. It was as if she was so much in control of the situation that it wasn't worth her while, and that scared him. Women, in his experience, didn't act like that. Perhaps he didn't know as much about women as he would like to think. Joanna, for instance . . .

Had she really known nothing, suspected nothing? Never heard the gossip, never been troubled by his own distaste for the emaciated body which had somehow become a weapon used against him in their childless marriage?

He stole a glance at her. She seemed perfectly relaxed in the silence which had lasted since they left Knockhaven, her small neat hands with their pink-tinted nails clasped loosely in her lap. And – or was it his imagination? – the gaunt contours of her face seemed softer, somehow, more rounded. He realised he hadn't seen her in the gym since it all happened.

Aware of his regard, she turned and smiled. He smiled back, somehow, but the thought having entered his head couldn't be shaken out. It had never occurred to him before to wonder what Joanna was like, as a person; she was just his wife, a fixture in his life, until the day came when Ashley had changed all that. After that, Joanna had become an encumbrance in his eyes, treated almost with contempt.

Had she *really* noticed nothing? he asked himself again. What if she had known, all along? What if she had watched, and waited and then – acted? Someone had.

There was the house now. He turned in and as he parked

the Mitsubishi by the front door, Joanna leaned across to pat his hand. 'You go into the sitting room, darling, and I'll bring you a stiff whisky. You need it, after all that. It's been a hellish day.' She jumped down and let herself into the house ahead of him.

The perfect wife. He followed her more slowly. Perhaps whisky was the answer – a lot of whisky. He couldn't think of any other way of dealing with the problems that were making his head feel as if it might burst.

There wasn't much pleasure in a night down the pub when you could barely raise your elbow for the heaving, sweaty mass of bodies and you were having to drive back afterwards anyway, Tam MacNee reflected morosely. He'd managed to take part of the day off, seeing it was Sunday, and he hadn't felt a bit like leaving Bunty and his own fireside.

Most of Knockhaven seemed to have turned out to show support and in the Anchor this evening, the condensation running down the inside of the windows was almost as bad as the rain now streaming down the outside. Behind the bar, Willie Duncan and three of his mates were hard at it, in-expertly pulling pints and serving shots in hastily washed, smeary glasses.

The worst of it was, MacNee wasn't getting anywhere. He'd had a lot of grief from the punters – jokes, questions, sly remarks and downright aggro about the lack of progress. Even the jokes had an undertone of uneasiness; the whole town was on edge even as they made a show of going about business as usual. He hadn't picked up anything either new or useful from the general conversations, which rapidly took refuge in the safe topic of football, and while he had nothing against discussion of the Beautiful Game, it wasn't enough to justify a car journey on a dirty night like this. Shandy had a limited appeal too. He might as well cut his losses and head for home. He was edging his way gloomily towards the bar to return his empty glass when a burst of raucous laughter made him turn his head.

A group of young men had colonised the corner to his right. They weren't quite drunk yet, just well on the way. MacNee was familiar with several of them, including Willie Duncan's son Ryan, all jobless and at least a couple with drugs raps on their record. He'd be astonished if the rest of them were clean.

He didn't recognise the one who was the centre of their attention, wearing a ripped black T-shirt and with hair gelled into spikes. There was a stud glinting in the side of his nose and he had a cluster of dull metal earrings; a vivid snake tattoo coiled up the side of his neck. 'Here, mate – it's your shout!' he called to a red-haired boy with a nasty case of acne, then he added a remark which MacNee couldn't catch, but which provoked another burst of laughter.

The accent – MacNee couldn't quite place it. Scots, obviously, and definitely not local, with that sort of urban edge to it. Alarm bells jangled: someone new on the patch, down from the big city, hanging around with this lot – he might just as well be holding a placard above his head with 'drugs scene' written on it. Things were messy enough here already without a turf war starting. He was beginning to edge discreetly closer when the spike-haired youth, as if feeling eyes upon him, turned his head.

MacNee felt his jaw physically drop. Blandly, DC Kingsley allowed his eyes to slide off the other detective's face, then turned back to take his pint from his red-haired companion. 'Here – you've slopped this, Dougie!' he complained. 'Gie's a wee sook of yours to make up.'

The voices rose again in joking argument as MacNee set down his own empty glass and shouldered his way through to the door, oblivious to the drinks he too managed to slop on the way and to the imprecations that followed, half-blind with rage.

Operation Songbird had been his initiative. He'd been working on it for weeks now, getting to know the players, getting accepted as just another bloke in the bar even if he was in the polis, cannily pulling together all the tiny scraps of information until they led him to Willie Duncan. Willie wasn't the big man, but he was working for him and knew who the big man was. MacNee had been close to breaking him too; the last time they'd talked he could see Willie struggling between fear of reprisal and desperation to have the questioning stop. He'd seen it in a hundred criminal confessions – the moment when the balance tipped – and he'd been almost there. With all that had happened, the moment slipped away, but MacNee would get back to him again. And again. And again. And he'd break, eventually.

Kingsley had been told, in no uncertain terms, the limits of his brief, and he'd blatantly ignored them. That could be a great big black mark on the cocky sod's precious professional record.

His head down, MacNee ran along Shore Street towards his car in the darkness and teeming rain. Its stinging freshness was almost welcome after the stale, unhealthy atmosphere inside. As he licked at the raindrops trickling down his upper lip, his temper began to cool as well.

After all, what could he really claim to have achieved recently? Tonight had been a complete bust and the plan to bring more pressure to bear on Willie had to be at best medium term, if the man was refusing to speak to him at the moment.

Kingsley was in there talking to the right people and he looked the part – even the tattoo looked kosher. And the bastard had managed to sound the part too, which was harder still. It was a classy operation. Sooner rather than later, he'd be put on to a supplier, getting hold of that elusive end of the thread. To make a complaint would make MacNee look jealous and spiteful. And unprofessional – the very charge he had felt the boss was unfairly levelling at him when Kingsley first arrived.

It genuinely wasn't that the man was a Sassenach. Tam had had some rare nights out with English lads who took the jokes and gave as good as they got, to mutual satisfaction. It wasn't even the degree and the toffee-nosed manner. Well, maybe it was a bit, and he'd bristled too because Marjory had seemed to suggest Kingsley merited special treatment. But he'd have got over that if it wasn't for the man being only out for himself. He'd no interest in being part of a team. He wanted to do it all, get all the credit going, keep everyone else out of it as if the investigation was his personal property – MacNee stopped. The rain was trickling down the inside of the collar of his leather jacket but he didn't notice.

'*O wad some Power the giftie gie us, To see ourrels as ithers see us!*' Why was it that on the occasions when the Power chose to confer that gift, it so often spoke with Bunty's voice? 'You daft fool!' it was saying to him now. 'You're like two cocks crowing over the same midden!'

He walked on and reaching his car, let himself in. His hair was dripping into his eyes; all he could find to mop it with was the duster he kept to wipe the windows, but it was better than nothing. When he could see again he drove off.

Maybe the boss had been right about lack of professionalism. Maybe, if he hadn't been so touchy to start with, they could have been working together on this, actually getting a result. They were on the same side, after all.

It wasn't too late. Tomorrow he could go in and congratulate the man, tell him to keep up the good work. It would be the generous thing to do, the right thing to do.

And, as another voice – which certainly wasn't Bunty's –

whispered wickedly in his ear, he could fairly enjoy seeing the feet ca'ed away from under Jon Kingsley.

In his bedroom at the back of the flat above the Anchor, Nat Rettie could hear voices and laughter filtering up from the bar below. He had been playing computer games most of the evening, to blot out his uncomfortable thoughts.

He'd been less than thrilled to see Kylie this morning. For God's sake, he was in trouble enough already, without the silly little slapper suggesting taking his mother's car and going off somewhere while everyone was at the funeral tea. With the Filth all over the town like a rash!

It was always the guy that got done for under-age sex – what about the girl? It should be illegal for her to do it too, but oh no, all she would get was sympathy while he took the rap if he got her pregnant. And he'd a nasty feeling Kylie quite fancied that, what with one of her sixteen-year-old pals with a baby having her own flat and everything. Nat wasn't getting into that kind of crap.

But he daren't dump her. She could really drop him in it, so he'd just have to sweet-talk her a bit longer, make sure she knew what to say if she was asked. Anyway, he was counting on moving away from here, disappearing for a bit. If he could get his mother to sell the pub there'd be money and she'd probably give him half just to get rid of him. She'd made it pretty clear after she married Rob that Nat was in the way.

She'd just ignored him since he came back. She didn't cook for him any more, or do the shopping. Luckily the neighbours were still handing in food and she'd had money in her purse so Nat could buy stuff for himself. When that ran out he could probably nick some from the till in the bar, but what he really wanted was some serious cash so he could get away from this minging place. Certainly the last thing he needed – the very last thing – was all those helpful bastards downstairs interfering, propping her up to keep the pub going till she was ready to take it on again herself.

He'd taken her a cup of tea a few times, been really nice and asked how she was and all that stuff, but she only looked at him as if she didn't know who he was. She spent all her time shut in the lounge reading old letters and looking at photographs and newspapers about every lifeboat rescue there had ever been and how great bloody Rob had been and all.

Nat tore angrily at the skin round his thumbnail; he'd no nails left to bite. He hated feeling trapped, helpless, with the police sniffing around everywhere. It made him scared, gave him a sort of savage feeling inside.

He started another game – one of his favourites, this was. In this he could do what he liked, satisfy every violent impulse. And if it all went wrong – well, with a game you could just crash it and start again. But his mind wasn't entirely on the screen in front of him.

He sat back from the screen, frowning. Then he looked at his watch, jumped up and left the room.

With some relief, Willie Duncan chased out the stragglers at the end of drinking-up time, then with the two men who had been helping him in his bar duties began to collect up empty glasses and full ash-trays.

'I never kent what hard work it was, being on this side,' one of them said ruefully. 'I'd rather a Force 10 in the Irish Sea – at least you're spared the backchat.'

'We've taken good money tonight, though,' the other pointed out. 'She'll be needing it, poor lassie.'

Willie grunted, dumping another tray of glasses by the sink below the counter and running in water to wash them, set grimly about his task, ignoring the jokes about his domestic talents.

It was gone half-past eleven before they were finished and the two helpers went home, leaving Willie to put the bulk of the takings in the safe and lock up. He switched off the lights and let himself out, locking the double doors behind him.

Outside, the heavy rain had settled into a steady drizzle. The yellow street lights had a misty halo as he walked along the deserted Shore Street with its darkened houses, the only sound his own footfalls on the wet, glistening pavement. He'd left the bike behind tonight; he might have taken a chance on his blood alcohol level normally, but not with all these coppers coming out of the woodwork. And Tam MacNee hadn't given up either – oh, he'd seen the way he was round everyone in the pub, even though no one seemed to be giving him the time of day. That problem hadn't gone away, but at least Willie'd come clean about it so he was in the clear as long as he kept his mouth shut. He wasn't scared now like he had been.

He cut round to the back of the pub, then crossed the open area to Baker's Brae, the steep, cobbled wynd which was a short-cut to his home at the top of the town.

He didn't see the car, with no lights and number plates obscured by mud, suddenly appear from a shadowed corner formed by the angles of the buildings round the rough square and turn up behind him between the high walls. It was only the sudden roar of the engine that made him turn, and then there was nothing he could do except give one desperate scream of terror, then agony.

A moment later the car, its hideous work done, accelerated away.

Marjory Fleming was very deeply asleep when the phone rang. Her heart pounding in alarm, gasping like a swimmer breaking the surface, she sat up, groping for it in the dark. Her eyes were still closed as she mumbled, 'Yes?'

A moment later, she was wide awake. Listening with horror to what she was being told, she switched on the light and swung herself out of bed.

As she replaced the receiver, Bill opened his eyes and said groggily, 'Problems?'

'Mmm. Tell you tomorrow. You go back to sleep.'

She rapidly found underwear, trousers and a thick sweater and crept out to change in the bathroom, switching off the light as she went. Almost immediately, she heard him start to snore gently.

It felt very lonely in the dark, silent house at one in the morning, faced with disaster. Tomorrow she would have a furious Superintendent and the jackals of the Press tearing her apart for failing to give Willie Duncan round-the-clock protection after what anyone equipped with 20/20 hindsight could see had been an attempt on his life. But worse than that, so much, much worse, was the knowledge that a woman was a widow because she, Marjory, had failed to find the killer in time.

14

Superintendent Donald Bailey's brow was so deeply furrowed that the creases were running right up into his bald crown, while the lines of disapproval round his mouth extended themselves into his second chin.

'This is a disaster, Marjory, a disaster! It'll mean questions, you know, about our fitness for that most fundamental of police duties – the protection of our citizens! What are you planning to do about it?' Fresh from an uncomfortable phone conversation with his own superior officer, Bailey was working on the pay-it-forward principle.

'We', Fleming reflected sourly, would have been a nicer word than 'you', keeping up at least the fiction that they were all in this together. The shower she'd had here at six in the morning had been less than wholly effective as a substitute for a proper night's sleep; her eyes were gritty and her tongue felt thick in her mouth.

'There's no simple answer to that, Don,' she said wearily. 'As you know. The only thing I can say is that it gives us a bit more we can focus on – we know that the murderer was on the spot this time and we know precisely when.'

'And with luck, there should be car damage and paint samples to follow up on?' Fleming did not comment and he went on, 'As I said to the Chief Constable, at least we know now who was the intended victim, and why. Shocking to think of those three brave souls dying so unnecessarily.'

'Indeed.' He had to be right about that, and Fleming had

to accept that her own instinct had been wrong. 'Naturally we're homing in on the drugs angle.'

'Naturally. And it might even give us a breakthrough there – the victim being a local man like Duncan, people may be more ready to come forward—' Bailey was cheering up; he was possessed of an optimistic nature, even if events rarely allowed him to indulge it.

Feeling brutal, Fleming cautioned, 'It's hard to say. It could work in the other direction – scare them even more.'

'Yes. Yes, I suppose so.' Gloom returned. 'Anyway, what's young Kingsley saying about this? I'm impressed with him – very much on the ball.'

'I'll be catching up with him later,' Fleming said evasively. Not that it wasn't true. And when she did, she'd fillet him with a blunt knife. She wasn't amused by constables who didn't report for duty and switched their phones off. 'I'm seeing MacNee and Kerr as well and we'll be heading down to Knockhaven straight away.' She got up. 'Unless there's anything more . . . ?'

Bailey rose too and went to open the door for her. A good sign – it suggested forgiveness.

He said, disarmingly, 'Good luck, Marjory. Don't think I underestimate the onerous nature of your position, ground between the upper and the nether millstone. I've done the job and my Super was a bastard too. It goes with the territory.'

It was why she could never truly dislike him: every so often a very human aspect popped out, like a tortoise's head, from within the carapace of his pomposity. She smiled at him but as she walked back to her office the smile faded. Where the hell was bloody Jon Kingsley?

MacNee and Kerr, waiting in her office, had both, of course, heard the news about Willie Duncan, but it was her task to fill in the details.

'He'd nowhere to go; the lane – Baker's Brae – runs between two high walls and it's only two feet or so, three at most, wider than a car. Someone heard him scream and went out to see. Nasty – very, very nasty. From the pathologist's initial observations, it looks as if he half-turned when he heard the car, then tried to run and slipped on the wet cobbles.'

'Just went under the wheels?' MacNee's face was very sombre.

'Twice.' Fleming swallowed, trying to put out of her mind the face, contorted in mortal agony, and the savage remark from one of the SOCOs – 'Treated like roadkill, wasn't he?' 'Apparently the bastard reversed and went over him again to make sure.'

Kerr shuddered. 'That's horrible.'

'Yes. And the other thing is that it doesn't look as if there was damage to the car, unless by any chance it caught the walls of the lane before or after. No paint samples, nothing needing garage attention.'

'Nothing a good hose-down couldn't sort out?'

'Right, Tam. I couldn't bear to tell Donald – it was the only straw he could find to cling to. There's a possibility the make and the tread of the tyres just might be identifiable –' and she didn't like to think why – 'but that's only going to be useful if we have someone in the frame. I've ordered every local car-wash to close for the same reason – if the car has to be washed at home there should be traces on the ground and in the pipe crevices in the drains. But again, that'll only be useful when we can finger someone. It's not a lead. And of course, everyone in the village knew what Willie was doing that night – we were all there at the tea when he announced it to the assembled company. So that's not a lead either. Story of our life, on this case.

'Now, on another tack, does anyone know where Jon is?'

MacNee and Kerr exchanged surprised looks. 'We thought he was at Knockhaven already,' MacNee said. 'He was there last night, and I reckoned he must have been on the spot when it happened.'

'Where was he last night?'

'Ah.' MacNee paused. 'I was going to mention that sometime. He was undercover in the Anchor, chatting up some of the likely lads.'

Fleming's brows rose. 'He'd no authorisation—'

'Right enough. And to be honest, it got right up my nose. But I have to say he was good – gelled hair, tattoo, earrings, the lot, and if it's going to get results you can't haver on about procedure.'

'That's all very well, but it still doesn't answer my question – where is he? He certainly wasn't at the scene last night.'

MacNee coughed delicately. 'Given what I saw of the way he was getting into his part, I doubt he'd not be wanting to drive home.'

It didn't impress his boss. 'You mean, he's down there somewhere nursing a hangover? He's going to have to learn to hold his liquor or else drink a bit more slowly.'

'You don't think anything's – well – happened to him?' Kerr broke in anxiously. 'You said he was hanging around with the druggies, Tam. Maybe he wasn't as convincing as he looked to you?'

There was an appalled silence. Then MacNee said, 'The lads he was with were convinced all right. But what may have happened after . . .'

'Right.' Fleming grabbed her bag and car keys. 'We're on our way.'

The screens were still up, blocking Baker's Brae at both ends, and men in white coveralls were coming and going from a couple of big white vans parked in the area at the bottom, behind the Anchor Inn.

A crowd had gathered too. The morning after the wreck, the village had been all but deserted, the few shoppers shocked and subdued; today it was buzzing. Almost like a swarm of bees, unpredictable and threatening, Fleming thought as she got out of her car and walked across to give her name to the constable recording visitors to the scene. The hum of talk swelled briefly at her arrival, then died as she moved out of sight behind the screens.

The lights which had been brought in last night were still in place, but all the investigation and photography involving Willie Duncan's sad, broken body must have been completed, and it was gone. It would be lying now, tagged, on a mortuary slab awaiting the attentions of the pathologist; attending herself, as she would have to do later, was one of Fleming's most disturbing duties.

A tarpaulin had been spread out to cover the area which would still be showing the terrible evidence of the crime, and the reason for this delicacy became apparent when Fleming realised there were two women standing just to her left with a policewoman she didn't recognise, most likely from the local station.

The older of the two, with starkly black hair untidily gathered into a bunch at the back, seemed a little more composed than the artificially blonde girl who was hanging on to her arm and sobbing. Duncan's wife and daughter, Fleming guessed, and bracing herself she turned to speak to them.

'DI Fleming, the Senior Investigating Officer. Good morning.'

The policewoman spoke first. 'Good morning, ma'am. PC MacLean. This is Mrs Duncan and this is Karyn. There's a son, Ryan, as well, but he isn't here at the moment.'

Fleming shook Jackie Duncan's hand and Karyn, still crying, held out hers too. 'I'm so sorry about this – your husband, your father . . .' She spoke warily; it was never easy to predict the reception you would get following a death. Responses ranged from physical violence to, even more unnervingly in Fleming's opinion, humble gratitude that you were there. It was the first time she had encountered embarrassment, evident as Jackie's face, bleak and tearless before, suddenly flared scarlet and her eyes filled.

'Oh, Inspector, he wasn't a bad man, really! I'm so ashamed – I know what he was doing was wrong and wicked and I told him he'd be punished for it. But I never thought of this – he didn't deserve this, being run down like a stray dog in the road!

'He just wouldn't listen to me, wouldn't even admit what he was doing. I used to get angry with his bare-faced lies, but he was angry too, angry for a long time because with them killing off the fishing he'd to take handouts instead of doing a proper job of work. "I'm on the scrap heap," he used to say – that's a terrible thing for a proud man.

'When he went out it was always just for crabs and lobsters, he said, but it was all round the village what he was up to – him and others too. I've lost friends because of that, and clients too.'

'Mum!' Karyn's tears had stopped and she was shaking her mother's arm urgently. 'You shouldn't be saying these things – you're just upset—'

'Why shouldn't I? Do you think someone's going to come after me? At least then I might find out who's behind it, who did this to Willie, even if all I could do was curse them with my dying breath—'

She broke down. MacLean put an arm round her shoulders and Fleming said, 'Mrs Duncan, I think you should let Constable MacLean take you back home now. I hear what you say and I promise you we won't rest until we find whoever is responsible for this. Unless there's anything more you think you can tell me now that might point us in the right direction –'

'Oh God, I wish I did!'

'– I think we should leave it there. Someone will come and talk to you later when you're not so distressed. And you too, Karyn.'

The girl muttered, 'Sure,' without looking up. Fleming raised her eyebrows; she and the constable exchanged glances. As the Duncans went out, Fleming murmured, 'You'll pick up on that?' Then, as the other woman nodded, added casually, 'Oh, by the way, you haven't seen DC Jon Kingsley this morning, have you?'

MacLean looked blank. 'Don't think I know him, ma'am. There certainly hasn't been anyone in plain clothes around while I've been here.'

'Fine.' There was no point in starting a hue-and-cry if Kingsley was quietly sleeping it off somewhere; on the other hand she was beginning to feel it would be a considerable relief when he appeared. And if he'd recovered from his headache by then she'd make damn sure it came back, with a vengeance.

After a brief conversation with the scene of crime manager and the constable whose record, when she asked to glance at it, showed no note of Kingsley either, she turned to go back to her car and heard a screech of brakes. A big 4WD, a Mitsubishi, had come to a sudden standstill. Leaving it double-parked, Ritchie Elder jumped down from it and came across to intercept her.

'I hoped I might find you here,' he said roughly. 'How can you have failed to prevent this latest disaster? There are questions needing answers.'

He looked terrible. She had thought him tired and strained

at the funeral, but this morning, unshaven, dishevelled and wearing a thick navy sweater and lightweight brown trousers apparently snatched at random from his wardrobe, he was barely recognisable as the suave and stylish man she had interviewed the morning after the wreck.

'I have one or two of those myself, Mr Elder. Perhaps we could make use of your office at the lifeboat shed? I can follow you along and you can move your car before it causes an obstruction.'

She walked away from him, well aware that by so forcefully taking control of the situation she was putting him at a disadvantage – not that it looked, at the moment, as if getting the upper hand was going to be a problem.

On her way along Shore Street she spotted Tam MacNee, with Tansy, talking to a small group of men, and on an impulse stopped. 'Hop in, Tam, I've got a job for you. All right, Tansy?'

Kerr nodded and MacNee got in. 'Good timing, boss. It was all getting kinda nasty there but they won't take it out on Tansy – she looks such an innocent wee soul. Could fool anyone with those big brown eyes.'

'Her Majesty's Constabulary not top of the pops, then?'

'First to be voted out of the Big Brother house, I reckon. They all think they're about to be murdered in their beds and for some reason they seem a bit fashed about it.'

'At this rate, they could be right.' The Mitsubishi went past them and she pointed as it drew up outside the lifeboat shed. 'That's Elder. I thought you could ride shotgun on this interview. He says he wants to put us on the spot.'

'That's what you'd call a coincidence, isn't it?'

'Are you thinking what I'm thinking?'

'If that's what you're thinking, I've thought that for weeks now. Who around here's loaded, with a business that could fairly have been designed for money-laundering? Who's got interests in Ireland, where we reckon the stuff's mostly coming from? Who was at school with Willie Duncan and would know he could rely on him to do as he was told and keep his mouth shut?'

'Absolutely. But Tam, why would he wreck a boat knowing it would mean killing the woman he was in love with?'

'I've been thinking about that. Do we know that it *wasn't* just a rumour? No one seems to have any evidence. And maybe he'll be thinking it's quite a convenient cover story now.'

'But he denied it, Tam, when I spoke to him.'

'Didn't think he'd be suspected at the time? Keeping it in reserve?' MacNee shrugged. 'You have to remember he went daft when he heard Willie hadn't gone out with the boat.'

'To play devil's advocate, that could just be because he was worried about her going out in bad weather with an inexperienced cox.'

'Maybe. So what'll he say, then, when we pin him to the wall in there?'

'If he's guilty, he'll start trying to convince us he was in love with her so he wouldn't have done anything that could harm her. And that Willie was a good mate and he wouldn't harm him either. And if he's innocent—'

'He'll say the same thing.'

She groaned. 'Come on, we'd better get on with it.' As they got out of the car she said, 'It's like that puzzle about the two identical tribes – one lot can't tell the truth, the other can't tell lies, and you meet one at a fork in the road. You have to know which way leads to the town instead of a crocodile-infested swamp and you're only allowed one question. You know that one?'

'No, what—?'

Elder was standing waiting for them. 'Tell you later. Oh – any word of Jon?'

MacNee shook his head. 'He'll turn up. Only the good die young.'

As they reached the shed, Elder said frigidly, 'Do come in,' holding open the door. They went ahead of him, the sound of their footsteps echoing in the soaring emptiness above them, and Fleming led the way into the tiny office where she and MacNee sat down on two small upright chairs. Elder took his seat behind the desk and with an assumption of authority began, 'Now, Inspector—'

'Yes,' Fleming said. 'Mr Elder, we're looking for a drug trafficker who's behind all this. And we're coming to the conclusion that it may well be you.'

Even MacNee blinked in shock. Elder recoiled, as if she had physically struck him across the face.

'What – what – I don't know what you mean—'

'Don't treat me like a fool. Of course you do.' He was starting to sweat already. Good.

MacNee leaned forward. 'I think the inspector means that in a situation like this, where two very serious crimes have been committed, both needing local knowledge, and where there is suspicion that it may be drugs-related, anyone who's wealthy and in a business using a lot of casual labour, is bound to be a suspect.'

This time it was Fleming's turn to be startled. It was only when Tam turned a bland face towards her that she remembered her challenge to him. Well, if he fancied the 'nice cop' role, she knew what hers was.

'That's the mealy-mouthed way of putting it. Let's start with where you were, precisely, at eleven-fifty last night, when the owners of a property adjoining Baker's Brae heard screams of agony and ran out to find Willie Duncan's body, flattened by the tyres of the vehicle which had run over him.' Seeing the look on his face, she added, 'Twice,' for good measure.

Elder was fighting for composure. 'At home in bed. You
– you can ask my wife—'

'And I take it there would be no objection to offering your
vehicle for inspection?'

He jumped at that. 'Certainly. None. I will give you the
keys, and I won't even ask for a warrant.'

'Mind you, it's not just the one you've access to, is it?'
Tam broke in. 'What about the business cars? And the vans?'

'Check any you like.'

'And that wee sporty number your wife has?'

There was a slight hesitation, then he said, 'It's her car.
You would have to ask her.'

'That's a fine cop-out,' MacNee sneered and Fleming
had to bite her lip. The nice-cop resolution hadn't lasted
long. She wasn't about to step in to fill the vacancy herself; she didn't think Elder would be dumb enough to fall
for it anyway.

'Let's move on to the other occasion, Mr Elder. The evening
the lifeboat was wrecked. What precisely were your movements on that occasion? If I remember your statement and
the statements of the saleswomen in the showhouse, you were
at Fuill's Inlat, although they didn't see you until you went
in to tell them there had been a call-out and you were leaving?'

'That's right. Yes.'

'Perhaps you could expand on that a little for us. I have to
confess I can't recall, offhand, how much time elapsed between
the call from the coastguard and when you spoke to them?
Though it will, of course, be a matter of record.' She really
had him sweating now; he'd taken out a handkerchief and
was dabbing his brow.

'I – I was talking to some people – prospective clients – I
don't know who exactly—'

'Strange,' Fleming mused. 'I don't recollect a report of any
of them mentioning that. We can always ask them again—'

'They – they might have forgotten—'

'Oh, come on, sunshine, you can do better than that! The big man himself, chatting up the punters, and they wouldn't remember?' MacNee's laconic drawl was pure, distilled scepticism. 'What were you doing – skulking around the bay, putting the lights in place?'

'No!' It was an animal-like howl and Fleming eyed him sharply. She'd been keeping him off balance to stop him thinking calmly enough to clam up and send for his lawyer, but she didn't want him falling apart altogether. It was like trying to land a salmon; this might be the time to cut him a bit of slack.

She said, much more gently, 'I wonder, Mr Elder, if you are beginning to feel you wish to – adjust some of the information you gave me on the occasion of our last meeting?'

He mopped his face again. His lips were trembling and he dabbed at his mouth before he spoke. 'Yes. I – I wasn't open with you. I rubbished the story about Ashley and myself because she was dead. What would be the point of admitting it? It would have meant trouble all round – her husband, my wife. And I have no reason to embark on a divorce now. But yes,' he bent his head, 'she and I were very much in love. We were together that night when the call came in. She'd just agreed to marry me—' He put the handkerchief to his eyes.

'Well, that's all very fine and good.' MacNee's tone was vicious. 'It's a nice performance. But you see, Elder, we've only your word for it. There's plenty of rumours, but no one's seen the two of you together. And your own wife said you chatting up Ashley at a party would be enough to get a story like that started.'

'You've spoken to my wife?'

'Oh aye. That was before this latest business, though. See here, Willie was into drug dealing – we know that fine. And he'd been worried about being seen talking to me – did that scare you? Just in case for once he'd discovered he'd a tongue?'

'You think I would have done something like that, to silence Willie?'

'Someone did,' Fleming pointed out.

'But not me! Look, the reason no one saw Ashley and me together was because we were careful, for God's sake! We both had positions in the community. We met, mostly, at the showhouse, once it was furnished.'

That suggested an interesting thought: was the ersatz domesticity of a showhouse bedroom a reflection of their relationship, a shallow illusion of glamour and the good life? From what Fleming had heard of Ashley Randall, true love would have been unlikely to strike if Ritchie had been the lifeboat mechanic instead of the Honorary Secretary, but looking at the wreck of a man in front of her, she could almost believe that what he was saying was genuinely felt.

'So where do you claim you were at the time the call from the coastguard came?' MacNee pursued.

'I don't *claim*, we met at a pub near Glasserton – the Black Bull.'

MacNee made a note of that. 'So they'll remember you there? We can check that out.'

'We deliberately chose a pub where we wouldn't be recognised. And it was a busy evening – the barmaid was more interested in her social life than her customers.'

'I see. Someone else who might have forgotten you being there? Funny, isn't it, the way all these people you meet seem to be suffering from memory loss?'

'No, no! It's only that girl—' He stopped.

'Oh, of course. Sorry, sorry. You've got me forgetting things now.' MacNee was having a fine time. 'The other people who'd forgotten you were there were right, you weren't there. You just told us you were, briefly, before you changed your mind. Now, before you get me even more mixed up, did you mean to say you were really down on the shore, fixing those lanterns?'

Elder put his head in his hands. 'This is intolerable!'

'Queer the things people find intolerable,' MacNee said conversationally. 'What I call intolerable is a man flattened on the road, and a wreck that killed two men and left one woman dead with her face smashed in.'

At these words Elder looked up, his face taking on a greenish tinge. He jumped up, his hand pressed to his mouth, and stumbled out of the room.

'Gone to boak,' MacNee said with coarse satisfaction.

'Tam, you went too far,' Fleming said. 'That was genuine enough, you know – you can't fake that kind of revulsion.'

'Maybe. But if you were cold-blooded enough to kill your oldest friend and the woman you were screwing – we've only his word for it about the touching proposal scene – thinking in detail about the result might easily make your stomach heave.'

He had a point there. 'Laura talked about pathological solipsism,' Fleming said thoughtfully.

'What's that, when it's at home?'

'Selfishness, to the degree where no one else matters in pursuing your own interest. And what you just said would be a perfect illustration.'

'She's not daft, Laura.'

Fleming nodded, then glanced at her watch. 'He's taking a long time. I hope this hasn't just given him time to think and get himself organised, before we move on to the drugs stuff.'

MacNee looked crestfallen. 'Maybe. He's been a while, right enough.'

A little silence fell, then MacNee said, 'What was the question?'

'The question?'

'The one you ask to find out which road to take.'

Fleming laughed. 'Oh, that question! You have to say, "If you were a member of the other tribe, which road would you tell me to take?" The lying man will tell you the wrong one, the truthful man will tell you the wrong one as well, so you take the opposite road.'

It took a moment for MacNee to digest it, then he said, 'I like that. I could see it working in interrogations – ask the lad who's protesting he's innocent what he'd say if he wasn't, and since you can assume he's lying, because they always do—'

'I think you're taking me out of my depth here, Tam. Anyway, that's him coming back.'

Elder was still pale, but he looked much more composed. 'Can we conclude this interview for the time being? I'm not well – I've been under a lot of stress lately, obviously.'

'Oh, just a couple more things,' Tam said. 'I've a question to put to you. We've as good as accused you of being a drug trafficker. Supposing, just supposing, you were, what would you say?'

Elder looked down at him contemptuously. 'I would say exactly the same thing as I would say if I were innocent. As indeed I am. I would say, "This is a ludicrous suggestion and since you haven't arrested me I can only assume you have no evidence to back it up. I am therefore refusing to say anything until my lawyer is present." And that's what I'm saying now.'

As they went back to the car, MacNee was looking crestfallen. 'Och well, you win some, you lose some.'

'We weren't going to get him so upset he confessed anyway,' Fleming said, 'and he's given us quite a bit to follow up on. Though I have to say it's all pretty negative stuff – he might not be able to prove he was where he said he was, but it won't be easy to prove he wasn't to the Fiscal's satisfaction.

'Oh, there's Tansy. I wonder if she's caught up with Jon?'

But Kerr's worried expression told them she hadn't. 'No one's seen him. And I checked discreetly with HQ and he hasn't turned up there either.'

'So we have to start taking this seriously.' Fleming's face was grim.

'I recognised some of the lads he was with last night,' MacNee said. 'I could try and find them – see if they know where he is without blowing his cover. But if I draw a blank—'

'I know. Then I think the balloon will have to go up.'

15

Lewis Randall came out of his surgery and on his way out for lunch stopped at the reception desk. Enid Davis was there, neat as always in a pale blue shirt-blouse; she looked up and smiled at his approach.

'Enid, I'm just going to look in to see Mrs Duncan on my way home. She must be in a terrible state of shock and she has to watch her blood-pressure.' He looked shaken himself, with dark shadows under his eyes.

'You are good. I'm sure she'll appreciate that. I know how difficult it was for poor Katy Anderson to have to come in here after the last tragedy.'

'Yes, all those people staring at her!' Muriel Henderson, who had been working at one of the filing cabinets, came over with the speed of a heat-seeking missile. 'So intrusive!'

'Yes indeed,' Randall said, without emphasis. 'Anyway, I'll have my mobile with me if I'm needed.' He went out.

'Muriel, I'm off now too. Mrs McNally's still in the waiting room – Dr Matthews is running late this morning. And Cara should be back in half an hour to let you away.' Enid headed for the back office to collect her coat.

'Thank you, Enid,' Muriel said frostily. She had not forgiven her for the way she had spoken, and she hadn't forgotten her suspicions either. That little exchange had been quite blatant – her leaving whenever he did, and him reminding her he had his mobile so he could let her know when he'd finished at the Duncans'. She must remember to pass *that* on to the constable, next time she saw him.

This would have to stop. Katy Anderson looked wearily about at the litter of memories she had surrounded herself with, all she still had to prove that her life with Rob hadn't been a dream: the photos, the pressed rose from her wedding posy, the programme from the Glasgow show they'd gone to on their first date . . . It had been her relief from the rest of the sorting out she'd had to do, removing Rob's pyjamas from the pillow, throwing out his toothbrush and shaving things. His clothes . . . she'd just had to shut the door of his wardrobe and leave that, until at some unimaginable future date the pain became bearable.

It had helped at first to blot out the intolerable present with the past, reliving the presentation of Rob's RNLI medal from the yellowing report and photo in the *Galloway Globe*, the surprise weekend in Paris from an old, sweetly sentimental birthday card. But it wasn't working now. Last night's tragedy had shocked her back to the reality that was this terrible new life.

What was happening, in this peaceful, friendly place where she had been so happy? Somehow, after Rob's death she had been too numbed with shock to ask questions; now, 'Why? Who?' was a constant beating inside her head.

Could she bear to go on living here, with the front windows of this very room giving a view of the sea which had taken Rob from her, and the back one of the place where Willie Duncan had died, where without even turning her head she could see the police screens and the gathering pile of flowers beside them? Could she walk down the street there and meet her neighbours, while she wondered if it was one of them who had done these awful things? It was horrible, horrible – but where else was she to go?

Then there was Nat. Sooner, rather than later, she would have to confront the problem. She had tried to blot out her terrible suspicions, and she'd been grateful to Enid Davis, who had made a case for him. Grateful – but not completely convinced. To someone naive, of course mothers and sons loved each other and estrangements were no more than mis-understandings. And perhaps she did love him really, even if all she felt about living with him, without Rob's presence to protect her, was a shrinking fear.

She had seen hatred in Nat's face when he looked at Rob – yes, and at her too, sometimes, hatred and contempt. In the initial shock, she had hardly noticed whether he was in the house or not, but now she was becoming aware that he was trying to make up to her, with cups of tea and sympathetic enquiries. Perhaps he did feel sorry for her, did feel guilty about his past behaviour, and perhaps she should be giving him the benefit of the doubt, but yesterday she had caught a look on his face as he turned to leave the room which was neither kindly nor apologetic.

She needed a breathing space – maybe they both did. She couldn't send him back to his father, of course, who was responsible for much of the damage that had been done to their son, but she'd always got on well with Dave's mother, a decent woman who might find Nat a suitable place near her in Glasgow for the time being. Or would that only make things worse? Oh, she needed Rob, Rob who was kind but tough, to put things in perspective . . . She pressed her lips together, hard. She couldn't have Rob, that was all, and she'd have to get used to it.

When the doorbell rang, it occurred to Katy to wonder if it might be Enid Davis. They'd talked a bit at the funeral tea; she'd discovered that they had both suffered badly from an unhappy first marriage, and she'd been helpful about Nat before, too, even if Katy did think she might have a rather idealistic notion of teenage boys. It would be a lucky coincidence if it was Enid.

It wasn't. When she opened the door it was Joanna Elder who stood there, stylish as always in a cream wool coat with a luxurious fake-fur collar. She had a basket looped over one arm and was carrying an elaborate floral arrangement of pink and white lilies.

'Mrs Elder!' Katy said, showing her surprise. Her acquaintance with the Honorary Secretary's wife had always been of the most formal kind.

'Oh, Joanna, please! How are you?' Her smile was charmingly sympathetic. 'I just brought you some flowers and one or two sort of foodie things.'

'How very kind! Do come in.' Katy had repeated the words so often that the response seemed programmed, like a mechanical doll's. She led the way upstairs to the kitchen so that her visitor could set down the 'foodie things', in the faint hope that with that duty done she might go away.

In the kitchen there was plentiful evidence of neighbourly concern: there were boxes and tins piled up and potted plants and flowers everywhere, some faded, still in their cellophane wrapping. There was no heating on and the lounge, with the electric fire on, had been very warm. Katy, her arms wrapped across her chest as if in protection, shivered as she watched Joanna set down the elegant arrangement on the dresser.

Joanna noticed immediately. 'My dear, you're cold. I'm sure you can't be sleeping properly and I did wonder if you felt able to eat? I hope you won't think it's impertinent, but I've got soup here, and sandwiches. I haven't had my lunch either.'

'That's very kind,' Katy said again, managing to smile. Joanna took off the smart little coat to reveal a gilet – real fur, this time – over a caramel-coloured sweater and trousers and draped it over the back of a chair. With a swift glance round the kitchen she found a pan and tipped in soup from the Thermos flask in her basket, then while it was heating set some exotic-looking packets and jars on the table and unwrapped a very professional-looking pile of sandwiches. Katy mutely fetched a tray, plates and mugs while Joanna chattered on.

'Ritchie's been so worried about you – well, we both have, of course – and he wanted you to know he's there for you, if there's anything he can do. I've been meaning to come before this, but you know how it is – it's been bedlam, with the police and the Press and all the arrangements.' Then she too shivered. 'Goodness, it is cold in here, isn't it?'

'I'm sorry. It didn't seem worth heating the house when I've mostly just been in the lounge with the fire on.'

'Then we'll take it in there, shall we?' Joanna said briskly, and Katy led the way across the landing.

Seen with a stranger's eye, the room looked untidy and sordid. The contents of her memory boxes were spread out over the chairs and floor; the dust of neglect filmed the surfaces and there were even dirty mugs and plates from the coffee and toast she had been living on. Katy looked about her helplessly. 'Sorry,' she mumbled. 'I've just been . . . going through things.'

'Not to worry!' Joanna set down the tray on top of one of the less cluttered tables, cleared an untidy pile of papers off one of the chairs beside it and sat down, handing Katy a mug and a sandwich. Dutifully Katy sipped at the creamy mushroom soup and was surprised how good it tasted and how hungry she felt.

'I promised Ritchie I would look in to see you today, to see if you were all right after this latest ghastly business. Right on your doorstep, too!'

'That was very kind.' Again, the all-purpose phrase.

'It's such a dreadful thing – poor Willie! We just couldn't

believe it – couldn't believe all this could happen in Knockhaven!'

'I don't want to believe it,' Katy said slowly. 'It seems like, if it's true, then my time with Rob was just sort of a bad joke, to kid me on that life could be good and happy. It isn't, is it? I was right before and Rob was wrong. It's cruel and ugly. All Willie was doing was helping me out, and this happened to him.

'Rob tried to tell me it wasn't, that bad stuff happened but you coped and things would get better again. But this won't ever get better, as long as I live. And it's the same for Jackie Duncan.'

'Yes. Poor Jackie.' Joanna's eyes went to the window at the back as she spoke. 'Did you—?' she said, then broke off as the doorbell rang again. 'Oh, are you expecting someone?'

Katy shook her head, putting down her mug to go and answer it, but Joanna was on her feet. 'Let me get that for you,' she offered, and went out without waiting for a response.

Enid Davis was on the doorstep and looked surprised to see Joanna. 'Oh – I didn't know you would be here, Mrs Elder! I spoke to Katy at the funeral and after yesterday – I just brought her a few things—'

'Come in, we're upstairs. I had the same idea myself – we're just having some soup. Ritchie made me promise to come and see her today. He was very worried about her, with all this on her doorstep—'

'I know. It's all so dreadful. I keep thinking it must be some sort of bad dream and we'll all wake up soon.'

'It beggars belief. And what's going to happen next? It's a horrible feeling.' She glanced at the bag Enid was holding. 'Do you want to put that in the kitchen?'

'I've just made a casserole for her to heat up – they both have to eat and she probably doesn't feel up to cooking for him.'

Joanna stopped. 'Oh yes,' she said slowly. 'I'd forgotten. There is that boy – her son, not Rob's?'

'That's right, Nat. I can't help feeling sorry for him, even if he has been in trouble. You know how difficult it is when there's a step-parent. Katy's all on her own now – she'll need his support.'

From what Joanna remembered of the boy she had seen a couple of times this seemed unlikely. But, 'I'm sure,' she said diplomatically, then led the way to the lounge.

There was no mistaking Katy's pleasure at seeing her guest. 'Enid, how nice of you to come,' she said warmly, holding out both hands. Enid took them, then went to sit beside her on the sofa. She had to displace a bundle of old newspapers; she picked them up, looking helpless.

'Oh, just dump them on the floor. Sorry – I've been trying to sort things out.'

'Mmm,' Joanna said, and Katy coloured. She hadn't asked the woman to come here and start disapproving.

Enid said, 'Oh, Katy, it must have been so dreadful for you, all this last night on top of everything else! I could have come then, if I'd heard.' She sounded genuinely distressed.

'I didn't know anything about it until the morning. The doctor's given me pills and I just crash out. My bedroom's to the front anyway – it's only Nat's at the back here.'

On the other side of the room, Joanna looked almost excluded from the conversation. *She doesn't like not being the centre of attention*, Katy thought as Joanna said loudly, 'Oh dear! Did he see what happened?'

'How is Nat?' Enid asked. 'He must have been very upset too.'

'I don't think he was there at the time. I heard him going out before I went to bed myself and he never bothers to open his curtains anyway. But I don't know – I haven't spoken to him yet.'

Enid hesitated. 'Look – perhaps I shouldn't say this, but he's all you have left!'

Katy sighed. 'I know what you're saying, Enid, and you're right, of course you're right, but Nat's – difficult. He really hated Rob and he was quite threatening to me. I was really thinking about seeing if his grandmother would have him for a bit—'

'You know your own son, of course. But you know, from a psychological point of view he probably felt he'd lost you when you remarried. You could build bridges now, surely, but if you send him away—'

Joanna got up. 'I'll leave you two to chat. Katy, if you've any problems on the business side do let Ritchie know – he's very good on that sort of thing. No, don't bother to show me down. I'll pick up the Thermos and the basket on my way.'

It was with some relief that Katy saw her go. She'd never found Joanna easy and her Lady Bountiful act seemed somehow phoney, though perhaps she was being oversensitive. Anyway, it was a help to talk to Enid about Nat. She didn't want to suspect her own son, of course she didn't.

The conflict of emotions raging within her was familiar to Marjory Fleming. She had experienced it every time one of her children didn't appear when they were expected to: a violent rush of relief from terror, thankfulness that they were unharmed and pure, incandescent rage. It overwhelmed her when the door to her office opened at half-past two and DC Kingsley appeared. She jumped to her feet.

'Kingsley! How dare you put us through all this?' she yelled. 'Do you realise I was right on the brink of announcing a public search for you? Can you imagine it – you breezing in ten minutes later, everyone cracking up because Galloway CID can't find one of its own detectives?'

'Sorry, ma'am.' With his hair in its normal style and his person innocent of any metal attachment, though showing a suspicious-looking patch of blurred colour on the side of his neck, Kingsley stood to attention in front of her desk. His impression of someone truly penitent was not entirely convincing.

'Don't try to apologise – I haven't finished with being furious with you yet.' She sat down again. 'Explanation?' she said icily.

'Yes, ma'am. May I stand at ease?'

'No.'

'It's sort of a long story.'

'Oh, I have all the time in the world, Constable.'

'You see, I was following up on Operation Songbird.'

'The brief I gave to Tam. Yes.'

He reddened. 'I suppose I should have cleared it through him. But anyway, I'd got the undercover bit all worked out and I thought I'd try it in Knockhaven before the gossip mill caught up and it was all round the place who I was.'

'Tam told me.'

'Yes, I was pretty sure he'd recognised me.'

'That, you see, was why we were so worried. You'd been in the town already working as a policeman so there was no guarantee that Tam was the only one to see through the disguise. You were in the company of known drug-users, you must have been asking questions, then you disappeared.'

'Oh! Sorry, I never thought of it like that.'

Dear God, it was like explaining to a teenager why you might be anxious if they missed the last bus and decided to walk home! Heaven send her patience!

'So here you are, in the pub, undercover. Take it from there. Oh, and I suppose you can sit down.'

'Thanks, boss,' he said with marked relief. 'Really, I mean it – I am sorry it caused so much trouble.'

'So am I. OK – but this better be good.'

His eyes lit up. 'It is, I promise you! It was all going pretty well last night. I told them I'd just come to the area, doing IT work locally, and where could I get hash – the usual line. Actually, I've done it in two or three pubs all across the area over the last bit, picked up some heavier stuff as well – thought we could run comparisons on whether it seemed to be coming from the same source.'

He was certainly cutting corners, a high-risk strategy, but just at the moment she wasn't going to worry about playing it by the book. 'Go on.'

'It was just luck that one of the lads I'd fallen in with was Ryan Duncan – Willie's son, you know? And when his old man kicked us out at closing time we bought a few more beers and went back to this lad Dale's house. Smoked a bit of pot – which, incidentally, to coin a phrase, I didn't inhale – then sat around, talking football mostly. They were all pretty drunk by then—'

'You, of course, were stone-cold sober?'

He grinned. 'I've got quite a good head. Evidence of a misspent youth. Then suddenly Ryan's sister came in, hysterical, saying what had happened to her dad. And I have to say, people sobered up pretty quickly. Ryan went off home and I was left with the rest of them.

'They were all shocked rigid. There was a lot of talk about what Willie had said originally about being a marked man and I noticed one of them, Dale, was keeping pretty quiet. When the others decided they'd better go, I asked if I could doss down on his sofa – the place was going to be crawling with cops and I didn't want to lose my licence, I said. Actually I think he was glad of the company.

'I led him on a bit after that and he and Ryan were obviously in on it through Willie, though the rest of them weren't. He was scared, but he was angry too, not angry enough to name names, but I stoked it up, went on about how the big men had it all and didn't take the risks and reckoned everyone was expendable, told him the best revenge was to shop him so everyone else would be safe . . . That sort of stuff.

'But I didn't push it – he was still edgy, so I just said I needed to crash out. Then when I woke up – a bit late, I'll admit that – he offered me breakfast and I didn't want to go off to make a call and lose the momentum.'

'Fair enough. I'll accept that.'

'Thanks. We were going back over it all when Ryan appeared. He was looking terrible and he wasn't best pleased to find I was still there, but I just sort of went quiet and made coffee and toast in the background while he and Dale started talking.

'After a bit they almost forgot about me. Dale said, "Are you going to let him get away with it?" and Ryan said, "No, I'm effing not." Then it got pretty obvious who they were talking about. There's a network outside the area, of course, but here he's a one-man band, runs a tight operation with just himself and men like Willie who distribute.'

'Ritchie Elder?'

'You were on to him already?'

'Only suspicion. But if we've got those two lads, we know who to lean on—'

'Better than that.' Kingsley's face broke into a triumphant smile. 'I've got them downstairs.'

'They're ready to talk?'

'Better than that, even. If you can persuade the Super to do a bit of horse-trading with the Procurator Fiscal on the question of charges, they're ready to sing, just like canaries.'

For the third time, the phone rang and rang until it rang out. Dorothy Randall, who had been tapping her fingers on the table as she listened, set down the receiver with an impatient sigh. She looked at her watch: ten to one, and Lewis should have been home for lunch just after twelve-thirty.

She had always been scrupulous about not phoning him during working hours. She had always been sensitive, too, to the faint sigh of irritation, the slight furrowing of his brow, that indicated he felt she was crowding him. As a result, theirs had been a close, happy relationship; she needed to be careful that in this time of anxiety and stress she did not jeopardise it. Dorothy had already made the mistake of going to his house, uninvited, to cook a meal for him, but she hadn't done it twice.

However, she badly needed to talk to him, after last night. If he wasn't coming home for lunch, she'd just have to phone him at the surgery after all. She'd give it one more try.

This time, her persistence was rewarded, though Lewis's 'Hello?' at the other end of the phone sounded almost tetchy.

'Lewis, it's me.'

'Yes, I thought it might be.'

She was immediately apologetic. 'Darling, I'm sorry to interrupt. Is that you only coming in for your lunch now?'

'Yes. I looked in on Jackie Duncan on my way home.'

It gave her the opening she wanted. 'It's quite shocking, isn't it? Lewis, I really need to talk to you—'

'Mother, I have to be back at the surgery in half an hour. Surely this can wait?'

She backed off hastily. 'Oh yes, of course.' Then she added, with artistic hesitation, 'It's – it's just I've had a little heart flutter that's been worrying me this morning . . .'

She couldn't hear the sigh, but there was an appreciable pause before he said, 'I'll be with you in a couple of minutes.'

'Oh but Lewis – your lunch! That's too bad. I could make you a sandwich—'

'Don't bother. I have some.'

He wasn't pleased, but at least he was coming. Going into the sitting room to wait, Dorothy caught sight of herself in the mirror over the mantelpiece. She was looking gaunt, her eyes were heavy from lack of sleep and her face looked blotchy. She'd always taken pride in keeping herself fit, but even leaving aside the imaginary heart flutter, she didn't feel particularly well, and with a twinge of alarm she reflected that it wouldn't do any harm to have Lewis check her over. At her age, this level of stress could be positively dangerous.

When he saw her, it was clear that Lewis thought the same. There was no sign of annoyance now as he opened his medical case and took out the sphygmomanometer he had taken for Jackie Duncan. But when he had completed the test and sounded her heart he sat back on his heels saying with some relief, 'Your blood-pressure's up a bit, but not badly – nothing to worry about. It's been an upsetting time – you just need to take it easy. Stop running round after your son, who's really perfectly capable of looking after himself.'

He smiled at her, and she smiled back. 'That's my pleasure. But Lewis, this awful business about Willie Duncan—'

'You've obviously heard all about it. Were you out this morning? Oh no, let me guess. Muriel phoned.'

He didn't sound pleased. Dorothy said, 'Oh, I know what you think of her. But she does keep me in touch with what's happening.'

'And quite a lot of things that aren't,' he said dryly.

'What's poor Jackie saying?'

'She's sobbing, mostly, and still in shock, of course. But she knew the risks he was running, getting involved with drugs, though her worry I think had mainly been about prosecution rather than something like this.

'And terrible as it is, I can't say it isn't a relief that this will draw a line under Ashley's death – and the others', of course.'

'But Lewis!' She leaned forward urgently, putting her hand on top of his. 'That was what I wanted to speak to you about. Don't you see – it hasn't?'

Shock was evident in his face. 'What nonsense is this, Mother?'

'We can't afford to be caught off guard. Muriel says that Willie's death could easily be a blind. Willie said himself that he wasn't in danger, and everyone knows that if there wasn't a drugs connection the police would be looking for someone else. So if you were the killer and you wanted to throw them off your scent, you'd have to kill Willie, wouldn't you?'

Lewis got up. Dorothy couldn't remember the last time she had seen her son angry, but he was angry now. 'That woman is pure poison! I don't want you to have anything more to do with her. Her one aim in life is to cause trouble.'

'Lewis!' She was on her feet too. 'You don't see, do you? Oh, I know what Muriel is. I don't trust her, I only believe ten per cent of what she tells me, but if she's thinking that way, sooner or later the police will too. And then you'll be back under suspicion again. Don't think you won't be!'

She could tell he was sceptical. 'Don't you remember that incident at university?' she said. 'I've never been sure they accepted your innocence. They've probably still got you on a file somewhere.'

When he didn't say anything, she pursued her advantage. 'So where were you last night? What were you doing?'

'I was at home, Mother, as I usually am at the moment, working in my study alone.'

'No, you weren't.' Dorothy had moved closer to him, fixing her eyes on his. 'You were here. We had supper. Steak and kidney pie, then fruit salad. Then we chatted over coffee and decided to watch a film on my video – *Lawrence of Arabia*, I think. You'd seen it before, but we both enjoyed it. It's a long film, of course, so it was after midnight when you left here. You walked, naturally, so no one would have heard you arriving or leaving, and they might have seen your car still parked outside your house. You probably left the lights on too, to discourage burglars.'

'You're crazy,' he said flatly.

'No, I'm not. We just have to sort this out before the police come round asking more questions. Of course you're inno-cent, but if you believe in British justice, given the amount of compensation they pay out for wrongful imprisonment every year, then you're a fool.'

Dorothy could see him wavering. 'Did you have any phone calls?'

He shook his head. 'No. Nor visitors,' he said slowly.

'Then you had supper here.' Her voice held a tone of firm command she had not used to him since he was a child.

Lewis moistened his lips. 'Yes. All right.' He bent to pack his instruments in his case then straightened up, the ghost of a smile on his lips. 'And a very good steak pie it was too.'

When he had gone, Dorothy Randall slumped back in her chair. If Lewis had been checking her during the course of that conversation, he might have been alarmed by the way her heart was racing, but it was slowing down now. She'd go upstairs and lie down for a nap and after that she'd be feeling *much* better.

16

'That's all fine and dandy,' Tam MacNee said as he sat in one of the chairs by Marjory Fleming's desk; it was Jonathan Kingsley, this time, who was perched on the table having taken up this position to wait for MacNee and Kerr appearing in answer to the inspector's summons. 'And I'm not saying you haven't done a good job. You have. I've been trying to get a handle on that bugger for weeks and it looks like you've nailed him. Congratulations.'

'Thanks, Tam, that's generous.' The younger man's smile was just a fraction too smug.

'You'd have to admit you could hardly have done it if Willie hadn't got himself killed,' Tansy Kerr put in sharply, since he didn't seem to be going to say it himself.

'Of course,' Kingsley acknowledged. He could afford to be gracious.

MacNee went on, 'But I've been chewing over our interview with Elder. Did it strike you, boss, that when we were questioning him about the murders he was all over the place? But the drugs – he was shocked, right enough, at being accused at all, but when we tried to press him on it later he'd all the answers about getting in his lawyer off pat. Och, I know he got time to pull himself together, but even so . . . It just seems kinda funny that if he was guilty of the killings too he wouldn't have worked out a smarter way to handle it.'

Fleming, who had observed the interplay between her detectives in watchful silence, said, 'I hear what you're saying. It wasn't the being prepared that struck me, but I did think that if either the story about your mistress was a fabrication, or you were ruthless enough to kill her, just the mention of the state of her face would be unlikely to make you physically sick. As he was,' she added in explanation to the other two.

Kingsley's face stiffened. 'But surely, with the greatest respect, you can't be saying you don't think he's guilty just because the gory details revolted him? It's been clear from the start it's a drugs scenario.'

'Oh, I know he's claiming an alibi in both cases, but they sound pretty flimsy to me – his wife and a barmaid who won't remember him. If we start from the premise that we know he did it and work backwards from there, I promise you we'll find the evidence to fit.'

There was a silence. MacNee and Kerr exchanged glances, then Fleming said coolly, 'It's not really the way we work here, Jon. It's too close to stitching someone up for comfort. Miscarriages of justice happen when coppers believe that all they need for a conviction is the conviction that they know who did it.

'I agree, everything points that way. He's got the motive, the knowledge and unless the alibis check out, the opportunity. So let's just talk about procedure – not as exciting as jumping to conclusions, but it's a hell of a lot safer for everyone concerned.

'Tansy, I want you to get statements at the Black Bull and then take a crack at Joanna Elder – it's on your way anyway, and you were talking to her at the funeral tea, weren't you?'

'She was rather obviously doing her social duty by Katy Anderson. Katy just looked bemused.'

'I meant to ask – did you pick up anything useful there?'

Tansy shook her head ruefully. 'My job on this case seems to be drawing all the blanks. Every conversation I overheard was just as you would expect.'

'You never know, given the woman's touch, Joanna may crack. She'll be shaken anyway, with her husband being arrested. See if the alibi stands up, and you might just try and find out whether she knew where all the money was coming from.'

'You'll be lucky,' MacNee snorted. 'That one can lie as well as a dog can lick a dish, if you ask me.'

Fleming smiled. 'There's a lot of it about. Now Tam, can you find out who our expert is on mobile phones? Elder claims he took a call from the coastguard at the pub; they should be able to pinpoint the area from the records. And you might brief a constable about getting a warrant for the house and the offices – cars, vans, drains and all.

'You'll be kept pretty busy here, Jon. We'll need official signed statements from your lads and they'll be bringing Elder in even as I speak. Have a shot at questioning him before we have to allow him access to his solicitor, though I doubt if you'll get more than name, rank and serial number.'

'Yes, boss.'

He was looking sullen. With an inward sigh, Fleming said in the interests of peace, 'Jon, I don't want you to think I don't appreciate that you've made remarkable progress on this. I'm not accusing you of anything unprofessional. All I'm asking you to do is to keep an open mind.'

'I wasn't suggesting for a minute that we should rig the evidence,' Kingsley said stiffly. 'Of course we have to be absolutely scrupulous. But having a clear hypothesis can very usefully give structure and direction.'

'Oh, I'm all for those. I think I saw one at Glasgow Zoo once,' MacNee said merrily, earning himself a warning look from his superior. 'Kind of cumbersome, though – might take up a lot of space that could be used for thinking, if you got one into your head.'

Fighting the temptation to say, 'Children, children!' Fleming changed the subject rapidly. 'By the way, I've had the report from the lab about the decoy lamps.' She sorted through a pile of papers on her desk and pulled one out. 'I'm not sure how helpful it is. The lamps came from Argos and they can tell from the serial numbers that they were bought in Argos in Dumfries on September third. Cash sale. There are no fingerprints of any kind – they'd obviously been polished – and the glass paint that was used was a standard one you could pick up in a DIY superstore. The only oddity was that on one of them they found faint traces of citric acid powder.'

'That's for wine-making, isn't it?' Kerr said brightly. 'Stuff like that.'

'Stuff,' Kingsley said. He was smiling. 'Oh yes, stuff. But we're not talking about wine-making here. That's what you mix heroin with for injecting. Quickest way to get it into the bloodstream. Right, Tam?' He couldn't conceal his triumphant satisfaction.

'Oh, right enough,' Tam said. 'But—' He stopped.

Kingsley raised his eyebrows. 'But—?'

'Oh, nothing. I'll away and put the enquiry about the mobile in hand, boss.'

The others rose as well, and when they had gone Fleming too got up and went to stand in her favourite thinking position by the window. Keeping this lot working as any sort of team fairly took it out of you, but in a curious way it was working. The animosity between Tam and Jon meant that whatever theory one of them put forward would get aggressive scrutiny from the other; too often when detectives cooperated closely, a theory reinforced by the team's backing was given too much weight. And Tansy – well, someone had to be civilised. It would be good if her interview with Joanna Elder turned out to be productive; she was clearly feeling dispirited at the moment about her investigative role having been so peripheral.

Fleming should have been feeling pleased. Don Bailey certainly was, rushing off to hack out a deal with the Fiscal. Elder's conviction on both charges would be the ideal solution, and on the face of it everything hung together. With the entire community, led by her own mother, looking to her for justice for the victims, it should have been a load off her mind. But it wasn't.

Justice: that was always the itch under her skin. It didn't matter how often it was explained to her that a court case was about proof, not guilt or innocence, she clung stubbornly to her conviction that her job was to seek the truth. She'd seen wicked men grin at their victims as they left the dock, acquitted on a technicality, but somehow, because she had been instrumental to the conviction, it had been much worse on the couple of occasions when she'd seen a bewildered innocent trapped in a skilfully woven web of Crown evidence. One had since been released; the other still languished at Her Majesty's Pleasure in Perth prison.

Police work nowadays seemed to be all about targets and initiatives; there was nothing in the handbooks about gut feeling, the instinct that was telling Fleming right now that this didn't quite add up. She struggled to articulate it.

There was no problem with the drugs rap. Even without the testimony of the sad and angry lads Jon had brought in, Elder's attitude during the interview had pretty much confirmed her own and Tam's suspicions that he was Mr Big. But what it had also confirmed, in her mind at least, was that he had been in love with Ashley Randall.

Was it possible that he could so separate his heart and his head that he would sacrifice his beloved to his own security? Could this be an example of what Laura called pathological solipsism? She must go and have another talk with her; she'd been so busy she hadn't so much as spoken to her friend on the phone for days now.

Maybe Laura could convince her that this was entirely possible. If it wasn't . . . it scarcely bore thinking about. If Elder's admittedly shaky alibis stood up to examination, where were they? Searching round for someone else with a power- ful reason for killing Willie Duncan? Or looking for someone smart enough to realise that killing Willie would shape the police investigation in exactly the way it had, away from the real victim – whoever that might be. They'd been there before. On Day One.

She rehearsed the case against Elder. He had been furious that Willie hadn't gone on the boat. He had given conflicting statements about his relationship with Ashley. He had lied about his whereabouts. He'd offered his wife and an in- attentive barmaid as alibis – the one with a vested interest and the other unlikely to be able to say definitely that he wasn't there. He was a drug dealer, which meant having no moral scruples about the deaths of the innocent. And now the citric acid link with heroin . . .

Tam hadn't been convinced, though. What had his 'But—' been about? She frowned, watching idly as a car, double-parked and blocking the road below, provided a bit of street theatre. She had little doubt that he'd be back to explain it now Jon had left, on the excuse of reporting progress on tracing the call, and trying to second-guess him was wasting time. She had an appointment with the pathologist later that she was doing her best not to think about and there was paper she had to shift before she left. With her usual wild enthusiasm, she returned to her desk.

Tansy Kerr was in a gloomy mood as she drove back from Glasserton to the Elders' house. Yet again, hers had been the enquiry which drew a blank.

At the Black Bull, its proprietor, a blue-chinned man with a beer gut and dirty fingernails, had directed her to Donna

Donaldson in the village, who had been manning the bar on the night in question.

Donna was a big girl, slow-moving, with an abbreviated T-shirt exposing a roll of pale fat round her midriff, straggling red-brown hair and a complexion sallow with yesterday's make-up which had smudged all round her eyes.

Feeling she should have brought a supply of bamboo shoots to offer her, Kerr put her question. Donna listened with a glazed expression, her jaws moving rhythmically.

'Dunno. They could of been there, I suppose.'

'Can you remember that evening? The evening the Knockhaven lifeboat was wrecked – a very stormy night.'

There was a prolonged pause, during which Kerr could have sworn she heard cogs clanking and gears grating, then a look of almost human intelligence came to Donna's face.

'That was, like, the tenth, right? Oh, I mind that fine. It was my pal's birthday and she goes, "Donna, you're working, right? Why don't we all come round the pub and blast a few breezers?" We'd a great laugh. Everyone was, like, stotting.'

'Do you,' Kerr persisted patiently, 'remember seeing the couple I was asking about? Older couple. She was blonde. Pretty. Looked a bit like Nicole Kidman.'

The glazed look returned. 'Nuh. There were some people in, prob'ly. Don't know, really.'

And that had been that. The barmaid's memory had certainly confirmed Elder's prediction, but there was nothing to say he hadn't noticed what she was like on some previous occasion when he'd been there, with or without Ashley.

Kerr wasn't looking forward to her next assignment either. If your husband had just been arrested for drug dealing you would be in quite a state, whether you were in on the act or not; a police officer would hardly be top of the list of visitors you would welcome with enthusiasm to your home. It was with considerable trepidation that she turned in at the

imposing entrance to Bayview House, parked her car beside
the powder-blue Mercedes and rang the front-door bell.

After a pause long enough to make Kerr wonder if Mrs
Elder was in hiding, the door was flung open by the woman
herself, wearing a sports top and shorts, sweating and breath-
less, as if she had been interrupted in the middle of a workout. It was obvious, at first glance, that she was in a towering
rage. There were two bright red spots in her cheeks, she was
scowling and Kerr almost felt her eyes might shoot sparks
at any moment.

'What do you want?' she snapped.

Despite a temptation to say, 'Nothing, thank you,' and
make a dash for the car, Kerr held her ground. 'DC Kerr,'
she said bravely, holding up her warrant-card.

'I know who you are. I asked what you wanted.'

'I have just one or two questions about Mr Elder—'

'One or two? Get in line, sister! The list of questions I
have about that pernicious bastard would run to more pages
than the telephone directory.'

Paydirt at last? 'I take it you knew nothing about this,'
Kerr said sympathetically.

Joanna glared at her. 'Do I look that kind of stupid? To
risk all this,' she gestured at the building behind her, 'when
you're making a fortune already because people are dumb
enough to pay good money for houses with walls you could
spit peas through and a cardboard roof—'

'Perhaps I could come in and you could tell me all about
it?' Kerr suggested delicately and Joanna shrugged.

'Why not? The minute there's a warrant your lot will be
trampling through the place like a herd of buffalo. One more
won't make any difference.'

Stealing interested glances about her, Kerr followed her
hostess across the wide expanse of hall and into the soaring
height of the swimming-pool area. She'd never seen this sort

of luxury in a private house before, only once been in a hotel that had a pool like this. At the farther end there was a collection of exercise machines which looked like instruments of torture to Tansy – though maybe now she'd given up smoking she'd have to do something if she wasn't to get fat.

Round the pool, though, there were glass tables and loungers with sharp lime-green cushions and even, bizarrely, a beach umbrella – presumably for those days when the burning heat of Galloway became too much. She could go along with that, if you added a nice chilled pitcher of something with vodka in it.

Today, however, only the last rays of pale autumn sunshine glinted on the improbably blue water and bathed the whole place in a bleak, cold light, mocking the fantasy of a tropical idyll, an idyll which was even now being ruthlessly destroyed by the evidence of two young men bent on vengeance.

'Take a seat,' Joanna said curtly, going to the farther end to take a lime-green towel from a pile in a white wicker cabinet and rubbing herself down.

Putting her shoulder satchel down on one of the glass tables, Kerr gingerly lowered herself on to one of the loungers. She was sure that never before had their immaculate cushions been contaminated by contact with distressed jeans and Primark trainers, considering the designer velour tracksuit her hostess had just pulled on, and her top-of-the-range Nikes. She swivelled so that she was sitting awkwardly on the edge.

Joanna flung herself down on the next-door chair. 'All right. Can I ask you a question first? Will all this be taken away if you can prove he was dealing?'

Well, that told you where her priorities lay, didn't it? 'I don't know,' Kerr said truthfully. 'There's new legislation coming in about confiscation of assets and directives to get tough. It all depends, first of all, obviously, on a conviction, and secondly on what he can prove comes from his legitimate business.'

'Right.' Joanna's expression was thoughtful. 'I'd better contact my lawyer immediately to safeguard my interests. So what do you want to know?'

Kerr had been debating the first question. The most important one – could she confirm her husband's alibi? – suggested itself, but she had a feeling the woman could be led on to talk about her husband and it seemed unlikely she'd want to do him any favours. It was chancing her arm, but . . . 'Was your husband having an affair with Ashley Randall?'

This wasn't the best position for conducting an interview. It was easy for Joanna, lying down, to turn her head, as she did now, and look straight in front so that Kerr could not easily see her expression. The length of the pause before she spoke, though, told its own story of calculation.

'He – might have been, I suppose. My cleaning ladies "felt I ought to know" – people are always so helpful that way, aren't they? – and yes, I should think they were right.'

'Was he in love with her?'

Joanna didn't turn her head away this time, meeting Kerr's gaze with wide, innocent eyes. 'Goodness, of course not! It was hardly the first time. I've just learned to accept that ours is that sort of marriage; he comes back to me in the end.'

'But it won't be such a happy ending now, will it?' Kerr slipped the knife in.

Joanna's eyes narrowed. 'It depends what happens, doesn't it? If you lot can't prove anything—'

'Oh, I think you'll find we can. You don't think we'd have charged him if we couldn't?'

'Right,' she said again, but she accepted Kerr's uncompromising reply with impressive coolness. 'Well, before you ask, I knew nothing about it. I never saw bags of curious

white powder lying around the house, we didn't have car-
loads of dubious people ringing the bell after dark. I'll be
astonished if all your searching comes up with anything
around this house, unless it's on his computer – my ladies
clean every corner. And believe me, at this stage I'd tell you
anything I knew.'

Kerr had no brief for the scum who dealt in death, but
this was a fairly breathtaking level of callous disengagement.
'You wouldn't feel you maybe should "stand by your man"?'
She indicated the quotation marks ironically.

'If he was drug dealing? Dear me, no.'

Was that a moral position, or had the phrase 'and got
caught' somehow been omitted from her statement? It was
hardly a question to which Kerr could expect a truthful
answer. Time to change tack and go for the big one. 'Mrs
Elder, your husband said he was here at home with you all
last night. Can you confirm that?'

'Last night? Oh – Willie Duncan,' she said slowly. 'You –
you have him in the frame for that too?'

'It's simply a routine check on people's movements. Was
he here?'

Joanna shrugged. 'He might have been. I wouldn't know.
I was here, but we don't see much of each other these days.
He's sleeping in one of the spare rooms at the moment.'

Kerr wanted to punch the air and cry, '*Yes!*' Instead, she
said calmly, 'Do you mean you didn't see him all evening?'

'I saw him around seven. I asked when he wanted to eat
but he said he wasn't hungry, that he'd grab a sandwich
later.'

'But you didn't hear him leave the house, or take his car
out, or anything?'

'I was in the sitting room at the back, and then I went up
to our bedroom which looks out that way as well.'

'Where did you think he went, after you saw him?'

'I don't know – to his study, probably. That's at the other end of the house.'

'And did he seem on edge?'

Joanna laughed with what sounded like genuine amusement. 'On edge? My dear girl, Ritchie has been a neurotic heap since the day the lifeboat was wrecked.'

It was said so innocently that it took Kerr a moment to realise that her attention was being very skilfully redirected. This needed a blunt response; she wasn't going to start playing games. 'Mrs Elder, are you telling me you think your husband was behind that too?'

'Behind what? The wreck? Good God, no – do you think I'd have been prepared to share my bed with a *murderer*?' Her outrage was beautifully done.

'Of course not,' Kerr said soothingly – though of course, by her own admission Joanna hadn't been sharing a bed with him anyway. 'But leaving that aside, you're saying you can't confirm he was in this house between, say, seven-thirty and twelve-thirty last night?'

'I'm afraid not, no.' She screwed her face into a small, regretful pout.

Kerr briefly imagined it framed in fur, wearing just that expression as the troika rattled over the rutted snow and Joanna Elder pushed her husband off the back to be torn apart by the waiting wolves. 'Thank you for your cooperation,' she said, getting up.

As she started her car, Tansy could see Joanna, stripped off again and heading towards the gym area. That was one fit, determined lady.

Elated at her success, Tansy drove back to Kirkluce. At last she felt she would be able to make a real contribution to the investigation; while the lack of confirmation of Elder's alibis didn't prove anything, at least it meant that there could be no possible objections to their taking his entire life apart.

And to a limited extent she agreed with Jon – once you looked hard enough, in the right direction, sooner or later you found what you were looking for.

Fleming was running late for the autopsy, but she really had very little incentive to hurry. They all knew, only too well, what had happened to Willie; it would have been different if useful information was likely to emerge, but as it was she was content to be as late as possible. The less time she had to spend in the mortuary, the happier she would be.

So when Tam MacNee accosted her in the corridor on the way out she was quite prepared to be further delayed, not least since she wanted to satisfy her curiosity about his stifled objection.

'I was on my way to see you to tell you they managed to intercept Sheriff Dobbie on his way home to his tea and got the warrants sworn out, and the mobile guys are going to get to work on tracing the coastguard call now.'

She smiled. 'Oh, sure. Now tell me what you were really coming to say.'

He shrank back dramatically. '"*She shook baith mickle corn and bear, And kept the countryside in fear!*" Witchcraft!'

'That's ten pence.' She held out her hand. 'We're getting quite a nice wee collection. It's going to the first charity I can find that supports single mothers – that seems appropriate, somehow.

'So – tell me what it was you didn't want to say in front of Jon.'

MacNee was indignant. 'I should be getting a gold star for good behaviour,' he protested. 'There'd been a bit of a stushie already when I didn't go right along with him and I didn't think you'd be best pleased at another one.

'But the thing is, you know what Kingsley said about citric acid?'

'That it's used along with drugs? Yes.'

'You don't need to go to a dealer for it. You can buy it in quantity on the Internet if you don't fancy drawing attention to yourself at the local chemist's. It's used at the point when someone's preparing heroin to inject, and if Elder's mainlining, he's the first Mr Big I've known who's daft enough to take what he's selling.'

'I see what you mean,' Fleming said slowly.

'The thing is,' MacNee persisted, 'Kingsley took that as more or less final proof of his guilt, but it's actually a link to drug taking, not drug dealing. And the man claims he's got an alibi, anyway.'

Fleming winced. 'Don't say that, Tam! You don't believe he's the Wrecker, do you?'

'Since you ask me, no. And,' he said shrewdly, 'if you ask me, neither do you.'

She put up a feeble defence. 'Maybe his alibi will collapse. And being in the drugs trade, there could have been someone around him doing drugs—'

MacNee gave her a pitying look. 'And him doing his craft work with glass paint on the lanterns at the time? Do me a favour!'

'So where do you go from there? Start looking for someone who brews home-made wine, like Tansy suggested?'

'Or,' he said with heavy emphasis, 'look for someone connected to the case who might well be doing a bit of H on the side?'

Fleming stared at him. She had no difficulty in following his reasoning, but it didn't make her happy. 'You think we eliminated him from enquiries a bit too soon? But Tam, if Rob was the intended victim and Ashley and Luke and Willie were killed for no other reason than to divert suspicion, and the Wrecker has any reason to feel threatened again . . .'

'Aye. Who's next?'

Shaken, Marjory said, 'We're getting ahead of ourselves, Tam. Tansy may come back with evidence that his alibis don't stand up, and looked at objectively, the citric acid isn't really evidence one way or another. Just for the sake of argument, the lamps could have picked up traces from a surface that had been used by an addict previously.

'Anyway, I'd better go. I'm calling in at the mortuary – briefly, I hope – then going straight home. I'm going to have a long, scented bath to try to get the smell of the place out of my nostrils, and then I'm going to pretend I have the sort of job that you sometimes don't think about for a whole evening.'

17

Refreshed after a bath which she almost felt had cleansed her mind as well as her body, and wearing her oldest, softest jeans and a mohair sweater retired from front-line duties, Marjory came downstairs to the farmhouse kitchen. Her mother, heaven bless her – and she must make time to phone her for a chat this evening – had been out yesterday and left a casserole Marjory had put into the Aga when she came in, and already there was a wonderful smell coming from it. She'd only had to add baked potatoes for the main course, and when she'd looked in the Tin there were even some meringues there for pudding.

Cat's favourites. That was good. There had been far too many evenings lately when Marjory had not been there to see for herself exactly what her daughter was – or wasn't – eating. To her anxious eyes, the child was looking thinner, though today when Cat came in from school she was wearing an outsize cardigan nicked from her mother's wardrobe, so it was hard to tell. Bill had said he was sure she was fine, but then Marjory hadn't specifically spelled out her worries to him. And perhaps this was making too much of it – a function of her own guilt at her absences, perhaps. Her mother always noticed everything; she could ask her about it when she phoned. She'd probably just say, reassuringly, that the child was 'off her food', a phrase Marjory remembered being used in her own childhood.

She was whipping up some of the rich yellow cream they

always got from the Raeburns when Cammie, declaring himself ravenous as always, came in and started raking about for biscuits to stave off the pangs in the interminable interval between now and the moment when his supper would hit his stomach. His mother opened her mouth to say he would spoil his appetite, then realising that he wouldn't – fat chance of that! – shut it again. You had to yak on often enough about the important things; it was pure masochism to nag when you didn't have to.

Through the window Bill came into view, crossing the yard and raising his hand in greeting. He came into the kitchen with Meg at his heels; she trotted across to sniff wistfully at the oven door and her master, too, snuffed the air as he padded across in his stocking-feet to kiss his wife.

'Now here's a treat – all four of us in for supper, and better still, it's Granny's cooking, eh, Cammie?' he said disloyally.

'Traitor!' Marjory accused him. 'How do you know this isn't just a little something I whipped up when I came in from work?'

'Because I saw her leave it in the fridge, covered with foil.'

'And anyway, if you'd made it, Mum, it wouldn't smell that good.'

'Cheeky brat! Why don't you learn to cook yourself? They have cookery classes at school.'

'They're for *girls*,' Cammie said with chauvinistic scorn.

'I've told you before that you can be a pukka chap and make loads of money too as a chef but even I'm getting bored with going on about Jamie Oliver.

'Where's your sister? Go and give her a shout, Cammie, while I dish up.'

Even so, Cammie was half-way through his heaped plateful before Cat appeared, still in the enveloping cardigan, and sliding into the room in the way she had developed lately, as if by staying close to the wall she might become invisible.

She took her place at the table and said to her mother, waiting by the stove, 'Not too much for me, Mum, OK? I'm not feeling so great – there's this bug going round at school.'

'It's a long time since lunch. You'll feel better when you've had something to eat,' Marjory said firmly, but she spooned out a small helping; if, for whatever reason, you weren't very hungry a brimming plate was very off-putting. 'I'll just give you half a potato,' she compromised, 'but I want to see you eat it.'

'Can I have the other half?' Cammie said quickly. 'And please can I have some more stew?'

Shaking her head, Marjory took the dish out of the Aga again. 'All right, bring over your plate,' she said. 'And I expect Dad probably wants some more too.'

Bill and Cammie had embarked on an animated discussion about Scotland's prospects – dismal, it appeared – for the new international rugby season, and when Marjory sat down with her own food she noticed with some relief that Cat had eaten quite a lot – not much of the potato, but most of the stew seemed to have disappeared. Then, when the meringues appeared, she saw Cat look at them hungrily and watched her demolish every mouthful. As the children disappeared, allegedly to do their homework, and Bill went out again to finish up some chores, she relaxed in her chair. She'd been making a mountain out of a molehill after all.

And then she realised where Meg, who had gone out with her master, had come from. At mealtimes Meg always lay by the Aga patiently keeping a weather-eye open for any delicious leftover that might come her way. She hadn't been there tonight; she'd been under the table, sitting by Cat's place. It was a strict rule that no titbits were given at mealtimes and Meg would have had to be encouraged, probably over a matter of days, to expect to be fed. Marjory was alarmed all over again – but on the other hand, Cat had definitely eaten the meringue; she decided not to say anything to Bill until she'd talked to her mother.

She'd often suspected that her mother was telepathic, so when the phone rang she wasn't surprised to hear Janet's voice at the other end. Not wanting to worry her, Marjory had planned to wait before introducing the subject of Cat being 'off her food' in a non-alarmist way. She didn't have the chance. After the briefest of greetings, her mother said, 'I'm so glad you're at home tonight, pet. I've been getting awful worried about Cat.'

Marjory's heart sank. 'Cat?' she asked hollowly. As if she didn't know.

Katy Anderson, too, was heating up a casserole for supper. Shamed by Joanna Elder's ill-concealed distaste at the state of the sitting room and almost more by Enid Davis's kindly offer to stay on and help her tidy everything away, she had taken up the reins of her household again. They felt strange in her hands, but she realised she must move on to the second, almost more painful stage of grief: accepting that life continued, even in this mutilated form when you had lost half of yourself.

She opened the windows in the sitting room, picked up the scattered newspapers and untidy bundles of memories to sort through and put away tomorrow, then vacuumed and dusted and polished. In the kitchen, she washed up the dishes Nat had left, threw out dead flowers and watered thirsty pot-plants, putting away the kindly offerings from her neighbours (and Joanna's almond-stuffed olives and balsamic vinegar). At the end of it she was feeling tired, but to her surprise hungry too. Enid's casserole, a sort of all-in-one hotpot, must be almost ready. Perhaps she'd open a bottle of wine and see whether the theory about a new beginning, which had sounded plausible at the time, would work.

Katy had heard Nat come in earlier and go straight across to his room. When she called him he came in looking surprised, his eyes flicking round the now orderly kitchen. He was wearing jeans with a hole in the knee and a V-necked T-shirt and he looked grubby, with a fluff of adolescent beard; she'd always had to nag him to shower and shave.

'Oh – feeling better, then?' he said, going to sit down.

'Well . . .' It was oversensitive to feel he was suggesting grief was like flu, to be got over in a week. 'I thought we ought to get back to proper meals. A friend of mine handed in this casserole.'

Nat peered at it distrustfully as she brought it to the table. 'S'pose it'll do.'

Don't react, she told herself. 'Would you like a glass of wine?'

'Any beer?'

'Not up here, no.'

'Oh, whatever.'

Katy served the food, opened the wine and poured out a glass for each of them; he drank his in two mouthfuls, then, unasked, helped himself to another. That alarmed her; perhaps wine hadn't been such a good idea after all. His father had been a mean drunk.

He was eating in silence. 'What have you been doing, then?' she asked, feeling foolish but unable to think of a less banal way to open the conversation.

'Nothing much. School – the usual. Having to look after myself.'

She ignored the implied reproach. 'Was everyone talking about what happened to Willie? I can't bear to think about it – on the way back from helping me out in the bar, just being kind. Did – did you see anything?'

Nat's eyes flickered to her face for a moment, then back to his plate. 'Nuh.'

'Nat, think about it! Your room looks out that way – if you noticed anything, a car parked in a funny place, say, or anything, however small, you should tell the police.'

He set down his knife and fork and leaned across the table towards her, scowling. 'Look, I said I didn't see anything, OK?'

She could feel her heart start to race in fright, but she wouldn't show it. 'Fine,' she said lightly.

This wasn't going well. How could you build bridges with a son whose every instinct was aggressive? He was making no attempt to talk to her, though he had taken a third glass of wine and helped himself to the remains of the despised casserole.

Desperately, she said, 'This is pointless, Nat. We need to talk, to get things sorted out between us. I know you resented Rob and I know too that I've neglected you this last bit. I'm sorry about that. But there were faults on both sides, you know.

'So let's put all that behind us. We can't go on like this.'

For the first time, he smiled. 'Sounds good. Let's do that.'

'I'll tell you what I was thinking—'

'No, why don't I tell you?' He put down his knife and fork, sat back with his glass in his hand. 'First off, we get this dump sold, right? Go back to Glasgow, maybe, where there's some sort of scene for me. There'll be a bit of cash—'

Katy swallowed. 'Nat, I don't see it quite like that. First of all, there's a mortgage—'

'Oh, sure. But I'm not daft – I know what the property market's done. And don't tell me Rob didn't have money he put in himself.'

'Invested it, yes, in the business. And I need a business to earn my living.'

'Nothing to stop you going back to your old job, is there?'

Waitressing – terrible hours, worse pay, no future. 'What about you, Nat – what would you do?' she asked quietly.

'Oh, leave school, get something, I suppose. I'm still a kid – entitled to have a bit of time to enjoy myself. Gap year, they call it. If we split the money—'

She had been undecided about her own future, until now. She was still afraid of what Nat might do but it was almost as if she could feel Rob's steadying hand on her shoulder. 'Any money there is was Rob's money. He put it into the pub to provide for our future, his and mine. If I waste it – or let you just throw it away – I'd be betraying him, and I'm not going to do that. The Anchor's the business we built together and we've had good friends here. I'm not selling it. That's final. And if you don't like it, Nat, well, there's plenty of young men your age earning their own living.' She braced herself for his response, ready to move out of the danger zone if he flared up.

He didn't. There was anger in Nat's face, but also un-certainty. He gave a tight-lipped smile. 'Well, let's cool it for now. See how things go.' He set down his glass, unfinished, and got up. 'I'm going out. Don't wait up.'

As he shut the door, Katy found that she was trembling. She buried her face in her hands. What sort of awful mother was she? Was there another woman in the world who so disliked what her child had become that she could no longer be sure she loved him? She tried to reach back for the memories other mothers seemed to keep preserved like rose petals in pot-pourri, memories of sunshine and laughter and chubby little hands, but Nat's childhood seemed to have passed in a fog of fear and anxiety. The Nat she remem-bered was a frightened kiddie she'd taken blows for, to pro-tect him from his drunken father – and what he had learned was that violent bullies got what they wanted. Both Nat, and her relationship with him, had been deformed as a result. It was her fault for being weak – she should have left, with Nat, before that damage was done – but no one who hadn't suffered abuse would ever understand how hard it had been.

Her every instinct was to send him back to Glasgow, now. It was only, really, her promise to Enid that she would try again that was stopping her – that and his unexpected reaction to her ultimatum which had suggested that perhaps he was still scared of the world outside, still reluctant to leave his home.

Or – something else? Something more calculating? She shivered. One more chance, but she'd phone Dave's mother meantime and have a chat with her about renting a room for Nat somewhere near enough for her to keep an eye on him. Just in case. Because she knew that if she let herself be abused again Rob would feel that she was letting him down.

At least the smug bastard had the sense not to gloat openly at the morning briefing when he heard what Tansy Kerr had to say, even if Tam MacNee was scunnered by the modest smile Kingsley had chosen to adopt instead. Tempted though MacNee felt to point out that an unconfirmed alibi wasn't the same as a false one, he managed to keep his mouth shut. There was still the evidence of the mobile phone to come, though not for a day or two, apparently, for some technological reason he hadn't even tried to understand.

Meantime, there was no choice. They'd have to wheel out the big guns against this their most promising suspect in the hope that sooner rather than later they could find something – anything – to link Elder with the more serious crimes. When the man got out today on bail, as he certainly would, and returned to his executive palace, he'd find JCBs digging up the drains – and, according to Tansy, a wife who'd been *'nursing her wrath to keep it warm'*. He grinned inwardly at the thought; it was a pound to a dud penny that Joanna Elder could be a right little hell-cat when she got going.

There would be a lot of legwork today too – more interviews, lots more, with everyone you could think of and probably a few that never even crossed your mind. He hated jobs
like this, particularly when he was far from convinced that
they were heading in the right direction, but there was no
doubt he was in the minority. The rest of the troops were
enthusiastic: Ritchie Elder was just the sort of guy everyone
liked to see fall on their face, and the flatter the better. Jon
Kingsley's stock was high this morning.

At least, at the end of the briefing, the boss had reminded
them of the status of unconfirmed alibis and warned them
to keep an open mind, though when MacNee brightened
and said, 'In that case, if it's unconfirmed—' she just said
firmly, 'No, Tam.' So that was that. He'd be expected to put
his heart and soul into his allotted task of checking the
schedule for every vehicle operating out of Elder's company.
Oh, he was looking forward to it already.

As he left, he found himself in the company of Jock
Naismith, sergeant of long standing and deep-dyed cynic.
He jerked his thumb back over his shoulder to where Kingsley
was the centre of an animated group. 'See him? Thinks he's
Archie, and he's not even Archie's *dog!*'

Grinning, Tam slapped him on the back, then went to
collect his detail in at least a slightly better frame of mind.

PC Sandy Langlands was feeling cheerful this morning as
he drove away from the showhouse office at Fuill's Inlat.
Right enough, it would have been good to feel he'd had
more of a hand in bringing Elder to justice himself, but like
all the lads he was glad to know that the bastard who'd
flooded the district with drugs and killed four people to protect his trade would soon be having an intimate acquaintance with the inside of one of Her Majesty's less glamorous
properties. Peterhead, maybe. He fancied the thought of

Elder away up on the bleak East Coast. They still had slopping out there, didn't they?

His mission this morning had been to make quite sure that the girls working in the showhouse office could confirm that they hadn't seen Elder until he came in to tell them the lifeboat had been called out, and that the time they'd given in their previous statements was correct. They could: one had moaned to the other that it was all right for the boss – twenty-past seven and there he was away, when they'd be on till ten. He'd noted that down and thanked them warmly.

Their case was still on track; the coastguard's call had gone out at five-past seven, so if no one had seen Elder until twenty-past, he could have parked his car, reckoning if anyone noticed it they'd assume he was somewhere else on the site, and then in the rain and darkness slipped behind it and down into the cove to place the lanterns, which would have taken ten minutes, max. Seven-twenty, and he'd have been ready to stick his head round the showhouse door and go back to Knockhaven.

Langlands's next task was to go back to the couples who had been viewing the houses. Several hadn't arrived until after Elder had left but there were four he had to see again to question in more detail. Ideally, they too would confirm he hadn't been in any of the houses and just maybe someone might remember seeing the Mitsubishi parked well before seven-twenty. You never knew your luck. His problem would be getting hold of them at this time of day – out at work, probably. He'd maybe have to call HQ to see if their work addresses were on file as well.

His mind on this problem, he was driving just a shade too fast up the narrow lane. Suddenly, just short of the point at which it joined the main road, he saw a woman come out of the cottage on the corner and with a fine disregard for her safety place herself in his path. He braked to an untidy stop.

She was elderly, in her seventies, perhaps, with rigid rows of curls covering her head; her mouth, he noticed with a sinking heart, was pursed up like a cat's bum. Now she was placing her hands on her hips.

Langlands drew the car into the side, put on his diced cap and got out. 'Good morning, madam. Were you wanting to speak to me?'

'I should have thought,' she said shrilly, 'that the boot would have been on the other foot – that the police would have been wanting *me*.'

His sense of humour threatened to get the better of him, but he realised in time that the brief pleasure of saying, 'Shall I fetch the handcuffs, then?' would not be worth the consequent pain. 'Now, why would that be?' he wondered gravely.

'You've asked everyone else about the night that lifeboat was wrecked but you've never asked me. Or my husband. For whatever good *that* would do you,' she added darkly.

'I'm sorry, madam. I suppose it was felt that you wouldn't have seen much from the top of the road. And of course we always hope that anyone with useful information will contact us.'

'Huh!' she snorted. 'Well, now you're here you'd better come in.' Without waiting for his response she went back inside and he followed her meekly into a small sitting room with a window which gave directly on to the lane.

A depressed-looking, grey-haired man in a beige cardigan was sitting in one corner by a meagre fire, a red-top open at the sports pages in his hand. He set it down, looking over it at his visitor with glum indifference. 'What are you after now, Jeanie?' he asked his wife but she behaved as if he hadn't spoken.

'There – see?' Jeanie had picked up a brown exercise book which had been lying, with a pen beside it, on the windowledge. 'See this jotter? The traffic down here's been a scandal ever since those gomerils in the Council were daft enough to agree to the houses. And a few wee backhanders slipped under the table too, I've no doubt, so there was little chance they'd pay any mind to what *we* had to say about it. Well, I've been keeping this log of every car that's been up and down here since. It's maybe too late to change it now, but if they think they've shut me up they've got another think coming.'

Her husband gloomily gave it as his opinion that if they did manage, it would be a first, but again was ignored.

Langlands took the book from her and started leafing through it, then stopped, drawing in his breath sharply. 'May I take this, madam? It could be very useful.'

With a triumphant glance at her husband, Jeanie said, 'See, Ron? And you telling me I was just wasting my time!' She turned her beady gaze on Langlands. 'Now, I'll be needing it returned, mind!'

'Of course. I'll give you a receipt.' He fished a pack of forms out of his pocket.

'Could you not take her too?' the melancholy voice said from the corner. 'I wouldn't be wanting her back.'

Repressing a shudder at the thought, Langlands went back to his car. He got in, then hesitated. He'd been given his orders, but there was no point in being in the Force if you didn't use your initiative sometimes. He was going to head back to the nick to tell Big Marge. From what he'd seen, this could change everything.

It was the blaring of a car's horn that shocked Ritchie Elder back to full awareness. He slammed on his brakes as, in a flurry of obscene gestures, the driver of a Renault Clio vented the adrenaline rush caused by Elder's Mitsubishi pulling incautiously out of the side road which led to the cells under the Galloway Police Headquarters in Kirkluce.

Elder's hand went to his brow and found that he was sweating. He wouldn't have believed, if you'd told him before-hand, what the effect of a night in the cells could be. He'd have said he was a hard man, but when the door slammed behind him and he was alone in that bare, bleak, harshly lit space with its seatless lavatory and its uncompromising mes-sage about the power of the State – no belt, no tie, in case he should decide to string himself up from the bars on the tiny window – he knew the panic of helplessness for the first time in his life. He'd never before been in a situation where money couldn't buy you, at the very least, the ordinary decencies of life.

The only other occupant last night had been a drunk brought in shortly before midnight, shouting and swearing and then being violently and noisily sick in the adjoining cell. Elder couldn't sleep; he got up and through the observation window saw a policeman with a mop and bucket going to clean it up.

'Bad luck!' he said sympathetically.

The man turned. 'Compared to you,' he said, 'he's Mother Teresa.'

Elder had never before bothered to consider what anyone thought of his dirty trade. He'd been in denial, too, about his own responsibility for Willie's condition on the night of the wreck; after all, he'd told the moron often enough that only a fool samples the wares, and he'd trusted the man not to let him down when it mattered. And of course he didn't believe in the garbage about one day answering before the Throne of Justice. Yet here in this blank hell-on-earth, you did begin just to wonder . . .

Qualms of conscience had never bothered him much, easily quelled by the usual arguments: nobody makes them buy the stuff; if I don't do it, someone else will . . . And there was a seedy glamour about it, too. At Kirkluce High he'd seen himself as an edgy sort of guy, lead singer in the predictably terrible rock band when Lewis Randall was a swot and Willie Duncan was a thicko with no ambition but to go to the fishing as the Duncans had done since someone first thought of putting a worm on a bent pin.

But now he was going down, no question. His lawyer, whom he employed because he knew every trick in the book, had been blunt. 'The difficult, we do immediately. The impossible – well, there's bugger all we can do about that.' He thought he was funny. Whether he'd think it was so funny if Elder decided to take his custom – worth tens of thousands, in his present situation – elsewhere, was another matter.

He'd known the risks, of course he had – theoretically. He'd even worried a bit, initially, but the trade had been running like clockwork for so long now that in his mind it wasn't a lot different from his legitimate business, which anyway wasn't entirely above board when it came to compliance with health and safety and building regulations. What Elder had never believed was that they'd get him. There were hundreds of them in his game, thousands more likely, and how often did anyone other than the poor pathetic runners ever get caught?

He probably knew enough about the supply routes to bargain down his charge in exchange for cooperation, but as his lawyer had pointed out, it might be better to take the rap and not spend your life after you came out waiting for the bullet in the back. Though, he'd added helpfully, you probably wouldn't have to wait that long. Newly sensitive, Elder realised that it wasn't only the police who despised him.

The murder accusation was something else. Murder was different. Murder – and they were talking multiple murders – meant they locked you up and threw away the key until you might as well be dead. Probably better dead, at that.

And dead was what he would be, or someone else would

be, if he didn't pay attention to his driving. He headed for Bayview House at an uncharacteristically sober speed.

When he turned in, the drive was already being dug up. His beautiful, elegant house, the crowning glory of his career – no shabby corner-cutting here – was being reduced once again to a building site. There were men in white overalls with clipboards observing as a man with a pneumatic drill broke up the concreted area beside the garage where there was a stand-pipe and a drain, while a group of workmen with spades and pickaxes stood by. Sick and shaken, Elder let himself into the house.

It was unnaturally quiet inside. Every window was, naturally, triple-glazed and the sound of the drill outside was muted to little more than background noise. Inside, all he could hear was a faint thud-thud-thud coming from the pool area.

Elder was all too familiar with that sound, made by Joanna's feet on the treadmill. He'd managed to blank her out of his mind. Slowly and reluctantly he crossed the pools of light that lay on the pale wood floor of his lofty hall and opened the door on to the artificial paradise he had created. It looked no more convincing than a stage set now.

Joanna, her delicate features contorted with effort, was running, but when she saw him flicked a switch, slowed down and got off. Red-faced and sweating, she confronted him. 'You stupid, stupid bastard!' she snarled, and slapped him.

Somehow, that helped. If she'd cried . . . 'Did you enjoy that?' he said. 'Other side, to balance it up?' He turned the other side of his face towards her.

She shook her head. 'You really are something else,' she said wonderingly. 'You couldn't be satisfied by what you cream off from your rubbish houses – you had to risk this whole thing—' She waved her hand.

He sneered at her. 'You don't really think I paid for this

from the business? The money that comes from the business covers the lifestyle, more or less. That's it.'

Joanna's eyes widened in shock. 'You mean, all this . . .'

'All this,' he said with relish. 'Yes, my sweetheart, when they freeze all the assets and then start unravelling the books there won't be much to get your sticky little fingers on.'

'My lawyer . . .' she faltered.

'Oh yes, your lawyer. Well, perhaps he's familiar with the old saying, "You can't take the breeks off a Highlandman." You'd be better phoning your mother to see if she can find a job for you in the shop.'

It was only then she began to cry and he could view her tears now with total detachment. 'There's just one other thing. You didn't confirm my alibi for the night Willie was killed.'

'How – how could I? I – I didn't set eyes on you, after seven o'clock,' she sniffed.

'Oh yes, of course. But then, that means I didn't see you either, doesn't it? You might have been tucked up in bed that night, or again you might not. And while I can still hope that they'll find I really couldn't have put the lanterns in place on the night the lifeboat was wrecked, I would question whether you can produce an alibi. What were *you* doing, Joanna, that night?'

Her tears forgotten, she spat, 'Bastard!'

'You said that already.' He was almost enjoying himself. 'And do you know what they're doing out there? They're digging up the drains to see if they can find traces of Willie Duncan's blood left there, washed off a car. You know, just like they did with Dennis Nilsen house.'

Elder realised he had lost her attention. She was looking over his shoulder.

'They're not,' she said. 'They're going away. What's that about?'

He turned to look. Then he said, with sudden conviction,

'They've written me out of the script.' He laughed harshly. 'And they haven't written you in yet.'

Perhaps he only imagined that under the glow of exertion she had turned pale. The truth was, he didn't really care any more.

18

It was clear, from the moment that PC Langlands opened the door to Fleming's office, that he was pleased. His eyes were bright, his tail was wagging – no, no, of course it wasn't.

She liked Sandy Langlands. His resemblance to a Labrador puppy might be so pronounced that you started looking for doggie treats, but enthusiasm was all too rare in a police officer and seldom lasted.

'Sandy.' She smiled at him. 'What can I do for you?'

He beamed back. 'Well – I think I've found something that's really important, boss.'

Was she sure she didn't have a Bonio somewhere? 'Tell me about it.' She waved him to a seat.

He was clutching a brown jotter, which he handed across the desk to her. 'There was this woman,' he said, 'in the cottage at the top of the road to Fuill's Inlat . . .'

She leafed through it while he gave her the back story, and suddenly she wasn't feeling flippant any longer.

'You think this is accurate?' she said slowly.

'I checked when she'd logged me in on my way down the road this morning, and it was spot-on. And you see, if you look at what she has marked, "Boss's big car" on the night of the tenth—'

'Went past at 7.19, with the comment, "Driving far too fast"—'

'That's right. And the girls in the office were absolutely definite that he went into their office at 7.20.'

Fleming ran her finger down the list, written in a firm if old-fashioned hand. 'And then she has him coming back up at 7.22. It's a pity she doesn't appear to have known anything about cars – Elder's is the only one she seems to identify apart from lorry, van – then big car, small car sometimes. And no numbers, of course, just the occasion rude comment about their driving. She's logged fifteen cars coming down to the site that evening from 6.15 on – two close together at the earlier time, then the rest at intervals.'

'That would be the two girls arriving to open up the houses,' Langlands suggested eagerly. 'There were eleven couples viewing, then Ritchie Elder. That's . . .' He paused to calculate.

'Fourteen,' Fleming supplied. 'It isn't news, of course. We know already that the Wrecker had to have driven down that lane. But we could get a time-fix on him from this.' Tapping her pen on her teeth, Fleming considered. 'Right, Sandy. Get back to the people who were there legitimately. Let's hope they can remember when they arrived at the site.'

Langlands was on his feet already. 'They were interviewed the day after it happened so they probably will. I'll get right on to it, boss.'

As he left with a spring in his step, Fleming looked down at the flimsy notebook on her desk. Was she going to change the whole thrust of the enquiry on the evidence of a cantankerous elderly lady with a bee in her bonnet? When it chimed precisely with her own unease, and Tam's, and considering the cost of the operation going on at this moment at Bayview House, you're damn right she was.

The atmosphere in Galloway Police Headquarters was charged when Tam MacNee came in, so charged that he could hardly believe that there were actually members of the public sitting peacefully unaware in the waiting area. They must be brain-dead, or cyclists, maybe, reporting the theft of their push-bikes. Or one of their anoraks. MacNee was politically incorrect on the subject of cyclists.

'Tam!' Jock Naismith hailed him from behind the front desk. 'What's going on? Big Marge has pulled everyone back—'

'I was hoping you could tell me.' MacNee walked briskly through the hall, left his notes in the CID room, then took the stairs to the fourth floor two at a time.

Fleming glanced up when he came in, then said abstractedly, 'Take a seat. Be with you in a second.' She had a big sheet of paper in front of her and she was scribbling on it with a frown of concentration.

One of her 'mind-maps' – that was what she called them, something she'd picked up at one of the training courses he had always avoided when he could. His first sergeant, God rest his black soul, had warned them all to be careful of the sort of thing they might pick up on residential courses.

At last she looked up. 'OK, Tam – what have you heard?'

'All I know is that when I passed the CID room Jon Kingsley was sitting alone at a desk looking as if someone taken his Saturday penny. So whatever it is, it can't be all bad.'

She gave him a quelling look. 'I had to tell him before it became general knowledge. Take a look at this.' She pushed a brown jotter across the desk and while he flipped through it went back to frowning over the scribbled sheet in front of her.

It didn't take him long. 'If this is accurate—'

'I don't see any reason why it shouldn't be. And the Super agrees.'

'He was jake with this?'

'Not exactly. He – er – whimpered a little.' She couldn't resist adding, 'I think it helped that when he'd called Jon in for a pat on the back yesterday he'd felt patronised.'

'Go on, what did he say?'

She wouldn't be drawn. 'He agreed, that's all. You know, Tam, I should be feeling depressed – and after Don and the Chief Constable see tomorrow's headlines I probably will be. After all this time the only progress we've made has been negative, but somehow I feel liberated.

'I've been thinking.' She indicated the paper in front of her. 'One of the good things Jon's done is have the drug samples he picked up in pubs around the area analysed, and what they're telling us is that they've all come from the same source – Ritchie Elder's operation. He didn't have rivals in the area who might have taken out Willie in a turf war, which was something that had crossed my mind. So if it isn't drugs behind this, someone, in all probability, killed Willie to make us believe it was.

'So I've been focusing on the other deaths. Luke, poor lad – there's absolutely nothing suspicious. Which leaves us with either Ashley Randall or Rob Anderson as victim.

'Of course we have to dig deeper. But looking here,' she pointed to a circle with the name Ashley Randall at its centre, and lines coming from it, 'what catches my eye is this – the figure in the shadows.' She tapped Lewis Randall's name. 'Jon's talked to him, you've talked to him – neither of you came back with anything to say.'

MacNee grimaced. 'Funny bloke. Either there's nothing there, or under that cool exterior there's a seething mass of passions.'

'That's almost poetic, Tam. See, you can do it yourself – you don't have to quote Burns. And it's cheaper. Anyway, there are the women to consider too in that area. Dorothy Randall, Joanna Elder, Enid Davis.'

'Enid Davis?'

'Yes,' she said firmly. 'No one's talked to her yet. Oh, I know what you said about Randall's attitude to her, but if he's a seething mass he may be secretly harbouring a passion for her – the most improbable people inspire timeless love. Look at Camilla Parker Bowles. And if Enid could be sure that only Ashley stood in her way—'

'OK, OK, Enid. And Dorothy, if you ask me, would cheerfully strangle anyone with her bare hands if they so much as looked at Lewis sideways—'

'And Tansy says Joanna would auction her grandmother for ten pence on her maintenance cheque,' finished Fleming. 'Do you reckon it could be a woman's crime, Tam?'

He shrugged. 'Why not? But aren't you forgetting someone?'

'Nat Rettie,' she said slowly. 'No. No, I'm not.'

'Maybe we need to pull him in again.'

'I'll give it some thought. What I need is some space to think this through, and I won't get it here at my desk so I'm going to take off. I want to have a chat with Laura too, if I can get hold of her.' She glanced out of the window; the sky was clear and white clouds, driven by a brisk breeze, were scudding by. 'Maybe she and Daisy would fancy a walk on the beach. I've a couple of things I want to ask her advice on.'

MacNee looked at her sharply. 'Bill all right?'

'Oh, Bill's fine. We're working our way back to where we were and I reckon we'll make it. No, it's – it's Cat. I think I told you she's far too chummy with Kylie MacEwan.'

Nat's girlfriend. MacNee nodded. That maybe explained Marjory's hesitation about him.

'There's something upsetting Cat and she's not eating properly. And I can't get her to tell me what the problem is.'

'Laura's just the lass you need to talk to, then.' He was one of Laura's big fans.

'That's what Bill said, when I told him last night.'

'That's good.' Tam had detected a certain constraint in Bill's attitude to his wife's friend; Marjory would be pleased if Bill was coming round. 'Away you go, then. Say I was asking for her.'

Her eyes watering in the wind, Marjory Fleming pulled up the zip of her weatherproof jacket as far as it would go, and sank her chin into it. Laura Harvey's small figure beside her was bundled up in a pink wool coat with a striped beanie hat pulled down over her ears and a matching scarf wound three times round her neck, while Daisy raced in circles round them on the hard sand below the tideline, her ears blowing back like small furry pennants.

Laura sneezed, then laughed. 'It's this air! It tickles the inside of my nose, like the bubbles in champagne.'

Marjory looked about her. 'Glorious, isn't it?' Her gesture took in the wide majesty of the sky, the deserted beach, the spits of rock running down into the sea, the low, wind-barbered shrubs on the other side of the road where their own parked cars were the only vehicles in sight. Above their heads, seabirds leaned into the wind, with the occasional keening cry.

Laura paused to stare out to the empty ocean with its white-capped waves foaming in, to vanish in a flurry of spent bubbles in the coarse sand. 'Alone in the universe!' she declaimed.

'I wish!' Marjory said with feeling, and her friend turned to look at her.

'How's the case going?'

It was a measure of Marjory's maternal disquiet that she waved aside the investigation which had been occupying most of her waking hours. 'I do want to ask you about that later, but what's worrying me most at the moment is Cat.'

She filled in the background, then went on, 'We haven't been happy about Cat's friendship with this girl, even before all the worrying stuff about Nat Rettie came out. But it's only very recently she hasn't been eating. Last night I think she fed her supper to the dog when no one was looking and then when I'd comforted myself with the thought that she'd eaten a meringue, I smelled sick in the bathroom. Mother's worried too. You know how it is with adolescent girls.'

'Anorexia nervosa.' Laura nodded. 'And you're right to be concerned – it's a psychological cliché that it often afflicts conscientious, well-behaved girls like Cat.'

'Not at the moment.' Marjory laughed shortly. 'You should have heard what they said at her Parents' Evening! I tried to talk to her about it at bedtime last night, and she just denied it flatly. She doesn't seem to have lost a lot of weight yet, but I don't understand, Laura – what's it about? What can we do?'

'The nervosa bit indicates that it's got an emotional rather than a physical origin. Sometimes it can happen when the family – especially the mother – has an obsessive attitude to food, dieting or not eating anything that isn't specific-ally "healthy".' She caught Marjory's eye and they both laughed.

'Not *exactly* Cat's problem,' Marjory said ruefully.

'Nonsense. You're perfectly in proportion for your height,' Laura said robustly. 'The other theory is that it's sexual, a subconscious fear of having to deal with the problems of being a woman. Extreme weight loss means you don't men-struate, effectively becoming a child again. From what you've said, it wouldn't be at all unlikely that she's feeling threatened by her friend's precocity. There must be a lot of conflict between what she knows is right and sensible, and loyalty to her peer.'

'So how do we tackle it?'

'Don't worry. Cat has to sit down to meals – you'd be astonished how many children don't – so you've spotted it before it's had a real chance to affect her physically. I don't believe this is an on-going family problem; I think if we tackle the situation she's in at school, try to take away the pressure she's feeling, it would sort itself out.'

Marjory sighed. 'I feel so guilty – she had such nice friends, before all the foot-and-mouth fuss. She says they talk to her quite pleasantly again now, but of course she's cut herself off by her friendship with Kylie.'

'Why don't you ask her to walk round tomorrow after school and have tea with me? I might manage to get her talking. Say I wondered if she'd like to see Daisy.'

'She'd love to. She and Bill were both wondering how she was getting on. Thanks, Laura.'

'No problem.' The dog, perhaps hearing her name, had come panting back to her mistress's feet and Laura bent to pick up a seaweed root to throw for her. 'So – what about the case? Everyone's talking about it, of course. The rumours in this place fascinate me – it's like a flock of starlings, all wheeling one way and then for no apparent reason wheeling round all at the same time and heading in the opposite direction.'

'What's the latest?' Marjory asked with interest.

'Ah! The latest but one was that Willie had gone around saying definitely he wasn't a target, so his death had to be just to divert suspicion. But then, with Ritchie Elder being arrested, they've decided Willie was wrong.'

'You've no idea how relieved I am that they're not up-to-date yet with the latest development. I was beginning to think they had my office bugged.

'Keep it to yourself, but we've got evidence that Elder couldn't have set up the wreck of the lifeboat. So I'm going to assume, at least for the moment, that he didn't kill Willie either.

'Laura, I need you to talk me through it, from a psychological point of view – did I ever think I would hear myself say these words? But the thing is, we just can't get a proper handle on it – tiny bits and pieces of information are coming in, but painfully slowly, and all that any of them seem to do is prove a negative.'

'If you're talking psychology, actually having a negative instead of a wishy-washy maybe this, maybe that, would be a rare treat. Oh God, Daisy's found a dead bird! Daisy, drop it!' Laura rushed ahead to drag the reluctant dog away from her trophy.

Marjory followed her, arguing. 'Yes, but no one expects you to bring someone to court at the end of a therapy session, do they? Bear with me. There isn't the faintest shred of evidence to suggest that for all his personal problems, poor Luke Smith wasn't just in the wrong place at the wrong time. If what we're talking about is the deaths of Ashley Randall and Rob Anderson, a group of suspects suggests itself.' She outlined them, then added ruefully, 'Of course, if we manage to eliminate all of them, Knockhaven has a population of around two thousand who could have heard the lifeboat being called out and decided wrecking it would be fun, but at that point I resign from the Force and start doing farmhouse B&B instead.'

Laura smiled, but her brows furrowed in concentration. 'You said the last time that you believed the killer thought the wreck would be put down to an accident – but once it wasn't, to be so determined to protect yourself that you'd mow another person down in cold blood . . . Though of course, the idea was probably suggested by the stories flying round about Willie saying it was meant to be him.

'It's not hands-on stuff. It's not psychopathic killing for the perverted pleasure of direct violence. The methods suggest a sort of dissociation, a reluctance to get your hands dirty, squeamishness, even. The wreck, for example – you could almost persuade yourself that you had invoked outside agencies to achieve the execution. And even the car – that's at one remove too. Sort of, "I don't like what I'm doing, so if I pretend I'm not . . ."'

'But if you felt like that, how could you kill innocent people?'

'Certainly, it would present problems for anyone who wasn't a full-blown psychopath. Unless you somehow convinced yourself that the others weren't innocent – or I suppose the way you could square it might be by arguing that killing someone who in your eyes was fit to die unfortunately resulted in collateral damage, like dropping a bomb. The second death – to continue the military image, you'd class that as shooting someone in self-defence. But all I'm doing here is thinking aloud. Were you leaning particularly hard on any of your suspects at that time?'

Marjory considered. 'Not specifically. Asking questions all round, which I suppose might make anyone feel uncomfortable.'

'So it's an extreme reaction to a low-level threat. It all suggests a very high degree of self-love, self-preservation.'

'Solipsism. That was what you said.'

'It's not a clinical term, just a way of describing someone with a vastly inflated idea of the importance of their own wishes – someone who sees life as a play in which they're not so much the leading character as the only character. The killer here seems to be egocentric to a seriously dangerous degree. And you don't need me to tell you that the first death is a taboo broken. The second one is easier – and, if you're threatened again, a wasted investment unless you eliminate the next equally ruthlessly.'

'So somehow we have to be sure of getting to the truth before someone stumbles on it?'

Laura's shrug was eloquent.

'So – why are you doing it at all? You love yourself – why do you expose yourself to a risk like this?'

'Love, hatred, gain, revenge – the usual. Or a combination.'

'Well, that covers most of our suspects. Couldn't you just be a bit more specific?'

'What you want isn't a psychologist, it's Gypsy Rose and her crystal ball. Or one of these profilers who can tell you the killer is five foot eleven, with a taste in sharp suits and an Oedipus complex.'

Marjory stared at her. 'You could be describing Lewis Randall. Except he must be at least six foot.'

Laura burst out laughing. 'There you are, then! But realistically, he could just have divorced her, couldn't he? And if you hated your wife enough to kill her instead, you'd probably want to put your hands round her throat.'

'I take the point. But his mother – she hated Ashley, who was a bad wife to her son. If he wouldn't divorce her . . .'

'More plausible motivation, certainly. Who else have you got under the microscope?'

'Enid Davis – allegedly in love with Lewis, though Jon swears he's not interested.'

'Killing the wife would be quite a speculative venture unless you were sure he wouldn't seize his freedom and go off with someone else. But Joanna Elder – is she still in the frame?'

'Very much so. She had a lot to lose, if Ritchie turned her out. Oh, he'd have to pay her off, certainly, but it's not the same.'

'So you think it was aimed at Ashley, then?'

'Not necessarily, I suppose.' Marjory pulled a face. 'There's

Nat Rettie, Cat's friend Kylie's boyfriend and Rob Anderson's stepson. Big problems there, and there's a trace of evidence that makes Tam think we might have been a bit hasty in writing him out on the basis of an alibi provided by Kylie, whom I wouldn't trust round the corner.'

Laura considered that. 'You wouldn't put the wreck down as a teenage crime, would you – too meticulous? But then again, they all spend hours on computers playing these intricate fantasy games, so elaborate planning mightn't be as unnatural as you'd think.'

'So – let me get this straight. You're saying it could be anyone, but if you were placing a bet you wouldn't put it on Lewis Randall or Enid Davis?'

'Oh, I'm not sure I'd go as far as that.' Laura was laughing. 'I did warn you long ago, you needn't expect answers from psychology.'

'Don't know why I bother, really. Seriously, though, that's helped straighten a few things out in my mind. And I heard what you said, about the next killing being easier.' Perhaps it was only because the sun had gone in that Marjory shivered. 'Brr, it's cold! The nights are really drawing in now.'

'Daisy's managed to run herself into the ground, anyway.' The puppy, trotting wearily beside her mistress now, looked up at the mention of her name and Laura picked her up, averting her face to avoid a succession of grateful licks. 'We'd better be getting home. Do you want to come back for tea?'

'Thanks, but no. I'm going to drive on down to Knockhaven for a chat with Lewis Randall.'

'Good luck! Don't forget to tell Cat to come to tea.' Laura waved goodbye and hurried back to her car.

Marjory lingered a little longer. As so often in the early evening, the wind had dropped and daylight began to yield to a creeping darkness that blurred the edges between the sky and sea. The birds had gone; a hush fell and it almost seemed as if that great silence was louder than the swishing of the waves at her feet. It was going to be a cold, clear night and across the bay the lights of the little townships down the Mull of Galloway studded the dusk.

After a moment or two she sighed, then looked at her watch. She should just have time to pick up a few things at the '8 'til Late' in Knockhaven – bread, potatoes and loo rolls, mainly. Wasn't it always?

She should have time for a chat with Lewis Randall and still be back for supper. For the next while, however difficult it might prove to be, she was determined not to miss the family meal, even if it meant going back to her desk afterwards.

She took a last look before she turned reluctantly to go; as the darkness encroached she could just see the stabbing beam of the Mull of Galloway lighthouse. With her mind on those who had their business in deep waters, she went back to the car.

There had been considerable industry in the CID room this afternoon. As officers returned, recalled from their details, a place at one of the computers was in high demand; most, if not all of them, had arrears of reports to make up and this pause for breath before the investigation spun off in a different direction was precious found time. Hot-desking was the order of the day and taking a comfort break, when you were in possession, was a high-risk activity.

With the double advantages of an early summons back to HQ and a good bladder, Tam MacNee had managed to stake out a corner desk and, ignoring both pleas and imprecations, was smugly finished by half-past five.

He got up. 'Anyone fancy a wee bevvy?' he said provocatively as there was a rush to take his place. He hadn't really
expected there to be any takers; he could go and have a quiet
jar, trading insults with the landlord – an old mate – and
time his arrival home so that he didn't see any more than
he had to of his brother-in-law, a banker, who with Bunty's
sister had been bidden to supper this evening. They always
behaved as if letting Tam eat at the same table was a big
favour and it took him all his time not to tell them what he
thought of that toffee-nosed besom and her lardy husband.
But since Bunty had the same inexplicable fondness for
her sister that she had for mangy dogs and flea-ridden
cats, he kept his trap shut for her sake. He just didn't like to
try himself too far, that was all.

It was only as he came out of his corner that he noticed
Jon Kingsley. He was sitting at the big table in the middle
of the room, apparently engrossed in paperwork, but he
looked wretched. In fact, he reminded Tam of nothing so
much as the deflated Mr Toad in a pantomime Bunty had
made him take her to, which he'd never have done if he'd
known it involved suffering for any of God's creatures
which – even when played by a man in a loud green-
checked suit – invariably wrung his wife's tender heart.
Perhaps it was in deference to her that he felt uncomfortable
seeing the man there, with a space about him on either
side, a sort of no-man's-land, as if all those who had been
hailing him as a hero this morning were trying now to dis-
sociate themselves from him – The Man Who Backed The
Wrong Hunch.

Tam's lip curled. He yielded to no one in his dislike of
cocky little sods who thought they knew it all, and if anyone
had it coming to them it was Kingsley. But when a man was
down . . .

'Come on, Jon,' he said roughly. 'Come and have a jar

and leave these tossers to get on with their homework nicely.'

Startled, Kingsley looked up. He didn't seem exactly thrilled, but after a moment he said, 'Why not?' and followed MacNee out.

The pub most favoured by the constabulary was a small, old-fashioned establishment about 500 metres along the main street. The Salutation had two long rooms side by side, separated only by a chimney stack where a fire, open to both sides, burned summer and winter. It made no attempt to attract a white-wine-spritzer clientele with its rough wooden flooring and its walls yellowed by years of kippering from smoke; you could get a good pint, sausages, decent pies and sandwiches, but towards the gastropub concept there was not so much as a nod.

It was early enough to be very quiet. 'Grab the table by the fire and I'll set us up,' Tam instructed his colleague, and while Jon sat down, holding his hands to the blaze as if its comforting warmth was not only physical, went to the bar to engage in some ritual abuse of the landlord, before coming back with a pint glass in either hand.

Jon took his with a twisted smile. 'Cheers. Payback time, I suppose.'

'*Slainte.* No, not really.'

Jon looked up sharply. 'I don't need pity!'

'You're not getting it. You stuck your neck way out, the axe came down . . . Tough.'

'Yeah, sure!' Jon's tone was bitter. 'It's the name of the game. But what's really got to me is the way the top brass are all over you one minute, then when I met the Super in the corridor today, slapping you down because something seems to have come unstuck – not that I'm convinced yet that it has, frankly, just because some dotty old biddy—'

'Ah. I wasn't sure if you'd heard yet. Some dotty old biddy, plus the cutting edge of modern technology.'

'What do you mean?'

'A report came in from Vodafone today. They've traced the call the coastguard made to Ritchie Elder's mobile, and it was answered in Glasserton, just where he said he was.'

'Oh.' Jon took a sip of his pint, but he didn't look as if he were enjoying it. 'So that's that, then. The Super seems to have marked me down as a total prat already and this will have finished it. Not that I understood what he said – he seemed to be saying it was a bummer – and I certainly agreed with him there. But he said something broad Scots about a bee as well—'

So that was what Marjory wouldn't tell him. Tam tried not to smile. 'Bummer and bees? Perhaps, "It's no' aye the loudest bummer's the best bee"?'

'That's right! What on earth does it mean?'

'In Scots, bees don't buzz, they bum. The bee that buzzes loudest isn't always the best.'

'I – see.'

Tam was beginning to regret his kindly impulse. 'Look, laddie, I'm going to tell you something they don't teach you at the university. If you're going to swan in and tell everyone you're better than they are, you'd bloody better get it right. If you keep quiet, never say boo, and don't get up anyone's nose, no one'll mind if you're wrong. Most of us come somewhere in the middle, and if you don't rub it in when you're right, they won't rub your nose in it when you're wrong.'

Jon smiled, a wonderfully polite smile. 'Thanks, Tam, that's very helpful, of course.

'Do you know what Big Marge is planning now? Presumably there'll be a morning briefing . . .'

Well, sod him! Tam dispatched his pint with unaccustomed

speed and, even more unusually, refused the other half, on the excuse that he had people coming to supper.

Bunty would be surprised. Tam's normal form was to appear just as the plates were put on the table, and disappear back to work with the arrival of the coffee cups.

19

'Oh, I'm afraid he's not here. He's off this afternoon.' The doctors' receptionist discreetly lowered her voice as five patients in the waiting area visibly strained to hear what the tall woman who had announced herself as DI Fleming wanted to know, and Fleming looked at her with interest.

She'd seen Enid Davis before, at the funeral tea, but had gained only a fleeting impression of the person who'd figured in rumour as a scarlet woman. Today she was wearing something nondescript and suitable in brown, which did nothing for her mousy hair and pale colouring. The polite, professional smile didn't quite reach her eyes and the lines about her mouth suggested that a real smile wouldn't come readily; you'd guess life hadn't been exactly kind to her and she'd stopped expecting that it would be.

'Would you know where I could find him?'

'Not really. I know he goes for long walks sometimes – or he could be at home. Or perhaps at his mother's. Do you need addresses?'

'I have them, thanks.' Fleming hesitated. Perhaps she should question Enid now too, to save someone else from having to come out to do it tomorrow even if it did mean being later in getting home than she had planned. She was wrestling with her conscience when another woman appeared from behind a bank of shelves. She had a helmet of grey curls and her eyes were bulging with curiosity – or perhaps she just had bulging eyes anyway.

'Who's this, Enid?' she demanded, loudly and rudely.

In a colourless voice, Enid told her.

'Oh, an inspector! We are going up in the world, aren't we?' she tittered. 'I'm Muriel Henderson.'

'So I see.' Fleming indicated the badge sitting on the sloping shelf of her acrylic-clad bust.

'I'm the most *senior* receptionist. I'll take over now, Enid.' With a quelling glance at her colleague she neatly edged her aside. 'Now, what did you want to know, Inspector?'

Enid moved obediently, but the look Fleming saw her direct at Muriel's back was eloquent. Of course, this was the woman who had told Jon the rumour; a high-ranking officer questioning Enid now would fuel a brushfire of specu- lation when she looked as if she'd suffered enough from that already – and it gave Fleming all the excuse she needed to duck out. 'It's all right, thanks. Mrs Davis has given me the information I need.'

'But—'

Pretending she hadn't heard, Fleming turned to go. As she shut the door behind her it was clear Muriel was moving in to give her colleague the third degree. What a fearsome crea- ture, like a spider at the centre of her web of intrigue, trussing her victims with the sticky threads of smear and innuendo before she sucked them dry. Fleming grimaced as she walked back to her car.

Randall's house was in a housing development built in the 1990s which was a mixture of smaller houses, built with gar- dens adjoining back to back, and a few larger ones with a bit more ground, like his. The streets were all, confusingly, called Mayfield something; she took a couple of wrong turn- ings before she drew up outside the big, ranch-style house with its white picket fence. There were lights on inside. That looked promising.

In the light from the street lamps, she could see that the

garden was quite bare – just paving slabs, with spaces left for a few shrubs. She went up the concrete path and rang the doorbell.

Lewis Randall was slumped in one of the big leather chairs in his study. He had an empty tumbler on the table at his side and there was a bottle of Bladnoch on the floor at his feet. He was dozing; the sound of the doorbell took a moment to register. Then he groaned, blinked blearily and heaved himself to his feet, swaying a little. But he steadied himself, shaking his head in an attempt to clear it, and went to answer the door.

He was better now he was on his feet, not so drunk that he couldn't carry on a civilised conversation with whoever it might be – no doubt one of the neighbours, who had all been treating him to kindness so relentless that it reminded him of a child loving a hamster by squeezing it till its eyes popped out. Still, as Lewis's calm, ordered world disinte-grated round him, he should be grateful for their constancy – and he was, in general. He licked his dry lips and ran a hand over his hair to smooth it down; the last thing he needed was to have it all round the village that the doctor had a drink problem. He might be working on developing one, but that was beside the point.

He didn't recognise the woman on the doorstep. At this time of night you occasionally did get cold-callers, though somehow she didn't look as if she was selling double-glazing. She was tall, nearly as tall as he was himself, but it was her eyes he couldn't help noticing – hazel eyes that seemed to be taking in at a glance what he was trying to hide.

'Detective Inspector Fleming,' she said. 'I wonder if I could have a word with you, Dr Randall?'

His heart gave a single, heavy thump of alarm. His mother had warned him . . . And perhaps he should say no, that it wasn't convenient. He ought to have all his wits about him before he talked to the police. But what would be inferred from that?

'Of course.' His tongue felt thick and unwieldy. 'Would you like to come in?'

He could take her into the sitting room, cold and dark at the moment, but without the evidence of glass and bottle. He was probably just about asphyxiating the woman with whisky fumes anyway, so with a mental shrug he led her through to the study where the lamps were lit and the ceramic stones in the bowl of the gas hearth glowed in fashionably ironic imitation of an open fire.

'Can I get you a drink?' he offered.

She smiled. 'I share your taste in whisky, but unfortunately I have a car at the door.'

'Do sit down, anyway. I'm just going to get myself a glass of water. Can I get you anything else?'

She shook her head and Lewis escaped from the room. In the kitchen he ran the tap cold, then splashed his face. He filled a glass with water, drank it, then refilled the glass, noting clinically that his hand was trembling slightly. He took several deep, slow breaths before he went back to submit to inquisition.

Best to take this one head on. As he sat down he said, 'I hope what I say to you is going to make sense. As you will have noticed, I've been drinking.'

'You're a doctor. I don't need to tell you it's not the best way to cope with problems. But it's entirely understandable.' She had a low, attractive voice and she spoke sympathetically. 'You must be under a great deal of strain.'

'Yes. Yes.' Alarmingly, he felt tears prickle the backs of his eyes. He hadn't cried, had hardly felt tempted to cry, but alcohol was notorious for loosening constraint. 'Everything is just – I don't know where I am. I'm not very good at uncertainty.'

'Were you and your wife very close?'

Lewis knew the shutting-down answer to that question –
'Yes, naturally' – but his tongue wouldn't frame the words.
'Not exactly – close, no. I feel sort of at a loss without her –
hence this, I suppose.' He gestured to the bottle and glass. 'We
didn't quarrel or anything, we worked together, had a lot in
common—' He stopped. 'It's not really much of a testimonial
to our marriage, is it?'

'Did you love each other?'

The chair the inspector sat in had lugs which cast a shadow
on her face so that the quiet voice seemed disembodied,
anonymous, like a priest's in the confessional. He had never
discussed his marriage; there was a delicious release in doing
so now.

'I guess we did, in a sort of way, though I'm not sure I
ever understood exactly what that means – or that Ashley
understood either. Perhaps that's why it worked as well as it
did. Oh, I know what you're going to ask me next – was she
having an affair with Ritchie Elder? Both of your colleagues
asked me that.

'I gave them the honest answer – I don't know. I never
saw any evidence of it, though I'd gathered from barely veiled
hints that there was gossip.' He rubbed at his forehead, as if
that might help banish the lingering alcoholic fog. 'But perhaps I didn't go looking for it – didn't, if I'm being absolutely honest, care enough to turn everything upside down
for the sake of finding out that my wife was having what
might be a temporary fling.'

'And you? Did you go looking for love elsewhere, since
you didn't seem to have found it in marriage?'

'It's what most men would do, isn't it? But – well, it's never
seemed worth it, somehow. What was lacking in our marriage
was something I didn't especially miss. I was quite content
with our life here the way it was – comfortable, predictable . . .'

He trailed into silence, then as Fleming didn't speak, went on, 'To tell you the truth, I've wondered sometimes if I'm a latent gay, but I can't see it. I've never been remotely attracted to another man and there was never anything wrong with Ashley's and my sex-life.

'There's a vogue for describing people as asexual just now, and perhaps that's me. I wouldn't actually argue.'

Why was he telling her all this? Perhaps it was the drink talking, but it was a huge relief to give voice to the thoughts which had been chasing round and round in his head.

'Did you ever consider divorce?'

'Ashley might have, though she certainly never mentioned it to me. If she had, I wouldn't have wanted to hold her to vows that had become meaningless.'

'That sounds very level-headed. Where does Enid Davis come in?'

'Enid Davis?' He was startled by the question. 'The receptionist – what do you mean?'

'Is there anything between you?'

He didn't know whether to be amused or uneasy at this change of direction. 'Between us? I have a warm relationship with her rock cakes, but that's the extent of it.'

'Have you ever spent time alone with her?'

The warm, soothing voice had sharpened. He began to feel the first twinges of real concern. 'No, never.' He took a sip of water, feeling more sober by the minute.

'Do you think she is in love with you?'

'No, I don't. She's worked with us for a couple of years or so. I know she had an unhappy marriage and I suspect she is lonely, but she has never by word, look or deed suggested that she wanted to initiate a closer relationship.'

The inspector sat forward in her chair, and now the light from one of the lamps caught her face. It was a strong, intelligent face and again, the eyes . . . He wondered if she had moved deliberately so that he would feel impaled on her direct gaze.

'Where were you on the night the lifeboat was wrecked, Dr Randall?'

He said flatly, 'As I said in my statement, I was here. On my own, working, though I gather my mother came round and looked in to see if I was busy without disturbing me, so she can vouch for that.'

'Is it a habit of hers?'

He avoided a direct answer. 'She is very protective of me and very considerate about not intruding.'

'And the night Willie Duncan was killed?'

He was dreading that question. He'd always been a useless liar; his mother was so adept at spotting a lie at a thousand paces that he'd seldom even bothered to try. He licked his lips, then looked up to meet her eyes squarely – it would never do to look shifty now.

'I was at my mother's. We had supper together, steak and kidney pie, then watched a film – *Lawrence of Arabia*. It was quite late when I got home – well after midnight.'

Fleming wasn't smiling, but somehow he had the uncomfortable feeling that she was amused. 'Can you remember what you had for pudding?'

'Yes. Fruit salad.'

'And the vegetables?'

'Look, what is this?' He was getting angry now. 'Are you trying to be funny?'

She smiled. 'Do you know what people tend to do when they're telling lies, Dr Randall?' she asked conversationally.

He felt suddenly cold.

'I'll tell you, shall I? First of all, they often lick their lips. Someone would probably tell you it's symbolic, so that the difficult words will slip out more easily. Then they meet your eyes very, very directly. Normally people look slightly to one side, since a stare tends to mean either a come-on or a challenge.

'The next giveaway is the tendency to elaborate – back it up with a lot of needless detail. It's rather well described in *The Mikado*, if you saw it when the Kirkluce Operatic put it on last year: this is "intended to give artistic verisimilitude to an otherwise bald and unconvincing narrative".

'Are you with me so far?'

'Yes, I'm afraid I am.' He had never felt more sober in his life.

'So let's pretend you didn't say all that, shall we? I'll ask again. Dr Randall, where were you when Willie Duncan was murdered?'

He had his head in his hands, and he spoke without looking up to meet her eyes. 'I was here, by myself, working late. I didn't speak to anyone on the phone, or see anyone, and my mother was afraid that if I had no alibi I would be wrongfully accused, probably convicted and locked up for the rest of my life.

'There was an incident at university, in the halls of residence, when the guy next door reported his camera had been stolen to claim the insurance. It was a scam, of course, but I was the chief suspect, which was pretty unpleasant. They dropped it eventually, but it's made my mother very protective.

'Anyway, since I knew I wasn't guilty, it seemed a harmless enough lie – might even save your time, in trying to prove that I wasn't where I said I was.'

'Very public-spirited, I'm sure,' Fleming said dryly, 'but we prefer to do these things in our own bumbling way.

'Where were you working that night?'

Lewis gestured to the desk under the window at the back of the house, a large birchwood desk with a computer on it as well as wire baskets piled with papers. 'There, as usual.'

'Using the computer?'

'Yes, I should think so, probably.'

'A touch of uncertainty – that's much more convincing,' she said approvingly. 'Do you think you could find what you were working on that night for me?'

He frowned. 'It was – what, three days ago? Oh yes, I remember, I was working on a report for a drug company about side-effects.'

'Would you mind opening the computer to Documents and finding it for me?'

Puzzled, he went over to the desk. Fleming followed him across as he found it and indicated the file. She leaned over his shoulder, took the mouse from him and pointed it, without clicking. A box sprang into view, with lines of information. At the bottom an entry read, 'Date modified: 20/10/02 23.40.'

'There, you see – there's your alibi. You couldn't be at your desk, modifying a document, and lying in wait for Willie Duncan at the same time.'

'Good God,' he said blankly.

'And if you'd like to track down the work you were doing on the night of the tenth, we could clear that up at the same time.'

When the inspector left at last and he shut the door behind her, Lewis slumped against the wall feeling totally drained. He'd always had, if he was honest, a faintly patronising attitude to the police, but she was good. God, she was good.

And she'd cleared him. His world was still disordered, but the fear at the back of his mind that his mother might have been right about British justice had gone. He must phone and tell her—

Then he stopped. Perhaps he'd just say they'd accepted he was in the clear. It seemed pathetic, to have been so easily caught out, and he wouldn't have to lie to her – all she would want to know was that her son wasn't under suspicion any longer.

Katy Anderson sat alone in her sitting room, listening to the noise and laughter coming up from the street below as the last of the drinkers left the pub. She should have been down there helping; the pub had been busy, and it wasn't as if she was ill, even though it felt as if she was. She couldn't rely for ever on the kindness of friends.

But she was scared. When she went back into the lovely wee pub she and Rob had created between them, his stocky, bearded ghost would be round every corner. She'd be listening for his hearty laugh, expecting his arm to come round her waist to give her a squeeze in passing.

The longer she left it, though, the worse it would be, and she'd have to take the plunge sometime, unless she gave in to Nat's bullying and sold up. He'd gone on at her again today, even in the morning on the way to school, then aggressively in the evening over supper. He'd been very late coming in and he'd been drinking or something; she'd tried to ignore it, but it was scary. She'd stuck to what she'd said, but how long would it be before either she gave in or he lost the heid because she wouldn't? She'd been there before, with the pressure and demands getting worse and worse until one day a fist came into the argument, and when they'd done it once they were never feart to do it again . . .

And then there was the other scary bit. She'd told herself Nat couldn't have had anything to do with Rob's death, he couldn't – but how sure was she? And if she went down and looked at the cars – Rob's in the garage, her own in the street – would one of them have traces of Willie's blood? She was too afraid to look herself while Nat was around, but she couldn't go to the police and accuse her own son with nothing to go on but what might just be a daft notion.

It couldn't go on like this. She'd made up her mind even before he slammed out of the house half an hour ago. She didn't know where he was away to, didn't know when she'd see him back. Didn't really want to see him. For now, they'd do better apart; she'd phone his grandmother in the morning, offer Nat enough money to persuade him to go. She didn't think it would actually be difficult, if she promised him there would be more to come later.

Katy had done a lot of thinking in the last twenty-four hours. She knew she needed to keep busy; sitting here alone, leafing through her past, was just asking to be miserable. This morning, screwing up her courage, she'd ventured out to coffee with her friend Ellie, who'd drawn up a programme to keep her busy and get started in the pub again ('And you've to tell everyone you're doing it, so you can't get cold feet and back out, OK?'). Then she'd gone along Shore Street for some messages for the first time since the disaster and every second person had stopped to speak as if welcoming her back from somewhere. Even Joanna Elder, coming out of the dry-cleaner's, stopped to ask how she was getting on, and when she'd taken the casserole dish back to give Enid at the Medical Centre she'd managed to stay calm when Muriel Henderson, in her rude way, demanded to know what she was going to do now.

It had all been encouraging, and Ellie was right that talking about it up front to everyone meant she would have to stick to the plan: tomorrow, she was to check the stock and make a trip to the Cash and Carry, and when she came back she was to go through everything, ruthlessly throwing away what she didn't want to keep, then go in to work in the evening. She'd told Nat all that as well, which was what had got him storming out; he'd taken it very badly that she was sticking to her decision not to sell the pub.

Today's activities had been tiring, though, and tomorrow would be busier still. There was no point in waiting for Nat to return; if he'd been out drinking it certainly wasn't the time to talk to him about Glasgow. She'd feel safer anyway, in her bedroom with the door locked. She was wishing already she hadn't listened to Enid; if she'd followed her own instinct he'd have been gone by now.

At least there was a pill waiting for her upstairs. She had only half a dozen more; Dr Matthews had told her kindly but firmly that he wouldn't give her any more after that and she knew he was right. In her situation, oblivion could become dangerously addictive.

'Fancy a nightcap? I've been doing the accounts and I deserve a reward.'

Marjory, who had spent the evening tackling a pile of ironing which seemed to have ambitions to rival Ben Nevis for the title of highest mountain in Scotland, looked up wearily as her husband put his head round the kitchen door. There had been nothing on TV she could bear to watch; her mechanical occupation had left her with too much time to think about her problems, and the surge of optimism about the change of direction in the investigation which had buoyed her up this afternoon was long gone. They'd almost got out of the nightcap habit lately and she'd been thinking longingly of her bed.

'The fire's not on,' she said. It sounded ungracious; aware of the still fragile state of their repaired relationship, she added hastily, 'but we could make it a quick one. I don't suppose either of us is looking for a late night.'

Bill nodded and vanished while Marjory put the iron away

along with what was left of the laundry, reduced now to Ailsa Craig proportions.

The sitting room looked sadly uninviting when she opened the door. Bill had put on the overhead light instead of the lamps, which showed up a film of dust on the polished surfaces, and the ashes of the dead fire added to the bleak impression. Meg, expecting the usual comfortable blaze, stood on the hearthrug looking accusingly from one to the other, then curled up into a tight ball.

Impelled by guilt, Marjory adjusted the lighting so that her failures as a housewife weren't so embarrassingly apparent, then, carrying the tumbler Bill held out to her, took her usual seat.

Bill, too, was out of sorts. The accounts were his bugbear; somehow invoices always disappeared, which demanded a lot of irritable scrabbling about in improbable places. Marjory sympathised, and in her turn deplored the state of modern broadcasting. They drifted on to the worrying situation with Cat and, with reference to her friendship with Kylie, the difficulties young people faced in their lives today.

But somehow, the warmth of the whisky and the peace of the room did its soothing work. Marjory, mid-grumble, looked up and saw Bill grinning at her.

'Is it your turn to say, "I don't know what the world is coming to?" or mine?'

She burst out laughing. 'We didn't believe we'd ever be like that, did we? And of course, we're not – not really. We're still young, still edgy, still risk-takers – and just to prove it, you can give me the sort of top-up which will make a mockery of government health guidelines while I endanger the planet by lighting the fire. And, as a final, reckless touch, I'm ready to stay up past my bedtime.'

'And *that* will show anyone who says we've forgotten how to party!' Bill topped up the glasses while Marjory, with the swift efficiency of long practice, got the logs blazing. Meg, with a sigh of satisfaction, stretched out to the warmth and Marjory relaxed back into her chair.

'Bill, could you bear it if I talked through some stuff?'

She said it lightly, and Bill's 'Sure. Fire away' response was casual too, but they were both aware how long it was since she had turned to him for advice in the old way.

'I asked Laura for a psychological slant on it this afternoon.' She was determined to be open about this, whatever Bill's reaction, but he only nodded gravely. 'She gave me a few pointers – helpful, though very indefinite, as always. But when I was thinking about it this evening – the person who did this near as dammit pulled off the perfect crime. That's what we're up against.'

He raised his eyebrows questioningly.

'The wreck of the lifeboat: but for Tam seeing the lamps, we'd never have known it was murder. And the lamps were bought in Argos, with a service system so impersonal there's not a chance you'd be remembered. That's clever. And even Willie's death – opportunistic, without the same level of planning, obviously, but still we've no hard evidence except for a partial tyre tread. And they've probably been changed by now anyway.

'Luck comes into it too, of course – you can't be sure there isn't an eyewitness somewhere, and if the lady at the top of the road who turned out to have been logging cars going down to Fuill's Inlat had jotted down the numbers as well we'd be home and dry. But this one seems to have the luck of the devil as well as a really cool head.'

'Cold heart, too. You might feel someone was so bad they deserved to die, but killing people you believed had done nothing – that's something else.'

'I've got a sort of sick feeling that the only way we'll get him – or her – is if they strike again, but all we really have to work on at the moment is motive. If we find one of our principal suspects hasn't got an alibi, we could probably clear them or nail them by digging up their drains and taking swabs from their parking area – as we started to do at Elder's house today – but the chances of getting a warrant for what would blatantly be a fishing expedition are nil.'

'You wouldn't catch me volunteering to have the yard dug up.'

'Quite. Always supposing Donald would authorise the expense, which he wouldn't.'

'So – next step?'

She groaned. 'Lewis Randall's in the clear, anyway. But he's such a strange man, Bill! It's almost as if something had been missed out of his personality. Why on earth would someone like that – good-looking, successful – be so thrown by uncertainty and the unfamiliar?'

'From the sound of his mother, he's probably always been scared of failing her. Do what you know and it won't go wrong.'

'Sometimes you sound almost intelligent. So – where would *you* go from here?'

'That's your job.' Provokingly, Bill didn't rise to the dangled bait. 'You talk, I listen.'

Marjory took a sip of her whisky and brooded for a moment. 'This time I haven't a gut feeling for it at all. Lewis was my strongest candidate and he's off the list. The only thing that struck me, talking to him, was that he was very naive not to have noticed that his mother giving him an alibi was a two-way process. She lied to Tam about not being out when the lifeboat went down and the story she gave him even then was pretty unlikely. She's been ready to lie about last Saturday too. I saw her at the funeral tea – a formidable woman. You'd cross her at your peril, and Ashley must have been a real thorn in her flesh. She's not young, of course, and you wouldn't think scrambling over rocks would be her scene, but Tam seemed to think fitness wouldn't be an issue. I think I'll sick Tansy on to her this time, and Tam wants another go at Nat Rettie – there's a straw in the wind he thinks is significant.

'The other two in the frame are Joanna Elder and Enid Davis. Joanna – well, killing three people seems kind of extreme. I mean, what do you do for an encore if your husband takes up a new fancy-piece? There'd be such a trail of bodies that even us plods would smell a rat.

'Enid—' She wrinkled her nose. 'I'd go on oath Randall's never looked at her twice, and you'd have to be clean daft to think getting rid of his wife would mean you could take her place. Added to that, as far as we can make out the rumour about them isn't widespread and the woman who fed it to Jon is the most poisonous besom imaginable.'

'She's probably the one who's done it, then,' Bill offered.

Marjory blanched. 'Don't even joke about it! What's haunting me is that we may manage to eliminate all our current suspects – and then what do we do? That's the stage when they call in another Force to see where you've gone wrong – the ultimate humiliation, if they find something obvious you've somehow missed.

'What I really need is time – just to go steadily right through every scrap of information we have and analyse it properly with a clear mind, with no phone calls or meetings or briefings or pressure from Donald and the Press. Like I can see it happening.'

'Put someone on to it. Your bright young what's-his-name, maybe?'

'I suppose I could. It's not the same as getting a handle on it myself. Still, needs must when the devil drives.'

The logs she had put on the fire were burning through,

and Bill gave a huge yawn. 'Are you determined to boogie on till dawn?' he asked. 'In which case, of course, I'm your man, but—'

She got up, laughing, then yawning herself. 'We've struck our blow for youth and freedom. At least, all the blow we're going to strike. If you're going to do your rounds, don't lock up till I'm in. I could smell a fox when I went to shut up the hens so I'm going to take a shotgun and see if I can scare him off, if he's hanging around.'

Bill looked at her with amusement. 'You won't shoot him though, will you, even though you're a better shot than I am and the beast's vermin?'

Marjory went pink. 'Well, I know it's feeble. I'll cheer on the hunt and I'll eat any pheasant anyone's kind enough to put my way. But I just don't like something that was alive being dead a minute later because of me.'

'And you a farmer's wife!' Bill teased her. 'Come on, Meg! You wouldn't have any scruples about sorting out a fox, would you?'

Marjory made a face at him, then went to the study to fetch the keys to the gun cupboard from the safe.

Bill was at the farther end of the farmyard when he heard a shot, and grinned. There was a long silence, then, just as he reached the house again, another one.

'Oh, she's a wild woman, your mistress,' he told Meg as they went back into the house. He pulled off his boots, then, after waiting a moment or two for Marjory to appear, went through to the kitchen to settle Meg down.

It was only when he had done that and there was still no sign of his wife that he went to the back door and looked out.

'Marjory!' he called, then, with mounting unease, 'Marjory!'

20

'Here, is this right – Big Marge has shot herself?' From behind the reception desk, Sergeant Naismith hailed Tam MacNee as he crossed the hall on his way out of the Kirkluce HQ at eight-thirty, carrying a laptop and a bundle of files.

MacNee gave him a scathing look. 'It's small wonder we can't get our convictions in court, with the folk here who can't get a story straight. Sprained ankle is all.'

Naismith looked disappointed. 'Andy Macdonald swore a gun came into it somewhere.'

For the third time that morning, MacNee explained. 'She took out a shotgun, just to scare the daylights out of a fox that was lurking round her hens. She fired once, then jinked around to see where it had gone and fell over a big stone, OK?'

'I heard that. But did she not shoot herself in the foot as well?'

MacNee sighed. 'No, she never. She fired again, after, so Bill wouldn't think she was still waiting round to give the fox the other barrel and go off to his bed. Sound sleeper, Bill, apparently.'

Fleming, on the phone to him at seven-thirty this morning, had been eloquent about the unpleasantness of being unable to walk and afraid crawling would do irreparable damage to an ankle that could be broken, on a clear night with the temperature dropping like a stone and the prospect of no one looking for you till the alarm went at six-thirty next morning.

She hadn't appreciated his comment that at least the fox would be getting a good laugh.

'She's working from home for today. She's wanting Kingsley and Kerr to report to her there – tell them when you see them, will you? And maybe you could remember which story's the right one when you catch everyone on their way in?'

Naismith was unabashed. 'Och, I liked the other one better. Kind of dull, just a sprained ankle.'

MacNee contented himself with another withering glance as he left. He dumped his burdens in the back of the car, then headed off on the road to Mains of Craigie. The gritters had been out but on this frosty morning the road surface still glinted white except where other cars had passed already and MacNee, with his early experience in Traffic, drove with suitable respect for the conditions. The sun was no more than a yellowish gleam behind a veil of cloud; it would be a good while before the temperature got above freezing today.

Mains of Craigie was about five miles out of Kirkluce, heading towards Stranraer. He turned in to the rutted farm track by the wrought-iron name sign and bumped up the hill. It was good to see the white dots of sheep back on the low hills round about: not as many as before, but time would take care of that, and at least enough of Bill's hill flock had been spared to teach the young ones where they belonged.

He parked at the back of the house as usual. As he got out he could hear the sound of a tractor; Bill must be doing whatever it was farmers did at this time of year. MacNee had never concerned himself overmuch with the finer points of agriculture.

He let himself in at the mudroom door, stopped off in the kitchen to look after his own interests by putting on a kettle, then opened the door to the hall and called.

'Sitting room!' Fleming's voice called back.

She was on a couch by the fire with her feet up and a rug over them; she was looking pale, with dark circles under her eyes, and it was obvious she was still in some pain. MacNee had been all ready with a burst of Burns involving mice, men and schemes that gang aft agley, but he was taken aback by her appearance – Marjory, who was normally the picture of robust good health and famously never took a day off sick.

'Here! Have they not given you something to take for it?' he said roughly, putting down the laptop and files on a table beside her. 'You look as if you should be in your bed.'

Fleming smiled wearily. 'Oh, they have. But if I take it it'll put me out cold – by the time A&E was finished with me it was two in the morning and I can't say I got much sleep after.

'But Tam, this is my chance. I was saying to Bill last night what I needed was a day's peace to get a grip on the case – and as my mother always said, "Be gey careful what you say you want because you'll maybe get it." I've got it now and I want to go through everything. We've missed something somewhere, Tam – we must have!'

'It'll keep till you're feeling better.'

'But will it?' She sat up in her eagerness to make the point, then yelped with pain. 'I'd my chat with Laura yesterday. She pointed out that this is someone who reacted with deathly violence to what was no more than a low-level threat of suspicion. Once it's all round the place that Ritchie Elder's in the clear for the murders, is the Wrecker going to panic? And then what will happen?'

MacNee digested that. 'So—?'

'Maybe we're on the wrong track. Maybe we've boxed ourselves in, defined it all too tightly. But for the moment, until

I've reviewed the evidence, I can't see any other lines open. We just have to plug away at the suspects we have, try to establish them in a time and place frame, see if there are any cracks—' She broke off. 'Is that the others arriving?'

MacNee went to the window. 'That's Tansy anyway. Can we go and brew up a cuppa? I wouldn't think Jon'll be far behind.'

She'd done it. At least, she probably had. She'd told Nat, anyway, first thing in the morning when at least he wouldn't be drunk or – or anything. Katy slid over the 'anything' in her mind as she'd done before now.

He'd been angry that she still refused to sell the pub, so angry that she could see his neck muscles bulging. But then she'd said about him going to Glasgow, and money, and he'd calmed down. 'How much?' had been his immediate question and 'Not enough' his prompt response to her answer. It suggested, though, that there might be a way for-ward, and it certainly showed she'd been daft to imagine even for a minute that he might not want to leave her. That hurt, a bit.

He'd asked for what he called a 'down-payment'; Katy had nearly £50 in her purse but she meekly gave it all to him. He left, saying he'd be back later 'to talk some more' as he put it. She knew what that meant, but she'd find whatever it took. Worth it, to feel safe in her own home.

Katy felt drained already, though, and it was only ten o'clock. Her programme, neatly written out, lay on the kitchen table, though it was tempting to tell herself she was too tired, too sad still, to cope – but then, she'd gone public just so she wouldn't take the easy way out.

The first item on it was to go to the Cash and Carry. It might be a chore but there'd be people around and she didn't fancy solitude just at the moment. It would be better than sitting going through all those memories that would get her crying again and she was feeling low anyway; she'd been more upset than she had expected to be by Nat's making it plain that his only use for her was as a source of cash. She'd need to do a check on the stocks first; with all these people in and out helping they would be getting low.

Picking up a notebook and her keys, she went downstairs to the little hallway where a door led into the back premises of the pub. The store was a small room with metal shelves floor to ceiling and opposite the door a narrow window looking out to the quiet street at the back.

Notebook in hand, Katy bent down to check on cleaning supplies. They'd gone through a lot of Barman's Friend and washing-up liquid; she was just making a note when she had a sudden thought. She hadn't been aware of looking out of the window, but she must have glanced out automatically as she came in and now it occurred to her that there had been something strange.

She straightened up and looked again. No, she'd been right: her car was missing. She could see Rob's, there in the garage where she'd asked her neighbours to put it when they brought it back from the hospital, but of her own small Peugeot there was no sign.

Katy felt sick. She knew what had happened; Nat had taken it again. She'd assumed he'd gone off to school as usual, but he wouldn't have turned up at school in a car. And why had he wanted that money this morning?

She tried to banish the thought, but it wormed its poisoned way into her mind, to fester there. It had been all round the town yesterday that they weren't going to be charging Ritchie Elder with murder and they'd be looking elsewhere now. Had Nat taken the car away to have it properly cleaned, somewhere far enough away from Kirkluce not to arouse suspicion?

You don't know that, she told herself. Of course you don't. He's taken the car to go joyriding before. And you're such a bad mother you don't even know what's happened about reporting him the last time; if you tell the police now you could get him put in jail for a second offence. And if that's all he's done . . .

Her carefully planned programme forgotten, she stumbled back upstairs to the kitchen and made herself tea with a shaking hand.

'Is Mrs Elder at home, please?'

It was Ritchie Elder who had opened the door to Jonathan Kingsley, though if he hadn't been in his own home Kingsley doubted if he would have recognised him. He was wearing jeans and a shirt that looked as if he'd slept in it, the greying stubble on his chin was well past the designer stage and his eyes were bloodshot and bleary. He'd lost weight and the flesh around his chin was sagging into jowls.

'How would I know?' he snarled. 'You don't think she tells me what she's doing, do you?'

He turned and walked – no, shambled away, disappearing down a corridor to the right of the hall, leaving Kingsley standing uncertainly on the doorstep.

He was feeling uncomfortable in his skin this morning anyway. Being made to feel a failure was a new experience and he didn't like it. He was suffering from a burning sense of injustice; he'd brought Operation Songbird to a brilliant conclusion for them, after all, but that seemed to have been forgotten because he'd gone out on a limb about Elder being the Wrecker and had been proved wrong, which could happen to anyone. And MacNee's patronising kindness last night had made it worse. As it was probably meant to, Kingsley reflected sourly.

And today, when they'd all had to have their briefing in a shabby farmhouse sitting room – and how professional was that? – he'd made a play for doing the interview with Dorothy Randall. He'd read a lot of stuff yesterday afternoon when he'd been sitting in the CID room trying to ignore the sideways looks, and his money was on her. If they were looking for someone with tunnel vision, no scruples and steely determination, she was your woman, and what he badly needed now was to be associated with a successful outcome.

But oh no, Big Marge wasn't having that. He and Tam had both spoken to Mrs Randall before and she was looking for a fresh take on it, so Tansy was to have a crack at her after she'd spoken to the receptionist woman. Tam had been banging on about Rettie for days and he was welcome to him, as far as Kingsley was concerned. He was a lot less happy about his own assignment, interviewing Joanna Elder; it hadn't seemed to occur to anyone that it could put him in an unpleasant, even dangerous position if Elder had discovered who was behind his arrest. He hadn't wanted to mention it himself; he could just imagine MacNee's curled lip at this evidence that Kingsley was, in his native *patois*, 'feart'.

Still, it didn't look as if Elder had even recognised him as one of the officers present at his interrogation. And he'd left the front door open, too; that must constitute permission to enter.

Kingsley felt a right idiot, though, wandering around the huge entrance hall, feeling he ought to tiptoe because his footsteps echoed so loudly. He stopped in the middle, listening. There was the faint sound of women's voices coming from somewhere towards the back of the house, then a burst of laughter which seemed incongruous in this troubled place. He was just heading towards a door under the staircase when he heard a loud splash from somewhere to his left where, as he drove up, he had noticed there was a swimming pool. He tapped on the door on that side, then opened it.

Outside the long windows there was still frost lingering where the shadows fell on the drive and the lawn outside, but the sun was just breaking through; with its rays touching the blue of the water and the warmth inside, the Elders' tropical paradise seemed particularly exotic and inviting.

Kingsley glanced appreciatively at his luxurious sur-roundings – yup, if he became a drugs baron he'd defin-itely want something like this – then saw the small figure in the pool, powering away from him at a fast racing crawl. He wasn't a bad swimmer himself but even so he reckoned she could beat him over the first length or two. He went forward to stand by the edge of the pool.

She didn't notice him, even after her kick-turn, until she drew almost level, then, turning her head to breathe caught sight of him, gasped, took in a mouthful of water and came up, spluttering and coughing.

'Who the hell are you? What are you doing here?' Joanna demanded when she could speak again, treading water.

He flipped out his warrant-card. 'DC Kingsley. Your husband let me in.'

He saw her mouth tighten. 'Did he?' was all she said, then swam with long, economical strokes to the steps at the end. She was wearing a dark pink one-piece, the same colour as the varnish on her toenails, and there was a pale pink robe lying nearby which she fetched and belted round her. Her hair was plastered to her head and she was, by his reckoning, a bit too skinny, but she had grey eyes with long lashes still spiky with moisture which, after an assessing look at him, she was now employing to great effect. The mouth which had been a tight line was now smiling widely, exposing a row of cosmetically perfect and very white teeth.

She towelled her hair vigorously with a bright green towel that matched the decor, peeping up at him provocatively. 'At least, if I'm to be subjected to still more police interrogation, the standards have improved. Come and sit down. Would you like me to send for some coffee?' She stretched out on one of the loungers and patted the one next to her invitingly.

'No thank you, Mrs Elder.' Kingsley made no attempt to sit down. He didn't want a nice, cosy, manipulative chat; from their reports, she'd done that to both Tam and Tansy. He planned to see what a bit of aggro could do and looking over her was quite a good start.

The smile disappeared but she said lightly, 'Fine, Constable, let's do it your way. What do you want to know?'

'I want to know why you lied to DS MacNee.'

'Did I?' The perfectly groomed eyebrows rose in a quizzical arch.

'You told him you didn't know your husband was having an affair with Ashley Randall. What other lies have you told?'

Joanna gave a gasp of outrage. 'Just because I chose not to admit to having heard what was, after all, only a rumour, you're suggesting—'

'You see, Mrs Elder, you told MacNee that just after the wreck of the lifeboat when we were looking into motives, and knowing about the affair with Ashley would have given you quite a powerful one, wouldn't it? It was only after Willie Duncan was killed and your husband was charged with drug dealing that you admitted to DC Kerr that you did know, after all. It's a question of timing, you see: at that point you might reasonably have thought it was safe to assume your husband would be charged with the murder as well. Not only that, you made a point of telling her that you couldn't confirm his alibi.'

Joanna had been leaning back, in ostentatious relaxation;

now she sat bolt upright, her face pale and the muscles in her jaw visibly tense.

'I told her I *didn't* believe he was a murderer!' she protested.

'Not entirely convincingly, as I understand it. Though of course it transpires you were right, so we're now looking elsewhere.

'What precisely were you doing on the night of October tenth, between the hours of seven and ten? And again, on the twentieth, between eleven and one?'

'The tenth – the night of the wreck, presumably?' Her voice was steady enough; she had swung her legs to the floor now and was sitting looking up at him, her head back in a defiant pose. He noticed, though, that her hands, clasped tightly in her lap, had fingernails which were not manicured like her toenails; they were raggedly bitten to the quick.

'The best I can offer you is to say that I was here, by myself, as I am most evenings unless my husband and I have a social engagement. I expect I had supper, exercised, then watched television. That's what I normally do. Then, of course, Ritchie came back, absolutely distraught, and told me all about it.'

'You have no children?'

'No.'

The reply was flat, but somehow Kingsley had the feeling he might have touched a nerve. He persisted. 'No visitors? No long, chatty phone calls with girlfriends?'

Her thin smile suggested contempt rather than amusement. 'I'm not that kind of woman, Constable. No.'

'That's a pity. Leaves you sort of exposed, doesn't it?'

'You reckon a judge would accept the physical possibility that I could have been there as proof of guilt?' she said sarcastically. 'The dock could get fairly crowded, on that basis.'

'Absolutely. But you see, it's a starting point. If you'd been able to prove you were here, there'd be no purpose in pursuing our enquiries, would there? Since you can't . . .' He shrugged. 'And then of course, there's the twentieth—'

'I was here, with my husband,' she said quickly, then stopped.

'Yes, of course. It cuts both ways, doesn't it? You didn't see him; he didn't see you. Such a pity.

'Do you ever make your own wine, Mrs Elder?'

'Make *wine*? Are you mad? My husband has a cellar—'

'You deny it? Thank you. Have you ever been to Argos, in Dumfries?'

She was getting flustered now. 'Argos? I – I don't know, I might have. I think I bought a heater there once—'

'Do you have the receipt?'

The agitation she was displaying could be the normal confusion such apparently random questioning might produce. Or not. 'My – my husband might have it filed somewhere. Why do you want to know?'

He ignored that. 'Have you ever used craft paints?'

Joanna got up, shaking visibly. 'I don't understand what this is all about, but you seem to be trying to trap me somehow. No, I have never used craft paints. But if you are going to go on asking me questions like this I shall refuse to answer until my lawyer is present.'

'Just one more. Mrs Elder, did you arrange the wreck of the lifeboat, then kill Willie Duncan?'

She burst into tears, jumped up and ran out.

'He doesn't seem to be in school today,' the headmaster said, consulting his computer screen. 'Is there a problem?'

MacNee grimaced. 'Hard to say. I can probably get hold of him at home this evening but there's a few things he could maybe clear up for us and I'd hoped to get it done this morning. Unless he's likely still to be in Knockhaven?'

Peter Morton shook his head. 'Not if his mother's at home. She's a nice woman, always very concerned about his education.'

'Any idea where he might be?'

'He's got a poor attendance record anyway. Better lately – this is the first absence in the last couple of weeks – but I don't know what he does when he's not here. Hangs out with some of his mates who've decided to bunk off as well, I'd guess. If the parents are out at work you get the house to yourself – TV and video games and a few cans of beer, bit of a laugh with your mates . . . Could fancy it myself sometimes, instead of coming in here.'

'Me and all.' They both laughed as Morton checked what he called 'the usual suspects' but he drew a blank. 'Oddly enough, they all seem to be subjecting themselves to the risk of learning something this morning. Sorry.'

'What about the girlfriend?'

'Kylie MacEwan? Yes, that relationship's definitely a problem. Her social worker's very stressed about the child. The family background isn't exactly ideal – mother has three children by three different partners – and they're trying to get the father involved. He's living in Lanark now in a stable relationship according to the reports and at least he's making concerned noises. Ah!' He pointed at the screen. 'There! She's off as well.'

'Right. So Nat could be at her house, maybe?'

'Could be. But Mum's on the dole and Granny lives there too – not that they'd make a fuss about truanting but the house wouldn't be empty, which kids usually prefer.'

'If you can give me the address I'll away round there and see.'

'I'll get my secretary to find it for you.' He phoned through the request then said hesitantly, 'Would it be in order to ask how the enquiry's going? We have a particular interest in it because of poor Luke.'

'Luke. Yes.' They'd tended to forget about Luke. 'There was absolutely no way Nat Rettie, or anyone else, for that matter, could have known he'd be on that boat. He was just an accidental victim.'

'That pretty much sums Luke up,' Morton said sombrely. 'He was bent on killing himself anyway, wasn't he, thanks to Rettie? I know he's my pupil, I know he had a difficult start in life, but I could find it in me to hope that this can be laid to his account. It might stop his talent for destruction ruining someone else's life.'

After the detectives had gone, the house fell silent, apart from the crackling of the logs in the fire and the soft creaks and sighs old buildings always make in a low-voiced conversation between stone and timber. Marjory almost felt like an intruder as the tinny waking-up music of her laptop interrupted their tranquil exchange. She had switched off her phone, though; she'd collect the inevitable messages later, but having been forced to take this day off she was determined to make the most of it.

Not that it was easy. Her head was aching as well as her ankle and she had that light-headed, unslept feeling. What sleep she had got the night before had been made hideous with dreams of struggles with mountainous waves and deep darkness, and of a woman raking her face with her nails until the blood welled up in the scratches. Somehow, in the way of dreams, she knew this was a distraught mother – Luke's perhaps, or even Lewis's, though she looked like neither. Lying awake had been preferable.

Where to start? Turning to the table at her side, her eye caught the glistening mother-of-pearl shell with a tiny hole in the middle which Tansy Kerr had taken out of her pocket and put there just as she left, saying, 'That's for luck, boss.' Fleming touched its smooth surface with one finger. She was certainly going to need all the luck she could get.

She flipped through the file which contained some of her own rough notes, reports that hadn't yet found their way into the system and the famous jotter, with a follow-up report from Sandy Langlands attached.

He'd done a good job. He'd tracked down the prospective buyers and eliminated their arrival and departure times from the list; the unattributable arrival time, 7.23, was consistent with someone hearing the maroon and driving out immediately from Knockhaven. The unaccounted-for return was at 7.31: time enough to park, place the lanterns in their pre-determined places and drive back up.

At least it confirmed that they needn't look further than Knockhaven. The road to the north, of course, had been blocked by that accident and anyone coming from beyond Knockhaven to the south couldn't have reached it in the time available. Except, of course, Joanna Elder. The first call from the coastguard had been to the house at 7.04, before they reached Elder on his mobile. Fleming made a note of that, with a star, on the pad at her side.

Langlands had also highlighted Elder's visits to the site in the evenings, which were consistent with his claim of taking Ashley to the showhouse: each time another car either directly preceded or followed the Mitsubishi – Ashley's own, presumably, described in one of the entries as 'sporty'.

Fleming flipped back to the beginning of the book. The first two entries, which were logged on the same date though some hours earlier than the first recorded visit by Elder and Randall, detailed a car which had gone down to Fuill's Inlat and returned nine minutes later. A comment in the margin read, 'Much too fast – in fog!' What would someone have been doing there for nine minutes? The Wrecker had taken eight, on the 10th . . .

Fog! She remembered something about a rescue in fog.

She accessed the RNLI website; it wasn't difficult to find the account of the *Maud'n'Milly*'s previous call-out, to rescue a boat adrift in fog. And the date tallied.

Had this been a trial run, or a first attempt, thwarted by the thickness of the fog which would have meant the cox steering on radar, even in these familiar waters?

There was no note, though, of a car returning to retrieve the lanterns, as surely it must have, so presumably this had been late in the night. And of course there was the car that had appeared at three in the morning after the wreck – to do just that, they had reckoned – and then swiftly disappeared. She'd almost forgotten that car.

It didn't feature in the jotter. Since the good lady seemed to have recorded every one of the passing rescue vehicles, she had probably collapsed exhausted into bed to sleep the sleep of the smugly self-righteous.

Fleming scribbled a rough timetable. It all hung together, which was always useful when you were constructing a case to present to the Procurator Fiscal. The only problem was that you were talking alibis again. Been there, done that.

The feeling of making progress waned as the hours passed. She had been so sure that analysis would yield a new focus for the operation, yet the more she read the more she felt it was all slipping away from her. She had a few notes to show for her morning's work, but what she still didn't have was a feel for the sort of person behind it. Most crimes, even the most trivial, fitted a pattern of one sort or another, had a signature that defined their perpetrator, but these contrived to be anonymous, leaving a blank where the personality should be. It made her realise the extent to which she always relied on her skill in reading that signature.

If she hadn't that instinctive feel for direction, she knew the alternative. Boring, plodding police work, sifting through the evidence more meticulously each time, riddling it first, then sieving it and finally using that thing her mother had for sifting icing sugar. With a groan that was only partly because of the pain in her ankle she settled down to it.

21

Yet again, Tansy Kerr was feeling on the outside of things, like she was sitting at home on a Saturday night with the party going on somewhere else. The only consolation was that she didn't think anyone else was at the party either. She hadn't seen Tam, admittedly, but she'd seen Jon Kingsley, on his way back to HQ to work on the drugs case, and he didn't seem to have got much further with Joanna Elder than she had herself, though he was talking it up like he always did.

She'd done her interview with Enid Davis in the staffroom at the surgery, feeling guilty because the old bag who worked there too had almost wet herself with excitement at her co-worker being under suspicion.

Awkwardly, Kerr apologised for it all being so public, but Enid had said only, with a sort of tired distaste, 'If you'd come to my house in disguise in the middle of the night she'd have asked me tomorrow what you were wanting. I suppose this is to do with what she's been saying about me and Dr Lewis?'

'That's right.'

Enid sighed. 'Look, I think Lewis Randall is a lovely man. I thought his wife was a complete bitch who didn't know how lucky she was. But I'm not kidding myself that she was somehow standing in my way. If she was Dr Lewis's taste in women, I'm not exactly the obvious next choice, am I? Oh, don't feel you have to make a polite protest. After my divorce

I decided I'd had enough of marriage – more than enough – and I'd more important things to do with my life than look for another man.'

The pain of that divorce had obviously gone deep. There was enough feeling in her voice to convince Kerr that it had the ring of truth, but even so she persisted, 'I have to ask you—'

'I know – what was I doing when these things happened? I was at home – I usually am – but I certainly can't prove it.'

Kerr jotted that down. 'You've said you disliked Dr Ashley. Why?'

'Oh – how long have you got? None of us could stand the woman. Poor Dr Matthews – he was always having to cover for her lifeboat absences if Dr Lewis couldn't but she was never grateful. She treated her husband like a servant, she was snooty to the patients, and she behaved to the rest of us, even Muriel, as if we'd come in on the sole of her shoe. Always giving orders, with never a please or a thank-you.'

Kerr had dutifully recorded that as well, though it didn't seem the strongest motive for killing not just your boss but another three people as well. If it was, there'd be a serious shortage of sergeants in the police force.

All in all, she didn't feel she'd made much progress. There was only one thing; just at the end of the interview, Enid had said hesitantly, 'I don't know if I should mention this, but—'

Kerr's ears pricked up. 'Definitely,' she said firmly.

'It's probably stupid. But I've got to know Katy Anderson since all this happened. She's a nice person and I'm just afraid I've given her bad advice about that son of hers. I'm on my own now; to have a son . . .' She bit her lip. 'Well, perhaps I'm a bit inclined to see it through rose-coloured spectacles. She'd been having difficulties with Nat and wanted to send him away and I convinced her not to – a stepfather's always hard for any child to adapt to, I said, and this would be her chance to put things right. But I've heard a lot more about him since and I'm very worried. I think she's actually afraid of him, but I can't exactly ring her up and say, "Sorry, I was wrong. Your son's a bad lot," can I? But maybe you could sort of check up?'

Kerr had made soothing noises and written that down too; she'd pass it on to Tam, though it would be confirmation rather than news to him. She'd left hoping that she hadn't spent long enough with Enid to give Muriel Henderson more food for gossip, but judging by the look on the woman's face as Kerr left it was a vain hope.

Now she had to tackle Mrs Randall – a right old battle-axe, according to Tam and Jon, who'd be happier drowning innocent folk than having them in her house asking questions. Jon had obviously had his money on her, trying to push the boss into letting him give her a going-over, though he seemed to be wavering after talking to Joanna Elder. Kerr couldn't see it, herself – a woman in her sixties scrambling about on rocks in the dark! Sixty was really old. You got your bus pass at sixty.

On the way into Dorothy's sitting room she changed her mind. There were a number of photos on a side-table – you could learn a lot from photos and Kerr always clocked them when she went into a room – with among them one of a slightly younger Mrs Randall doing some vigorous crewing on a sailing boat and another two which looked quite recent: one of her on top of a hill with her son and one with her in tennis whites in a ladies' team.

'Do you still play?' Kerr asked, gesturing towards this last one as Dorothy Randall escorted her in, doing a good impression of someone with a bad smell under her nose, despite the fact that Kerr had on her best jeans today and a very respectable top her mother had given her for Christmas which she'd never liked much.

'Not at the moment, obviously. In the summer, yes.' The way she said it suggested that, recognising a sadly limited intellect, good manners forced her to be patient.

Don't give me that, you stuck-up old bat? Well, perhaps not. 'That's a very careful answer, Mrs Randall.' Kerr could do heavily polite with the best of them. 'But why I'm here is because you weren't quite so careful about what you told us before.'

Dorothy was wearing a raspberry-coloured polo-neck that looked like cashmere; it almost seemed as if the dye was seeping out of it, up her neck and into her face.

'I can't imagine what you think you mean.'

'Oh, I'm sure you do, if you think about it.' Surely the woman had to have prepared herself for this line of questioning! Big Marge had called her son's bluff last night and by now he must have tipped her off.

'I'm sorry, Constable, you'll have to be rather less cryptic.'

'OK, if you like. Could you tell me what you were doing on the night of October twentieth, when Mr Duncan was killed, please?'

This was Dorothy's opportunity to play her 'senior moment' card. 'Oh, of course, I'm terribly sorry, I'm afraid I got it confused with another night – silly me!' Kerr could have written the script for her. Instead, she said, 'I've made a statement about that already.'

With unholy joy, Kerr realised she didn't know, after all. Had Lewis been afraid to tell Mummy he'd failed to convince?

'Maybe you could repeat it to me,' she suggested. 'Just briefly.'

Dorothy sat straighter in her chair and repeated, in a firmer voice now, the account her son had given. It was, as far as Kerr could remember of what the boss had said, almost word for word the same. She let the woman finish, then contrived a lengthy pause, with her own head bent over the notebook she was holding as if in contemplation.

Then she looked up. 'I've got a wee problem with that. Your son told DI Fleming that same story, and then had to admit there wasn't a word of truth in it.'

The flush of colour drained so rapidly from Dorothy's face that Kerr thought for a moment she would faint. 'My – my son said that?'

'Yes. And you see, there was a record of him working on his computer so he couldn't have been here. Or down in the town murdering Willie Duncan either.'

'Oh God! He told me you said he was clear, but I thought . . .' She was visibly shaken.

'You thought he meant we'd swallowed your story? The thing is, your son seemed to think it was all designed just to deflect any suspicion from him—'

'It was, it was! The moment you found out that – that *creature* was betraying him, you'd have made up your mind that he killed her! And after that, you wouldn't bother to look for another solution. The police never do – oh, we've had experience of this in the past! That's why I wanted him to say he was with me. I'm his mother – I had to protect him!'

'Yes, we always look a bit sideways at the alibis mothers give their sons. But in your case there's another way of looking at it that didn't seem to occur to him. His story was protecting you just as much as yours was protecting him.'

'But I swear to you—'

Kerr laughed. 'Now, if I had a fiver for every time some villain's said that to me I'd be having smoked salmon and champagne for my lunch every day. We're not daft enough to think that the words "I swear" mean you're going to tell us the truth.

'So can I take it you are stating you were here on your own that evening? And that no one can confirm it?'

Dorothy nodded as if speech was almost beyond her, but she was making a visible effort to regain control. Tam had warned Tansy this wasn't a stupid woman; despite her agitation that brain was working furiously. It would be a mistake to lose momentum.

'Let's move on now to the night the boat was wrecked. You were out of the house in your car, down at your son's house, you said. But you see, we think that's kind of a fishy story. It's not where you were, is it?'

'I – I was only trying to give my son an alibi for that night too. For the same reason – because of Elder and Ashley.' She spat out her daughter-in-law's name.

'That's all very well. But you didn't come up with this great alibi till DS MacNee told you he knew you'd been out in the car that night. I'm not dumb, Mrs Randall. Come on, what did you really do that night? Take a wee trip out to Fuill's Inlat, to get rid of the daughter-in-law you couldn't stand?'

Dorothy got up and began to pace the room. Perhaps it was anxiety that drove her, perhaps it was to give her time to think up her cover story, away from Kerr's direct scrutiny.

'I didn't go to Fuill's Inlat – of course I didn't. That's a most ridiculous insinuation. But I admit that I didn't go to my son's house either. I went down to watch the boat being launched.'

Oh, sure! 'The last time I checked, that was still legal,' Kerr said acidly. 'Why wouldn't you just have said that at the start?'

'Because I was *spying*!' The woman spun round and snarled the word. 'I'm not a sensation-seeker, for God's sake! I went down and mixed with the crowd in the darkness because I wanted to see Elder and Ashley together – you can always tell when something's going on. Muriel Henderson told me it was but she has a wicked tongue and Lewis had warned me off – he was always defensive about his marriage – but if I saw it for myself, I'd have risked telling him outright to stop him looking a fool.'

If she'd made that up on the spot, it was quite good going. There was a glaring flaw, though. 'I can see you'd maybe not want your son knowing that. But why wouldn't you tell DS MacNee – an innocent wee trip down to see the boat launched?'

'And have him mention it to Lewis? When I've never done that in my life? He'd have known immediately, and what would it have done to our relationship – with his wife just newly dead he finds out I'd been spying on her? Anyway, why should I tell anyone? – I hadn't done anything wrong.' Her confidence was returning. 'And then, when I was challenged about it, it struck me I could safeguard Lewis by saying I had seen him at home, which was all I wanted.'

It hung together, in that messy sort of way the truth often did. But Kerr reminded herself that this was the woman who on being caught in a lie by Tam had been quick enough to use it to provide an alibi for her son. 'What did you do after the boat went out?' she asked, knowing already what reply she would get, and yes, Dorothy claimed she had come straight home, and it didn't seem likely anyone could prove she hadn't. They could ask around, too, to see whether anyone could confirm her story about being at the launch, but even if no one had, it didn't prove she wasn't. The enquiry seemed to have been bogged down with this sort of problem right from the start.

There were the other two questions they'd been told to ask; she posed the first of them.

'Citric acid?' Dorothy looked surprised. 'Yes, I should think there's probably some in the kitchen cabinet. I sometimes make elderflower wine, for instance—' She broke off. 'But what is all this about?'

Without answering, Kerr went on to ask about the glass paint.

This time Dorothy was much more cautious. Her eyes narrowed; she said flatly, 'I can't think what you imagine I might use it for. Perhaps you could be a little more specific?'

Kerr declined that invitation too, but chancing her arm, asked if she could take the packet of citric acid. It had occurred to her that chemical analysis might be able to match it with the trace they had found on the lamps.

There was a long pause, then Dorothy Randall said with a return to her former hauteur, 'No, I don't think so. One is always anxious to help the police, of course, but proper procedures are there to protect the public from over-zealous officers with a case to make.'

Banging her head against a brick wall didn't appeal. Kerr left, warning Dorothy that she might be summoned to police HQ to make a formal statement and cautioning her not to destroy the packet of citric acid. She didn't know what she thought herself; quite a lot of that had sounded convincing, but the woman had proved already that she was an unscrupulous and fluent liar. And if there was one thing that wasn't in doubt, it was that Dorothy Randall would consider that no one's interests mattered except her son's, which were clearly, by extension, her own.

Still, she'd love to be a fly on the wall the next time Dorothy spoke to her son. Smacked bottom and straight to bed with no supper for Lewis, having dropped his mother in it like that, she reckoned. She was grinning as she got into her car to drive back to Kirkluce.

★　　★　　★

The MacEwans' house was on a small council estate on the southern edge of Knockhaven, a decent enough area compared to places Tam MacNee had known in Glasgow, but they seemed to be doing their best to lower the tone. As he drew up outside, he realised he had been here before. He recognised the rusting motorbike on the side path and the patch of what might loosely be termed a garden, which seemed to produce only a handsome crop of empty bottles, crisp packets, cans and a particularly colourful selection of polystyrene fast-food cartons. The front door still bore the marks made by one of the MacEwan boys when he was resisting arrest.

It was Gladys MacEwan, the matriarch, who opened the door to his knock, her brick-red face taking on a belligerent look when she saw who stood there. From the house came the sound of waves of laughter and applause from a TV on its highest volume setting.

'What are you after now?' she demanded, adding, 'Scum!' as an afterthought.

'Well, Gladys, maybe we could have a wee guessing game? You think what the boys have been up to and then you could jalouse which one I might have come for.' MacNee was smiling broadly; this was where he felt at home, not pussy-footing about in drawing rooms with china ladies on the mantelpiece.

A volley of obscenities was the only response. 'Don't fash yourself, Gladys!' he said soothingly. 'That was just my wee joke. I'm needing to have a word with Kylie – is she here?'

A younger woman appeared at Gladys's shoulder, a cigarette in her hand and bright green baffies on her feet. Her hair was metallic blonde, with the dark roots showing, and she was wearing a grubby-looking lycra tracksuit.

'What are you wanting with my daughter? Kylie's at the school anyway,' she said sullenly.

'Not so's you'd notice.'

Gladys said, 'Oh, the wee besom. I'll give her laldie when she gets back,' but not in any way which suggested that the promised punishment would have much effect.

'Do you know where she is?' MacNee asked, though not hopefully.

'How would I know? Can't blame the bairns, can you? It's that boring at the school – waste of time, mostly. I blame the teachers.'

'Funny, that. They blame the parents. Maybe it's time you got together and blamed the kids when they bunk off?'

The two women stared at him blankly; he shrugged and left. Now what? He tried phoning Marjory but she'd switched off, so he left her an encouraging message. Just as well if she got some peace, probably; they needed some really sharp thinking on this one. The local paper he'd picked up this morning was pretty inflammatory stuff that was going to stoke the flames of local anger about their lack of progress.

He might as well go back to HQ and try to get some thinking done himself. Two heads were better than one.

Bill brought them both soup and sandwiches at lunch and ate his quickly before going back to lifting neeps for winter feeding. Marjory had rather expected a clucking visit from her mother, but when she'd phoned to tell her what had happened Janet had seemed preoccupied; she'd been sympathetic but hadn't immediately offered to rush to the patient's couch of suffering, leaving her daughter with a faint, unreasonable sense of hurt. It was just as well she hadn't come, really; it would have been easy to be tempted to a long chat, in time she could ill afford.

Doggedly she went back to her task, trying to stifle the whispers of self-doubt. Her ex-policeman father had always told her scornfully that she wasn't up to the job he was still determined could only properly belong to a man; she knew it wasn't true, but only intellectually. Her less rational self, while accepting that she was giving it her best shot, always feared that best still wasn't good enough. And the first crime in particular, the wrecking of the lifeboat, had struck right to the heart of her own community; failure would be bitter and extremely personal.

Her tiredness was becoming a problem now too. She could only hope it wasn't making her miss something important. What she was reading seemed, as it had when she'd read it before, uninformative, unhelpful . . .

Suddenly she stopped, stopped and went through again what she had just read. She circled it with her pen. It was a trivial inconsistency, but suddenly she felt that shiver of recognition, that sixth sense she had always had when she was on to something.

It might mean absolutely nothing, but even if it did, it had prompted her towards a whole new angle of enquiry. She should have thought of this sooner, much sooner. She grabbed the phone and switched it on, ignoring the sugary voice that told her she had seven messages.

When she had given her instructions, she lay back on her cushions, frowning. If there *was* something there, there was a whole other dimension to this which might mean the past two weeks had been totally wasted time looking in the wrong place. Discounting some massive coincidence, it would eliminate almost all of their present suspects. Almost, but not quite. There was one who would suddenly be in prime position.

With her mind racing on, she thought of a remark made by Laura, and something Bill had said too, both of which did suggest a sort of warped rationale. She searched for the sheet of paper where she had scribbled her mind-map; she added to it, drew arrows and loops, and at last encircled a name.

It could be a false dawn. This could be quite as trivial as it appeared to be. But she didn't think it was. Maybe the little silvery shell there on the table had brought her luck after all.

Tam MacNee hurried out of the Kirkluce HQ, grim-faced, dialling Fleming's number on his mobile. If she was still switched off, he'd better get out to the farm to brief her on the 999 call which had brought the news of the latest disaster.

The line was engaged. That was a step forward, at least. She was most likely picking up her messages. He'd try again in another couple of minutes.

Fleming cut short Jon Kingsley's message urging his suspicions of Joanna Elder. She was getting tired of all his geese being swans, and what had clearly emerged from her own researches was that it was pretty unlikely that Joanna could have driven back to the scene of the wreck at three in the morning, when she'd still have been coping with a husband who had arrived home, distraught, well after midnight. It was one of the things she had down on a sheet of paper headed 'Mistakes', which was going to form part of a debriefing paper when all this was over.

There were a few messages from HQ, which she also checked briefly, to make sure there was nothing demanding immediate action; she smiled as she listened to Tam's message saying he hoped all this peace was proving useful and was she getting fish for her lunch to help her brains? She'd contact him shortly, but she was waiting anxiously for a call which just might confirm her new theory. It couldn't take that long to check up on, surely.

When the phone rang, she snatched it up eagerly, but it wasn't the call she'd been hoping for.

Tam MacNee was at the other end, and when she heard what he had to say her face stiffened.

'Come and get me, Tam. No, I'll manage somehow.'

She switched off, then, wincing with pain, swung her feet on to the floor and reached for her crutches.

22

'Aaah, it's so cute!'

'Isn't it sweet? What's its name?'

'Daisy.' Laura, waiting at the gates of Kirkluce Academy, smiled at the group gathered round the puppy, which was making a gallant effort to lick the faces of all these new friends simultaneously. There was nothing like a puppy for breaking the ice; she had, with calculation, come to meet Cat taking Daisy as bait and the girls were rising like trout to a tempting fly.

There was Cat coming now, walking alone and a little apart from the noisy, chattering groups of youngsters. There was no sign of anyone with her fitting Marjory's description of Cat's undesirable friend Kylie.

Cat's face lit up when she saw Laura. 'Hi, Laura! Oh Daisy, haven't you grown!' She dropped her bag and crouched down to pat her.

'Pick her up, if you like,' Laura urged, and as Cat straightened up with Daisy in her arms the girls clustered round, crooning.

'Is this one of Meg's puppies, Cat?' she heard one plump, cheerful-faced lass say. 'Dad's sheepdog's old now but he's going to buy one that's trained instead of a pup – it's so mean! I love them when they're puppies.'

One of the other farmers' daughters, presumably. 'Another day,' Laura suggested cunningly, 'why don't you see if Cat would bring you for tea, and you could play with Daisy?'

'Would you, Cat?' the girl asked hopefully, and another said, 'Oh, me too!'

'Sure.' Cat gave the assurance casually but there was a flush of pleasure in her pale cheeks. Marjory was right, Laura thought; the girl was looking peaky and definitely thinner.

Marjory had phoned that morning to tell her about the accident, and on a suggestion from her Laura had bought home-made meringues from the Copper Kettle in the High Street, caramel-tinged, cream-filled, delectable. While Cat played a squeaky-toy game with Daisy, she fetched them out from the kitchen with a pot of tea for herself and a can of Pepsi, Cat's favourite tipple.

'Do you want a glass, or will you drink it straight from the can?'

It was clear that the girl's mind had been on seeing the puppy, and that the other implications of 'going to tea' hadn't struck her. Her face took on a hunted expression. 'The can's fine. But have you any Diet Pepsi?' she asked awkwardly.

'Heavens, no!' Laura said cheerfully. 'Can't stand that sort of stuff.' She opened the can and handed it to her guest. Cat touched it to her lips and set it down on the table beside her. 'And now – ta-ra!' Laura presented the plate of meringues with a flourish.

It was instructive to see the child's reaction. Her tongue came out and licked her lips, then her eyes slid away from the plateful. 'I'm not really hungry, thanks – I had a big lunch.'

'Oh, you don't have to be hungry to eat a meringue. Just greedy. Come on – I went and got them specially for you.' Piling on the pressure, she helped herself, then held out the plate; years of conditioning in the guest's duty of politeness should make it impossible for the child to refuse.

She took it. 'Cheers!' Laura said, raising the cake before biting into it, and Cat, with an obvious effort, did the same.

But after an initial reluctance she devoured it while Laura chattered inconsequentially on about Marjory's accident and Daisy's most recent misdemeanours. Cat responded with a certain vagueness, then five minutes later asked if she could go to the bathroom.

Laura gave her a level look. 'No, I don't think so, Cat. You see, I know what you're going to do. You're going to make yourself sick, aren't you?'

Cat's eyes widened in shock, then she burst into tears.

It was Daisy's distress, rather than Laura's attempts at comfort, that brought the fit of sobs to a hiccuping close, even producing a watery smile as Cat reassured the dog.

Fetching a box of tissues, Laura said, 'Cat, I'm not going to ask questions, I'm going to tell you what I think first. I think that this is all to do with your friend Kylie, and perhaps her boyfriend. I think you feel so uncomfortable about it that it sort of screws you up inside and you feel you don't want to eat.

'Shall I tell you what I'd say professionally? I'd say that things in your world are scary and out of control and you feel there isn't anything you can do about it. Eating is something you can control so there's a sort of triumph when you manage not to eat. And if you do – like now, with the meringue – you panic and throw up to feel back in charge again. So it sounds as if it's a problem about food, but the only way to sort it out is to give you back power over your own life.

'Does that make any sort of sense?'

'Kind of.' Cat, her head bent, mumbled the words, as if reluctant even to consider what Laura had said. But she looked up sideways a couple of times, then as Laura waited, went on, 'I suppose – it is Kylie, sort of. She's like – well, you know – doing it, with Nat. And she says I'm just a dumb kid, because – well, one of Nat's mates fancies me, and I won't. And now – well . . .' She hesitated. 'She said I mustn't tell . . .'

Laura knew better than to get into an argument about the teenager's honour code. She said nothing. Cat took a deep breath and said in a rush, 'She's pregnant. And she's like, "Oh, it'll be really cool to have a baby," but Nat's trying to make her – you know, get rid of it. And I don't – I don't know what I should do. Neither of them's in school today.' She began to cry again.

It was a nasty mess, that was for sure. It gradually emerged that Nat Rettie was a serious problem, with a drug habit financed by stealing from the till in the pub, and if the police pursued the driving charges he'd soon have a criminal record too. Cat swore that neither she nor Kylie had taken drugs, though Laura was far from sure that Cat would know what her friend got up to when she wasn't there, since Kylie didn't seem to have a problem with joyriding or under-age sex. It took Laura quite some time to convince Cat that, however loyal she might be as a friend, this was something she didn't have to cope with.

'It's up to Kylie and her parents to deal with this, not you,' she said firmly. 'There's absolutely nothing you can do about it. And anyway, you could still be her friend without her being your only friend. Those girls today – they seemed OK.'

'Yes,' Cat sniffed. 'They used to be my friends, until Mum—' She broke off. 'But at least they're not being mean to me now. And when Kylie was off today, Fiona – that's the one who asked if I'd bring her to tea – came and sat beside me in English.'

'It's a start. What about bringing a couple of them here next week? And Cat, you really should talk to your mum about this—'

Cat's face hardened. 'Mum? She'd probably just go out and arrest them, or something.'

'Right,' Laura said hollowly. That was a whole other problem; she wasn't going to go there at the moment. What she expected was that Cat would go on to ask her to promise not to tell Marjory, but she didn't, which was encouraging in itself. Laura was satisfied with the initial groundwork; there would be tricky times ahead but having the problem out in the open was the first step towards solving it.

It was beginning to get dark when MacNee and Fleming reached Knockhaven. Following the main road south, about half a mile beyond the town MacNee turned off on to a single-track road leading directly towards the sea, where there was a right-angled bend with only a fringe of grass separating it from the edge of a low bluff, about fifteen feet above the rocky shore.

Police cars, summoned from Kirkluce, lined one side of the road, making it awkwardly narrow, so that MacNee had to bump along, half on the verge, to get Fleming as near to the scene as possible. He drew up behind an ambulance and a fire-engine which were blocking the road; Fleming got out with some difficulty and leaning on her crutches, winced her way across to look down over the edge.

The tide was full, but the wreckage of Katy Anderson's small green Peugeot was lying immediately below, above the high-water mark and nose into a long ridge of rocks. The front of the car was no more than mangled metal; firemen with cutting equipment were working at the driver's side and the lights they had rigged up highlighted a slumped figure.

Tansy Kerr, standing in a group of policemen, came across when she saw them arrive. 'They've taken Kylie off to hospital. She'll be all right – broken leg, bit of concussion – but of course she's in a hysterical state, trapped there since this morning with Nat—'

'Dead?' Fleming asked grimly.

'Oh yes. Broke his neck on impact, they think. They weren't found until this afternoon when someone was walking their dog along the beach – there's not much traffic on this road, and even if you did pass you wouldn't see the car unless you happened to peer over.'

'So do we know yet what happened?'

'One of the front wheels came off, just as he reached the corner, probably coming a bit too fast – look.' She pointed to a wheel, lying a short distance away. 'He lost the steering, of course, and the momentum took the car over. The second front wheel came off as it landed.'

'Not an accident, then,' Fleming said heavily.

'Doesn't look like it, I have to say.' Kerr glanced anxiously at Fleming; this was the last thing she needed, standing there looking as if she should be going to her bed for a week.

'I didn't suppose it was, really. Though of course if you wanted to kill someone this is a pretty haphazard method – the car might have just collapsed more or less harmlessly. Do we know what they were doing out here?'

'Finding somewhere quiet for a snog, probably,' Kerr offered. 'There's a wider part further along that's quite popular with courting couples. And no, Tam, that's not from personal experience.'

'Never said a word!' MacNee was protesting when Fleming's phone rang. Balancing awkwardly, she got it out of her pocket and answered it; Kerr saw her weary face come alive as she listened intently to the report from the other end.

'Right,' she said. 'Thanks,' and snapped it off. She turned to MacNee. 'That's the answer I needed. We've got enough to do some serious questioning. I'll just fill you in on this, then go and bring her in. Take one of the patrol cars with you and I'll get another sent from Kirkluce.' Her voice was strong and decisive. 'Katy Anderson – she's been told about all this, has she? I'm going to have to talk to her anyway.

Tansy, you've had dealings with her – you can drive me along there now. It'll only take a couple of minutes.'

The patients' records had been sorted out and returned to their places in the filing system, the repeat prescriptions had been arranged in alphabetical order for giving out next day and the appointment book opened to the next page, ready for the morning. Dr Lewis had finished his surgery and gone home; all that Muriel Henderson and Enid Davis, on late shift today, were waiting for was for Dr Matthews to get rid of his last patient so that they could switch on the answerphone and lock up.

'Whatever you said about Dr Ashley,' Muriel said crossly, 'at least she didn't go encouraging them. You could always reckon that the surgery would get shut up at six o'clock sharp. Dr Matthews just lets them walk all over him – well, that's his privilege, but he's no consideration when it comes to us—'

The ringing of the telephone interrupted her rant, and she scowled. 'Now what? By rights, that thing should have been switched off ten minutes ago. If it's someone wanting attention they can just ring the night service, that's all.' She picked up the phone. 'Yes?'

But from the change in Muriel's expression, this wasn't a professional request. 'Well!' she said, two or three times, and 'Would you credit that?' At last she said, with great solemnity, 'Oh yes, terrible, terrible!'

Enid Davis, needlessly sorting a pile of letters as distraction from her companion's monologue, looked up sharply. It had been a long, long day.

Muriel replaced the receiver with almost reverent awe. 'You'll never guess! That was Janine,' she said, naming one of her most favoured sources of local news. 'You know Katy Anderson's wee green car? Well, it went off the road and down a cliff!' She paused for effect.

Enid's face became a mask of concern. 'Oh no, how awful! Is Katy all right?'

'Oh, *Katy*'s fine.' Muriel was enjoying her telling of the story. 'But that son of hers, that Nat – bunking off school, and away joyriding with his girlfriend, Janine says, and her only thirteen and a wee hizzie. He's dead and she's at death's door!'

The blood drained from Enid's face. 'Nat – dead?'

'Good riddance, is what I say. Save his mother a lot of grief, and us taxpayers a fortune. I read in the papers you could send them all to Eton for what giving them the jail costs, and that's where he was headed, I've no doubt. But see you – you're shaking! No need to take on like that – he's no loss.'

Enid said, through stiffened lips, 'I'm going. Katy's – Katy's going to need a friend.'

'And *then*, if you please,' Muriel said to the patient who had emerged from the consulting room, at last having come to the end of her 'And-another-thing-doctor' list, 'she just walks out without a word, leaving me to set the answering machine and sort out Dr Matthews's patient records and do all the checking and locking up. That woman has never in her life given a thought to anyone but herself.'

It was Katy's friend Ellie who admitted Kerr and Fleming to the house, looking faintly surprised at seeing a woman on crutches, wearing a grey jersey tracksuit, who declared herself to be a detective inspector.

The stairs presented something of a problem but clinging to the banister Fleming hopped up doggedly, Kerr following with her second crutch. MacNee had offered to do her questioning by proxy, but she'd refused. 'I won't know what I want to ask till I see what she's able to tell us. And I know you're every bit as competent as I am, Tam, but I want to do it myself. I don't think with my ankle, so stop looking like that.'

He'd muttered something about '*glaikit Folly's portals*', but she'd chosen to ignore it. A bit of pain and exhaustion would be worth it if they could get corroboration that at last they were on the right track. And that – ouch! – was the top of the stairs at last. She'd worry about getting back down later.

Fleming heaved herself back on to her second crutch with some relief and swung across the narrow landing as Kerr held the sitting-room door open.

The room was a testimony to the failure of Katy's plans to tidy the past back into its boxes and pick up the threads of her life. The photographs, letters, cards and newspapers still lay in untidy piles on the floor and Katy herself was sitting on the sofa, her face grey with shock. She turned blank, incurious eyes on her visitors as they came in.

Ellie went to sit beside her, taking one of the unresisting hands in hers. 'Katy, it's the police – Inspector Fleming and – er . . .'

'Tansy,' Kerr supplied. 'We know each other already.' She went across to drop to her knees on the hearthrug, looking up into the stricken woman's face. 'Katy, I'm sorry – so sorry.'

Katy nodded, as if someone had pulled a string.

'Look, my boss here wants to ask you something – something terribly important. We wouldn't be intruding at a time like this if it wasn't. All right?'

This time, Katy simply looked back at her as if she had hardly heard what was being said and certainly failed to understand it. Watching, Fleming realised she was traumatised; she wondered whether she would be physically capable of answering questions. Katy needed a doctor, but a doctor would almost certainly send the police packing and there was too much at stake. It seemed unlikely, in any case, that anything they could ask Katy would damage this damaged woman any more.

Standing over her on crutches wasn't going to help the atmosphere. Fleming backed to a seat opposite and ungracefully collapsed into it.

'Mrs Anderson – Katy,' she said in her low, persuasive voice, 'this is going to be very tough for you, but what you can tell us might let us find the person who killed your husband Rob and your son. Do you think you're strong enough to help us?'

At the mention of her husband's name a flicker of animation came to the woman's face. 'Rob,' she said with a deep, shuddering sigh. 'For Rob. Yes.'

'It's about Rob I want to talk to you.' Fleming paused; she was treading on eggshells here. 'I never met him, but he was obviously a wonderful man. Everyone we talked to here seemed to love him.'

'Except – except Nat.' Katy was starting to look distressed, her lips quivering.

'Let's not think about that now,' Fleming said hastily. 'Katy, how long were you and Rob married?'

'Four – four years. That was all we got.'

Another dangerous topic. 'Did he ever talk to you about his life beforehand, about things that might have happened before he met you?'

She looked bewildered. 'Sort of – yes, I suppose he did. Mostly we talked about the future, what we'd do, our life together . . .' Her eyes filled and tears began to spill silently over, pouring unchecked and seemingly unnoticed down her cheeks. Ellie, a troubled witness, gathered tissues from a box and dabbed with tender ineffectiveness at her friend's cheeks.

God, this was even worse than Fleming had imagined! Still, she had to go on with it now. 'Did Rob ever talk to you about an accident he was involved in?'

'Accident?' That connected; Fleming could see her thinking about it. 'Yes, there was something, I remember – he didn't like to talk about it, though. We'd both had a bad time in the past and he always used to say not to look back, that every day was the first day of the rest of your life.' She gave a convulsive sob. 'He said he'd show me stuff about it sometime – but we never got round to it. I think he forgot – we were just busy and happy.'

'Stuff?' Kerr and Fleming spoke together. Fleming's eyes went to the pile of newspapers on the floor; there would be officers working on accessing newspaper archives by now, but this would be a lot quicker. Hardly daring to ask, she said, 'Did he keep the Press reports about it, Katy?'

'I don't know. Probably. That's a pile of his things there – I was going to have gone through it and sorted everything out today, before I found out that Nat had taken my car again and I just knew something bad would happen.'

Kerr got up. 'This pile?' She picked it up and took it back to Fleming's chair, handing half to the inspector. While Ellie murmured comfortingly to her friend, they both started flipping through the cards, the cuttings about lifeboat rescues, the *Galloway Globe* with pictures of crew dinners and Rob, looking self-conscious, having his hand shaken by some lifeboat dignitary.

Kerr said suddenly, 'Here it is!' She held up a yellowed newspaper, the *Helensburgh Clarion*, and Fleming read the headline at the foot of the front page.

'Naval officer in child's death crash.' And there was a photograph of the nine-year-old boy who had been killed and one, too, of his grieving mother.

Enid Davis sat in her car in the gathering darkness outside Katy Anderson's house. It was parked where she had parked it before, more than once, in the patch of deep shadow formed by the angle of two buildings, where the light from the one street lamp did not reach. Here she had waited for Willie Duncan; here she had watched last night until all the lights went out and she could be sure that no one would see her in her thin surgical gloves deftly loosening the wheel nuts of Katy Anderson's car with a spanner. She'd always been good with her hands; she'd had to be, with her useless husband.

She'd been cool enough then, but now she was close to panic. It had all gone so terribly, horribly wrong. Her heart was racing and with her medical experience she knew she was hyperventilating. She had to take slower, less shallow breaths. The game wasn't over yet; if she could just stay calm, get in to see Katy alone, she could still save herself.

There was a strange car outside now. A friend, most likely, having heard about Nat. Enid would just have to wait till she left, that was all, then make her own neighbourly visit to sympathise over the tragic accident and condemn the carelessness of garage mechanics. Not that she'd harm Katy – of course not. She wouldn't want to harm anyone, not directly like that, in cold blood with her own hands. Not unless she really had to. She just needed to persuade Katy she ought to be in bed, then Enid could get her hands on those newspapers and destroy them.

She still didn't know how she'd managed not to gasp audibly when she saw them first, lifting up the pile to sit down next to Katy and catching sight of the masthead of the *Helensburgh Clarion*. There had been a photograph of her in more than one edition and if Katy saw it . . .

It was the most cursed luck. You'd have thought the Bastard would have been ashamed of what he'd done, not kept the reports of it like some sick souvenir. She'd had no chance to remove them under Katy's nose and Katy had obstinately refused her help in clearing and sorting, said it was stuff she had to go through herself. So it was all Katy's fault, in fact;

this latest disastrous mistake would never have happened, if she hadn't been so stubborn – which was bad luck too. And Enid hadn't even managed to reach Katy before anyone else did, so she had to sit here, fighting her fear in the encroaching darkness. She'd always known she was the unluckiest person in the entire world.

Muriel Henderson walked home, still in a bad temper. It was high time something was done about Enid, more than high time. She was barely civil to Muriel these days and once or twice she'd been downright rude. Then walking out like that! It simply wasn't good enough. As *senior* receptionist Muriel was due proper respect.

Of course, if there was hanky-panky going on with her and Dr Lewis – as Muriel was still sure there was – he would stand up for her. Well, if it came to that she'd just have to say it was either Enid or her. That would settle it; without Muriel, the whole practice would collapse into chaos and none of the doctors could afford *that*. Dr Lewis would have to change his tune.

She'd speak to Dr Matthews about it tomorrow and put an end to it. An unpleasant smile came to her face as she reached Mayfield Gardens. Enid's days were numbered.

The car was still there. Enid looked wretchedly at her watch, for the hundredth time. Quarter of an hour – what if they decided to stay all evening? What if she couldn't get Katy alone? What if . . . ? *Stop it,* she told herself. *Stop it, stop it!*

It was so unfair, the way it had all turned out. It was to have been her beautiful, elegant, secret revenge for what the Bastard had done to Timmy. He'd got off scot-free; nothing he could have done, the police said, when Timmy came flying out of a side road in front of him on his bike. Nothing he could do? He could have swerved, avoided him, couldn't he? He'd killed *her son*.

Though it was just like Timmy, too – never a thought for the pain his carelessness would cause his mother, though she'd warned him often enough what it would do to her if anything happened to him. The impotent anger bubbled up in her even now: anger against him; anger against the police who wouldn't punish the man who had ruined her life; against her husband who had, typically, refused to consider a civil case, knowing how important it was to her; anger against Anderson. Above all, against Anderson, the Bastard. Well, he was dead now; he had his rightful punishment at last, but it was all wrong that Enid should be having to suffer too. God knew, she'd suffered enough already!

She had watched him obsessively from that day on. She knew when he left the Navy, knew when he took up with Katy. Unrecognised, she'd even watched him from the other side of the road coming out of the registry office with his new bride, and mouthed a curse on their happiness. With the help of local gossip, she'd tracked him to the pub in Glasgow where he was working to learn his new chosen trade, then found out from them, oh so casually, where he'd gone, and subscribed to the local paper.

The advertisement for the medical receptionist's job – a job she'd done before – seemed like a sign, one of the few pieces of luck she'd had. Her marriage, stormy at the best of times, had collapsed into acrimonious divorce; she reverted to her maiden name, applied and was accepted.

It was a novel that gave her the idea, shortly after she arrived in Knockhaven, some foolish historical romance about wreckers in Cornwall. The beauty of it was that his death would be an accident, just as Timmy's had been, and actually, in the final analysis, not even her responsibility. After all, the man at the helm was accountable for the safety of his craft.

And if fate was kind, who would suspect anything but a deadly misjudgement? She'd taken every precaution, though, in case it didn't quite work out like that – especially being as unlucky as she was – and she'd meticulously covered her tracks, buying the lamps with cash in a chain store, the glass paint from a DIY warehouse. She'd worn the gloves from the surgery to handle them, and polished them as well, just in case; she'd roamed the shelves at Stranraer Library to find *Reid's Almanac*, which a book on sailing had told her gave details of navigational lights, rather than asking a librarian who just might remember her. She'd established the sites for the lamps while apparently scrambling innocently along the rocks, as people often did, admiring the views and peering into rock pools, picking up the occasional pretty stone or shell as an excuse. She'd rather enjoyed the planning, as a matter of fact.

Enid had no scruples about the others who would die along with the Bastard. She was just a little uncomfortable about the young lad – what was his name? Luke? – though of course that wasn't her fault; he would never have been there if Willie Duncan hadn't taken drugs. It was Willie who should have died then; drug dealers were trash, and the world would be a better place without Ashley Randall. Poor Dr Lewis! His wife had been selfishness personified, and if there was one thing Enid hated, it was selfishness.

A movement caught her eye and she turned her head sharply. A young woman had just come hurrying round the corner and Enid sank down low in her seat; no one would pay any attention to a parked car. She went straight to the door of Katy's house and rang the bell. Another of Katy's friends!

Enid bent her head, catching her breath on a sob. How long must she endure this torture of waiting?

★   ★   ★

There was a chilly wind and the woman standing on the doorstep jiggled from foot to foot and huddled her jacket more closely round her as she waited. When Ellie opened the door, the two women hugged.

'Oh, Ellie! Isn't this awful? Poor, poor Katy! I came round as soon as I heard to see if there was anything I could do.'

Ellie shook her head. 'Not at the moment.' Then, glancing over her shoulder, she lowered her voice. 'The police are with her just now.'

'Right, I'll come back later, shall I?' The other woman turned to go, and Ellie came out to walk down the path with her.

'I don't think they'll be long. I'll tell you what's been going on later, but I'd better get back to Katy now.'

Ellie watched her friend go, then with a final wave went back into the house and shut the door.

Enid brought her fists down on the steering wheel in frantic frustration. For a moment there her heart had leapt, believing they were both leaving, but she should have known better. She never got the lucky breaks.

The fog that first time was bad luck too, though at least she'd retrieved the lamps, exactly according to plan. The second time, there had been the shock of finding cars there, lots of them, and people about looking round the new houses. She'd almost considered turning back, but once the houses were occupied people would be even more watchful about strange cars lurking around their homes, so steeling her nerves she'd gone ahead, the raging storm and darkness her friend. Indeed, Enid told herself, the other cars were good cover; who could possibly notice an extra car? Her deadly mission complete, she had gone home to wait.

She knew it had succeeded when she heard car after car racing up the High Street past her little house. She only had the first warning that, in an important sense, her luck had failed her again, when she went out, as before, in the dark of night to retrieve the lamps and found a police car on guard.

And the terrible thing was, once it wasn't an accident, the police had to look for a reason. With Muriel supplying one by telling everyone Willie had been the real target, it was plain enough what Enid needed to do.

Not that she liked doing it. Having to mow someone down, having to see him fall, and scream – horrible! She shouldn't have had to do something like that. She'd been quite upset about it afterwards, but at least she had been sure she was safe. Until she saw those newspapers.

She'd felt sorry for Katy's son, with the Bastard as a step-father. She'd tried to persuade Katy to build bridges with him; perhaps if she and Nat got close again he'd convince her that her precious Rob wasn't so wonderful after all.

But once Enid had realised that the Bastard was trying to reach out from the grave to grab her, she'd had to think quickly. As long as Nat was around, if anything happened to Katy he'd be the first suspect and she knew the police had him on their list anyway; she'd emphasised that, quite skil-fully, she thought, when she was talking to the policewoman with the ridiculous hair.

But after Katy had come into the Medical Centre, full of her plans to sort out her papers, Enid knew she had to act at once. The police would know by nightfall next day, if Katy couldn't be stopped; maybe loosening the wheel nuts wasn't the best plan in the world, but the situation was desperate.

There was a chance Katy might be killed, though natu-rally, Enid would have preferred not – she wasn't some kind of monster, for heaven's sake – but most likely she'd just be hurt or shaken, and when Enid heard about it she'd go round to sympathise and persuade Katy she needed a nice lie-down.

Get her out of the room, even for ten minutes, and she'd have the evidence safe in her bag. Just as she would do now, as long as Katy was prepared to listen to reason.

It was her unique brand of bad luck that Nat had taken the car – however could she have foreseen that? And what would the police make of it? Vandalism, perhaps. Yes, vandalism; that was certainly more plausible than a careless mechanic. She'd push the vandalism angle to Katy and she could even arrange some over the next bit, to direct their minds that way.

Oh, the game wasn't over yet, if luck was with her, for once. If she could just get in to see Katy, on her own. Was the visitor going to stay all night?

But at last, at last, the door was opening, light spilling out on to the paving strip outside. A woman on crutches appeared – Enid didn't know who that would be. Then behind her came someone she did recognise, someone with ridiculously streaked red hair. The one on crutches, she saw now, was the inspector who had asked her about Dr Lewis. And the younger policewoman was holding a bundle of newspapers.

The game was over, after all. Or very nearly.

23

The road from Knockhaven to Kirkluce was so familiar now that Marjory Fleming could almost anticipate every corner as Tansy Kerr came up to it at speed and brace herself, which was just as well considering the protests from her over-used ankle. The combination of adrenaline, pain and exhaustion was a powerful cocktail; she was feeling positively light-headed, but there was no way she was going to miss out on the endgame. There had been one police car outside Enid Davis's house in the High Street as they drove up it to join the main road which crossed it at the top; the other car she'd assigned should have arrived by now and gone with Tam to pick her up at the surgery. With this, and the fatal accident, every copper on patrol duty tonight in the Galloway area was going to be tied up in this one place; she could only cross her fingers and hope that something wasn't about to break elsewhere.

Fleming spent the first five minutes of the journey arranging for a search warrant for Davis's property to be sworn out and giving instructions for the digging team which had been pulled back from Bayview House to be on standby, ready to move in at first light; blood and tissue could often be found in drain traps and joints. Her next phone call was to Superintendent Bailey; it might have been more flattering if he hadn't sounded more surprised than delighted that progress had been made. Then she sank back against the headrest and closed her eyes.

'Boss,' Kerr said, 'can I just ask—?' Then, glancing sideways, she broke off. 'Sorry – were you trying to sleep?'

Fleming sighed. 'That's OK. I don't think I could anyway.'

'I suppose once we'd eliminated everything else, we'd have gone wider and got round to digging into Rob Anderson's past – even Ashley Randall's, come to that. But why just now?'

Fleming smiled. 'Just a tiny thing, nothing in itself, really, but it caught my eye – you know how discrepancies sometimes do? I was reading your transcript of what Rob said to Katy in hospital, and one thing caught my eye. He was talking about the lights and then he said, "Three of them – too many." But we know there weren't three lights, there were two – if there had been another the SOCOs would have found it, and in any case the signal for the harbour entrance is only two lights. He was in shock, of course, but it was only that remark that made you believe he was confused.

'So assume he wasn't. What *was* he talking about? What was preying on his mind to such an extent, when he probably knew he was dying? I started to wonder what there were three of. Three crew in the boat, but that was unremarkable. He was still alive so there hadn't been three deaths – and anyway he said "them", not us.

'If he'd known the other two had died—'

'He did. Someone at the funeral tea said he'd been told, and how awful it must have been believing he'd caused two deaths because he got it wrong.'

'Right.' Another piece of the speculative jigsaw slotted into place. 'And he was racked with guilt – "My fault," he kept saying. If their deaths were so much on his conscience, I just began to wonder if there could possibly be something we didn't know about – some third fatality. OK, it could have been a complete red herring. Maybe I was reading too much into the confused maunderings of a dying man, but what had we got to lose? We'd been focusing on the current situation and we were running out of options. He'd an unknown past which would at least bear investigation. And – well, I had a sort of feeling . . .'

Kerr stifled a smile. Big Marge's 'feelings' were the stuff of police legend.

'He was a naval officer until he went into the licensed trade, so there was no problem accessing his record up to that point. It turns out he'd been serving at Faslane, just along the road from Helensburgh where the accident happened, five years ago. According to his file, he was completely exonerated. He'd actually stopped when the child lost control of his bike and swerved into him – came over the handlebars and cracked his skull on the edge of the roof.

'Of course it needn't have been connected to this but if it was, there was only one person on the list of suspects – though for quite the wrong reason – who wasn't living here in Knockhaven long before Rob ever appeared on the scene. It would have had to be quite a coincidence if he had chosen, more or less at random, to come to a place where someone happened to be nursing a deadly grievance against him. But Enid followed him here.'

'Tough for her to accept him being in the clear.' Kerr pulled out to overtake another car, neatly and safely enough, but Fleming caught her breath. She didn't like being driven.

Letting it out again, unnoticed, she hoped, she went on, 'Demonstrably impossible. And if you were, to use Laura's word, so solipsistic that your need to punish your son's killer was all that mattered, it wouldn't be hard to persuade yourself that taking a drug dealer and an adulteress with a deeply unpleasant personality along with him would be a positive service to the community. And what followed you'd just put down to what Harold Macmillan once called "Events, dear boy, events."'

'Yes,' Kerr said slowly, 'I can see that. But Nat? Why should she want to kill Nat? She described him to me as a thoroughly bad lot, but surely even she—'

'Come on, Tansy, think!' Fleming said crisply. 'You can do better than that!'

Kerr thought for a moment, then bit her lip. 'Oh – Enid wouldn't have expected him to be in the car, would she? In fact, she'd set me up – if Katy came to grief I'd be meant to think of Nat immediately. Probably would have, too.

'I'm not starring, am I – not picking up on what Rob said either. Sorry.'

'You recorded it, it was in the files, and that's your job. It was my job to pick up on it, but if I hadn't been stupid enough to wreck my ankle I'd never have had the time to analyse the evidence thoroughly. We'd have got Davis in the end, you know, by the long, slow elimination process – but God knows what mayhem she would have felt inspired to cause by then.'

They had reached Kirkluce; as Kerr slowed down to make the turn into the police car park, she laughed suddenly. 'I was just thinking, it's as well she's not on a mission to improve society. Muriel Henderson would definitely be the next to go.'

'That's not even funny. We'd better go straight to the CID room – Tam should have Davis safely in custody by now and I want to map out the interview before we start.'

She wasn't there. They'd tried the Medical Centre first, but it was in darkness, the outer doors closed and the car park deserted. They went back to the High Street; its handful of small shops had shut their doors and in the flats above and the terraced houses between them, lamps glowed behind drawn curtains as their inhabitants settled in for the night.

But the windows of Enid's little house were dark, and knocking, ringing and even shouting through the letter-box brought no response, beyond bringing the next-door neighbour out to say, 'I don't know what all the stushie's about but if you'd the sense of a flea you'd know she's not in.'

Enid should have been innocently at home, having returned from work half an hour ago. How the hell could she have known they were on to her?

The sight of two police cars, an unmarked car and five officers was creating a stir. Doors were opening and Tam MacNee, deprived by the presence of the paying public of a bout of cathartic swearing, gritted his teeth.

'I'm sorry, madam. Would you have any idea where we might be able to find Mrs Davis?'

No helpful answer was forthcoming. 'Was it her that did it all?' someone shouted from across the street.

MacNee ignored that. 'You lot stay here. I'll have a scout around the back.' He jumped into his car and at the T-junction at the top of the hill turned right on to the main road, then immediately right again into an unpaved lane that ran down the backs of the old houses. One or two had doors opening directly on to it while others had small gardens with garages and sheds; Davis could have gained access to her house this way unseen.

It was frustrating, though. Without numbers to guide you, and with ground plans so irregular, it was difficult to work out which house might be hers. He knew the rough location and most houses by now had lighted windows. If Davis had returned, he could assume she would be cowering in the dark.

Provokingly, in the approximate area there were two houses in darkness, side by side, each with a garage built across the end of the garden. He tried the doors of both, but they were locked.

Certainly, even now a sheriff somewhere would be granting a warrant – might have granted it already, in fact. It wouldn't bother him to jump the gun and break into Davis's property; on the other hand, only a copper who was tired of life would risk kicking in the wrong door without a warrant clutched in his sweaty fist.

He'd need to go back to the High Street and count down from the top. '*The idiot race*', as he scornfully termed the onlookers, should have gone back inside by now, reluctant to miss the unfolding drama of *Neighbours* or *EastEnders* or whatever other brain-rotting soap they were addicted to, not having the patience to wait for the final act of the much more riveting drama being played out right on their doorsteps.

As MacNee reached the junction of the lane with the main road, a blue Honda on the farther side slowed down as if to turn in, then speeded up again and drove off before he could read the number plate. His suspicions aroused, MacNee made to follow it, but was prevented first by two cars coming along on his side of the road and then by another going slowly in the opposite direction. By the time he got out of the lane, there was no sign of his quarry. He swore, and pulled into the side of the road.

Perhaps it hadn't been Davis, trying to get into the back of her house. But he was getting as bad as the boss – he had a feeling that it was. But where did you go from here?

The panic that had made Enid Davis's head feel like a pin-ball machine, with lights flashing and thoughts like random balls banging about, subsided once the police had driven away with the evidence that would damn her. Instead, an unnatural calm descended. She had heard this happened in near-death experiences: detached, you found yourself looking down on your body from a great height. She could see herself now, a small, huddled, frightened woman in a darkened car in a dark place. A very dark place.

She had no coherent plan beyond heading for the sanctuary of home, forgetting to stop at the turn on to Shore Street, lurching out in front of a car which was forced to stop with a screech of brakes. That brought a grim smile to her face; it would have been an ironic fate, if she too had perished in an accident like Timmy's. But she hadn't. She drove on, into the High Street.

It was only as she turned the corner that she saw the police cars, right outside her front door. It had crossed her mind that they would come looking for her quite soon, but the reality was more shocking than she could have imagined; for a moment her foot hovered disastrously close to the brake. With a gasp of fear she lifted it again; they couldn't have her number yet, surely, and they hadn't stopped the car ahead of her. As long as the drum-like beating of her heart wasn't audible outside the car, she would be all right provided she didn't draw attention to herself. She drove normally, looking straight ahead, until it occurred to her that a normal person would turn curiously to look at the police car; she managed that too and reached the top of the High Street without provoking any reaction.

Enid turned randomly left on to the main road, towards Fuill's Inlat, where this had all begun. She drove blindly, mechanically, trying to think what she could do, fighting against the answer that was screaming inside her head – nothing.

She had to get into her house. She had only a few pounds in her purse. She didn't believe in credit cards, but in one of the drawers of her desk she had a passbook with her nest-egg in it, a couple of thousand pounds. They'd put a stop on her current account immediately but this one was in her married name; she'd likely be able to withdraw most of it before they traced it, enough to establish herself in Birmingham, say, or London, even, where it was easy to disappear. People were always looking for someone respectable to clean their house while they were out at work, cash left on the table, no questions asked.

But she hadn't a moment to lose. Enid stopped suddenly, to more screeching of brakes and a blare on the horn from the car behind, which swung out to pass her with an obscene gesture from its shaken driver. She didn't even register the sound.

A gateway offered a turning space. They were watching the front of the house but there was a chance, just a chance, they didn't realise there was a lane behind. And surely they couldn't have a warrant yet. Her spirits rising just a little, she drove back.

A glance down the High Street as Enid passed the T-junction was encouraging. The cars were there, of course, but the house was still in darkness. She slowed down to turn into the lane. Perhaps her luck was changing at last?

Just as she did so, a car came nosing its way along the lane towards her, a car she knew wasn't one of her neighbours' cars. It wasn't a police car, but she saw the driver sit forward and stare at her and knew with absolute certainty who it must be. Her last chance had gone.

'Roadblock!' Tam MacNee was shouting into the police car's radio phone. 'Priority – get one in place on the Glasserton road. Old blue Honda Civic, last seen heading south out of Knockhaven. If we can move fast enough we might get her. I'll speak to HQ about more blocks if we don't have a result in ten minutes. OK?'

He switched off and set it back in place. 'Even if she slips past that one, we've got her bottled up. That's the good thing about this place – you can seal it tight as a drum.' He spoke with exaggerated conviction.

'Unless she finds a wee back road, or dumps the car and goes on foot,' a plump, lugubrious uniform said. 'Or public transport. Or maybe even kills herself, now she knows she's had it.'

MacNee glared. 'Do you not get tired of Ingles always being so cheery?' he said acidly to his partner, who grinned.

'Are you heading back to tell Big Marge then, Tam? She'll not be best pleased,' he said, helping matters along.

He was spared MacNee's verbal vengeance by a message coming in that the warrant had duly been granted. PC Ingles's heavy face lightened.

'Here, Sarge, can I get to kick in the door?'

'Be my guest. Though you'll most likely dislocate your knee. Or break a toe. Or topple over backwards and dunt your head on the kerb. And then of course,' his generous gesture included the other patrol officers, preparing to follow on behind, 'you lot'll be here till midnight, going through everything with a fine toothcomb. Later than that, probably. If you're lucky you'll get ten minutes off for your tea, but the chipper here's rubbish. Famous for its soggy chips.'

He got back into his car and drove off. 'It's never worth it with Tam. He aye gets his own back,' one officer said gloomily. 'Come on, Keith, swing the boot.'

Her stomach churning, looking fearfully in her rear-view mirror, Enid drove through the maze of small streets in the old part of the town, taking a right, then a left, making arbitrary choices to shake off any pursuit.

It was a shock suddenly to find herself in a narrow lane between high walls, a lane she knew all too well from her troubled dreams. Shuddering, she could almost hear Willie Duncan's scream as if it were still reverberating from the walls. She had come full circle, back outside Katy Anderson's house again. And, with Shore Street a dead-end once you reached the lifeboat shed, there was no other way out except past the police in the High Street. She dared not risk that again.

No, her only alternative was to drive back up Baker's Brae, just as she had done that night which now seemed so long ago. Her hands clammy on the steering wheel, she forced herself to turn the car and retrace her route, past the wilted pile of flowers lying at one side.

The flashback was so vivid that she braked abruptly, gasping. The car slewed on the cobbles, greasy from the damp night air, and the wing scraped against the wall. It didn't matter now, but she gave a cry of dismay, as if it did. It took all her strength to restart the car and drive on. A minute later she was on the main road again, heading south. She was shaken, but she had escaped.

Escaped – to what? Without money, she had no escape. Soon they would have her car registration. They would search her house. Rummage through everything, her desk, her chest of drawers in the bedroom . . . Her eyes widened in horror. How could she have forgotten the little notebook, the one where she'd written down her meticulous research on the harbour lights and the tides, and the timings for getting to Fuill's Inlat and setting the lights in place? How could she have been crazy enough not to destroy it? Fear seeped through her again, like a cold finger stroking slowly down her spine.

Enid drove more and more slowly, then stopped in a lay-by just outside the town, tears of self-pity standing in her eyes. It was so unfair! She had been the victim, after all. It almost made her want to put an end to it, though she'd never been able to understand how people could actually harm themselves.

Would a women's prison be so bad? She remembered Muriel Henderson complaining about their luxurious accommodation after seeing a documentary, and the women there would be mothers too; they would understand that if the State wouldn't do its job, there were times when you'd no alternative but to take the law into your own hands. There might even be public anger when it came out that the police hadn't taken action over Timmy. She'd read about cases like that in the papers . . .

It was no good. It didn't convince even her. One death, perhaps, while the balance of her mind was disturbed by tragedy. But they would say she was responsible for the deaths of four – no, five, people, even though the last one was just an accident. No one would listen to her. They would throw away the key.

She bent her head down to the steering wheel and sobbed. It wasn't how she'd planned it, how she'd seen it in her head. She was a loving, grief-stricken mother, a respectable woman. How had she become – *this*? There was a sort of darkness round the edge of her mind, a fog of despair that threatened to engulf her.

She fought against it. It was his fault. None of this would have happened, if it hadn't been for the Bastard. Because of him, she'd lost her son, her home, her friends. Anger began to replace misery, anger and hatred. That was better; it warmed her, made her feel somehow less helpless.

They couldn't do worse to you than lock you up for life. When you thought about it like that, it gave you a strange but wonderful sense of freedom. They said she was a killer? Then a killer she would become, instead of a woman seeking the justice the law had denied her.

She had nothing with her that she could use as a weapon

and she couldn't get into her house. What she did have, though, were the keys to the surgery. Enid turned the car and drove back into Knockhaven.

'We'll need one just before Wigtown on the A746 and another at Auchenmalg on the A747. If we don't get her there in, say, forty minutes, move from Wigtown to the A75 between the turn-offs for Shennenton and Benfield and send the other car to the Glenluce crossroads. We're guessing she's most likely to head for Stranraer, but we don't want her getting through to the M74 either. You've traced her registration? Good.'

As Kingsley, across the CID room, arranged with Traffic for the roadblocks to be put in place, Fleming and Kerr waited uneasily for developments. Kerr was fidgety, aimlessly picking up files then putting them down again; Fleming, sitting uncomfortably in a swivel chair, was just feeling deathly tired. Having thought they were entering the home straight, she hadn't the energy left to start tackling obstacles again. She hadn't broken the bad news to Donald Bailey yet either and she was going back, fretfully, over their procedure in the failed attempt at arrest. The woman's incredible good luck was still holding; she must have been walking home from the surgery by some back route when they'd gone there to pick her up, and spotted the car waiting for her. Yet she'd have had to have fetched her car – when had she done that? Unless she'd had it at the surgery already, which seemed unlikely given that it was barely a five-minute walk . . .

When a phone rang, Fleming nodded to Kerr to pick it up, with the negative thought that this was probably some fresh piece of bad news. But the message from the officers searching Enid Davis's house was encouraging: they had found Davis's cheque book, Switch card and a passbook in her desk, and there was no record of any credit card.

That was, undeniably, a huge bonus. Fleming perked up again. 'She can't have a lot of money on her. So there's no point in heading for the Irish ferries. And even driving south—'

She broke off as Tam MacNee came in, looking crestfallen. 'Sorry, boss. I don't know how she was on to us – she's made a pact with Old Nick, that one – but we shouldn't have lost her. I'm pretty sure I saw her car but she got a head start and I didn't see much point in chasing after her when she could easily have turned off and got behind me.'

'Cheer up, Tam!' Fleming said bracingly. 'As you said to me once, "*You never died a winter yet!*"'

He gave her a dirty look and she said, 'Yes, it irritated the hell out of me too. Here, listen – they've found she's no money on her, to speak of. What's she going to do?'

'Kill herself,' Kingsley said. He had been subdued since Fleming had taken him off the work he was doing on the Elder file and brought him back into the case, but he delivered the suggestion now with a certain satisfaction.

That had occurred to Fleming, of course, and to the others too, no doubt, but saying it bluntly made the possibility more real. It might be perfectly understandable that someone should prefer death as an alternative to permanent incarceration, but from a professional point of view the suicide of any suspect was serious bad news. There was a silence which no one seemed keen to break, then Fleming said suddenly, 'I'm going to see if I can get hold of Laura.' She picked up the phone.

Laura greeted her with enthusiasm. 'Bill said you'd something on so I didn't like to call you direct, but I'd a good chat with Cat this afternoon. Incidentally, she confirmed that Kylie was with Nat on the night the boat was wrecked, so—'

'That's academic now, in fact,' Fleming said briskly. 'Laura, we're looking for Enid Davies. I'll explain later, but it looks almost certain that she's our killer. The thing is, she seems to know we're looking for her. She's disappeared in her car but doesn't have much money with her. We think she knows she's trapped. What's she going to do?'

Laura was taken aback. 'Hey! Crystal ball time again? Marjory, how can I tell you that, off the top of my head? I haven't so much as met the woman.'

'Take it from the other end. From what you know about the Wrecker, is she likely to kill herself?'

There was a moment's silence from the other end as Laura gave it consideration, then she said slowly, 'Don't take this as gospel, but my instinct would be that it's unlikely. That sort of egocentricity involves considerable self-love, and if you think about it self-love and self-harm are fairly inimical. She was prepared to kill ruthlessly to save her own skin, after all. That's just a guess, remember—'

'Yes, of course. But it's useful to know that's your opinion. Our problem is that we've got to move on. I can see you can't tell me what she's going to do, but what's she going to be feeling at this moment?'

Again there was a thoughtful pause. 'She'll have a burning sense of injustice – because she sees everything from her own point of view she will believe her actions were justified and blame external agencies for what has gone wrong. She certainly won't be repentant. She'll be feeling sorry for herself, and angry, probably – very angry. I'm not sure there's much I can add to that.'

'Thanks, Laura. That gives us a focus, at least. Speak to you later.'

Fleming put down the phone and related what Laura had said.

'So she'll be looking for a way out,' Kerr said thoughtfully. 'I can't see what, though. She's no money, she can't hide out for long—'

'Steal a boat?' Kingsley suggested, but even he wasn't

impressed by the idea; he shrugged when Kerr said, 'And then what?'

MacNee had been conspicuously silent. Now he said, 'Hmmm.'

Fleming turned to look at him hopefully. 'You've got an idea, Tam?'

'It may be daft,' he said slowly. 'Look, I'm Enid Davis. I know, somehow, that you've fingered me. I ken fine that if you investigate you'll find something. I'm going down for years, probably for ever. I'm angry. What am I going to do?'

'You're stretching our imagination here, but you'd better tell us.' Kingsley's attempt at flippancy fell flat.

'Go on, Tam,' Fleming said.

'I've nothing to lose. If the world was against me, I'd punish it. Take someone out as revenge. Several people, given half a chance.' He smiled his wolfish, humourless smile. 'I'm nasty that way, see?'

'Remind me not to put you in that position,' Kingsley said lightly, but Fleming felt suddenly cold. She and Kerr looked at each other.

'Muriel Henderson.' They spoke at the same time.

'Muriel Henderson,' MacNee echoed, getting to his feet. 'As sure's a cat's a hairy beast, Davis hasn't left the town. We placed the roadblocks on the assumption that she would be trying to get away.'

'Take Tansy with you, Tam. Police car, blues and twos. Jon, contact the lads at Davis's house and send a car over there immediately.'

It went against the grain for Fleming to stay here, stuck uselessly in a chair with her crutches by her side, but she would be a liability. A moment later she heard the two-tone siren start and she knew she wouldn't even have reached the car by now. She sighed, following them in her imagination as, blue lights flashing, they sped down the familiar road.

Kingsley came back over to her. 'I've set that up. Do you really think our Tam's on to something? Or has he just got us dashing madly off in all directions to make it look as if he knows what he's doing?'

Fleming looked at him coolly. She had been wanting an opportunity to talk to him; now was as good a time as any, when she hadn't anything to do except fret. 'Jon, you have a problem with understanding about team work. We're fighting together against crime, not against each other to see who comes out on top and who screws up. You're doing yourself no favours at all.'

Kingsley's good-looking face coloured. 'That was a joke,' he said stiffly.

'Half joke, whole earnest. Do you think I'm stupid?'

'Of course not,' he mumbled.

'I've a nasty feeling you do. I've a feeling that you think I don't notice you trying constantly to undermine Tam in particular, though you're not above doing it to Tansy too.

'You did a brilliant job bringing in Elder. I was impressed. We were all impressed until you started trying to rub in how impressive it was. What makes you feel you have to stamp over other people to get out in front?'

He didn't say anything.

'I'm not just sniping at you, Jon. I want to know what drives you – if you know yourself.'

Kingsley lifted his chin. 'Unless you're the lead elephant, the view's always the same.'

She was surprised into laughter. 'Well, Jon, you'll be looking at the backside of this particular she-elephant for the fore-seeable future. And don't bother trying to manipulate me. I'm a mother; I've seen every trick in that particular book, performed by the real experts.

'Now perhaps you could go along to Control and see what's happening with the cars at Knockhaven. Thanks, Jon.'

Fleming couldn't read his face as he went out. Perhaps he'd learned something, perhaps he hadn't and would put in for a transfer back to Edinburgh the next morning.

At least that exercise in plain speaking had taken her mind off her anxieties, briefly. She wasn't used to a silent and deserted CID room, wasn't used to not being where it was all happening. This was slow torture.

24

She had abandoned the car, tucking it into a parking place on one of the residential streets in the middle of a dozen others. It would take a while for them to look here; she'd heard the residents complain often enough that they never so much as saw a police car, let alone a bobby on the beat. Long before anyone noticed it, she'd have completed her mission.

Enid approached the Medical Centre cautiously, checking to see no one was watching it. There was a smirr of rain now, a fine, soft mist of droplets which clung to her skin and hair, and when she looked over the wall the tarmac of the car park was glistening black and wet under the street lights. It was empty, like the street outside.

Feeling in her pocket for the keys, she walked across the car park and into the shadow of the porch over the side door. If there was a twitching curtain on the far side of the road, all they would see was one of the receptionists on an out-of-hours errand, but a quick glance over her shoulder assured her that she had been unobserved. The keys turned easily in the security locks, the familiar warning buzz of the alarm system greeted her and she walked un-hurriedly over to the instrument panel with its pulsing red light to tap in the code. The light changed to green; the buzzing stopped. In the silence, she heard a car go past outside and tensed, but it went on its way without even slowing down.

Light from the street lamps bathed the room in an eerie glow, and familiar with her surroundings as she was, Enid had no difficulty in moving confidently to her objective. She unlocked the drawer that held the other keys, picking out the one for Dr Lewis's surgery. It seemed somehow fitting to involve him. Oh, they had such a lot in common, she and Dr Lewis! If only things had been different, over time, who was to say that he wouldn't come to look for more than glamour and a sexy body?

But that dream was dead now, like all her dreams. That was the past, and for her there was no future now. Only the present.

Enid knew exactly where to find what she wanted. She picked it up and left, automatically locking the door and replacing the key in its proper place. She was feeling quite calm now, calm and confident as she reset the alarm, then after a cautious check let herself out again.

The police car, with Tam MacNee at the wheel, sped into Knockhaven; on reaching the centre he slowed down a little and switched off the warning lights and sirens. As they crossed the T-junction with the High Street on the way to Muriel Henderson's house in the Mayfield development, he turned his head to glance down it, swore violently and braked. Tansy Kerr's eyes, shut tight for most of the journey, shot wide.

'Tam, for God's sake!'

The car rocketed backwards across the junction with a fine disregard for the Highway Code, then MacNee swung it down into the High Street. 'There's two cars outside Davis's house. How the hell's there two cars, when one's meant to be at Muriel Henderson's?'

He pulled up behind them, jerking on the brake and leaping out almost before the wheels had stopped spinning. Both cars were empty but there was a lot of activity evident inside the house. MacNee stuck his head in at the front door and bellowed.

The lugubrious Ingles shot out from the sitting room as if a cattle-prod had been applied to his plump rear. 'What's up, Sarge?'

'Who's at Muriel Henderson's?' MacNee demanded.

The constable's face cleared. 'Oh, she's fine. We went up to check – no problem.'

'When was this?'

'Oh – around twenty minutes ago, maybe?'

'And what do you think has happened in the last twenty minutes?' MacNee's tone was savage.

Ingles gulped. 'Has she – is there—'

'I don't know. But neither do you – that's the point. I'm away along there now this minute, and you better hope the answer's nothing.'

He stormed out of the house and reversed the car back up the road. A moment later the constable, now joined by his partner who had wisely kept out of sight, heard it being gunned along the main road.

'How was I supposed to know they thought she was needing a bodyguard?' he demanded plaintively.

'Right enough,' the other agreed. 'You'd think if that's what they wanted, they'd never have asked you.'

'This is Mayfield *Crescent*, not Mayfield Gardens!' MacNee snarled, shoving the car violently into reverse yet again. 'Why they give all these bloody streets the same name beats me. Get on to Traffic, Tansy – find out where we need to go from here.'

There was, she kept telling herself, no reason why the police should guess where she was going, but even so Enid's heart was thumping heavily again as she walked along the quiet street. It was a cul-de-sac of small modern bungalows and from behind the curtained windows she could hear gentle, domestic sounds: synthetic laughter from a television, music, the noise of a vacuum cleaner. At one window where there was a blind half-drawn she could see a woman working in her kitchen, but she didn't look up as Enid passed. There were cars parked in driveways and two or three parked by the kerb as well, but even to Enid's over-anxious eyes, none looked at all suspicious.

Muriel had never invited her home, but the house when Enid found it looked just as she had expected: tidy but tasteless, with a bulbous antiqued lamp above a meagre porch which high-lighted the door's purple paintwork. There were two tiny lawns on either side of the front path, bordered by weedless beds containing half a dozen cowed-looking plants at regimented intervals. A light was burning behind the curtains of the room to the left of the front door.

Her hand on the purple wicket gate, Enid hesitated, her breath coming in ragged gasps as if her throat was being constricted by a powerful hand. This was different from before. This was an unforced choice, a direct confrontation, an ugly and violent act. Murder. It was the first time she had accepted the word as a description of her own actions.

She needn't do it. She could turn back, even now, and walk away – to what? To a life where she had no control over even the smallest decision, like opening the door to a room and walking out. A life where she must live for ever with impotent anger and futile hatred and the bitter knowledge of injuries unavenged.

If it hadn't been for Muriel, the police wouldn't even have thought of looking in her direction. Slowly, her hand went down and she turned the latch. Slowly, she walked down the path, preparing herself. Muriel was a much bigger, more powerful woman; all Enid had was the advantage of surprise. And a surgical scalpel.

She would have to put her plan into action the second the door opened, bringing up the wicked little knife to slash across the carotid artery and have enough resolution to follow through and sever the windpipe as Muriel collapsed.

She had it ready in her hand as she rang the bell.

It seemed a long time before there was any sound of movement but then, something strange seemed to have happened to time and it didn't have much meaning any more, seconds stretching out endlessly and half-hours unaccountably disappearing. At last she heard the door open and tensed herself to spring.

But it wasn't Muriel who stood there. It was a man, of middle height but stocky, who was silhouetted against the light from the hall behind. His face, as he stepped into the little porch, was in shadow, only his eyes catching a glint from the outside light. He was breathing fast, as if he had been running. Then as he came towards her she saw, too, his threatening, gap-toothed smile.

Giving a gasp of terror, she lunged at him, but without conviction. A steely hand gripped her arm so that she cried out with pain and let go of the knife which arced out of her hand, light glinting on its silvery blade. It rang like a bell in its tinkling fall; in Enid's ears, it sounded like a knell.

She dropped to the ground with a keening wail and Tam MacNee, not normally imaginative, recognised in it the darkness of total despair.

'Not so much a confession, more a five-hour speech of self-justification,' Marjory Fleming said. 'When her brief arrived, he about burst a blood vessel when he found out what she'd been telling us. He's muttering about improper pressure but he hasn't a leg to stand on. Tansy Kerr just said, "Now, Enid, I know you've had great tragedy in your life," and she was away. And given the evidence of blood and tissue in the waste traps in her drains and the helpful DIY guide to wrecking lifeboats in Enid's bedside table drawer, she'll cop a guilty plea the next time it calls in court. We even found some citric acid in her kitchen cupboard – an essential ingredient in the lemon squash she makes, apparently – and they're analysing it to see if it matches up with what they found on one of the lanterns.'

It was a week after Enid's dramatic arrest, the sort of golden autumn afternoon whose warmth hints at a with-drawing sun and few more days like this before the dark, cold days of winter. It had prompted Marjory, on her much-needed day off, to try out the mending ankle on a short walk with Laura; from the valley below where Meg the collie was working them, the bleating protests of hill ewes, brought down to be dipped before they were put to the rams, wavered on the air. Daisy, running ahead, kept lifting her head to watch the sheep and barking while Marjory and Laura followed more circumspectly.

'I hadn't picked up on the obsessive side of it,' Laura admitted ruefully. 'Of course there was no hint at the time what had prompted it all, but clearly the thoughts and images of her son's death had recurred in her mind with such force and frequency that they took over her whole life.'

'But the egocentric angle that you did suggest came out pretty clearly in what she told us,' Marjory argued. 'What she felt about her son's death seemed almost to be less grief than resentment at what he had put her through. And the police in Helensburgh say her ex-husband seems to have been a long-suffering sort of bloke. From interviews with her neighbours they've got a picture of a woman so selfish and demanding that if he'd murdered her instead of divorcing her he'd still have found people to go on the stand as character witnesses.'

'I wish I'd seen Tam and Tansy scrambling through back gardens and over fences to reach Muriel in time,' Laura said wistfully. 'Did he find a suitable quotation?'

'I asked Tansy that, but she declined to repeat what he'd said when Traffic told him Mayfield Crescent and Mayfield Gardens were back to back and going round by the road would take a lot longer, so I think you can assume that if he did, it was from one of the poems you don't normally find in anthologies.

'Muriel, mind you, was most indignant when they arrived at her back door. She was positively looking forward to an encounter with what she described as "that shilpit wee nyaff" – that's a sort of puny, insignificant person, to you – and was mightily offended at the suggestion that she couldn't cope with any threat from her. And frankly, I wouldn't back Enid, even armed with a scalpel, if it came to a confrontation with Muriel in her height and glory.'

Laura laughed, then sighed. 'Poor, sad creature! I wonder what happened to Enid to make her feel so insecure and lacking in trust that she had to reduce her world to containing only herself?'

Marjory gave her an old-fashioned look. 'You've gone a long way to converting me to psychology, Laura, but every villain who comes my way could – and usually does – claim it's not his fault. But if you accept that . . .' She shrugged. 'Well, it makes you either a slave to your genes or the plaything of a malevolent God, and I don't believe either of those excuses. It's a hell of a lot harder for some than others, but I've seen enough decent people from backgrounds just as bad to feel that assumptions like that are demeaning.'

'I wouldn't argue. I still do believe everyone has a choice, but I guess I'd say I was looking for a reason, not an excuse. The moral dimension isn't the business of science.'

'Nor of the law, really. Lucky for Enid that the judge won't be sentencing her on the basis of the anguish she's caused.' Marjory was slowing down now, and Laura looked at her sharply.

'Is it time we were turning back? You shouldn't overdo it.'

'Discretion might be the better part of valour. As of today I'm driving again – they've been having to send a car for me and like everyone else I hate being driven, so I'm prepared to be careful. Still, it's been good to get outside again.'

She looked lovingly across the slopes of the low, rolling hills, then turned back towards the farmhouse. In the stone-walled orchard the apple trees were losing their leaves and only a few wizened apples still hung from the branches; a burst of cackling from the hens suggested there had been a new, hotly disputed windfall.

'How's Cat doing?' Laura asked. 'When she came in to see me on Tuesday she said Kylie had left the school.'

'Yes, gone to stay with her father. She's another poor, sad little creature; she actually had a miscarriage after the accident and at least that gave her social worker leverage to suggest she might benefit from being in someone else's charge. She certainly hasn't a chance in life if she stays with the MacEwans, though whether being with her father will give her one, I wouldn't like to say – the new partner will have to be very understanding. But in fact, Kylie seems to have been glad of a fresh start. She hadn't many friends in school apart from Cat and quite honestly I think Kylie felt she was a bit uncool – for which I have to say, I am profoundly grateful.'

'Is Cat eating any better?'

Marjory sighed. 'A little.' Then she corrected herself. 'Yes, definitely better, it's just still not the way she used to. But at least we've talked about it and we have a sort of contract, that she can discuss beforehand what she's going to eat and once it's agreed she'll stick to it and not go and throw up. The best thing is that she's going around with the girls who were her friends before—' She stopped. 'I still feel it's my fault that she's having this problem.'

'But you believe in personal choice, right?'

'OK, you made your point. It's just going to take patience, isn't it, which has never been my strong suit. Still,' Marjory brightened, 'the other day she came to me, rather sheepishly, and said her black bedroom was pants and if she used her own money could she do it over? I said I'd give her a present of the biggest pot of paint money could buy and help her put it on, too.

'I got started this morning. I hate to think how many coats of paint it's going to need, but,' she smiled at her friend, 'I will admit I'm enjoying it.'

'A therapeutic wiping out of the past?'

'Psychobabble,' Marjory said dismissively, reluctant to confess to just that thought as each successive coat covered more completely the darkness which had so dangerously touched her daughter's life. 'Look, there's Bill with the shepherd who's giving him a hand today heading back for their tea. I'd better get the kettle on.'

The sun was low in the sky, turning the sea to gold and dazzling Tam MacNee so that he had to put his hand up to shield his eyes as he walked down the High Street in Knockhaven and reached the shore. The sandstone of the harbour walls had taken on a honey-coloured glow and with the soft light on the white-harled houses it made a picture-postcard scene.

On the foreshore, two seagulls were having a raucous squabble over a crust of bread.

Tam's mouth twisted. You'd never know to look at it that this was a town in shock and still in mourning. You couldn't tell that the Anchor wouldn't be opening its doors for the evening session in half an hour or so, because Katy Anderson was in a hospital, silently staring at a wall. You would see the lifeboat shed, without realising that it was empty until a new cox and rescue team could be trained up to man another boat. You wouldn't be aware of the job losses because Ritchie Elder's building empire had collapsed and Jackie Duncan hadn't the heart to go on with her hairdressing salon.

Tam glanced at his watch. He'd arrived a bit early; he continued his walk, deep in thought.

You'd still find Muriel Henderson presiding over the Medical Centre, of course, revelling in her starring role in the recent drama, and for Lewis Randall and his mother life was probably going on in much the same controlled, bloodless way. And there was maybe a chance the new doctor they'd get would be a bit more patient-friendly than Ashley had been.

Thanks to Jon Kingsley, there would be an interruption to the drugs supply of – what? A few weeks, a couple of months if they were lucky, before someone else moved in and it started all over again. It wasn't what you could call a favourable balance sheet for this wounded community.

With a start, he glanced at his watch again. It was time he headed for his destination, instead of wandering along here in a dwam. He took the road leading to the back of the Anchor, cut up Baker's Brae with its sad ghosts and turned along the street at the top towards Willie Duncan's house.

He tapped on the door which had been slammed in his face on his last visit. This time, it was opened promptly as if Ryan Duncan, a tall lad with his mother's build and colouring, had been watching out for his arrival.

'Thanks for coming, Mr MacNee. D'you want – would you like to come in?' he said awkwardly.

MacNee, still in the dark as to what he was doing here, followed him into the sitting room. A big photograph of a younger Willie was propped on the mantelpiece, taken in the wheelhouse of his boat while he was still a skipper, and looking from it to his son Tam could see a resemblance there too: Ryan had the straight gaze of the man in the photograph, whose greatest high was the adrenaline rush that came from a rough night in the Irish Sea. Tam would be prepared to swear Ryan was clean now too.

He sat down on one of the black imitation leather armchairs. 'So what can I do for you, lad?'

Ryan perched on the edge of the seat opposite. There was a fine sheen of nervous sweat on his skin.

'You know I've had – well, a few bits of bother with the police, Mr MacNee. OK, I was asking for it. But I've seen what happened with my dad and I'll not touch the stuff again.'

'We'll get you help, no problem, if that's what you're wanting,' MacNee offered, but Ryan shook his head.

'I'm fine. What I wanted—' He broke off.

MacNee said nothing, and after a few moments the boy went on, 'You'll maybe just laugh, but I want to join the lifeboat. I know I'll have to tell them about my record and they'll maybe tell me to get lost, but I just thought if I could say to them you'd speak up for me, Mr MacNee . . . Oh, I ken fine I'll have to wait to show I've really put it all behind me, but one day I'd like there to be another Duncan cox of the lifeboat. To – to make up, sort of.'

Tam MacNee found he had to clear his throat. 'Och, I think we could maybe manage that, Ryan. Given time.'

   Later, as he walked away, looking down over the roofs
and gables of the ancient town, he found himself silently
repeating the comforting phrase. Given time, the wounded
community would heal itself, as communities always do.

Epilogue

When Laura left and the men had finished their tea and gone out to make use of the last of the light, Marjory glanced at her watch. Cat had signed on for a late hockey practice – another encouraging sign – and Cammie was having tea with a friend. She could pick them both up and still have time beforehand to look in on her parents.

She'd spoken to Janet several times since her accident but during the time she couldn't drive her mother hadn't been out to the farm. It was ridiculous to feel in the least resentful that she hadn't come dashing out to see how her only child was: a sprained ankle wasn't exactly life-threatening, Bill was more than capable of looking after her, Marjory was forty years old and anyway all she really wanted was the chance to say, as usual, 'Oh Mum, don't fuss! I'm absolutely fine.' Why should she feel so unhappy at not having had to say it?

She'd even wondered if Janet could be ill, but her voice sounded strong enough and when asked – casually, of course – if she was all right, had been robust in her insistence that she was. But then she would, wouldn't she?

It was with an unspecific feeling of unease that Marjory opened the front door. The house seemed abnormally quiet; usually the first thing you heard was the sound of the TV which her father affected to despise but watched incessantly. She put her head round the sitting-room door but there was no one there and the big screen in the corner was blank.

'Mum?' she called and heard her mother's muffled voice respond from the kitchen. When Marjory opened the door, Janet was sitting alone at a table set for two, with pots simmering gently on the stove.

Marjory did her Bisto Kid impression. 'Mmm! Smells good! Where's Dad?'

'He's out a walk.'

It was a simple enough statement. Why shouldn't Angus go out for a walk? Hadn't Marjory been telling him for years now how unhealthy it was to sit all day in front of a flickering image? It was just that she'd never had any success in persuading him to take exercise, apart from the occasional walk with Janet after Sunday lunch.

'Well, that's good,' she said with forced heartiness. 'A lot better than being glued to the telly.'

'Yes. Yes, it is, I suppose,' Janet said, and burst into tears.

Her mother's attitude to problems had always been that if you ignored them, they tended to go away of their own accord, and even if they didn't, by the time you had to deal with them you'd adjusted to the idea so that it didn't seem as bad as you would originally have thought. It was a principle which had served her well over the years; Marjory was far from being the only person to rely on Janet's calm, reassuring competence. Now her daughter, professionally experienced in dealing with human reactions to everything from being given a parking ticket to being told of sudden death, found herself completely at a loss.

'Mum,' she said feebly, 'so he's gone for a walk? Why shouldn't he?'

'It's – it's time for his tea!' Janet sobbed. 'You know what he's like – his dinner at half-past twelve, his tea on the table at five o'clock sharp. These last couple of weeks I've never known when he's coming back.'

The fear which lurks at the back of the mind of every

child with ageing parents gripped Marjory with a cold hand. 'What does he say when he comes in?'

She could see the struggle in her mother's face. Love, loyalty – even when Marjory's father was being unreasonable, her parents had always presented a united front. How many times, over the years, had her father been offered a graceful retreat from an untenable position? Janet might occasionally intervene openly, but never without the face-saving gloss which would leave his pride intact.

Which made it all the more shocking now that she should say helplessly, 'I don't think he knows where he's been. Marjory, I don't know what to do about Angus!'

Angus? She'd always called him 'Dad' or 'your father' when she was talking to Marjory. Suddenly, her mother was just another woman who had problems she couldn't deal with, asking for help. She wasn't any more the person who knew all the answers, if only you could persuade her to tell you what they were. Marjory had so often reflected, ruefully, that when she was at home she went back to being her teenage self; in that moment, she aged twenty years.

She didn't want to ask the next question. She wanted to say, 'Oh, I'm sure he'll be back before long – when he's hungry!' and laugh. She wanted to say, 'I'm still worried about Cat. Do you think she'll be all right?' so that her mother could make her feel safe with her assurance, 'Don't you worry, pet. She'll be fine.'

Instead, she said, 'What's been happening? Tell me all about it and we'll see what's to be done.'

Reluctantly, with a terrible finality, Marjory Fleming said farewell to the last, precious vestiges of her childhood.